'Till Time Do Us Part
Upon a Time
Book One

By
Stella May

Copyright

Editor: Sloane Taylor

Cover Artist: Kelly Shorten

Published by Draft2Digital

To Sloane Taylor, my fairy godmother, the wind beneath my wings.

PROLOGUE

Eight Years Earlier

"Nika, wake up." Alex maneuvered the car to a full stop.

When she refused to budge, he administered an elbow jab to the ribs, a sure way to get his sleeping cousin out of her slumber.

"What? Why?"

Nika sprang up, like a cork out of a champagne bottle, and banged her forehead against the dashboard in the process.

"Ouch!" she yelped, massaging her abused head.

He gave her his lopsided, pirate grin.

"Poor baby. Have a boo-boo?"

"Shut up, Cuz. Where are we? And why did we stop?"

"Well, my girl, according to the sign, we are in the fine old town of Fernandina Beach, Florida. As to *why* we stopped," he grimaced "The car has finally given up. She couldn't take it any longer, poor thing. So, here we are."

"I told you we should take my car instead of this heap. But did you listen?"

"What, take a red, brand-spanking new Ferrari to make our *secret* escape from Manhattan? Yeah, that would've been a very covert operation indeed!"

Nika shrugged off his remark, especially since he was absolutely right. In her car they would have been located and stopped in a matter of minutes.

"And why are we in Florida? I thought we were stopping in Georgia for a few days."

"Well, we reached the Peach State last night, while you were in a deep slumber, but I didn't feel like stopping. Why? Did you want to see something in particular there?"

"No, but we are supposed to talk and agree on things, both of us." She glared at him.

"What if I didn't want to go to Fernandina Beach?"

"Well, if you don't, we'll go somewhere else. As soon as we figure out how."

He patted the dashboard of the now dead car with his hand, and drew a deep breath. Then grinned at Nika. "Yeah, that would've been a very covert operation indeed!"

"You wanted an adventure, my girl. I'd say, your wish came true!

"Yeah, I'd say," she grumbled, pretending to be mad. Secretly she was as pleased as her cousin. But since the second-hand heap, camouflaged as a car, was his idea, and especially since he passed through Georgia without consulting her first, she wasn't ready to let him off the hook easily. She didn't want to stop anywhere in particular, or see anything in that state, truth be told. Principle. It was just a matter of principle to her. If they were true partners, they should make all the decisions together. Period. On that Nika was firm. When she first presented him with her idea of the Grand Adventure, or more accurately running away from their fathers, she made sure they both agreed on the most important basic terms. They were to share everything, tell the truth no matter what, and—the cardinal rule—make all the decisions mutually. He took an oath and violated it in a matter of days simply because he didn't care to stop in Georgia. The moron! Her annoyance evaporated as soon as she turned to her favorite cousin.

Just look at the idiot!

He was grinning ear-to-ear, happy as you please, sitting in a dead car smack in the middle of a street, in some tiny picturesque town at five in the morning. Was it any wonder she simply adored him?

"What do you say, my girl?"

She may never forgive him for being a jerk, but Nika was crazy about her cousin since childhood. She couldn't stop her grin even if she wanted to.

"I say, our Grand Adventure came to a screeching halt. What do you propose we do, *partner*?"

"Let's see, *partner*." He fluffed her hair in a familiar manner that had driven her nuts since they both were in diapers. Her crazy mane of curls probably resembled a crow's nest by now. "How much money do we have?"

Nika, who was their financial manager, replied without a pause, "Ninety-seven dollars, thirty-three cents in cash."

"Credit cards?"

"Two thousand, give or take. If the fathers didn't block them yet."

Their fathers, identical twins Joseph and Jacob, were the heads of the international Manhattan investment bank and financial services Morris & Morris and a formidable force to be reckoned with. By running away from home they had violated the Two Golden Rules of the Morris's.

Rule number One– the twins (as they were called by friend and foe alike) are always right.

Rule number Two – If you think otherwise, look at rule one or get out of the way.

And that is precisely what they did. They both disagreed with the rule number One, especially where their life choices were concerned.

"Let's hope for the best." Alex, always the optimist, glanced at Nika. "Or we could call one or the other?"

"What, call Dad? For money? Are you out of your mind?"

"Well, you could call my dad, and I could call yours."

"And tell them what? That they were right, and we can't survive without them constantly supervising our every step, or dictating our every move? And prove them right? Out of the question. I'd rather starve." Nika banged her small fist against the dashboard with a surprising force and winced. *"Never."*

"Yeah, bad idea." He nodded. "Well, there is always *Verochka*. She supported our cause and even bought this heap, as you call it, for us."

"Grandmother might back our decision to stand on our own and rule *our* lives, but even she won't go so far as to lend us money behind the twins' backs. Her conscience would force her to tell them our location." Nika gritted her teeth in frustration. "You know the cops would be after us, trying to capture the fugitive children."

"They won't go that far! Would they?" He turned his troubled eyes to her. Looking into those eyes was like looking in the mirror. Only two out of the six children the twins produced, had inherited the unusual violet-blue shade of eyes from their Grandmother Vera, or *Verochka* as everyone called her.

"You never know, and I don't want to find out for sure." Nika dragged both hands through the mess of her tangled curls. She shook her mane in a defiant manner and then smiled recklessly at her partner in crime.

"Hell, our luck has held up so far, Cuz. I say, let's stick to the plan and make it a true Grand Adventure. Let's stop here, in this town, and start building our lives from scratch."

"Here? In Fernandina Beach?"

He focused on her, then glanced out of the window at the sleepy town, quaint and picturesque, and somehow unreal, shimmering mysteriously in the first rays of the rising sun.

"Why not? The weather is always warm in the Sunshine State, or so they claim. A big plus. The ocean is right here, so the seafood and shrimp galore, a huge plus." Nika, warming to the subject, leaned forward. "The history is all around us, I can feel it! The houses, the streets, the atmosphere—it's where we are supposed to be, Cuz. I can see us here in three, five, even eight years from now. We'll start a business. Yes! A company we always wanted to start, just the two of us."

"And what would that company of ours do?" Alex asked with a chuckle. His own misgivings on the subject evaporated shortly after his younger cousin by a mere month spoke. He found it absolutely impossible to stay in a bleak mood longer than a few minutes in her presence. Her exuberance and enthusiasm were simply overwhelming, her thirst for adventure and her stubborn belief that life is beautiful were highly contagious. At least, it was always to him. Even as a boy, he shadowed his miniature tornado of a cousin, constantly in one trouble after another, but unable to resist the temptation. The most miserable period of his life was his four years of Harvard. Nika's grades were not good enough so she attended a local college. Now, they were both graduates with freshly minted diplomas and two sets of irate parents they managed to piss off by running away on the Grand Adventure. They escaped right after their graduation party the twins had thrown for them two weeks ago. It was a desperate and daring move and yes, a rebellion against the dictatorial regime of the Morris's households, where Jacob and Joseph reigned supreme.

Anyone unfamiliar with their fathers or their methods, might have considered their escape as an extreme measure. But to the members of the family, including the six children, who lived by the Two Golden Rules, and the staff of the Morris & Morris bank, such wasn't the case.

Even the twins' mother *Verochka*, their favorite grandmother, was in a state of a constant awe, not to mention bafflement, of her own offspring. It didn't stop her, however, from aiding and abetting Nika and Alex. *Verochka* had a strong independent streak along with a firm and unshakable belief in freedom. Her motto - every person has the right to shape his or her own destiny, and be happy. And, of course, because she absolutely adored the pair of them.

"We can do anything we want. We can try many different things before we find our own milieu. Well, what do you say, partner?"

"Heck, why not? Let's do it, partner."

Nika laughed and, launching at him, threw her arms around his neck.

"I'm so happy! I'm happy you decided to drive past Georgia, I'm happy our car has died on us, I'm happy to be here. I just know it's where we are supposed to be. We'll make it happen, Cuz. Just wait and see. We'll make it fine on our own. And we will show the whole wide world what Morris & Morris Jrs. are capable of."

"Please," he grimaced. "Not Morris & Morris. Whatever we call our future company, I want your solemn promise we absolutely *will not* mix the twins' name into it."

"You got it, darling." Nika placed her palm onto his face and gave it a light pat. She knew the ordeal was much harder on him than he let on. He was her almost-genius, soft-hearted, and serious cousin. A man who found it impossible to hurt a fly. Let alone defy their overbearing fathers. He might have entered Harvard Law School and finish it with flying colors, then join the family firm and be miserable for the rest of his life if not for her and her ingenious escape plan. Well, what was a younger cousin for. Nika was delighted for them both and the world in general.

"Let's name it *Before and After*, then. Before we came here—and after we settle here. Get it? And we make sure that whatever it is we'll do, it will make a lasting impact on this town and its people. How about that, Cuz?"

"*Before and After*. Holy cow, I like it!"

He reminded her of a little boy, happy, kind and joyous, who followed her every step and got her out of mischief more than she cared to admit. Or, the times he couldn't talk her out of it and joined her. Like right now. Was it any wonder she loved him more than her own brothers? Actually, more than anyone in the world. She couldn't imagine her life without him.

"Fate, you fickle bitch, here we are, and here we stay, for better or worse," he shouted through the open window of the derelict broken-down car, delirious and carefree.

"Here we are," Nika joined in, poking her head out through the passenger window, her own voice clear and sonorous like a silver bell, "and here we stay! And let's see how that fickle bitch Fate will dare to defy us now!"

PART ONE
The Coleman House

CHAPTER ONE

"Why are you so riled up? You wanted the Coleman house, you fought for it like a woman possessed for more than two years. And now, when it literally got dumped into your lap, you're getting all huffy and puffy. What gives?"

Alex stopped the car in front of the hotel and turned the engine off. To say that he was pissed off was the understatement of the century.

Nika kept silent, infuriatingly so, but her face and her whole demeanor screamed 'mad' with a capital M. At least, she went to the trouble to dress herself for the occasion. He wouldn't have put it past her to go to this dinner meeting in grubby jeans and a paint-stained t-shirt and crowned with her infamous baseball cap. He exited the car, handed the valet his keys, and turned to his aggravating business partner, his cousin and all-around best pal. But she had already reached the entrance of the Ritz-Carlton hotel where their anonymous client had invited them to dinner. A business dinner meeting, to be precise.

"Nika, seriously," he tried again after he caught up with her. Even though diminutive in size, her stride was that of an athlete, or a person who was accustomed to serious physical exercise or manual labor. Nika scored on both counts. "At least, let's listen to the man."

Nika halted in midstride. The stubborn frown that marred her high forehead was endearingly familiar. Her violet eyes were hot and blazing fire. Her infamous Morris temper, he concluded, was at a boiling point.

"Nik, please. And if you won't relax those muscles, you'll get a permanent line up there." Always a pacifist, he smiled at her mutinous, angry face and tapped the frown that etched between her brows. Usually it made her laugh. Not this time, though. Giving up, he drew in a deep breath. He put both hands on her shoulders, and kept them there. "Okay, Nika. If you don't want to, let's turn around and leave. We'll send a note with our apologies, saying that something came up at the last minute and we couldn't make it. And we refuse the job."

"You'll do it too. You'll lie and refuse an important project, because of me."
She covered his hands still lying on her shoulders with her own and gave
him one of her most brilliant smiles. She raised up on her tiptoes and then
plunked a sloppy kiss on his chin. "Thanks, pal. I love you, too."

"Hey, that's what families are all about." Alex let go of her shoulders after the
last squeeze. "So, partner, what do you say?"

"I say, partner, let's get this business—whatever this is—over with, and get
the hell out. What do you say we grab a pint of Guinness at the Palace?"

The oldest operating bar in Florida, the Palace Saloon, was the favorite local
watering hole that traced its history as far back as 1878. Both Nika and Alex
adored its unique ambience and had become regulars over the years.

"Say it's your treat, and I'm all yours."

"You such a cheap date, Alexander Morris!"

"But you're crazy about me, Veronika Morris!"

Together they climbed the last step to the ornate entrance doors of the
famous hotel.

Salt, an acclaimed restaurant at Ritz Carlton, was located on the main floor,
so it took them less than few minutes to get there.

"We are expected," he said as he gave their names to the hostess.

"We just don't know by whom," Nika added in a saccharine voice, getting her
hackles up once again.

"Nik," he growled in warning, his own smile strained at the corners.

Nika shrugged, annoyed. She didn't know why she was so pissed, but the
whole business with the Coleman house—the secrecy and the stupid
cloak-and-dagger games surrounding it—rubbed her the wrong way. Plus,
the fiasco with its acquisition. Alex was right, she wanted the house badly.
Something fierce, as her grandmother always said. For two years, she had
been doing everything in her power, and beyond that to get the current heirs
to sell the house to *Before and After, Inc.* To no avail. And now, just two days
earlier they had received an offer no sane person could possibly refuse to fully
restore and renovate the Coleman house to its former glory. The funds were
unlimited and they had carte blanche. The time frame of the work—as long
as needed. And the full cooperation of the current owner and the historical
society.

So, Nika summarized in her mind, no deadline, no limit on a budget and no roadblocks from the notorious organization and anonymous heirs. The sky's the limit. The ultimate dream-job. Why then, she asked herself for the umpteenth time, was she so uneasy to accept it? Or so frightened?

That's it! That what was making her so angry. Reality hit her like a jackhammer. She was scared. Unabashedly and unreasonably. For the first time in her career, she, a local legend aptly acclaimed by friend and foe as a "house whisperer" was afraid to... what? Fail? Ridiculous. The Coleman house 'spoke' to her as no other had for the longest time.

"This way, Mr. & Ms. Morris," the hostess said, interrupting her unwelcomed musings and invited them to follow her.

"Here goes," Alex muttered.

They were led to a faraway table tucked cozily into a corner. It was already occupied by a distinguished looking stranger in a dark suit who immediately got up as soon as they approached the table. Their mysterious host, Nika deduced. Even though the lights inside the restaurant were dim, he looked vaguely familiar.

"Thank you both for accepting my somewhat unorthodox invitation," the stranger said in his smooth cultured tenor with a whisper of northern crispiness in it.

As soon as they were face to face, both of them recognized the man. No wonder he was trying to stay anonymous!

"Senator," Alex said, momentarily taken aback. "This is a surprise, to say the least." He recovered quickly, though, and pumped heartily the outstretched hand.

Nika too was surprised to see one of the current Senators from Massachusetts standing in front of her, shaking hands with her cousin.

"I thought you looked familiar," she blurted in lieu of a hello when his quiet gray gaze settled on her. "What are you doing here?"

"Why, meeting you, of course." Senator Elijah Lauder flashed a courteous smile that didn't reach his eyes. He appeared even more uncomfortable than she. His uneasiness filled the air, even though his gaze never wavered and his manners were impeccable. But the good Senator from the North wasn't in his usual milieu, so to speak, and despite fitting seamlessly in the plush and posh atmosphere of the Ritz's famous restaurant, he was still not on his home turf.

He held the chair for her, and nodded at the waiter.

"I took the liberty of ordering the drinks for us. I hope it will meet with your approval."

"Champagne?" Nika eyed the label (Dom Perignon) and arched her brows. "Are we celebrating?"

"I hope so."

Senator gave another nod to the waiter. They waited until their flutes were filled. "I really hope that the two of you have read my proposal and came to an agreeable decision."

"The proposal came from the attorney's office, not from you, Senator," Nika countered before her cousin said anything. "And anyway, how are you involved in this?"

"Allow me to explain." Senator Lauder put his flute down without a sip. "My full name is Elijah Coleman Lauder. My grandmother, Margaret Coleman, was the only surviving child of Elijah— or Eli— Coleman, the original owner of the house. She married Maximilian Lauder in 1940, and my father was born after a couple of years. I was very close to my grandmother, who passed away just recently."

"I'm sorry," Nika murmured, lowering her eyes. The genuine sadness in the Senator's eyes was making her uncomfortable, like she was witnessing something personal and very intimate.

"Thank you. She was a very special lady. Very special indeed."

He took a small sip of his champagne, still obviously lost in memories, then put the flute down and focused his piercing eyes on Nika.

"She remembered her parents—her father Eli, who I was named after, and her mother, Daisy—vividly and in great detail. My grandmother was the only person I've ever met with the eyes of a very usual color: violet-blue. The same shade as yours."

More baffled than surprised, Nika sipped her champagne.

"That's... interesting. Then again, Alex has the same violet eyes like me. We both inherited them from our grandmother."

"Anybody else in the family, or just the two of you?"

"Only us. Why?"

"Just curious."

Nika had a strong hunch that it wasn't the case, but she chose to keep her thoughts to herself.

"I am sorry, Senator, but what does our eye color have to do with anything?"

"Maybe nothing, maybe a great deal." The last words were uttered so quietly that Nika almost missed them. A sudden chill ran up and down her spine, raising the fine hair on the nape of her neck.

"Anyway." The Senator sat straighter as if he had given himself a mental shake. "My grandmother had a secret. Or, more accurately, she made a secret promise to her father that she kept for many years."

"And that secret was?" Alex prompted after a pause. He, too, was intrigued, but puzzled by Nika's reaction. Her face became drawn and unusually pale. Or was it a trick played by the dim light? Alex turned his eyes back to the Senator, but took one of Nika's hands in his, and closed his fingers firmly around it. The sign of it didn't escape the Senator, and he gave both cousins a warm smile, that finally reached his expressive eyes and made his face simply arresting.

"That secret, my young friends, was a small envelope and a sworn promise to find Before & After, Inc. and its two owners, Veronika and Alexander Morris, and make sure they'll agree to renovate the old Coleman House."

"That's it?" Nika made a strange sound, somewhere between a croak and a chuckle.

"That's it. Oh, and the most important of all—it was supposed to be done no earlier or later than September 2019."

He squeezed his cousin's hand in a death grip and leaned forward. His usual cheerful disposition had evaporated in a flash.

"Senator, with all due respect, this is... nonsense."

Nika kept silent.

"I admire your restraint," Senator Lauder answered with a good-natured chuckle. "I myself reacted more in terms of crazy or delirious."

"And was she?" Nika finally broke the silence.

"Was she what? Crazy? No, not at all. My grandmother, God rest her soul, was sharp as a tack until her last day. She was the rock. Even confined in a wheelchair, she was the strongest, bravest soul I've ever met. She was totally in charge of her mental faculties."

"How did your great-grandfather even know about Before & After, Inc.? And why 2019?" Suspicion spread across Alex's face. "Why not 2009 or 2017?"

"That, my friend, I don't know. And neither did my grandmother. Yes," he answered the unspoken question, "I asked. She just shrugged and said that what her Father had asked of her."

"And she promised, just like that?"

"Yes, just like that."

"And she was the only heir of Elijah's," Nika said. It wasn't a question, but the Senator answered her, nonetheless.

"Correct. She was the sole owner of his estate, such as it is."

"And that's why the family refused to sell the house for so many years."

"Yes. She knew through her attorneys of your interest in it, and of your numerous proposals to buy it. But she refused. As I understand now, she was holding onto her promise to her father. When she felt it was almost her time." He stopped and cleared his throat before continuing. "She called me and asked me to come to her at once. She was living in Virginia at the time. I flew there immediately. At that meeting, which happened to be our last, she entrusted me with her secret and took a solemn promise from me that I will comply with my great-grandfather's wish, however crazy and delirious it might have seemed. So, here I am."

"So, here you are," Nika murmured as she studied the senator. "Do you have her picture?"

"Grandmother's? Of course." He produced a wallet out of his breast pocket, opened it, and removed a photo. He offered it to Nika. It was a snapshot of a woman in her late sixties-early seventies. She was smiling at the camera, her eyes crinkled at the corners. Nika's heart gave one hard thump against her ribcage.

"You said your grandmother had violet eyes."

"Yes."

"Do you know who she inherited them from?" But even before he answered, Nika knew.

"Her mother," the Senator answered. "It is family lore that my great-grandfather nick-named her Daisy, for she resembled a flower."

The chills ran down Nika's spine.

"And her real name?" she asked, holding her breath.

"Nobody knew. She was Daisy Coleman. Even on her tombstone her name is engraved like that."

Why do I feel like crying all of a sudden?

"Did your grandmother talk about her?"

"Not so much, come to think of it."

"So, what do you know about Daisy?"

To his credit, the senator didn't move a muscle at the catch in her voice.

"Very little." He frowned. "Nobody knew exactly where she came from, or who her family was. She was the second wife of Eli Coleman, the love of his life, according to all accounts. She was the mother of his only child, my grandmother Margaret. And that's about it."

"And she had the violet eyes and golden curls."

"Golden curls? How do you know that?" Alex asked.

"Yes, my dear, how did you figure that out?" Senator Lauder cocked an eyebrow.

"I...I don't know," Nika couldn't tear her eyes from the small picture. She raised her left hand to her blond hair with its springy curls she had struggled to tame since she was a child. A few years ago she cut them chin length, easier to hide under her baseball cap. As a result, her hair resembled a golden dandelion.

"It just seems right, somehow."

"I will verify with the family historian, but—"

"Family historian?" Nika's chuckle rung hollow even to her own ears. "Fancy that!"

"Well, when the family is one of the oldest and most prominent pillars of the Amelia Island community and related to the Carnegies, and the Father of Florida railroads, David Yulee himself, it's no wonder." The Senator shrugged without false modesty. "Anyway, I will do my research—"

"No need, Senator," Nika interrupted, reluctantly handing back the picture. "As the restoration project manager, it is my job to do all kinds of research, family pictures included."

She raised her flute in a small salute.

"So, you are taking the job?"

"Yes, we are." She glanced at her cousin. A twinge of guilt bit at her. Usually they made all decisions together, especially such an important one. This time, however, Nika took it upon herself to voice a decision without consulting her partner first.

"Are you sure, Nik?" he asked.

He probably didn't give a damn about her making a decision solo. Yet his actions were strange, his demeanor subdued. Something must have bothered him the entire evening. She had no idea what that was but eventually he may tell her.

"I'm sure." The image of their grandmother *Verochka* popped into her mind. "I am very sure."

"Well, then."

Alex took a deep breath, let it out, and raised his champagne glass.

"To the new project, then, may it be a smashing success!"

Senator Lauder clinked his flute with both of theirs. "To the Coleman house."

"To the Coleman house," Alex echoed.

"To the Coleman family," Nika said and upended her champagne in one gulp.

"Oh, I almost forgot." The senator drew a small yellowed envelope from his pocket. "I'm supposed to give you this."

"What's this?"

Nika's hands grew icy-cold as she reached across the table. Her heart beat erratically against her ribs, like a desperate bird trying to escape its cage.

She was suddenly as afraid as if she had seen a ghost.

"The letter from Eli Coleman, my great-grandfather. I promised Margaret to deliver it to you personally. But only upon your agreement to take on this project."

CHAPTER TWO

Sleep refused to come. No big surprise. Nika arranged her legs in her favorite position, her left knee bent with the right foot tucked under it. She sat outside on the second-floor deck of the house she and Alex owned together, and stared at the ocean. In predawn hours, the view of the Atlantic was a sight to behold. The glory of the water, indescribably beautiful, majestically overwhelming, spread in front of her to infinity and beyond. It was fiercely alive and unapologetically domineering. Changing, always changing its moods and colors. Calm and dignified one moment, angry and tempestuous the next. It always took her breath away.

Nika's mood was as turbulent as the furious waves that crashed and foamed on the beach a short distance away.

The mysterious letter lay on the small table in front of her, beckoning. She had yet to succumb to its demand.

If she was honest with herself, and she always was, she had to admit that she was more scared than curious. Which was absurd. What was so scary about a piece of paper, yellowed from time and almost a hundred years old, that she was reluctant to even touch it, let alone read it? But absurd or not, she couldn't bring herself to do it. Not yet. Deep in her gut Nika was confident that as soon as she read the letter, her life may change forever.

Elijah, or Eli Coleman. The man, the legend, the first owner of the house that was now hers and their company's first priority. His name in this part of Florida was revered as much, if not more, than that of David Yulee, the father of the railroad.

Eli Coleman, the philanthropist, the businessman, the engineer, the pillar of the community in the late nineteenth and early twentieth century, did many things for the prosperity of Fernandina Beach. The hospital, the schools, the first shrimping factory and paper mill, the modernization of the town's infrastructure, among other things. He was a pioneer and true revolutionary when it came to protecting the marine life and the fragile, unique environment of the town he called home.

He was born in Europe to a wealthy couple. Maybe Scotland or England. She made a mental note to check. He relocated with his family to Florida when he was still a child and lived there the rest of his life, except the three years he attended Oxford to earn his engineering degree. Married twice, thanks to Senator Lauder's information, but no details on the first wife, and very little on the second. er name, or nickname, was Daisy because, thanks to her golden curls, she resembled a flower and had violet-blue eyes.

Like yours, her inner voice whispered.

And what was so unusual about that? *Verochka* and Alex have the same eyes, she argued with her inner self, and so did Elizabeth Taylor. So what? So, nothing. She sighed and rubbed her forehead. Just a coincidence.

Yeah, you keep telling yourself that, my girl, her annoying inner self supplied.

"Shut up," she grumbled, and almost jumped out of her skin. While she was busy chatting with her bitchy self, Alex materialized like a ghost, and sprawled in the chair next to hers.

"Are you talking to me?" he inquired lazily, smirking in that way Nika adored, even though it annoyed the heck out of her sometimes.

Like right now.

"Dammit, Cuz, you almost made me pee myself!"

"*Moi*?" He pressed both hands to his heart, feigning wide-eyed, innocent surprise. "You wound me. Even though it would be an interesting, if a highly undignified, reaction to my humble self. So, you happy to see me?"

Barefoot and bare chested, dressed in his usual around the house attire of cotton shorts, he somehow managed to make an impression like he owned the world, or at least this small sliver of it. Which he did. A successful entrepreneur and part owner of their multi-million-dollar company, he was well respected in the business community, loved by friends and neighbors, and adored by his business partner.

Nika recovered quickly from her initial shock. "Happy-shmappy. How long have you been sitting here, spying on me?"

"Watching," he corrected, pointing an elegant finger at her. "And let me tell you, my girl, it's a fascinating and enlightening process, to watch that ugly face of yours during your silent discussion with yourself."

He knew her well. Too well. Sometimes, even better than she knew herself. It should be disconcerting, but instead was comforting. With Alex she didn't need to pretend. Didn't have to be anything other than herself. No wonder she loved him so much. The feeling was mutual. Nika drew a deep breath and blew it out noisily.

"You know me too well," she murmured, in half-accusation, half-acceptance.

"Well, spill it, brat. I already guessed it's the letter from our good senator's great-grandfather that gives you the willies."

"Yeah, you may say that again. I'm uneasy about it, about all of it."

"Same here, to be frank. But we agreed to take on this project. So, for better or worse, the Coleman house— and all its history, including this letter—are now ours to deal with. So, did you read it?"

In lieu of an answer, she shrugged, keeping her eyes glued to the ocean.

"Want me to do the honors?"

"No." Dammit. The coward in her wanted to do just that, let her cousin read it first. Especially because of that, she bore down and repeated, more forcefully, "No, I'll do it. It's for me, so I have to do it."

He nodded sagely.

"Take your time, babe. It was waiting for a hundred-something years, so what's another day or two in the great scheme of things?"

And that's precisely what Nika had been telling herself all these hours. Dammit, he did know her well. Too well. Sometimes, they didn't need words to communicate. They could read each other's minds, feel each other's emotions.

Lately, she wondered if their unique closeness was preventing him from forming a family. Not just a relationship, which Alex had had quite a few throughout their years here on Amelia island, but a strong, lasting, one-of-a-kind attachment to another human being. Come to think of it, the same could be said for her. Was their love for each other so huge that it didn't leave a place for another person? Were they both spoiled by the closeness they shared? Something to ponder about later, she decided, and, because the moment called for it, she stuck out her tongue at him. He laughed. Just as he always had.

That deep, rolling sound of a chuckle was uniquely Alex. Just like the deep cleft in his chin, or his clean-shaved head. A fashion he adopted before it went chic and trendy. His unusual violet-blue eyes. Like her own.

Or Daisy Coleman's—

Stop it, she ordered herself.

"It's her, isn't? Daisy Coleman that you're so hyped about?" He stopped laughing. Something in Nika's face and her overall behavior since yesterday, made him uneasy. So much so, that he had contemplated calling Senator Lauder and politely refusing the job. But if he did that, Nika would have his head on a platter. And not only because it compromised their Golden Rule of business, but because something *was* there, he couldn't put his finger on. Something elusive. Something clouded her face with bewilderment and sadness. And fear. Oh, yeah, that what was bugging the hell out of him. Nika was never scared. Ever. Even as a child, knee-deep in mischief and trouble, she was never scared of anything or anyone. Now she was. And it pissed him off.

"Nik, let's talk it over."

Because she refused to quit this project now, especially after they both gave their word to the senator, at least they could bring it, whatever *it* was, in the open and dissect it.

"Let's not," Nika answered after a pause, and curved her lips in a small crooked smile. "I know what you're trying to do but it's not necessary. I need to understand this, whatever *this* is, on my own. No offence, Cuz, but this is for me, and me alone, to deal with. I will read the letter that the great citizen of Amelia Island wrote for me in 1909. I will start my preliminary search on the Coleman house project tomorrow. And we'll see."

"Okay. Alright." There was something in her voice. Finality? Resignation? Whatever it was it closed the discussion and swept all his objections out of the way. Nika had made her decision, and come hell or high water, she intended to stick to her guns. Or die trying. And she was alone in this. The barriers she erected were as tangible as brick walls. She expected him to respect that.

The hell I will.

We'll see. A brewing uneasiness filled him. *We'll just see about that.*

"Do me a favor, Nik?"

"Anything."

"Call *Verochka*. She needs to hear about our new project, anyway, and I think it would be better if she hears it from you."

They always shared their professional news with *Verochka*. It was a tradition of theirs to get her blessing before starting a new job, any new job, but especially such a grand one as the Coleman house. And *Verochka*, Alex knew from experience, was the only person on earth who could change Nika's mind. He planned to see to that part. Because he had texted their grandmother earlier and expressed his misgivings.

"Yes, you're absolutely right. I will. By the way, where is she now?"

"Believe it or not, in New York. I think she's getting kinda tired of all her globetrotting, and ready to settle down."

"Cousin, are you talking about our grandmother, the one who circled the planet several times over, got stuck in the Great Pyramid of Giza, got bitten by a snake in the Amazon jungle, and swam with sharks in Bermuda? *That Verochka*?"

"Well, when you put it that way." He chuckled and shook his head.

He admired their infamous grandmother for her insatiable hunger to travel. She was the only one of the family without a permanent address. She never lived in the same place or country longer than a couple of months. Hence, her love affairs with the hotels. Ever since Amelia Island boasted its own Ritz-Carlton, *Verochka* was a favorite guest during the years she lived here. She even had her own suite kept especially for her. As the widow of the late banker Jackson P. Morris, she inherited his multi-billion-dollar estate and could easily afford it. Thank God for that, because if anyone deserved it, it was *Verochka*.

"I'll call her, and maybe talk her into visiting, since she's in the States," Nika answered as if warming up to the idea.

"That would be grand!"

He perked up. If *Verochka* came for a visit, she had the ability to put things into perspective and put his mind at ease. Because there was no one on this planet whose opinion and common-sense he trusted more. If she put her seal of approval on this project, then everything would be fine.

"Well, I'll take my magnificent self off, then," he declared and lazily rose to his feet. "Man, look at this view! I just fucking love it!"

"Yeah, it's spectacular. I'm so glad we bought this house," Nika smiled at him. "Despite someone's misgivings."

"And how long will you hold it against me? So, I was wrong, I already told you that a gazillion times."

Alex kissed the top of her head and then fluffed her springy curls with the palm of his hand. His action drove her crazy when they were children. Now it was a tiny bit annoying, as the man himself. Nika batted his hand off, and pulled her cell phone from the pocked of her shorts.

"Scram, oh you of little faith."

"I just couldn't envision us living in the circular house, that's all."

Their two-story home on the beach was built as a hexagon, but from afar it made an impression of a circle. The reinforced wooded stilts held up the second story like mythological Atlases. The winding staircases hugged it from both sides, so Nika and Alex had their separate entrances. Inside, were two master suites with two lavish bathrooms, equipped with their own small kitchenettes. But both preferred to use the main kitchen they had remodeled into a state-of-the-art masterpiece Nika called it every chef's wet dream. The open living/family space with its floor-to-ceiling windows that gave them a killer view of the Atlantic Ocean was the selling point. That, and the considerable distance from the historic district where Before & After, Inc. had its main office. Dealing with people in and out all day, every day, made her crave solitude. Not that she didn't like people, but she needed her own space and alone time. Both of which she found only near water.

Buying a house on the beach was a must. Buying this one, situated smack in the middle of Ocean Avenue, just a short walking distance from the water was a lucky draw.

"Circular-shmircular," she grumbled good-naturedly. "And I'll hold it against you for as long as you live."

"Shrew," he threw over his shoulder.

"Shmuck," she retorted on a chuckle, already speed-dialing *Verochka's* number.

Her merriment faded at the familiar childhood greeting.

"Hello-hello, Daisy-girl! How is my favorite flower?"

CHAPTER THREE

Nika cruised along Ocean Drive in her Corvette with the top down. What was the point in owning a convertible if you drove it like a regular sedan? For her job she drove a truck, a reliable, sturdy Chevy she respected from the moment she purchased it. It, too, matched her personality as it was fire engine red. Like her temper, Alex joked. The Corvette was a different matter. She was absolutely and crazily in love with it, considered it her baby and pampered it as much as was humanly possible. She even named it Coco and talked to it, kissed it good-night and petted it when no-one was around. The car was a comfort to her as much as a luxury. Maybe, even more so, since she bought it with her own hard-earned money. Today Nika needed all the comfort she could get, even from an inanimate object such as Coco-the-Corvette.

She turned left onto Dolphin Avenue. Luckily the Sunday streets were almost empty because her mind raced with a million different thoughts. There was no need to go to the office. She had a rule that weekends were free time for them. But she found it hard to settle down after her long phone conversation with *Verochka*. And she still couldn't bring herself to read the letter. So, what better way to kill a Sunday morning than to take a drive? An aimless and long one to clear her head and calm her jittery nerves.

Her grandmother was the only person on earth who ever called her Daisy. According to *Verochka*, the newborn Nika with her fuzzy mop of golden hair always reminded her of a wildflower.

Sound familiar? Elijah Coleman called his wife Daisy because she reminded him of a flower.

"Stop it. Just stop!" Nika banged the steering wheel with her fist. Regret for harming her baby shot through her. She patted the leather wrapped wheel gently. "I'm sorry, Coco. It's not you, baby, it's that bitch that lives inside me. I hate her, you know."

Hate me, love me, you know it's strange, and not a mere coincidence. Couldn't be.

"Yes, I know."

He wrote to you. You! The message that is supposed to be delivered in September 2019. Girl, you have to read that letter sooner or later.

"Yeah, I know that, too. Just... not right now."

Coward.

"Maybe, so sue me."

Nika sighed. She had been salivating after the Coleman house for two years. Dreamt about it, fought for it, for goodness' sake! Now she had it, and she was reluctant to start even the preliminary research, not to mention the actual job.

That darn letter!

One good thing that came out of the Coleman house deal was the upcoming visit from their adorable and beloved globe-trotter. *Verochka* was intrigued. And when she was intrigued, she got antsy. And when that happened, their grandmother was as unstoppable and unpredictable as a hurricane. No surprise to Nika if *Verochka* was already on her way to Amelia Island.

She smiled, and took the next turn toward the Fernandina Beach historical district where the office of Before & After, Inc. was located. She stopped in their parking lot and sat there for a moment, reminiscing. Was it a coincidence that their company's main office was across from the spot where eight years ago their battered old car had died on them? Did Fate, that fickle bitch, really interfere and make the decision for them by forcing Alex and Nika to halt their rebellious, childish 'Grand Adventure' and start a real adult life?

There was no such a thing as coincidence. Everything happens for a reason, however trite it may sound. And every situation in life has its purpose. The purpose of their car giving its last breath on the corner of this street eight years ago was clear to Nika: to make them stop and reassess their choices.

The reason, however, had yet to be determined.

A light breeze teased her hair, propelling the springy curls into a crazy dance. Right now she probably did have a striking resemblance to the wildflower her grandmother nicknamed her after. That darn hair was the bane of her existence. Nika had tried everything under the moon to tame them to be straighter, more presentable, but to no avail. They curled madly in every which way, and stubbornly refused to obey to any ministrations of world-renowned stylists, or submit to the restrictions of combs or hairpins. So, in defiance—or pure madness—she hacked them off to chin length bob. Now her hair resembled the top of a dandelion, or like *Verochka* loved to say, a nimbus. The color of her hair was another disappointment. It could, she supposed, be called blond, but loosely. Its shade was so dark it was almost bronze. *Verochka* called it tarnished gold. Alex called it nutty blond. Nika called it ugly. But the texture was silky smooth.

She blew angrily at the curls whipping around her face and started the car. She pulled out onto the street and made an illegal U-turn. She drove fast—too fast—to her destination, before she might talk herself out of it. In a few whirlwind minutes she was there.

She liked that the island was small and suspended forever in the Victorian era. Its charm and enchantment came from that time and was unapologetically locked in it. Nika loved everything about Amelia Island. Its history, climate, and captivating beauty that always enticed different types of people, from the aristocrats and royalty to the pirates and bootleggers.

As a result, the atmosphere and energy were a unique and fascinating mix of fairy tales, drama, and suspense.

Just like the house that loomed in front of her. *The Coleman house.*

A smile crossed her face as she drove past the old trees and then through the gate barely hanging on its rusted posts. She imagined the derelict building in its glory day all those years ago, when it proudly towered over the other houses nearby, so sure of its superiority, so comfortable in its glory. Majestic. It took her breath away from the very first moment she had laid eyes on it. She still had yet to gain it back.

Her research proved the legendary structure was erected by the best architect of that time, Robert S. Schuyler, local celebrity and Amelia Island native, under close supervision and to the detailed specifications of its owner, and was a testament to Elijah Coleman's engineering genius.

She loved searching through old newspapers and documents to learn more about the house that enthralled her. Located at the end of the so-called Silk-Stocking District, named for its famous sherbet-colored mansions, the Coleman house was as different from its genteel neighbors as night and day.

Governing over the northern part of the historical district, it stood three stories high, unblemished by any hue, regally white and unapologetically male. This 9,000 square-foot edifice with its three cottages and luxurious pool was a mixture of Italianate and Mediterranean villas, blended together in one unique mix. The native flora was presented in abundance. Century-old live oak trees with whimsical Spanish moss naturally co-existed with exotic palm trees. The one bit of family history that intrigued Nika was the story of a little butterfly garden built for Abigail Coleman, the younger sister of Elijah who had mysteriously disappeared in her early twenties. One day she was there, the next—she disappeared, never to be seen again. There were rumors she ran away with her lover, escaping a pre-arranged marriage by her brother to a member of the Carnegie family. There was speculation Elijah had learned of her indiscretion and disinherited her, then evicted her from the house. There were also whispers he killed her in a moment of rage.

Too far-fetched in her opinion, because according to all the records, Elijah Coleman wasn't prone to losing his temper. Quite the contrary. His biography described him as self-controlled, even rigid at times, and disciplined with little to no emotion. Highly intelligent, highly educated, the heir apparent of the Coleman clan, he was rumored to be terse, laconic, and an extremely private. His one and only weakness was his baby sister. Much older in years, he had raised her, doting on her, indulging her every whim. Hence the butterfly garden. Did he really pre-arrange her marriage? Probably. Did he kill her? Unlikely.

But whether the rumors were true or false, the history of the house was turbulent, multi-layered, and shrouded in secrets like its residents.

And now it stood in front of her, forlorn, neglected, but not defeated. In her imagination, the house was frozen in a self-induced sleep, hovering on the brink of awakening.

Waiting.

Yes, the house was waiting. Patiently. Tolerantly. Resignedly.

And now it was hers. Nika shivered at the thought.

Well, not *hers*. It was her responsibility for as long as it took her crew to awaken this sleeping beauty, restoring it to its former glory.

Nika lifted her eyes to the third story, then trailed her gaze down over the mansion, trying to take it all in. Magnificent!

"Hello, again," she whispered against the windshield of her convertible. "How have you been these couple of days?"

That was how long it had been since she last been to the house.

She visited it regularly, as often as she could. Like a magnet or a drug, the house pulled at her. And like an addict, Nika readily and gleefully succumbed to the seduction.

Every time she stayed away from the house longer than a few days, she became tense, nervous, almost sick, itching to see it, and yes, talk to it.

The house had talked to her from the moment she laid her eyes on it. Its murmurs, energy— pulsing, demanding— were a language she understood well. After all, Nika wasn't called the House Whisperer for nothing. Her famous sixth sense was at its strongest when it came to this particular home. *The Coleman house. Her house now.*

"You probably know already that I finally got permission, and I will be taking care of you from now on," she murmured. "I promise you won't be disappointed."

She was up to the task. Maybe it was bold, even shameless of her, but she had confidence she could do it better than anyone else. She could and would do the job, and do it with excellence. Deep in her gut she was dead sure that it was for her, and only her, to restore the house it to its former original splendor. Impossible for anyone to do it better, because...well, dammit, because she felt it deep in her marrow.

And how unusual and strange was that?

Well, not so usual since she experienced the same feelings about their projects Before & After, Inc. had the privilege of renovating during the last eight years. But she confessed to herself, not as strong or overwhelming as with this project.

She sighed, deep and resignedly. The Coleman house was special. To her.

While it wasn't strange or unusual for Nika to 'feel' almost any house and its atmosphere and energy, what *was* unusual and strange was that she envisioned in her mind's eye all the details of the interior of this particular house, even though she had never stepped a foot inside.

From the tiny spec in the Tiffany lamp in the library and the shade of the draperies in the master bedroom to the sound of the creaking steps, especially the third step on the main staircase, and the design of the mantels in each room.

Not to mention the colors and patterns of the wallpapers. Those were so popular in 1906-1909, Water Lily print in the family room and Bonaparte Cassique in the guest bedrooms. She also envisioned an imposing and ornate grandfather clock, the eight-day longcase masterpiece circa 1827 made in England that stood in a corner of the first floor, slightly to the left from the entrance to the formal dining room. The deep and wheezy sound of its chime was as familiar to her as her own name.

And how on earth was that possible?

Nika cursed as she jumped out of the car, slammed the door shut, and stomped toward the house. Each step created the sensation she was a woman approaching the firing squad.

What on earth? It's never been like that before.

Perplexed and shivering, Nika slowed her steps, but still moved forward.

She had come here many a time before, marveling at the house, coveting it, admiring it. And never been afraid. Then, why was she now so scared all of a sudden? When she wanted the job and knew she couldn't get it, she was okay, but as soon as her innermost wish and her dream became a reality apprehension set in her core. She started to dread it.

Stupid, she cursed inwardly. *It's the same house it was two days ago. Nothing changed. Nothing could.*

Determined to squash her totally irrational fear, Nika steeled her spine and stubbornly marched forward. She intended to prove to herself, if nothing else, that she was fully in charge of her own emotions, dammit it. Fear be damned. Premonitions are silly. And she wasn't a ninny, for goodness' sake!

Ignoring the hissing noise inside her head and funny jitters in her stomach, Nika plowed ahead.

Brutal nausea hit her like a sledgehammer.

Doubling over with pain, Nika stopped as throat wrenching gags gripped her. Cold sweat ran in rivulets down her face and into her eyes. Saliva pooled into her mouth.

What the hell?

Mad, sick, and trembling all over, Nika turned her back to the house. She spit foul tasting liquid from her mouth after the belly twisting retches slowed. She fought to catch her equilibrium.

No way! No way will I give in.

And all because the old cranky house had decided to show her its displeasure. Humiliated more than scared, she shut her eyes and tried to breathe deep through her nose, exhaling through her mouth. She didn't know how long she stood there, clutching her middle, desperate to regulate her breathing, but the sun still shined and the warm breeze swirled around her. Her throat was raw. The putrid taste of vomit unbearable.

"I'll be back," she muttered, glaring over her shoulder. "I'll be back soon, you cranky old bastard. And next time, I'll be prepared, and I'll stay. Whether you like it or not."

Her breath still hitched in and out, more embarrassing than annoying, because it almost sounded like whimpering. Not quite, but still. Aggravated, Nika struck out.

So there.

Flipping an inanimate object the middle finger, especially one that shook like a drunk on Sunday morning, wasn't rational or professional of her. She didn't care.

The house—that *bastard*—smirked at her. Really? Or was it because her brain was too muddled and her stomach too queasy? Feverish, trembling, Nika stumbled toward the Corvette and almost whimpered in the process. Once safely inside the car with her doors locked, Nika started to feel like herself. Doors locked. She drove a convertible and the top was down!

At once, her nausea disappeared and the shivers stopped. If not for the tremor in her hands, she may have imagined the whole episode.

But no, it wasn't a dream or hallucination. The Coleman house had declared its displeasure in the loudest and most conspicuous way.

Never before she had experienced something even close to what happened just moments ago. Never before had her restoration project announced its 'feelings' and reacted that strongly toward her.

Funny, but she never sensed the Coleman house's negative energy. Quite the contrary, in fact. Some old houses were cranky and whiny. Some were bitter and mean, emanating waves of negativity so thick it was almost tangible.

A few times Nika had to 'cleanse' the house first by burning white candles, sprinkling rock salt or scattering black tourmaline, before she could enter it. Alex joked at her attempts at white witchcraft, but never did he step inside of any 'mean' houses before she had a chance to perform her magic.

Not this house, though.

The Coleman house always greeted Nika with an utmost respect and acceptance, if you could use these expressions toward an inanimate object. She always sensed the Coleman house as the most dignified, distinguished southern gentleman, highly intelligent, kind, and soft-spoken.

But not, obviously, meek. Or forgiving. The house was mad at her. But for what?

What had changed? She got the project, she met the last descendant of the Coleman clan, Senator Lauder. She received the letter from Elijah Coleman. *And still didn't read it.*

So, that's the problem? That's the crux of it? Impossible!

But even as she debated the reason for the house's strange behavior, she was confident she had hit it square on the nail. As her cousin and grandmother gently but insistently nudged her to read the letter, the house gave her one angry, mighty push, demanding it.

Nika touched the pocket of her shorts where she had tucked the darn letter earlier.

Was she imagining it, or was it really warm to the touch, even through the layer of denim? She snatched back her hand as if the envelope had burned her and then clenched the steering wheel.

Dammit.

She will read the letter when she was good and ready. Not one minute earlier. And she wasn't ready. Not yet. Not by a long shot. And no one, not a living, breathing person, and definitely not a century old structure of bricks and wood, were to say anything about it.

So there!

The million-dollar question was, when exactly would she be ready, if ever.

And that posed a huge problem and put this project in perilous danger.

If she got sick each and every time she approached the darn house, how on earth did she expect to work inside of it?

CHAPTER FOUR

For the next week Nika worked like a woman possessed.

While she waited for all the permits' approval she started on more research. Their local library became her home away from home, where she poured over the pages of *The Florida Mirror,* that was published between 1878 and 1901, the books with old photographs, and tomes on the history of Amelia Island. She was usually the first one to enter the library in the morning and the last one to leave.

Even at home, after a quick shower and a bite to eat, she continued to scrutinize online catalogs and articles, taking copious notes, printing out a gazillion pages, copying a lot of data onto her computer. Architecture, fashion, design, art and music, drinks and culinary recipes, customs and gossips. She collected every little scrap of information she found on the era, and hoarded it onto her hard-drive.

A gal can never be too careful.

She laughed as she backed it all up on multiple thumb-drives.

Nika was driven, determined, relentless.

She was obsessed.

The house that took her breath away two years ago and spoiled her for any other work finally became her reality, her most coveted and important restoration project. Granted, it wasn't legally hers, but Nika never had such a pride of ownership or such a thrill of possession before. Or such a burning jealousy toward the real owners.

After her job was completed, they would be the ones to claim the house. To do with it whatever they chose. She never asked Senator Lauder, and he never volunteered the information, what his family's intentions were after the restoration. Hotel? Museum? Family winter residence?

No matter what it was no concern of hers.

The hell it wasn't.

It was her baby, her project! Her sweat and blood were about to be poured into it or spilled onto its grounds. So, it was her business. Her concern.

The hell it was.

Why did she care so much? Granted, she cared about all their projects, but not to the point that a mere thought of giving the fully restored house away, back to the owners, made her sick to her stomach.

Under normal circumstances, they were the owners of the house that Alex, as a licensed real estate broker, located and Nika, as a licensed contractor, thoroughly inspected. The plan was for Before & After, Inc. to buy it, restore it, and sell it. After that they walked away with a profit, ready and eager to do it all over again.

With the Coleman house, however, it was a totally different story.

Nika found it quite by accident. Or the house has found her, more accurate. One evening, returning from a party she didn't want to attend in the first place, mildly annoyed and headachy, Nika made a wrong turn. At the time she was busy with being mad at Alex, who, enamored with an exotic brunette he had met decided to stay and party some more.

When her mistake became apparent, Nika banged the steering wheel with her fist, cursed like a seasoned sailor, and then poured her frustration into imagining all the mischief she was now duty-bound to spring on him.

That calmed her down. As she prepared to make a U-turn on the narrow dark street, she turned her head back to make sure the road was clear. And there it was, the Coleman house.

It took her breath away and rendered her blind, mute and deaf for a good thirty seconds before Nika found her bearings. Her sniffles and headache forgotten, she stopped the car in the middle of the street and stepped out.

The old house in front of her called to her like no other structure before, or after. It stirred something inside of her heart and made it tremble.

It brought hot tears to Nika's eyes, and made her wonder and want.

It claimed her soul.

The very same evening, as soon as she finally found her way home, she jumped on the computer, and to make the inquiries about the abandoned house.

Her agitation proved to be highly contagious, and Alex joined her in the pursuit. With considerable effort by an attorney, they located the current owners and offered them an outrageous amount of money for the house. But, one after another, their multiple offers were rejected. For two years in a row. Only to be replaced by the more outrageous offer they couldn't refuse.

No, the house wasn't theirs. There was no need to market it afterwards and show it to potential buyers. The Coleman house belonged to the family that adamantly refused to sell it, but gave Nika carte blanche to restore it.

She stayed away from the house for several days. Instead, she took long walks along the historic district, down to the Fernandina Harbor Marina, the popular tourists' destination, and the starting point of all Amelia Island River tours and cruises.

She had been on many such tours when she first arrived here eight years ago. Fascinated with the island, drunk on her newfound freedom, she drove Alex crazy, dragging him on day trips, visiting museums and cruising on tour boats. She discovered her love for the small towns and various islands with their unique flora and fauna. Settling eagerly into the rhythm of life of her new hometown, Nika shed New York like a snake does old skin. She was surprised how easy it was for her to let go of the old habits, old life, old Nika. Her Ferrari, her prized and most adored possession, was long forgotten, as were her regular trips to the trending exhibits or sessions at the salons.

She embraced her new life in the small picturesque village-town, saturated with sun and local history. And, of course, the ocean. Her newfound love for it was another surprising discovery. In short, Nika was happy. Satisfied.

Until the Coleman house...

She still hadn't read the letter, even though she carried it everywhere with her. *On her*, to be more accurate, since she tucked it into the pocket of the outfit she happened to wear that day absolutely unmindful on the significance of the gesture. She slipped it out of her pocket every evening when she changed for bed. To protect the fragile century-old pages, she placed it into a Ziploc sandwich bag, painstakingly removing all the air from it before zipping it closed. Alex joked about it when he caught her in the act. Nika flicked her hand at him and lied through her teeth that she was protecting the historical document, nothing more.

Nika ached to go to the house, just to check on it, to make sure that it was still there, intact, waiting for her. That it talked to her again as before, and not reject her like the last time. But she was afraid. And mad at herself for her cowardice. So, she drove herself ragged, learning, preparing, searching. Absorbing.

Her research became her mission. She browsed the internet until her eyes became unfocused and her vision blurry, until her brain started buzzing with all the information she uncovered and committed to memory. Sometimes, she was so engrossed in her reading that the images and pictures of the people and the era she was researching swirled in her head, filled with snippets of conversations, smells, and sounds. Nika became disoriented at strange moments like that. A great amount of time passed before she shook the feeling and resurfaced from that murky world to reality.

She knew everything, or next to everything, about the Coleman household, its residents and various staff. She had learned how many servants there were at different periods and their names. She even managed to dig out accounting records of the household expenses and memorized exactly how much the Colemans spent each month from the cost of groceries to the tailor's bill. The learning experience was fascinating. But Nika failed to suppress a nagging sensation of deja vu, like she was reading a book she had read already, a long time ago, and had just forgotten the plot.

Her sense of uneasiness and irritation increased, but couldn't diminish the joy or the fever of pure, undiluted exaltation that signified the beginning of a new project.

"Look who I found wandering in the neighborhood!"

The excitement in Alex's voice was the first thing that registered in her foggy brain. The meaning of his words finally penetrated her mind and shattered her concentration. Nika tore her gaze from the computer screen, squinting, frowning. She had been hunched over it for a long time, completely absorbed in her reading.

In the next moment, Nika squealed with delight and jumped up from the sofa.

"*Verochka!*"

Like a compact tornado, she barreled forward and hugged her grandmother tightly. "I missed you, oh I missed you so darn much!"

"I guess she's glad to see you, Gorgeous," he said to his grandmother.

"I am, I am!" Nika squeezed her eyes tightly to fight the unexpected tears. "I'm so glad, so happy, so ecstatic!" Her voice hitched on the last word, betraying her turmoil.

Verochka's eyes met her grandson's with concern, but when she finally disengaged herself from Nika's hold, she smiled at her granddaughter, wiping the worry from her face.

"Hello-hello, baby girl. I have missed you, too." She kissed both of Nika's cheeks in a European manner then shook her head. With one delicate finger she slowly traced underneath Nika's eyes, tucked a lock of stray hair behind her ear. Nika could only imagine the picture she presented: red-rimmed eyes, disheveled hair, wrinkled shirt.

"Hard at work, as usual, I see," her grandmother concluded with a sigh.

Verochka's velvety soprano held a delicate murmur of her native French, adding an additional layer of sophistication to her impeccable appearance. Dressed to the nines, perfectly groomed, tall and willowy, she was the personification of the word elegance. With her effortlessly erect posture, a graceful swan-like neck and her long legs accented by a pair of snug pants, she personified the image of the ex-ballerina that she was, only aged to perfection, according to her own favorite expression. She even smelled perfect, subtle and classy, wearing her trademark, *Chloe.* The company should have made *Verochka* their muse instead of that young, skinny, freckled girl. Their loss.

"*Mon Dieu, babe, tu as un air terrible,*" *Verochka* scolded Nika, shaking her head. Since she spoke only English in her everyday life, sliding back into her childhood French rarely and only in moments of distress, Nika deduced that she indeed, looked a fright.

She grinned, carefree and joyous for the first time in weeks.

"I clean up good, I promise."

"See that you do, because I'm taking both of you for a dinner to that fancy new place I've read about."

"*Pogo's?*" Nika perked up immediately.

"Yes, I believe that's the one."

Nika boogied— or tried to— her apparent delight, because *Pogo's Kitchen* was her all-time absolute favorite place, and earned a swat on the butt from Alex.

"Don't, please. For the love of God, don't do that," he emphasized his words by a windmill motion of his hands, "especially in the presence of the Dance Goddess."

It was a known fact that Nika was born with two left feet and couldn't dance even if her life depended on it. She was the family klutz, pure and simple, but it didn't prevent her from trying some moves on occasion. Like right now.

"What? I can dance. Sometimes. Right, *Verochka*?"

"Daisy-girl, I love you to the moon and back," *Verochka* answered with a deep sigh, "but if you insist on showing that...body motion you just did in some public place, I'll swear on a stack of bibles that we're not related." But her violet-blue eyes danced with laughter.

"Fine, alright, okay," Nika grumbled, good-naturedly. "Be that way. Be mean to me. But one day, I promise, I'll waltz. You'll see. And you'll be ashamed of yourselves for making fun of me."

"It takes two to waltz. But I will gladly apologize to you, Daisy-girl," she said. "The day I see you dance. And I mean, really dance. Until then, please change your...whatever it is you're wearing, and oh, don't forget to take a shower."

"In other words, I stink," Nika snickered.

"Hmm," *Verochka* twitched her adorable, perky nose, but refrained from commenting.

"By the way, love the hair." Nika winked and gathered her things from the sofa.

Verochka's silver-blond mane that she usually wore twisted up in a knot, was now cut short in a smooth, silky cap of a chin-length bob. "When did you change it?"

"I thought you'd never ask." She touched gingerly her naked nape. "Just last week. I decided it was time for a change. Do you honestly like it?"

"It's uber chic. Classy, elegant, and sexy as hell! And it makes you look twenty years younger."

"Thank you," She smiled with obvious satisfaction. "I thought so, too, but it always nice to have your opinion confirmed."

Uh-oh, time to interfere. Alex shook his head. The subject of hair was one of the most favorite amongst the womenfolk, without any exceptions. Goddesses included. Nika's curls resembled a casualty after an explosion in a pasta factory. But she was so adorably ridiculous, sitting cross-legged on the sofa with her laptop balanced on her bended knees, wearing her reading glasses and a scowl. For the life of him, he couldn't explain why sadness had suddenly swept over him, or why his throat had gone tight and itchy. He chuckled, shaking off the strange sensation that whirled around him.

"Ladies, I hate to interrupt, but time." He tapped his wristwatch with a finger. "Scoot." He shooed Nika off, motioning with both hands for more emphasis. "Go make yourself presentable for our dinner date. After all, it's not every day we dine with the Dance Goddess."

Nika made a face at him, blew *Verochka* a kiss, and hurried from the room.

"Five minutes," she threw over her shoulder. "I'll be as good as new."

"Take ten. Better yet, twenty. You need it, and then some." Alex sighed and met his grandmother's gaze. "Drink?"

"Thank you, dear, I wouldn't say no. And pour yourself one, too. We both need it."

After pouring a glass of *Verochka's* favorite Chablis, Alex dropped two ice cubes into his own glass then splashed in vodka.

"Well, what's your verdict, Gorgeous?" He asked after a long sip, tilting his head.

"She is..." *Verochka* tried her wine then nodded her approval. "Preoccupied."

"Ya think?"

"Don't be sarcastic, Alexander. It doesn't become you." She continued to sip her wine.

"I apologize. But...preoccupied? She's obsessed is what she is," he said in a curt tone of voice he rarely used with his grandmother. "It's too much, too intense. She always gets up to her neck in a project. Sometimes I have to remind her to eat or to shower." He pointed his hand in a general direction of Nika's side of the house. "But this time...I don't know. It seems unusual, even for Nika. She doesn't sleep, or not enough. She practically lives in the library. When she's home, she's working on her computer, deaf and mute to anything around her. This project, this Coleman House is special, somehow. And I'm nervous. No, let's be honest. I'm freaked out."

"Oh? Why?"

"I can't put my finger on it. But one thing I know for sure is that Nika is not only obsessed with this house, she's afraid of it."

"Don't be ridiculous, darling." *Verochka* dismissed his concerns with a delicate shrug. "For one, our girl is not afraid of anything. You know that better than anyone. And I absolutely refuse to even entertain a notion that some inanimate object, a century old plus structure can make her afraid."

"It *talks* to her," he said after a long pause.

"Which is absolutely normal for her." His grandmother nodded, unfazed. "She is sensitive to energy."

"I know, but this time..." Alex stole a glance at Nika's side of the house. "It just seems strange and overwhelming. I'm afraid she's in over her head."

"You talk like she's in love with it," *Verochka* chuckled.

"But she is. She's obsessed with this house, I'm telling you. She thinks about it like it's a living, breathing person. And that damn letter." He skimmed his hand over his bald head.

"Alex, darling, you're getting overly dramatic for nothing." *Verochka* set her glass on an end table then took his hand in hers.

"Nothing?"

"Yes, I promise you. Nika is empathic, and always was. She feels too much, too deep. And she's always had this adventurous and reckless streak she got from yours truly."

She tugged at his hands still sandwiched between her own, and made him sit on the sofa beside her.

"This house, the history of it, the old letter addressed to her, which could have a very simple explanation to it, is just too irresistible and too delicious to our Nika. It makes her tingle and it makes her wonder. Simply put, it gets her juices flowing. Everything about this house seems so unique and special to her." *Verochka* wiggled her fingers like a magician performing an illusion. "Because it is shrouded in *mystery*. And only because of that, trust me. With time, when she starts the actual labor, she won't have time for anything fanciful, it'll pass."

"You sure?"

"Positive."

"And what about the name?"

"What name are you referring to?"

"The name of Elijah Coleman's second wife."

"What about it?"

"Daisy. Her name was Daisy, and she had violet eyes and dark blond curls. Like Nika."

"So? Just proves my point. A layer of mystery over something as trivial as a female name, eyes, and hair. There's nothing special about it. And again, it could have a very simple explanation."

"So, you think it just a coincidence, then?"

"My dear boy," she leaned over and kissed his cheek. "There is no such thing in the universe as a coincidence. Period."

"I hate to bring it up, Gorgeous, but you just contradicted yourself." He gave her a pained half-smile.

"On the contrary, my darling." *Verochka* patted the cheek she just kissed a moment ago in a self-indulgent gesture, "I have made my case."

"How so?"

Again, she took a moment.

"Have you heard of Fate?" she asked. "Or Karma?"

He blinked several times, momentarily thrown off balance.

"Well, for the sake of the argument, let's say the meaning of those two words are familiar to me."

"Excellent. We are all born with a free will, of course, but our paths are mainly predestined. Now, whether we *choose* to travel the path that was chosen, or predestined, is entirely up to us. With me?"

"So far," Alex nodded, both fascinated with her and dumbfounded by the subject. He made a circling gesture with his hand, inviting her to continue.

"Nika was predestined to discover the Coleman house. I'm sure of it. She fell in love with it, and wanted it badly, desperately even, for her next project, which is quite normal. But," she lifted her finger and pointed at him. "She was denied. The owners refused your offer again and again, and it only whetted her appetite and triggered her curiosity, not to mention her imagination. When the senator from Massachusetts approached you with his proposition, you both could have refused it. Correct? Especially after learning about Daisy, and the letter. But you and Nika accepted."

"And?"

"And that's all. You both have chosen to follow the path the universe had predesigned for you, and now you have to learn to live with it."

"So, there is nothing that strikes you as unusual? The house? The letter? The name?"

"I didn't say that."

"But you said—"

"I said it could be easily explained."

"How so? Enlighten me, for goodness' sake, because I'm even more confused than I was before this conversation."

"Delighted to," A serene smile touched her lips. "You see, everything can be explained very easily if our Nika *was* Daisy Coleman in her previous life."

CHAPTER FIVE

Alex blanched.

"Reincarnation?"

"And why not? That explains a lot, doesn't?"

"Are you serious?"

"Absolutely."

"You are serious." He stared at his grandmother for a long moment. "So, what should I do now?"

"Nothing. Live, work, go about your business, and let the situation unfold in its own time and rhythm. After all, nothing has changed."

"If you say so." He was unconvinced. And bewildered.

"It's hard to take it all in. Not the reincarnation stuff, mind you, because, sorry, Gorgeous, but I don't buy into it." He leaned forward and steepled his fingers, bracing both elbows on his knees. "What boggles the mind is that you truly believe in it. You, the most clear-minded, intelligent person I know."

"I'm also an open-minded person, darling. And one thing I've learned by now is that there are more things in heaven and earth. Thank you, Horatio. Call it the wisdom of my advanced age, if you will." She smiled.

"Let's say, you're right."

"I am."

"Okay. Let's assume for the sake of an argument that you are. Should we tell Nika? Get her any hints, or—?"

"I say or. I think she'll need to work it out on her own. Sooner or later, she will realize the truth."

"That she was Daisy Coleman."

"Right."

"In her previous life."

"Correct."

"What did I miss?" Nika walked into the room, fastening her slacks on the go.

"Nothing," *Verochka* and Alex answered in unison, quickly. Too quickly.

Oh-uh. Nika's hands stilled in midmotion. Her mild curiosity metamorphosed into heavy suspicion in a flash.

"*Verochka*?"

"What, dear?"

"Are you hiding something from me?"

"What could we possibly be hiding from you, Daisy-girl? By the way, you do clean up marvelously."

"Don't try to change the subject. I will torture it out of Alex later, anyway, so spill."

"There is nothing to spill, as you succinctly put it." *Verochka* picked up her purse and draped the long, delicate chain handles over her shoulder. "And if we don't leave in the next few minutes, we'll be late for our dinner reservation."

Nika switched her gaze to her cousin, who hurriedly gulped down his drink and made a production of checking his wristwatch. He deliberately avoided her eyes, which made Nika even more suspicious. She wouldn't get anything out of these two right now. She shrugged with a deliberate nonchalance and pretended to let it go. She decided to enjoy her dinner and the company of two people she loved most, and then she planned to round on him, or *Verochka*, or both, and flush the truth out. For now, she must go along and pretend that nothing was amiss, and enjoy herself.

As it happened, she didn't have to work very hard on uncovering the truth. Earlier, *Verochka* had accepted his invitation to spend the night in the guest bedroom instead of going back to her hotel, so after a delightful dinner at *Pogo's Kitchen*, all three of them returned to the house on the beach.

The drive back was uneventful, but Nika, even as tipsy as she was, still didn't forget her quest. The truth will come out as to why her cousin and her grandmother both wore identical expressions of guilt on their faces earlier. They were hiding something from her, but not for long.

Hiding-shminding, Nika snorted, *forgot who they were dealing with*!

When she wanted something, she became as single-minded as a bullet in a trajectory. The best course of action, she decided, was to divide and conquer.

Simple, efficient. Easy. She preferred to work on Alex. Her cousin was an open book to her. Plus, Nika had no problem reverting to dirty tricks with him, which she never allowed herself with her grandmother. Yes, he was easier, but she decided to take what she could, and play it by ear.

As soon as they were inside, Alex announced that he was beat, and scurried to his bedroom, the coward. That left *Verochka*. And that was okay, even if it required a slight change in her tactic. Her grandmother's biggest weakness was that she couldn't keep any secrets. At least, not from Nika or Alex. So, feigning nonchalance, Nika casually offered a walk on the moonlit beach. *Verochka* accepted.

Nika started the conversation by asking her grandmother about her last trip. And learned that it was Borneo, of all places.

"Why Borneo?" she asked, curious.

"Why not?" *Verochka's* bare feet were almost floating over the wet sand. "It was quite an adventure, let me tell you. Oh, I watched bat swarms! They're flying in a huge, single endless ribbon to confuse predators. Spectacular! Then, I spent a good part of my trip with a native tribe of blowpipe hunters."

"Blowpipe hunters?" She shouldn't be surprised. Nika was used to *Verochka's* amazing adventures by now, but her grandmother still managed to baffle and astonish her. Like right now.

"Yes. They're called Penan, the indigenous, ancient people that still live as they did hundreds of years ago." Her expression grew serious. "But it's sad and pitiful how the government treats them. They are removed from their remote villages and throw into poor settlements, and all because of the trees. The government almost deforested the whole country, destroying their most valuable commodity the rain forest. It's despicable. I wrote a protest letter to the prime minister but so far haven't heard any reply. I will try again." *Verochka* stopped walking and glanced at the moon. "I donated some funds to the tribe leaders, so at least they won't starve. That's all I was able to do, dammit. It's not enough. Not nearly enough to save these people."

"You did what you could, *Verochka*," Nika touched her shoulder. "You can't save everybody."

"I know, I know. It's just..." *Verochka's* eyes darkened with sadness. "Such a beautiful country, such an amazing people. Proud, independent, strong. They deserve better. And the kids...deplorable."

Time to change the mood.

Nika patted her grandmother's hand and asked, "So, where to now? After the rain forest, I'm sure you're ready for a change of scenery."

Verochka squared her shoulders and broke into a mischievous grin.

"Funny you should ask. I was thinking Iceland."

"Iceland, huh? Yes, I can see how it would be different from the rain forest," Nika chuckled. "Wait, didn't you visit there a few years ago?"

"Sure did. But you never tire of the geysers."

They moved along the beach once again. *Verochka* glided effortlessly on her long legs while Nika stomped on sand and dragged her much shorter ones with considerable exertion. All the while she mentally scrambled for an opening to introduce her subject.

"Well," Verochka said after they plowed across another half mile of sand. "You got me here. We've talked about my trip. Now, why don't you just ask your question instead of dragging me all over this beach, chatting and pretending that you forgot?"

"Nothing goes by you," Nika murmured under her breath. "And here I thought my scheme to get you all alone, in the most scenic spot at night, and gradually ease you into the conversation, was so clever."

"It would be clever, if it weren't me. Or you. We know each other too well, Daisy-girl. You know, for example, that I absolutely hate secrets, and can't keep them from the people I love, even if it's for their own benefit. And I know that you are like a bull terrier. If you want something, you grab and hold."

"So, you're saying, we are predictable?"

"At least, to each other, yes."

"I hate to be predictable," Nika frowned, "it's one step short of boring."

"There is nothing boring about you, Daisy-girl, in my humble opinion."

"And there is nothing humble about you," Nika parried with a crooked half-smile.

"True," *Verochka* grinned in return. "Very true. But getting back on track, you wanted to ask me a question. Ask away."

"And you'll answer truthfully?" Nika eyed her with suspicion.

"What's the point in lying? You'll know it, I'll know that you know it, and we both will be disappointed. I either answer truthfully or don't answer at all."

"Comforting. Okay, here's the question. What are you and Alex hiding from me?" She stopped, turned, and faced her grandmother.

"Nothing that you wouldn't figure out for yourself, if you'd think clearly and calmly about the situation." She studied Nika with narrowed eyes.

"Situation. As in—?"

"The Coleman house and your reluctance to read that letter you carry around day and night."

"Ah, the Coleman house." Nika's gaze traveled to the ocean, and stayed there. "It's strange and exhilarating, and scary as hell."

Verochka's hand landed on Nika's shoulder like a delicate butterfly. No words were needed between them. For a long moment only the sound of crashing waves disturbed the silence.

"I feel like I know it," Nika murmured quietly, almost as if she was talking to herself. "Inside and out. Intimately. I know everything about it. The pattern of the draperies, the feel of the wooden banister under my fingers, the sound of the creaking steps on the staircase. And how weird is that?"

"What else?" *Verochka* prompted her gently.

"I feel like I know *him*. Elijah Coleman, the original master of the house. I know his habits, his preferences in food and clothing. I know that he loves his baby sister very much, and worries about her. He wants her to marry into a wealthy family. Carnegies. He knows that she's reluctant, but he decided to overlook it and push her harder in that direction. I know that he's sad, deeply sad and that he's hurting, blaming himself for the death of his wife.

"I want to restore that house, and at the same time, I'm afraid of stepping a foot inside of it. I'm drawn to it like a moth to a flame, and fear I might burn like that moth if I get to close." Nika swept her fingertips across both cheeks. "This house can change me. Or hurt me. It almost did. The last time I was there, it smacked me silly, rejecting my presence."

"Smacked you? How? Why didn't you tell me about it?"

Nika shrugged. "I just did."

"Was it like a negative energy? Did you feel threatened?"

"No, it wasn't negative as much as angry. I didn't feel threatened. I felt sick to my stomach. I puked," she grinned, then she grew serious. "It was angry at me, because I..."

"Because you what?" Verochka prompted.

"It's silly, I know, but I feel that it was angry because I didn't read the letter. There you have it. Am I obsessed or just crazy?" She turned to her grandmother. "Tell me honestly."

"Neither." *Verochka* rubbed Nika's arm to offer comfort just as she did when Nika was a child with a problem. "You are one of the most level-headed people I know. Compulsive, yes, empathic, yes, passionate, oh hell, yes, but never obsessed or delusional."

"Thanks, Gorgeous," Nika patted *Verochka's* hand that still lay on her arm. "Then, how do you explain all this?"

"Easily. But I think, instead of explaining it, I'll strike a bargain with you. You read that letter, and if after that you still don't understand, I'll tell you my thoughts on the subject."

"Read the letter? Like right now?"

"Yes. And what a better time than now? Or would you rather be alone?"

"No. No, I'd rather be with you. Just in case in I fall to pieces afterward, you know." She shot her grandmother a wicked grin. "Promise not to freak out if I do."

"You'll do no such thing, Daisy-girl. My money is on you. Just do it."

Nika pulled the letter from her pocket. She took great care to unzip its protective cover and pull the envelope out.

"Would you." She swallowed hard before continuing, "Would you please break the seal and take it out? I'm kinda shaky," Nika confessed.

Verochka took the yellowed envelope from Nika's unsteady hand and after breaking the small seal, pulled out a single page folded in two.

"Now it's for you to read it, baby."

She handed the fragile page to Nika. Trepidation scaled though Nika as she unfolded the page and lowered her eyes.

"Well?" *Verochka* asked after a few moments. "What's in it? What did he say?"

Nika lifted her eyes and blinked several times before she burst into full-scale laugher. Still shaking from it, she passed the letter to *Verochka.*

"Can you believe it?" She managed between her laughter. "Can you believe that son of a bitch? Here I am, afraid to read the damn letter, and all he wants for me..."

Verochka scanned the now-wrinkled page:

Find the key. You know where it is. Hurry, for goodness'
sake!
Elijah B. Coleman

"Key?" She arched her brows. "What key? And how does he know that you know where it is?"

"I have not the foggiest. Any ideas?"

"Not at the moment." *Verochka* smoothed the page and tucked it back into the envelope. She offered it to Nika who took it on auto-pilot.

"Okay, I've read the letter, and I still have no clue. We made a bargain," she turned to her grandmother. "Pay up time."

"Well." *Verochka* braced herself. "My theory was, and still is because this letter confirms my hunch that you are, indeed, Daisy Coleman."

CHAPTER SIX

Nika didn't blink. Her heart didn't lurch. Her stare didn't waver. As a matter of fact, her body had no react at all, like her brain failed to process her grandmother's last words. But she heard them. There was nothing wrong with her ears, even if her brain temporarily blocked off.

Why am I so calm?

"I hate to tell you, *Verochka*, but Daisy—that Daisy—lived in the last century, not to mention she's been dead for many, many years. I'm here, alive. Shaken, but otherwise not worse for wear."

"And thank God for that. What I meant is that you *were* Daisy Coleman. Last time. In your previous life."

Why I am not surprised?

"Okay, that's better. Not much, but better." Nika shook her head in disbelief. "You know, if I didn't know you, I would think that you're suffering from some mental illness. But since I do know you, I'm sure that you have a theory to this madness."

"That's not madness, baby, just a simple logic. And an open mind."

"Explain logic," she asked after a moment. "We'll get to an open mind later."

"Well, for one, you felt familiar with the house from the start. You knew its décor even though you never stepped a foot inside. And you remember him, Elijah. You said so yourself just moments ago."

"Okay, but how do you explain the letter?"

"Again, simple. He probably wrote it to his wife, to remind her about some key she might've lost. She might've kept it with her paperwork and other mementos. With time, this letter got shuffled with some other papers of the estate, and voila."

"I would buy it, but for this." Nika lifted the letter in her right hand and tapped it with her left index finger. "How do you explain this? It was addressed to me, *Verochka*. Not his wife, but me. See?"

Veronika Morris.

The name—Nika's name—was penned in same flourishing manner by the same impatient hand. Elijah Coleman's.

"How do you explain that, Sherlock?"

"I don't know. But there too, might be some simple explanation. Like, for example..." she opened her mouth, then closed it, frowning.

"What? Nothing comes to mind?"

"No, dammit. But I'll think of something."

"Please do and share with me when you come up with *something*. *If* you come up with something."

"*Merde*," *Verochka* muttered under her breath. She was clearly exasperated. Her grandmother rarely swore, but Nika recognized a French swear word when she heard one.

"By the way, did you share your theory with Alex?"

"Yes."

"And?"

"And what do you think? He doesn't believe in reincarnation," *Verochka* huffed indignantly.

"I wonder why."

"Me, too." *Verochka* misinterpreted her remark and plowed ahead, warming to the subject. "It's an ancient belief, as much philosophical as religious. Hinduism, or Buddhism to name a few, were practically built on its concept. Think about it. We all are energy. The energy doesn't disappear to nowhere, that's elemental physics. So, where do we go after biological death of our bodies, which are no more or less than a shell? Huh? Right. The non-physical essence of us, spirit or soul or whatever else you want to name it, continues on and starts new life in a different physical form. So there."

"You truly believe it," Nika stated after her grandmother finally ran out of words.

"I do."

"Amazing. I wish I had your open-minded disposition toward all of this. But, I guess, I have my limitations."

"My dear girl, we all have our limitations. The most important thing is not to fight them, but to accept them, even embrace them, and then turn them to our advantage."

"How?"

"You'll have to figure it out on your own." *Verochka* smiled.

"I guess, I do. Okay," Nika tucked the letter in her pocket, deliberately closing the subject. "What do you say we head home? I feel like I need to think."

They turned and walked back along the moonlit beach. The sound of the slow rolling waves was muted and soothing.

"When I was growing up, I always knew that I was different from the rest of them," Nika said in a quiet voice after a few minutes of silence. "I wasn't beautiful like Mother, or smart like Father, or an obedient, perfect child like my brothers. I was different. I loved them, and I guess they loved me, too, but there was never a link between us, like there always had been between me and Alex, another misfit in his own family. So, we bonded early on, grew up closer than twins, and at the end, saved each other's sanity by running off and starting on our own. You helped us, *Verochka*. By being there for us, trusting us. Trusting in us. By just being you. You loved us without any strings attached, without any conditions. And we both treasure it. Treasure you. I'm so honored to be named after you."

Her own name Veronika meant little Vera.

She fell silent for a moment then reached for her grandmother's hand. "I don't remember if I told you lately that I love you? I do. I love you."

"What brought this up?" *Verochka* wrapped her fingers tight around Nika's hand. It was her gentle way to show love and support because she knew how hard it was for Nika to express her feelings in words.

"Just wanted you to know, that's all."

"That's far from all, Daisy-girl. Come on, it's me you're talking to. Tell me what is it, love. What's bothering you?"

"Oh, you mean, besides the situation with the Coleman house, Elijah's letter, and your conviction that I was Daisy Coleman in my previous life?" She gave one short, dry snicker.

"You'll fix the Coleman house, you already read the letter, and you will arrive at the same conclusion about being Daisy. So, there," she echoed Nika's words, linking their hands, and leading them toward the house. "And after this job is done, we'll go together on an adventure. How about Iceland? Or Norway? Or Italy? Or any-damn-where you want to travel. For a couple of weeks. Before & After, Inc. and Alex can fend on their own for a while without you. How about it, Daisy-girl? My treat."

"Two weeks in paradise with my favorite girlfriend, away from here? Now, twist my other arm!" Nika laughed.

"Seriously. Let's do it. Just you and me, what do you say?"

"I say absolutely, positively yay, and I'd even boogie, but wouldn't want to insult Your Highness's sensibilities."

"That's very considerate of you. But, seriously, promise me. I know if you do, you'll never break your word."

"What, you want a written contract sealed in blood?" Nika joked.

"No, your word will do."

"Then, here is my solemn word to you. When all of it is behind me, I'll go with you wherever you decide."

"Pinkie swear?" Verochka lifted her little finger.

"Oh, for God's sake." Nika mimicked the gesture and hooked her own pinky with *Verochka's*. "Now, satisfied?"

"Totally. Let's seal it with some good wine and go to our beds."

"More wine? It's too much! Even for your alcohol resistant titanium French stomach."

But Nika didn't offer any protest when, after opening the door to the house, *Verochka* went straight to the bar.

"Poor misguided child." Her grandmother feigned a sigh. "I'll have you know that there is no such thing as too much wine, and nothing that couldn't be rectified, cured or fixed with a glass of an excellent red."

"I'll remember that." Nika accepted the glass and then clinked it with her grandmother's. She really hoped her grandmother was right that the wine helped to cure her unquiet mind and rectify the nagging sensation of impending disaster.

The next morning Nika woke up before dawn, as usual. She was groggy from too much wine consumption and her mind refused to shut down, keeping her in a semi-delirious state all night. How else could she explain her vivid dream of a dark stranger—an absolutely delicious, devilishly handsome hunk—who gazed at her with the most incredible silver-gray eyes as he repeated *find the key*?

That damned phrase looped in her brain over and over. All night long. Big surprise after she finally read that strange letter the previous evening. And only after *Verochka's* nagging. But the man in her dream was familiar somehow. Tall, strong shoulders, black hair. And those piercing silver eyes. She recognized him. Or was she simply projecting the image she had formed in her mind onto the mysterious owner of the Coleman house? There was no doubt in her mind she dreamed of Elijah Coleman. No, she corrected herself, he preferred to be called Eli.

My friends and family call me Eli. I prefer it.

She crossed the bedroom to her bath. Once there she flipped the shower handle and then tossed her pjs onto the floor. Thoughts of Eli played in her mind. She stepped into the steamy water and then tipped her head back to let the water pulse against her tired scalp. She squeezed shampoo from the bottle and inhaled the fruity aroma as she worked it into her hair, praying to clear her troubled brain.

Her hands stilled when his voice, deep and rich baritone, sounded in her mind's ear. And how, for goodness' sake, did she know that? And why was it uber urgent, paramount even, for her to find that blasted key?

Find the key. You know where it is. Hurry, for goodness' sake!

Nika cursed out loud and hurriedly rinsed her hair, impatient now to jump start her day. She slammed off any more reminiscing about the damn dream that kept her in a constant state of trepidation, and finished her shower in record time.

She dressed in her usual working attire of jeans, t-shirt, and boots, then grabbed her favorite baseball cap and turned in backward on her head. Nika snatched her truck keys off the table by the door and ran out the front door.

The ocean was ink-dark, with the first rays of sun still hours away, but the sound of it reached her, soothing, comforting. It was majestic with its mercurial moods and spectacular power. The Atlantic didn't suffer fools and didn't forgive careless. Second chances were out of the question. It just was. Alive and infinite.

God, she loved the ocean. Nika closed her eyes and took a deep breath saturated with salt and fragrance of the water. Brilliant!

And just like that, her worries and misgivings disappeared. She forgot all about her mysterious dream and the dark stranger, and the troubling urgency to find the key.

She worked to forget *Verochka's* bizarre theory that she was—used to be—Daisy Coleman. The hell she was! She was Veronika Margaret Morris.

For the hell of it, and convince herself there was no such thing as reincarnation, she yelled out to the heavens, "I am Veronika Margaret Morris, so there!"

She was ready, quivering with excitement, trembling from the simple joy of *being*.

Nika jogged down the staircase and then turned toward the garage feeling strong and for whatever the day threw at her.

Before she got into the truck, she decided where she was heading. The Coleman house. Even though her permits were still in the works, she could do a little preliminary work, like visual inspections and measurements, like walking the perimeter and determine how sound the three guest houses and a gazebo were, and check the former butterfly garden. For some reason, she wanted to see it. *Needed* to see it. Nika swore to herself to do anything and everything to salvage and restore it. After all, it used to be Abigail Coleman's domain, her pride and joy, before her older brother decided her fate for her.

"I'm not going there," she firmly reminded herself, gunning the truck. "I'm absolutely not thinking of anything except the job. Renovations. Measurements. Inspections."

And who are you trying to fool?

"Shut up, you bitch. Perfect timing for you to pop out and start arguing." She glared into the rearview mirror as she backed out of the driveway.

The road was clear and thoughts bombarded her. Would the house once again reject her presence? If so, what was the best way to circumvent the problem? And circumvent it she decided firmly, because, for better or worse, she was getting inside and staking her claim.

Nika was primed for a good fight, but nothing happened when she approached the house.

The house was still the same: tired, dignified, and glorious. The old southern gentleman, fallen on hard times, but struggling to maintain appearances. Was it any wonder she simply adored it? "Here you are," she said gently. "Not mad at me anymore, are you?"

A quiet sigh, soft like a baby's breath. Her unruly imagination? Possibly. Probably.

Or the house is really pleased to see me.

With unsteady hands she unlocked the main gates and pushed them open. The squeak of rusty metal sounded like a cackle. She took it as a good sign.

The walk toward the main house was a long, wide path that split in three. To the right where the three guest houses and to the left Abigail's gardens and her favorite gazebo. The glassed-in pool was tucked behind the main building.

Nika decided to take a detour and check out the perimeter. Or so she told herself. Because she was reluctant to admit, even to herself, that she was still hesitant to enter the house that had haunted her dreams and waking hours for two years.

She turned right. The dilapidated guesthouses came into view. Nika's shoulders slumped as the full scope of work needed to restore them hit her. She headed toward the backyard and the pool. She cursed under her breath at the algae slime caked along the sides and bottom of the cracked, cement pool. Nika yanked her phone from a back pocket and texted Alex.

At the site. Will bunk here tonight. 2 much 2 do.

He won't worry or be concerned. She always carried her emergency duffel bag in the truck with a change of clothes and toiletries and her trusty old sleeping bag. More often than not she stayed in the house she was renovating, sleeping on the premises for days, until he dragged her dirty, overworked self back to civilization.

His reply pinged in a moment

'*What can I do?*'

That was so Alex! She could always rely on him in any damn situation, no matter what, where, or when.

"I love you, too, Cuz." She smiled and tapped on her screen.

Don't bother me for 3-4 days. And tell V.

His answer came back momentarily.

Will do. Tag me if you need me. Have fun.

She quickly replied with a thumbs-up emoji and stuck her phone in her back pocket. Nika scanned the property and then shook her head.

Fun indeed.

She wasn't kidding. The work was too much. Way too much. As a matter of fact, Nika never had a project of such magnitude before. All the more interesting, but the challenge was tremendous. The restorations—extensive and complicated, the time frame... Her mind whirled with the magnitude of this undertaking.

She eyed the three dilapidated houses ahead, then the gazebo barely visible from her vantage point, and the pool, and the house behind her.

Probably good eight to ten months if not longer, she calculated.

In short, Nika should be in her own private paradise. Would be, she mentally corrected herself, if not for that nagging sense of uneasiness.

She pivoted in a slow twirl and studied the looming three-story main house. Its single Gothic turreted tower rose on the northern side. That dark and gloomy appendage was in such a jarring contrast with the main style and design of the house, that the overall effect should be horrendous. Somehow, though, it wasn't. The tower *felt* organically correct, and managed to gel in into the main structure just right. It was...dignified, and subtly forbidding. Like its owner.

Eli's domain.

Now how did she know that?

No more procrastination! She walked back toward the house, following the path in a wrap-around way. Soon she stood in front of it, gazing at it, truly mesmerized.

"I'm going to take care of you now," she said in a soothing voice as she approached the oversized mahogany door. "But first, I need to check you out, just to see how badly you hurt. I hope not too bad. From what I see, the time was kind to you. You have strong bones, so there's a plus. Your roof and all your walls are intact, and it's a huge plus. Let's see about the flooring."

Nika always talked to a house as if she was speaking to a child. Calmly, kindly, softly. Sometimes out loud, like right now, sometimes inside her mind.

She wasn't called the House Whisperer for naught.

Nika pulled the cluster of keys out of her left pocket. They were attached to an old chain Senator Lauder gave her after dinner. Without a second thought she chose a rusted key. She didn't stop to think how she knew which was the right one. She just inserted it into the slot. Her hand moved, like it was on autopilot. Two full revolutions clockwise, a slight upward pressure, then a gentle wiggle to remove the key.

And just like that, the door was unlocked.

Nika stood for a moment with her hand frozen in mid-motion, gazing at the dusty, ornate frame, reluctant to move.

Was this how Alice felt seconds before she plunged into a rabbit hole?

But, unlike her favorite childhood heroine, Nika was fully aware she might never come be the same once she crossed the threshold. The moment stretched.

God only knew how long Nika might have stood there if not for a sudden screech of a crow. She jerked back, cursing, and then laughed at the huge bird sitting on a tree limb.

"Right, I know it's silly. Thanks for the push, buddy." With a last glance at the curious crow, she pushed the door open and stepped inside.

The smell assaulted her first, that unmistakable mix of neglect and abandonment so natural for the old historic houses. The fragrance of time, Nika called it. In reality, it was nothing more than a horrendous amount of dust accumulated for decades, and a lack of fresh air. But for her, the smell of every house was special and totally unique, kind of like a house's ID card.

The Coleman house had its own unique fragrance, for sure.

Her nose twitched as one olfactory sensation after another unveiled itself and mixed with fresh air, creating an echo of scents.

She recognized the faint aroma of lemon wax mixed with something so painfully familiar, so poignant that it brought tears to her eyes.

Shaken, unbearably sad, Nika sucked in a deep breath and then another.

"Okay, alright. Dammit."

She steeled herself, drawing on all the willpower she possessed to not turn around and run. But that was a weakness and a failure. Nika was neither weakling nor a loser. She bit her lower lip, straightened her spine and, with her heart thundering inside her chest, scanned the spacious foyer. She narrowed her eyes, focusing on the strong and weak structural points. She recognized the vaulted ceiling, the silk-upholstered walls and the parquet flooring laid in an intricate mosaic design. An uneasy sensation circled through her. Was that from memory or research? Everything around her was covered in a thick layer of dust, muting the once vibrant colors.

But I know. I remember. And how is that possible?

An image of the room in its glory days sprang into her mind's eyes.

Nervous but determined, she walked down the hallway, drawn to a large dark object in the far corner. Her breath hitched and caught in her throat.

The old grandfather clock, at least six feet tall, stood like a proud sentry. Her hands shook as she recognized the elaborately carved ornamental hood, that frontal part of the wood frame that covered the clock face. It was dark, almost black from the collected grime and dust.

It's called bonnet.

She knew it was called that because...

Because what?

Because she read about it? Probably. But how on earth did she know that before it struck an hour, it made a low hissing noise? How did she know the voice of the clock, that deep, velvety bong?

How did she know that the dial was inlaid with eighteen carat gold, as were the hands, curved and ornate, and the long pendulum with the disc in the form of a star at the end? This particular grandfather clock was made in England, by one of the best and famous masters, John Alker, in 1827, at the very end of his career, and was considered the most valuable heirloom in the Coleman family.

How on earth did she know all of that?

"My God," Nika pressed her shaking hand to her forehead, knocking off her baseball cap. "I'm either losing my mind, or..."

Or else, *Verochka* was right. Nika indeed used to live in this house once upon a time. Like a hundred years ago. Because nothing else, nothing whatsoever, made any sense otherwise.

CHAPTER SEVEN

Confused and shaken, Nika stood frozen to the spot, hypnotized by the old grandfather clock. Was it possible that she was, used to be, Daisy Coleman? *And why not?* That bitch in her brain teased.

"W-why n-not?" Nika sputtered. "Why the hell not, she asks! Because it means—hello, reincarnation! And that's impossible! It's...It's crazy!" Frustrated, she shouted at her annoying inner self.

What's wrong in believing that one could be brought back, in another body, time after time?

"What's wrong? I don't know what's wrong. But that's not right, either!"

Why?

"Because, dammit, it's not fair! It's confusing as hell, and... and..."

Nika groped for the right word, then gave up. "It's just too much," she whispered fiercely.

Desperate to leave, she turned, and started to retrace her steps. She had to get outside. To her own world. To fresh air, and yes, to assure herself that she was Veronika Morris, flesh and blood, and not a shadow of the woman who lived in this house in the last century.

She lived here, entertained here. Loved here.

The image of Eli Coleman swam in front of her eyes as if conjured by her imagination. Tall, proudly erect, impossibly handsome, he stared at her, his mysterious silver eyes flashing sparks. He was angry and sad at the same time. "My...my God..." Nika took an involuntary step back. Then she blinked and the image was gone. But the feeling of deep sorrow, his or hers was the question, still remained, throbbing like a fresh wound. Her heart ached, her eyes misted, and her head pounded. Nika clutched her abdomen. Was the house making her sick again? No, her pain had nothing to do with the house, and everything with its owner. Or her memories of him.

She had loved him. She had loved Eli Coleman. He was her husband, her hero, her best friend. He was the father of her only child.

Not hers, she reminded herself in fierce desperation, but Daisy's.

She was Nika, Veronika Morris. Not Daisy Coleman!

"I need to get out of here, I need to..." Nika ran to the front door and then flung it open.

Gulping a lungful of fresh air, she pushed the door shut and propped her back against it.

Now what? Should she continue? Or should she call Senator Lauder and refuse the job?

And what would you say? Sorry, Senator, but I just realized that I'm your great-grandmother reincarnate, and I'm afraid I'm going to lose my mind, if I work on this restoration?

"Yeah, right."

Well, how about, Senator, I inspected the house and it's way too much job for Before & After, Inc. to handle?

The latter might be less complicated, but it that was an outright lie.

To confess to the first reason was equivalent to signing her own professional death sentence, because no one after that would be willing to work with a crazy contractor, even if said contractor was the highly acclaimed House Whisperer.

"No way in hell," Nika muttered stubbornly.

What, then? Make up your mind, sister.

"Easy for you to say, *sister*!"

She desperately wanted to call Alex. Just to hear his voice. Just to re-assure herself that she was sane and grounded in reality.

She needed to share her discovery with him. *Guess what, Cuz? Me thinks that Verochka was right, after all.* She needed his perspective on this bizarre turn of events.

And to let him talk her out of the project, or more accurately, to take the dilemma of whether to continue to work on this project or quit off her hands. That was an easy way out. His immediate reaction would be an imperative order to get the hell out of dodge, before he called Senator Lauder and refused the job. He would do it for her, even if it meant a serious blow to the company's reputation.

Coward.

"The hell I am!"

Nika squared her shoulders and stuck her chin out.

She wasn't a coward, or a weakling. And anyone who said differently was a stinking liar! When did she ever look for an easy way *in* or *out* of anything? Never-fricking-ever.

She didn't like easy, period. It if was easy, it was more than likely not worth the effort. So, Nika ruthlessly squelched her need to call her cousin. No, she refused to involve him. No way. It had to be her decision, her responsibility. Because the house was hers and hers alone, whether she was Daisy Coleman reincarnate or not.

She sensed it two years ago. She knew it now without a shadow of a doubt. She gave her word to Senator Lauder. She promised the house to take care of it. She resolved not to renege on either.

And then, there was a matter of that letter.

Find the key. You know where it is. Hurry, for goodness' sake.

She had yet to uncover the meaning of that cryptic order. Nika lifted the bunch of keys attached to the thick keychain. What key? One of those? Maybe.

Find the key...

For what purpose? Why? And if, by miracle, she did find it, then what?

You know where it is.

The hell she did! The house was huge, like, seriously humongous. And if she was dumb enough to search for that darn key, she could spend the next decade at it.

Hurry, for goodness' sake!

The son of a bitch had the gall to put it like an order!

"What's your hurry? You've been dead for a half of century."

And he addressed the letter to her, Veronika Morris.

How did he know her name hundred years ago?

Why her?

And why to be delivered in September 2019? Not in October, or August?

And why, dammit, her?

"Questions, questions, so many questions, and not a single answer!"

Maybe the letter was a fluke, just to whet her curiosity. Maybe the Senator's mysterious great-grandfather hadn't written it. Was it fabricated recently and aged by a forger? After all, she had never authenticated it. The thought never crossed her mind. Okay, possible, but why? And to what purpose? To add a layer of mystery? To ensure that Before & After, Inc. took the job?

Nonsense. The Coleman family was aware, for the two years, that she and Alex were more than interested, and even eager to buy the house outright, and start restorations.

Or maybe, it was a joke, just to see her reaction.

Or maybe it has a much simpler explanation, just like Verochka *claimed, you know.*

She had no clue and the suspense was killing her.

No, she refused to quit. Until the origin of that mysterious letter was identified she couldn't step back. Just like the pro she is, Nika decided to continue with her initial inspections. And maybe, just maybe, that blasted key might appear.

Think back, Nika.

Had she come across some mentioning of a hidden space in the house during her research? Because she sure as hell had no idea where that key was supposed to be.

But she would be damned if she forced herself to hurry.

She pursed her lips, then lifted her hand to remove the baseball cap from her still pounding head. But her fingers encountered only the curling springs. Cursing like a sailor, Nika kicked the door and then clutched at her head with both hands when pain shot through her.

"Damn, damn, damn!"

It was her lucky cap. She wanted, no, needed it!

You're behaving like a brat, you know.

She knew, and it made her only more aggravated. Nika hated emotional outbursts. They were nothing but childish tantrums displayed by adults, and nothing was more ridiculous than that.

Very rarely did she indulge herself and only when she was alone. And only when she was really, really pissed off. And frustrated. And scared. Like right now.

Nika gingerly pressed two fingers to her right brow, winced from the vicious pain that had kicked in. That was all she needed for a full measure of unhappiness, one of her famous tension headaches. Where were her pills? Oh, yeah, the same place with her tools, the water cooler, and sleeping bag.

The back seat of her truck. She sucked in a deep breath, held it for a second, then noisily blew it out. A trip out to her truck was imminent. Because, ready or not, Nika was staying.

At least, tonight.

She turned toward the closed door. With a sigh she tugged open the heavy door.

The weather was hot and humid despite the fact that it was the middle of September. Autumn meant crisp, colder air, hot apple cider, and a beautiful red-gold colorful palette of nature. Anywhere in the country that is, except Florida.

Florida maintained ninety-five degrees in the afternoon, iced coffee was the most popular beverage, and tropical flora stubbornly recognized only one color. Green.

After eight years, Nika became accustomed to the constant perspiration and immune to the merciless sun. Well, almost immune. The weather forecast on her phone app just reaffirmed the fact that it was going to be another scorcher. A dazzling 96 degrees without a hint of a cloud.

Oh well.

Thankfully, she had a small but powerful fan in her truck, since the majority of Nika's jobs were AC intolerant by default. The pile at her feet was all the items she needed for the foreseeable future, grew rapidly. Nika resigned herself to a few trips between her truck and the house. What time was it? She shot another quick glance at the screen of her iPhone. It was barely eight in the morning.

Impossible.

She arched a brow and tapped the screen again to bring it back to life. But the numbers had only changed by a few seconds. She had been at the house forever. Had time stopped? Or did it pass slower on the inside of the Coleman house than outside?

Nika shrugged, picked up her water cooler and started the first of several treks to the main entrance.

Once inside, Nika contemplated where to set up her temporary headquarters. She walked into a semi-circular room that once upon a time was a parlor. She shook her head, shattering the mental picture of a lit fireplace with Christmas stockings hanging from the mantel. She closed her eyes, took a few deep breaths, then popped her eyelids open. The dusty, derelict room was empty and forlorn.

Ignore the fireplace. Pretend it's not even here.

The room's location was perfect. It was smack in a middle of the first floor on the left and directly across from the main staircase. It had Palladian windows along the one wall that were huge and perfectly arched, and all of them intact. Sunlight streamed into the windows and turned everything into a soft gold shade, creating an otherworldly, whimsical picture.

Like a daguerreotype image.

Nika switched off the thought.

The windows, hardwood floors, the fireplace, and ceiling were in decent condition. Most important, this room was the closest to the front door. As safety measures went, a fast exit was the paramount for her. You never knew when, not if, an emergency situation might arise dealing with a century-old structure.

Nika deliberately bypassed the fireplace. The same as she avoided the grandfather clock during her multiple treks between the truck and the house. Not that it emanated something dark and negative, or gave her creeps or anything like that, but just...just because.

It took her a tad under an hour to haul everything in. By then she was sweaty, winded, and famished. And no wonder, since all she had eaten was a banana. And that was ages ago.

Need to go grab some real food, Nika lectured herself, breaking the trail mix package with her teeth. *And coffee. The hot stuff.*

She opened her cooler and dug out a frosty bottle of Starbucks Frappuccino. *Gotta have the hot stuff. Can't survive without it. And that has to wait until later.*

She shoved trail mix packages inside her various pockets. She gulped one last chug from the bottle, set it on the floor, and tugged her toolbelt from the duffel.

The belt was custom made from the best imported leather and crafted by hand in Germany according to her size and specifications. It cost a little less than her Corvette, but not by much.

But its real value was unmeasurable in coins, because it was Alex's present to her on the day Nika passed her contractor's exam. That was six years ago.

And she has not been without it since. It was her talisman, her juju. She considered it her armor and shield. Nika hooked it around her hips and immediately became calm and in control.

All she needed now to feel one hundred percent was to find her good luck charm baseball cap.

She munched on her snack while compiling her mental lists of to do immediately tasks and to do as I go, prioritizing inspections and safety issues. She wandered out of the room to find her cap right by the doorway. Relieved, she picked it up and then gave it a few good whacks against her hip to flick off the dust. She plopped it onto her head, bill side backward, and then tucked her hair under it.

Nika continued down the hall, checking the condition of the plaster, wood, and stone. She braced herself when she reached the grandfather clock. She tried to act like an appraiser, cooly and detached, facing a beautiful *object d'art*.

And failed by a mile.

The golden hands, forever frozen in time, gracefully pointed at the number twelve. It stopped at afternoon sharp. Or midnight?

"So, what if I know you," she whispered. "Or feel you? It doesn't matter. I won't let it matter. I'm here do my job. And I will. Splendidly. So, let's make a pact. I won't interfere with you, and you won't mess with my head and memories, and everything will be fine. Agreed?"

The ancient clock was silent, but not dead. Oh, no. It heard her, loud and clear. But kept its judgement close to its intricately carved vest. At least, for now.

"Fine. You think about that while I'm making my inspection. Let me know when you come to a decision."

With that, she turned around and went about her job.

She spent several hours taking initial pictures, measuring, testing, making copious notes in her own shorthand, all the while keeping the lid on all of her senses firmly shut. Nika had mastered this skill and honed it to perfection during her years in the business as a professional contractor for historic houses.

The first visit was usually the hardest. Before she stepped inside any house it was a sleeping beauty, frozen in time, and, more often, in neglect.

When unlocked at last, it woke up, and all the time condensed to the maximum, the energy, positive and negative, the memories good and bad and everything in between, bombarded her, testing her, pushing her. Measuring her up.

And then, there was that fragrance of time...

Nika had learned to shield herself and keep her professional façade at all cost. The situation was completely different with this house. It didn't test her as much as remind her of the past. It didn't push against her. It pulled her in. Which was worse? Nika had no idea.

Bong bong.

She was in the northern section of the second floor, crouched in front of the ancient wardrobe, when it reached her ears. She sat on her haunches and turned her head toward the sound.

The grandfather clock.

So, you've made up your mind, after all.

A satisfied smile cured her lips. But only for a moment. The realization of *what* that sound actually was-the chiming of a clock that no longer worked and had stood frozen in silence for the past century—covered her skin in goosebumps. Someone must have nudged the pendulum to swing in order to wind the clock. She was alone in the house. On the second floor. The grandfather clock, that marvel of English watchmaker's engineering, was on the first floor.

"How..."

Her hands shook. Cold sweat ran in a rivulet along her spine. For the first time since she stepped into the Coleman house, Nika was spooked in earnest. And then, finally, it hit her. The key! This particular clock was unique because in addition to its manual mechanism, the usual three pulleys, it also had a key that brought the weight of those pulleys down independently.

The key!

The key she needed to find was the key from the grandfather clock! It had to be.

Nika jumped to her feet and took off on a run and charged down the stairs two at the time.

The urgency to find that key propelled her forward, pushing her to run faster toward her goal. She didn't understand why she needed that key, but she absolutely had to find it as soon as possible.

Winded, disheveled from her mad dash, and breathing hard, Nika came to a screeching stop in front of the clock.

It hadn't changed since she last saw it few hours earlier. Its golden hands still pointed at the number twelve and its three gold plated pulleys were frozen in upward position. How was it possible for the clock to make a noise? Any noise, much less the deep booming chime?

As Nika stood there, mute and shaken, the clock continued to count the hours with husky, melodious bongs.

I know that voice. It always reminded me of a tipsy opera singer.

"My God... But how..."

The clock's round gilded face was enigmatic and full of shadows. Or was she imagining things? Trembling, she stared at the clock as it continued to chime, louder and angrier, until Nika was all but deaf from the blasting, ear-splitting roar. The very walls of the house were vibrating, shifting, moving. Nika was caught in a nightmare, except she was wide awake.

As nightmares go, this one was a doozy. Nausea hit her like a fist, quick and unexpected, adding another layer to her misery.

Son of a bitch.

The ringing in her ears was unbearable. The tiny dots sprinkled her vision like furious black flakes. Bile flooded her throat.

Stop, stop, stop.

"Stop! Please," she screamed.

And just like that, the sound ended. The silence was deafening. It pressed at her from all sides, making her even more disoriented.

The key, looped inside her head, *the key...must find the key.*

You know where it is.

And she did. On shaking legs, Nika stepped closer to the clock and, half-hugging it, half-leaning on it, awkwardly reached with her right hand behind Its back. The tiny rounded bump from the hidden panel was cool to the touch. Nika pressed at it gently with her fingertips and the tiny panel jumped outward. Gingerly, blindly, Nika dipped her fingers into the gap. When she pulled back her hand, she clutched a key.

She had found it. She knew where it was.
Hurry, for goodness' sake!

CHAPTER EIGHT

The brass key on her palm was old, but gleamed as if it was just polished. For a three-inch-hunk of metal it was surprisingly heavy, and somehow... alive. It literally vibrated in her hand, pulsing with energy.

Hurry, hurry, hurry...

Astonished, she stared at it, then at the clock, then back at the key in her hand.

I know what this key is for. She shivered once, almost violently. *Well, Nika, there is only one way to find out.*

Her hands shook as she pulled open the glass panel that covered the clock's face and, finding the keyhole, inserted the key. It slid in.

"Okay, alright," Nika whispered, "and now..."

She gingerly tried to move the key counterclockwise. Smoothly, like it was waiting for the guidance of her hand, it turned once, then stopped. She held her breath and repeated the rotation one more time. Nothing happened. Disappointed, Nika let out her breath and pulled the key free. Or tried to. It refused to budge. Maybe she hadn't applied enough force, so she tried again. The key was stuck. She jiggled at it again with no success.

"Oh, for goodness..."

As if by magic the key jumped out on its own accord, and landed on the floor at her feet.

"You sneaky little..." Nika bent forward to pick it up and was thrown sideways so violently her breath was knocked out of her.

Stars danced behind her closed eyelids.

Must have banged my head on the floor.

But the blasted key was in her hand, and biting into her palm.

A strange smell, like wet dirt, filled her nostrils at the same time a thunderclap sounded in her ears.

What the...?

Nika opened her eyes to a blue-gray sky partially covered by...

Spanish moss?

She laid there for a moment, gazing at the strange picture in front of her eyes.

Is the ceiling covered in frescos?

Strange. She would have remembered. Squinting at it, Nika racked her memory, but came up blank. A blur of the movement in her peripheral vision caught her attention right before a male voice cut though her foggy brain.

"Get up! Get the hell up!"

Who was yelling? Why and who was supposed to get up? She braced her weight on her elbows then slowly lifted herself. She blinked several times, trying to clear her vision. Damn, she banged her head really good, otherwise how to explain the black stallion barreling straight at her?

The horse was a beauty alright, ink-black, enormous, gleaming under the sun. The rider was equally impressive. She squinted, shielded her eyes with her hand against the sun and tried to bring the picture into focus.

Magnificent!

They made such a splendid picture. Both dark, huge, and ...mad. The stallion's eyes shone, his ears pulled back, his nostrils spewed vapor. The rider's eyes were hidden from her, but his narrowed eyes and set jaw were enough to scare her. His bellowing voice added just the right amount of fear to make her swallow hard.

Why were they mad? And why were they still moving pell-mell toward her? Nika jerked herself up and tried to scoot backwards. Two things became abundantly clear, she was sprawled in the middle of a dirty road and about to get trampled under the hooves of the huge horse barreling toward her.

The sound of the thundering hooves was clear enough. The earthy fragrance of damp dirt filled her nostrils.

What the hell?

Was she hallucinating? She probably was, otherwise—

"Move! Move the hell away!"

The deep voice was loud and too close for her comfort, not to mention her safety. Nika tried to move, but her limbs refused to obey her brain's command. Hallucination or not, the rider on the huge animal was almost upon her. She was doomed. Nika closed her eyes. Her last coherent thought was of Alex and *Verochka*, they must be devastated—

"Are you insane, boy? What is wrong with you?"

Strong hands grabbed her collar and then a pair of muscular arms hoisted her off the ground.

I'm alive.

Relief swept through her, but it was short-lived. The identity of the person who held her in a death grip and shook her roughly was unmistakable.

Nika stared into his familiar silver-gray eyes.

Elijah Coleman.

"No," she sputtered. "No, no, no—"

"No? You're not insane? Could've fooled me, you little idiot!"

"No, I'm not..." Nika bit her lip before she blurted out the truth. For some ridiculous reason she didn't want him to mistake her for one. And how ridiculous was that? Her only excuse was a deep shock that held her in a state of mental and physical paralysis.

Elijah Coleman.

My God, she wasn't hallucinating. Had she completely lost her mind?

He still gripped her shoulders painfully shook her like a rag doll.

Half-delirious from shock, Nika started to drift in and out.

"I almost killed you. Imbecile!" he shouted, now almost nose-to-nose with her. He gave her another mighty shake that almost rattled her bones.

"Do you realize that if Sultan weren't such an intelligent creature, you would be a mangled corpse by now?"

He was visibly shaken, and seriously pissed off. His rage was hot enough to singe her skin. And being clutched, more accurately in such close proximity, with his nose almost pressed to hers, made that phenomenon even more possible. Even sliding in and out of a hazy mist, and half-blind from shock, Nika recognized danger when it stared her in the face.

Elijah Coleman, or his impersonator, was huge, hopping mad, and barely holding it together.

And we are alone. In the middle of nowhere. Oh-uh.

He shoved her aside. Flicked off like a pesky gnat—effortlessly, mindlessly—added to her fear. His great physical advantage over her was obvious without any demonstration. She would be damned if she made it easy for him. She was determined to scratch and bite and use all her pitiful arsenal to fight the brute. As soon as she got her breath back. Nika hazarded a quick glance in his direction. He was petting his horse, murmuring to it in a calm, deep baritone that sent shivers along her spine.

"Good boy, Sultan, good, smart boy. Here, now, here, everything is alright. Calm down, baby."

Under different circumstances, Nika may have admired his voice, a really exceptional, opera singer worthy one. Now, however, his gentle crooning terrified her. She wrapped her arms around her middle, holding onto herself. A thousand different scenarios, one scarier than the other, scrolled before her eyes.

Was she trapped in a parallel universe? Or a nightmare? She really hoped that whatever was happening was either a bad dream or a hallucination, and she would snap out of it.

But everything around her *felt* so real. Try as she might, Nika couldn't snap out of this nightmare.

She was sitting smack in the middle of a dirt road, compliments of rough handling by the magnificent brute, with her bruised butt singing a song of the wounded. She tried to rotate her shoulders and winced. They ached from the death grip of said brute's hands.

Not to mention her ego that was shot to hell when he mistook her for a boy. Frowning, she took a stock of herself: black unisex t-shirt, dusty jeans, ripped at the knees, workman's boots. Huh. Dressed like that, plus wearing a toolbelt, she *was* camouflaged as a boy.

My hair!

Nika's hand shot up, bumping her baseball cap askew, then quickly straightened it. Her curls were fully covered.

No wonder he thinks I am a boy.

If the situation wasn't so scary, even a little ridiculous, she might have laughed out loud.

Nika eyed Elijah who still crooned to his horse.

Only I could enter an old house in the morning, figure out a cryptic letter sent by a splendid brute, and end up in the middle of a parallel universe, or a nightmare worthy of Bosch's paintings, a few hours later.

And got mistaken for a boy!

Not to mention the time jump. Because, wherever she was, Nika wasn't in the twenty-first century. That fact was obvious by Elijah's clothing. The black riding britches, frilled white shirt, and high leather boots belonged in a historical museum.

By the way, where was she? What month, day? Year?

"What day it is?" she asked.

He speared her a single glance over his shoulder.

"Thursday."

"Ah, Thursday of what?"

"Of September. September nine. Are you unwell?" He frowned. "Did I damage you after all? Or are you that frightened?"

"I'm fine," Nika mumbled as she tried to match up the facts. So, the day was the same, September nine. But a Monday was when she went to the Coleman house.

"And what year?" She squinted through her spread fingers at him.

"Good Lord, did you hit your head, after all?"

Elijah Coleman came closer. His brow furrowed with concern.

"No, I—"

"Eli! Eli, what happened?"

The sound of the thundering hooves came to a short stop behind Nika. In a moment, the man was roughly pushed aside, and a young woman peered down at Nika.

The clear bell-like voice that interrupted their conversation belonged to a creature from a fairy tale. The girl who materialized in her line of vision was tall, slender, and beautiful with a cascade of dark gleaming curls. Her eyes, a dreamy, smoky grey, flashed with anger. She obviously arrived on that second horse Nika heard but still couldn't see. The girl had to be younger than twenty. She wore old-fashioned riding clothes, too, only the female variety. *Like in that old group portrait of the riders circa 1910 from the museum I saw the other day. My God, was it possible? Or these two are actors from some kind of historical re-enactment?*

"What did you do?" the girl asked the man as she studied Nika. The girl bent down and asked in a lower voice, "Did he hurt you, you poor creature?"

"No, he didn't, I just—"

"Why do you always assume the worst of me?" Elijah interrupted. He appeared to be more curious than offended.

"Because I know you, Eli." The dark-haired beauty cut him off, motioning with her hand as if dismissing the subject. "What happened here?"

"Nothing," he shrugged.

"Nothing?" She pointed to Nika. "You call this nothing? Look at him! He's frightened, poor boy, probably injured. And whose fault is that?"

"I didn't see him, Abby. He just ...I don't know, one moment the trail was clear, the next there was this lump of rags lying in the middle of it!" Eli racked his fingers through his hair.

"Excuse me." Nika and the girl, who must have been Elijah's younger sister Abigail, echoed each other in identical outcries.

Nika, her fear momentarily forgotten, was beside herself with indignation. To mistake her for a boy was one thing, but to insult her like that!

The gall of the brute, calling her lump of rags!

"The gall of you, you big oaf!" Abby exclaimed.

Well, big oaf was good, too, although Nika preferred brute.

"He is a boy, a human being, not a pile of rags!"

"Lump", Nika chimed in, "he called me a lump of rags."

"Sorry, lump." Abby nodded at Nika. "He's just a boy, and you probably scared him half to death."

"I would undoubtedly have caused his very death, too, if Sultan hadn't stop just in the nick of time." Eli shouted at both of them.

"And such a good boy he is," Abby murmured smiling at the horse, who came closer to investigate and was currently sniffing at Nika. Abby gently nudged the huge horse's nose out of the way. She gave it a pat, and offered her hand to Nika.

"Can you stand up, boy? Or do you need help?"

"I can get up, no problem," Nika answered, still a bit disoriented.

Abby, Eli...so, it was no re-enactment, after all.

She tried to lift herself up. Easier said than done, Nika admitted in a moment after her legs folded under her.

With a muted curse, Eli stepped forward and hauled her none too gently to her feet.

"Thank you," Nika muttered, pulling her hand away from his grasp. He glared at her. She glared back. At least, she gave it her best try.

"What is your name, dear?" Abby asked with a gentle smile on her face.

"Nik…" For some reason her kindness managed to do what Eli's brute handling and rudeness couldn't. It brought Nika close to a meltdown. She swallowed the lump in her throat and tried again. "Nik…"

Once again, she choked on the word and shut her eyes, willing the unwanted, embarrassing tears away.

"Stop it, boy," Eli ordered gruffly. "Stop it this instant. Men do not cry. And you weren't hurt that badly, so stop pretending."

"I'm not—" Nika drew in a lungful of air. She wanted desperately to shout that she was *not* a boy and that she wasn't pretending. And that she was hurt more than they could imagine, because she had no idea what was happening to her. But her vocal cords disobeyed her order, and her shout came out as a mournful mewling.

"There, there, dear heart." Abby curled her arm around Nika's shoulders. "Don't despair. You are not visibly hurt, just shaken. Your clothes are not torn. They're just dirty and dusty. We can clean you up in no time. First, we need to show you to a doctor, to make sure you have no concussion."

That sent Nika into a real spin.

"No! No doctor, please. I'm okay, I swear!"

"Perked you up right away." Elijah's smug remark cut through the haze of her panic.

"Okay, alright, Nick. You said your name was Nick, right? No one will force you to see a doctor, although Doc Schmidt is a very kind and experienced doctor, and he's visiting the island, too. If you change your mind—"

"I won't, thank you."

"Well, Nicholas, what shall we do with you?"

The shock was wearing off. Otherwise, how to explain her stupid grin after Elijah Coleman had called her Nicholas? Was she starting to enjoy herself? Or was it still the remnants of her delirious state of mind?

"Just Nick," she offered after a moment. To Abby, she said, "I'm not hurt, not badly, but I probably knocked my head, because I seem to have forgotten some things," she ended meekly.

"Things? What kind of things?"

"Well, I remember my name, but I forgot everything else," Nika quickly improvised. "What… what year is it?"

"We ought to show you to the doctor still, my boy. Amnesia is a serious after effect from the scare you've experienced." She shot an angry glare at her brother. "But to answer your question, the year is 1909. Today is the ninth day of September."

Nika's head started to swim in slow, lazy circles.

"What else did you forget?" Abby's smiling face zoomed in and out of her focus.

"Where am I?"

Nika lifted her eyes to Elijah Coleman's face. His stubborn chiseled chin was marred by a deep cleft, dividing it in half. Strange, but it didn't soften his features. Quite the contrary. He looked tough, strong, and ridiculously handsome, dimple, frown and all. And at the moment, he glared at her, as if she was the most appalling, disgusting specimen under his imaginary microscope. For some insane reason, that hurt her the most.

"Where the hell am I?" Nika choked under her breath, already sliding half-way into a gray comforting mist, holding onto her composure by the proverbial fingernails.

"On Cumberland Island," Eli answered, frowning even more. "And you are about to pass out."

"N-never."

Eli stepped forward just in time to catch the boy's unconscious body.

Thunderation.

The last thing he wanted was Abby's mutinous glare to make him feel like a leech. Guilt was already tearing him apart. And self-disgust.

But there was something peculiar about this boy.

Eli lifted the small body as if was weightless and then stomped toward his horse. The boy didn't stir even when Eli mounted the stallion. He cradled the little urchin as best as he could in his arms, and started galloping toward the house. No need to check for Abby over his shoulder. There was no doubt she was right behind him, matching his mad dash.

He glanced at the small pale face tucked between his shoulder and arm. There was something definitely strange about the creature. Eli realized he needed to be smart to stay away from him. And that was his plan, after he delivered the boy to the house and let Doc Schmidt check him out. If he was unharmed, then they ought to cut him loose, or deliver him to wherever it is he came from. Eli intended to see to it and keep his distance. Even if he could explain the boy's miraculous appearance in the middle of the road, he refused to accept his own reaction to the creature with the violet-blue eyes of a Madonna and a mouth that belonged on an expensive prostitute.

Eli swore under his breath. He had no business noticing these things. And on the child—a boy, for crying out loud! Too long. He had been living the life of a monk for too long if the mere sight of pretty eyes and a moist mouth sent him into such a carnal state.

But, consarn it, not for the boy!

Disgusted beyond all measure, Eli refused to accept that depravity.

He glared at the road ahead and nudged his horse into a faster gate. The sooner he deposited this boy into the careful hands of the Doc, the faster he could wash his own hands of the whole affair and forget about it.

Part Two
The Journey

CHAPTER NINE

An unfamiliar voice, high-pitched but undoubtedly male, penetrated Nika's confused mind.

"So, you are coming about. Good. Excellent. It is time to wake up, *mein Herz,*" the bell-like voice said in a cheerful singsong.

Who's coming about? Why is it time to wake up?

Nika didn't want to wake up. And who was the owner of that strange voice? She had been all alone in the Coleman house. She asked Alex not to bother her for a few days. Did he send someone to check on her, anyway? He could, the rat. Nika smiled. He was such a sweetheart, and such a worrywart. She just loved him to pieces...

Her eyelids grew heavy; she was drifting in and out of a silvery-grey mist, feeling languid, carefree, and lazy. She lay on something soft and smelled good. It was warm and comfortable. The aroma of fresh-cut flowers and some perfume she didn't recognize scented the air. Nika was comfy. She didn't want to open her eyes. Whoever he had sent to check on her will go away eventually. When her hand was touched and lifted off a bit, Nika tried to tug it back.

"Go away," she mumbled, burrowing deeper into the softness of the pillow. Her brain might be hazy, but something was off. But what?

A pillow? What pillow? She traced her fingertips along the lace trim. *Definitely a pillow, but where did it come from?*

By her last recollection, she was in her sleeping bag, on the hardwood floor, without a pillow.

The Coleman house.

She was in the Coleman house. The old grandfather clock had scared her.

Find the key.

But I did find it because I remembered where it was and held it in my hand.

Nika bolted upright, disoriented and slightly nauseated. A huge lump of fear lodged in her throat.

Where am I?

Frantic, she scanned her memory, but came up with a blank.

Okay, alright. Don't panic. Think, Nika, think.

But her foggy brain refused to cooperate. She slowly turned her head concentrated on her surroundings. Try as she might, she couldn't make sense of the picture in front of her eyes. The room was unfamiliar, soft and feminine, all done in muted shades of yellow with golden accents. The bed was adorned with a canopy. The cover silk and smooth as a baby's bottom. Everything overwhelmingly and unapologetically luxurious.

Where the hell am I?

The last thing that jumped into her mind was bending to pick up the clock key from the floor. Then like a thunderbolt it hit her: the jarring fall, the dirty road, and the rider on the black stallion...

"Oh, God." Her breath caught in her throat. Was it true after all? Had she managed, somehow, to jump through time and land over a hundred years back in 1909?

Impossible! She was just dreaming or...

Or else, she was crazy and suffering from some mental condition.

Both alternatives were unacceptable, not to mention insane.

"No," she moaned. "I'm not crazy."

"Of course not, dear child!"

That high-pitched tenor sounded familiar. She knew that voice. Yes, from her dream. It had pulled her back to reality, dragging her away from the paradise of slumber. Who did it belong to?

And then her gaze collided with a pair of kind hazel eyes. The smiling, round face belonged to... *Santa Claus*? Yes, definitely Santa Claus. Minus the beard. Plus a pair of gold-rimmed glasses that rode low on his beak-like nose.

Did Santa wear glasses?

And where was his red hat? And why Santa? Was it Christmas already? And why was he chuckling, looking at her, all amused and joyful?

I'm losing my mind.

"Are you...Santa Claus?"

"I have been called many things in my life," the jolly little man answered with a cackle. "But never that. However, it is a definite improvement over the 'stinking brute' you named me earlier."

"Oh...oh," Nika swallowed and closed her eyes, mortified. "I didn't mean...it's not...not you...I mistook you for someone else."

Someone much larger, and darker, and stronger. Someone who looked at me with barely concealed contempt and called me a 'boy' and a 'lump of rags.'

"I gathered that much, *mein Herz*," Santa patted her hand. "Do not fret. So, you are awake. Excellent! How is your head?"

"Head?" Nika gingerly touched her forehead. "Still attached."

"Such a wit! Marvelous, *mein erz.*" Santa dissolved into a high-pitched, laughter that shook his generously rounded body. His delicate tenor made such a great contrast with his general appearance that it should have been ridiculous. But somehow, the overall result was natural and organically balanced. And soothing. Nika felt better already.

"Who are you?" But even as she asked the answer popped into her mind.

"Doctor Schmidt at your service, my dear child," he answered, confirming her suspicion. "I have been tending to you since Mr. and Miss Coleman brought you here, unconscious, a couple of hours ago. Miss Abby said you had an amnesia and did not remember where you were. She was afraid you hit your head. But, after my examination, I can assure you, no bumps or lacerations on your head or any other part of your anatomy. You are in excellent health otherwise. So, how do you feel, my boy? Or should I say, girl?"

Doctor's kind, but shrewd eyes peered at Nika over his drooping spectacles. "How...?"

"*Mein Herz,* I have practiced medicine longer than you have been alive. And, believe me, I can differentiate a female body from that of a male." A deep chuckle jiggled his belly.

Nika blanched, forgetting all about modesty, she jerked away the sheet covering her body. She was dressed in her own t-shirt and panties, but her jeans, socks, and boots were gone. So, someone undressed her. Who? The doctor? His nurse? Self-consciously she tugged at the sheet, covering her breasts. Not that there was anything special to cover. Nika occasionally wore a kind of a sport bra or omitted it altogether because her meager cup size made wearing one more of a nuisance than necessity.

"Who undressed me?" she asked after a pause.

"That would be me. Your pants and socks were too dirty. They will be returned to you after a thorough washing and cleaning."

"My toolbelt!" Forgetting about modesty, Nika flung the covers over and attempted to jump off the bed until two surprisingly strong hands pushed her back.

"Your professional belt— and a fine one it is, by the way—is on the chair next to your bed." He pointed at the nearby plush chair. Nika recognized her toolbelt and her baseball cap. Thank God! Her favorite things were with her, nearby. Intact. She was almost herself again. Almost.

"Santa, er I mean Doctor Schmidt—"

"Call me Doc Schmidt, or just Doc. Everyone else does." He wrapped the sheet around her shoulders.

"Doc, okay." Nika drew a deep breath and started again. "Doc, I need to ask you..."

"You are wondering if anyone else in the household knows by now your true gender?"

Nika nodded.

"No, I did not tell a soul, *mein Herz*. Your secret is safe, but not for long, I am afraid."

"No, not for long," Nika muttered, rubbing her forehead. *What a mess.* For some reason that still eluded her, it was important that everybody took her for a boy. She couldn't say *why* it was imperative, just that it was.

How long could she keep up the charade? If one person knew the truth, sooner or later everybody had to learn it. She would probably give herself away the first chance she had to take a shower.

Shower? How long are you planning to stay here?

Her inner self grew frantic, manically trying to push through her rational mind.

In three or four days, Alex will check on her only to find her gone. He will be beside himself with worry. He undoubtedly will blame himself for not checking in earlier. First, he will call the police, and then the FBI because thoughts of her being kidnapped will charge through him. He has enough political pull to flood Fernandina Beach with law enforcement agents from several branches. Next, he will make TV appearances and promise outrageous rewards for any information about her. When all else fails he will beg and threaten, reason and blackmail. In short, the life and business he built from scratch eight years ago will turn to hell.

And all because of you!

And *Verochka*? Her grandmother's reaction was something Nika shuddered to consider.

In the best traditions of her motherland, she will start a small revolution, calling the mayor, governor, the Ambassador and probably the president himself.

The bottom line, Nika needed to get back. Like right now. Or as soon as possible. Her mind raced with questions. But how? The key! Where was it? Did she drop it in the middle of that dirt road? And where was that blasted road? Elijah Coleman mentioned Cumberland Island. Was she an unwilling guest of the Carnegies? Because, as far as she knew her history, Cumberland Island always belonged to that family. She knew her way around the island, had visited it many times. But that was in *her* time, in the twenty-first century.

Stop it Stop panicking and think. Nothing good will come if you insist on sitting here and behaving like a helpless damsel in distress.

She drew on all her resolve and straightened her spine.

Calm down, don't panic, think rationally.

The Grandfather Clock's key.

If that key got her here, one way or another, it was the key that got her back. What about the grandfather clock? Probably some kind of a portal in between the times...

Don't think about how crazy that sounds—just try to figure out what to do next. You need the key and the grandfather clock. Just concentrate on that for now.

Where was it? Still in the Coleman house, she supposed, in Fernandina Beach, on Amelia Island. In Florida. And she was in Georgia, on Cumberland Island.

So, Nika summarized, she needed to find the key and get to the Coleman house, from one island to another. No problem them being in two different states. Piece of cake! Hysterical laughter bubbled close to the surface, but she bore down.

You can do it. If you escaped from the twins, you can do anything you damn well please.

She just needed to keep pretending to have an amnesia. And that she was a boy. *What a mess!*

"I suppose, you have a good reason to travel like a boy, hiding your true identity and your gender." The good doctor interrupted her inner struggles. "That is none of my affair, *mein erz*. I just want you to know that Mr. Coleman and Mr. Carnegie, the host of this fine house, and yours truly, will help you any way we can. Providing, that you did not commit anything illegal, of course."

"Illegal? Like...like what?"

"Something criminal. A murder is a murder, even if committed in self-defense."

He knitted his white bushy brows in concern and stared down at her.

The situation was more and more absurd by the minute. She almost laughed. "No, no, Doc, no! I assure you, I didn't do anything illegal or criminal, just—"

"Just ran away? From an abusive male?"

"Something like that." She lowered her eyes. She hated to lie, but telling the truth to this kind and gentle Southern doctor with a funny accent was more dangerous than spinning a wild tale about an abusive spouse.

What a mess!

"That's alright, then." Doc Schmidt patted her hand. "May I make a suggestion, my dear? Talk to Mr. Coleman, tell him the truth. He is the one who found you and brought you here. From what I gather, he is very worried. Moreover, he considers himself responsible for you."

"No one's responsible for me but myself," Nika muttered while doing her best not to snap at this nice man.

"That is all well and dandy in theory, my dear, but in real life? In your current situation, you shall be needing help. And Mr. Coleman, not to mention Mr. Carnegie, are powerful, rich men. They both are more than able to protect you from whomever is it you are running away from, *mein Herz.*"

"Are you German, Doc?" Nika asked, partly because she wanted to change the subject and switch the attention from herself, and partly because she really was curious. The good doctor had an adorable accent.

"Guilty as charged," he smiled, then patted her hand again. "Born in Bavaria, in the grand city of Munich. Ever been to Germany, *mein Herz*? No? Oh, you must visit one day! It is such a beautiful country! Such a history, such an ambience! And the food..." Doc's eyes took on a faraway look, but then he sighed, and quickly returned to himself. "I came to America as a young fellow, full of dreams and illusions, fresh out of medical school. I wanted to explore The Land of the Free for a month or two. But," he shut his medical bag with a loud click, "I stayed for good."

"Why?"

"The girl, of course, why else?" He chuckled, his eyes crinkling with humor. "Ah, my dear child, it was the love at first sight. When I saw her, my Anna, it was like, 'Oh, here you are at last.' Do you know?"

"No, I don't," Nika sighed. She had never been in love, not even half-in-love.

"You are so young, my dear. You will definitely meet the love of your life yet."

"I'm not so sure." She lowered her head, feeling unbearably sad and totally alone.

She supposed at twenty-nine she was young compared to Doc's age— sixty-something at a glance— but never before had the weight of every one of those years pressed heavily on her shoulders.

"Oh, you will, my dear. You shall not despair. I am positive everything will work out for the best. In a meantime," Doc's eyes clouded with concern, "we need to decide how to proceed from this point onward. I can prescribe you a bedrest for a few of days. Think, *mein Herz*, think long and hard what you wish to do next. I will visit you daily, of course, but if you are not willing to take anyone else in your confidence "then it will be a bit precarious."

Doc took his watch out of his breast pocket, tsk-tsked after checking the time. "I am afraid, I need to get back to Dungeness, my dear."

Nika's eyes almost popped out of their sockets.

"To where?"

"To Dungeness. Did I not tell you? I am Carnegies' family doctor, and whenever they are in residence here on the island, I stay with them. Have you heard about their winter home, by chance?"

Nika opened her mouth and then closed it with a loud snap. She almost blurted that not only had she heard of the house, she had visited it often. Whatever was left of it, that is. But somehow, she doubted the good Doctor was ready to hear about the fire that destroyed the famous Carnegie mansion in 1959.

Instead, she half-nodded, half-shrugged, noncommittally.

"Oh, you must definitely see it! It is something amazing."

"How long have you been the family doctor for the...Carnegies?"

It was hard to make her tongue work around the famous name she had read books and watched TV documentaries about as casually as if she was talking about her next-door neighbor.

Doctor Schmidt, bless his heart, smiled and answered cheerfully, "Oh, too long to remember for sure, dear child. But a few generations of Carnegie babies were brought to this world by yours truly."

"Where do you live, Doc?" Nika blurted out. "I mean, when you are not vacationing with the family?"

"New York, *mein Herz*. City, that is. Our marvelous city on the Hudson river."

Ah New York. Nika sighed, suddenly homesick. She truly loved her new home on the divine island in the South, but New York, that marvelous city on the Hudson was in her blood. Like a dollop of poison, too diluted to bring real harm, but still very real to shorten the breath.

"You are a long way from home, Doc." She gave him a small, sad smile.

"And so are you, dear child."

"Me? No, I'm local. Well, almost. I'm from Amelia Island."

"If you insist."

"No, seriously. My name is Nika. Veronika Morris. And I live in Fernandina Beach. Just not..."

"Not?"

"Just not in this century," Nika finished in a rush. What in blazes prompted her to blurt out the truth? She was playing with fire by admitting her true identity, but she was also too sick and tired of this insane charade. If she wanted to get back, she really needed all the help she could get. Who was a better candidate than Doc Schmidt, a kind and highly intelligent man, to take into her confidence? And besides, he was from Germany, where rumor had it people still believed, and took a great pride, in their haunted mansions and folklore tales. As a scientist and a highly educated man of his time, he must have an open mind, right?

The pair of keen shrewd eyes focused on her, unblinking, for a long time, before Doc Schmidt cracked a smile.

"I am glad your sense of humor is back, *mein Herz*. It is a good sign. Good sign indeed."

So much for intelligence an open mind.

"Yeah, well," Nika sighed in defeat, trying to cover her mishap by a lopsided smile.

"But your toes gave me a pause for a moment."

"My toes?"

"Yes."

"What's wrong with my toes?"

"Oh, absolutely nothing, except that they are colored."

Heat charged across Nika's cheeks. Her painted toes were now embarrassing.

He probably thinks I am a floozy. Or worse.

Get a grip, girl. You're being ridiculous.

Doc had undressed her. Examined her body. So what if he noticed her pedicure? But for some insane reason she was unable to explain, such a small and intimate detail made her all the more vulnerable.

"Now, I have heard of such custom in ancient Egypt and China. Do you, by any chance, belong to any special religious groups, my dear?"

Panic charged through Nika. That was all she needed, to be written off as a member of a sect. And all because of her love of polish, no less.

"No, Doc, nothing as drastic as that. It just..."

Just what, for goodness' sake? Think fast, Nika.

"My grandmother...she is French, and she got me into a habit of...taking care of my feet and painting my toes. It's called pedicure, and it's a basic routine. In Europe," she added hastily. That was a hundred percent truth. But when exactly did pedicures started in Europe? Good question. By her vague recollection it was somewhere in the beginning of the last century. Or later? *Oh, crap.* With a beating heart, she held her breath.

"Well then, it looks quite fancy." He finally nodded. She let go of her breath in a single whoosh.

"French, huh? Must have given you all those gorgeous curls, your grandmother."

Nika smiled as an image of *Verochka's* exquisite face rose in her mind.

"No, but she gave me my eyes."

"Most unusual color, indeed," Doc commented. "Never seen that shade of blue before. Almost lilac."

A deep 'bong' of the mantel clock brought him out of his reverie.

"*Mein Got*, look at the time! I must be off, dear child. But I will come to see you tomorrow. Please think of my suggestion and talk to Mr. Coleman—"

"Talk to him about what?"

CHAPTER TEN

Nika sucked in a sharp breath. She turned toward the sound.

She knew that voice.

She had heard it so many times. But from her dreams or real memories from *before?*

My friends and family call me Eli.

He was larger than life and managed to dwarf all the furniture in the spacious room. The sensation of being small and fragile, and insultingly insignificant swept over her as she laid there under his steely glare. Was he still angry with her? Nika cringed, but didn't avert her gaze.

What have I done?

Was he angry because he almost trampled her under his horse's hooves? Or did she manage to displease him in some other way? Adding to her discomfort, she was in bed, almost naked, while he stood there, dressed to the 'T', towering over her. This dark and imposing stranger, one that she knew almost intimately, stood there, totally immobile, yet he managed to electrify the atmosphere in the room. Nika's ears buzzed. The fine hair on her arms and neck rose up and her cheeks were on fire. But she held the heavy glare of his eyes.

Call me anything you like, but in my house I'm the master and the reigning king.

His commanding presence accentuated by an almost military stance was overwhelming. Even the good Doc Schmidt was visibly uncomfortable, torn between the urge to flee the room and his professional duty to care for the patient. The duty won. With a deep sigh, he shifted his doctor's bag from one hand to another, and flashed a faint smile at their unexpected guest.

"Mr. Coleman! You startled me, sir. I was expecting to see Miss Abby—"

"Talk to me about what?" Eli repeated coolly, transferring his attention to the doctor.

"Talk to you? About what?"

"That's what I'm asking you, Doc. Before I entered, you said 'talk to Mr. Coleman.' There is only one Mr. Coleman, and that's me." He glanced at Nika and then turned to the doctor. "So, I repeat, talk to me about what?"

"Oh, that," poor Doc Schmidt frowned, obviously ill at ease. "You have to ask Nick. After all, the decision is h-his."

He stumbled at the last word, but Eli didn't seem to notice.

"What decision?"

"Well, whether to trust you or not."

Elijah's eyebrows shot up, his head tilted. The glare he aimed at Nika was positively charged with an insult. Then just as quickly he tucked it under the sheen of mild indifference. As if amused by the notion that a street urchin he picked up— literally—from the dust might find him untrustworthy, he smiled. The razor-sharp curve of his lips was cold and somehow rude. And scary as hell.

"So, have you decided yet, boy?" His voice didn't change its volume one iota. But his insolence resonated through her bones and chilled her blood. Nika barely suppressed a shudder.

"Well?" he prompted after a moment.

"I'm not...I have not..." she muttered then swallowed with effort past the lump of fear and misery lodged in her throat.

I'm not a boy, and I have not decided anything! She screamed silently.

"Mr. Coleman, if I may, sir?" Doc interrupted with a hesitant little cough. "My patient just recovered from a very nasty fall. Furthermore, he's suffering from the mild case of amnesia. May I suggest that you postpone your questioning for some future time? Give him a bit longer to assimilate his current situation. And to think some more."

Sparing one quick glance at Nika, Doc, immune to Elijah's current dark mood, patted him lightly on the arm with an air of familiarity. "I am sure there is no question in our guest's mind of your trustworthiness. He is just shy and confused, that's all, *mein Herz.*"

"If you say so." Elijah inclined his head.

"Oh, I do, sir, I do. Well, I must be off." But Doc remained in place, shuffling his feet.

"What are you waiting for, then?" Eli inquired.

"Oh, I was just wondering if Miss Abby..." Doc cleared his throat, switching his gaze from Nika to Elijah and back. "What I meant is, Ms. Abby asked me to wait for her return," he finished feebly.

"It's quite alright, Doc. You may leave. I will watch over our guest until Abigail's return."

When Doc still hesitated, hovering at the threshold, Elijah lifted his eyebrows in a familiar gesture, the first notes of impatience crept into his voice, "What is the matter? Don't you *trust* me with your patient, Doc?"

"I beg your pardon, sir. Of course, I do." With one last pointed glance at Nika, as if trying to convey some silent message to her, he quietly left.

Finally, they were alone.

The silence was oppressive. It sat heavily around the cheery room like a mushroom cloud after a bomb exploded and added to Nika's dismay. She tried to shrink her body to the smallest possible form, curving into a protective ball under the covers. Never before had she been at such a disadvantage. Yet there she was sitting in bed, almost naked, facing a fully dressed large man who appeared perfectly content to just stand there and watch her like a hawk.

She was the first to break under the pressure of that deafening silence.

"What?" Defiantly, deliberately, Nika lifted her chin, sought his eyes. But the slight tremor in her voice betrayed her inner turmoil and spoiled the picture of belligerence.

"Not a thing," Elijah answered after a long pause. His enigmatic silver eyes kept her pinned to the spot until hey stripped her of all her false bravado.

"Then stop looking at me that way."

"And what way might that be?"

"You know, like you're an inquisitor and I'm your prisoner."

"Prisoner?" Elijah curved one brow in a mock surprise. "You call this room a prison?"

"No, the room is fine." Nika nodded.

"What, then?"

"*You* You're standing there, accusing me of God only knows what."

"I didn't say a word."

"You don't have to!" She swallowed hard as she plucked the lace trim on the top sheet. "Your eyes are doing it. So, why don't you ask me your questions instead of just standing there and glaring at me?"

Elijah appeared to ponder that for a moment, then inclined his head.

"Very well, then. Who are you, and how did you happen to pop out of thin air?"

Nailed it squarely on the head, didn't you?

She did pop out of thin air, being thrown through time by some incredible force. One moment she was bending to pick up the key, and the next she was dropped smack in the middle of a dirt road, almost under the hooves of the galloping horse. Thrown back a hundred years, no less.

"My name is Nick." She recovered her voice enough to answer the first question. For some reason she didn't want to share her real name. "As to the second question..." She lowered her eyes. That was the tricky part.

"Yes?" he prompted patiently, coolly.

"I don't know."

"You don't know? Or don't want to answer?"

"I really don't know, honestly. One moment I was...and the next..." She raised her eyes to him and let him see the truth. "I don't know."

For a long moment he quietly observed her, then he sighed.

"It is a possibility, even though a slight one, mind you, that you did strike your head and forgot some things." He frowned. "What I find difficult to believe is that a small boy like you could be a cunning thief, acting on your own."

"A thief? What are you talking about?"

"This," he reached into his pocket and produced an object that he presented to Nika. She recognized it immediately. The grandfather clock key. The same blasted key she had found in the Coleman house. The same damned one that miraculously brought her here. She would recognize that key anywhere.

Nika did a double take, then lunged for it, grappling as the sheet twisted around her legs.

"Give it back! It's mine!"

He easily side-stepped her. Nika stumbled, sprawling at his feet.

"Yours?" He laughed then, a short bark that somehow was scarier than a shout.

"Yes, mine. Give it back."

"And how did you come about obtaining it?"

"I found it!"

"Where?"

"None of your business!"

"No?" He answered insolently as he tucked the key back into his breast pocket. "Funny because this key is the one of a kind. It's from the Coleman grandfather clock, the family heirloom that belonged to my grandfather, then my father, and now it belongs to me. This key is unique, and there is no duplicate to it. It was in my house, hidden in its special secret place that no one knows about. No one, that is, except me." He glared at her. "I didn't tell a soul about it. And I find it very peculiar that you, of all people, come to have it in your possession. So, I repeat, how did you steal it?"

"I did *not* steal it."

"Who gave it to you, then? Who is your accomplice? Someone in my household? Answer me, boy!"

"What on earth is going on here?"

If Nika was ever happier for an interruption, she didn't remember the occasion. Abigail Coleman stood in the doorway surveying the scene in front of her.

And what a crazy scene that must be: half-naked 'boy', sprawled on the floor, her brother towering over, his eyes spewing the wrath of God. *Poor Abigail.*

"Eli? What's all this? What in the name of God do you think you're doing?" She quickly crossed the room and crouched over Nika, hugging her protectively.

"Have you lost your mind? The boy is barely recovered from the nasty fall. Why are you questioning him like some kind of an inquisitor?"

Nika laughed, she couldn't help it. Tears streamed down her face, but whether from fear or defeat, she had no idea. But when Abby called her brother an inquisitor, echoing Nika's previous remark, she found the whole business hilarious. She was getting hysterical, and no wonder. She was also losing her mind.

What now?

Elijah Coleman had found the key that she probably dropped when she fainted. He accused her of theft. More, he suspected her of acting with an accomplice, or being a member of some nefarious gang! Sooner or later, they had to learn that the *boy* they recovered and brought to this house, was in reality a girl, and call the authorities. Arrest and questioning by the local police was in her near future. And what might she say? That she was an unwilling time-traveler from the future?

Oh, what a mess!

No wonder she was half-hysterical, half-bewildered. But her current emotional state was also a blessing in disguise, since Abigail Coleman took it as an aftermath of her accident. She was outraged by the manhandling her older brother had dished out and sympathetic to Nika. At least someone was on her side. But for how long? That was the million-dollar question. Nika shivered. Abby dragged the quilt from the bed and wrapped it around Nika's chilled body.

"Truly, what is wrong with you, brother? You are behaving like a monster!"

Eli walked to the window and then glanced out.

In truth, he needed some time to compose himself before facing his sister and that strange boy again. What *was* wrong with him? He worked his jaw as he pondered just what the hell was happening. It was so out of character for him to lose his composure and his temper this way. Something about the boy, he mused. Something wasn't quite right, and for the life of him, he couldn't understand what. His gut told him the boy was lying through his teeth. About everything. Maybe, even about his name. And how did he happen to have Eli's prized clock key in his possession? It was a mystery he was determined to solve, one way or another. And for that, he needed to have that boy close at hand. To watch him, to question him. To uncover his true identity and his real mission here. He hazarded a quick glance at him. The indolent creature was glaring back out of those uncanny eyes of his, his plumb mouth trembling. But his pointy chin was stuck stubbornly upward. And then there was that mane of fluffy golden curls.

The boy looks like a yellow daisy.

What a picture! Eli suppressed the chuckle that threatened to erupt, still uneasy by the mystery of why this boy was affecting him so strongly. But affecting him he did, damn him. Even now Eli unwillingly admired the boy's spirit, not to mention that unholy mouth of his that belonged on a whore.

An image of Annabelle in her black negligée, sheer enough to see every detail of her ripe body, emerged in his mind. And her mouth. A mouth that made men cry out in pleasure when she worked her magic. Desperation for companionship prompted him to pay good money, time and again, for an hour or two with her. Disgust and shame coiled through him, choking air from his lungs like the boa constrictor he saw in Brazil killing an ocelot.

Dammit all to hell and back.

He gave himself a mental shake and turned to his sister.

"We are leaving in the morning, so you would be wise to pack your belongings."

"Leaving?" Abby's shoulders stiffened. "What do you mean?"

"We are returning home."

"So, have you changed your mind, then?" Abby asked in a wistful tone.

"No."

"But, Eli, my engagement—"

"Will simply be postponed. Make no mistake, Abigail, you *will* marry Patrick. It's a done deal, whether you like it or not."

"Well, I don't, and you know it!"

"I do, I just happen to disagree with you on the subject."

"How dare you!" Abby stood and faced her brother with her hands on her hips as if she were ready for battle. "It's my life we're talking about. My future. My happiness!"

"I know, Abigail. I also know that you will be much happier as a married woman and the wife of a fine man like Patrick Carnegie."

"Happier than what?" Abby threw up her arms in frustration.

"Than a spinster, traipsing all over the Europe in false hopes of becoming an artist."

"Not just an artist, dear brother, a world-famous artist. And not all over Europe. Just France. I want to go to France and continue my education. You know I have a talent. You know that, Eli. Even you have a hard time denying that."

Her voice quivered on her last words and Nika's heart went out to the young woman.

"You do," he added, unruffled by his sister's dismay. "But that talent will not give you security and family, not to mention, children."

"I don't want any children! I don't want to marry, even though Patrick is a fine man—"

"Nonsense," he cut her off, unperturbed and seemingly unaffected.

"You are *impossible*." Abby's eyes welled with tears. "Sometimes I hate you as much as I love you, brother!"

"Go right ahead and hate me, if you will." Eli nodded. "Later you're going to thank me."

"*Never.*"

Totally forgotten by the Coleman siblings, Nika was the unwilling witness to this family drama as it unfolded before her eyes. Facts from her research popped into her mind. Abigail Coleman had disappeared in 1909 just before her engagement, never to be seen again. There were dark rumors that her older brother had murdered her in a fit of rage. But Nika couldn't imagine Elijah doing anything in rage. He was so controlled, so reserved. The man was maddening! If anything, the opposite rang a truer bell. Abigail was the one more capable of exploding.

So, what's really happened?

She studied each of them in turn.

And what business is it of yours? What's done is done. You must worry about your own predicament and not interfere with history. They are both dead. Remember?

But for Nika, they were not. They were alive and breathing, and in Abby's case, hurting. They were as real for her as Alex and *Verochka*. They both, for better or worse, had found her and brought her to this house, had tended to her. Was it any wonder she felt involved and, to some extent, responsible? How could she not interfere? How could she not even try to right the wrong? Because, even burdened with her own misery, Nika was still outraged by Elijah's tyrannical position toward his sister. Just like her own father, who always knew what was best for her.

Men! In every century, in every generation, always knew what was best for the women! Huh! If it were her...

"You are such a *tyrant*." Nika exploded, her words bounced off the walls. "How can you? She's your only sister. How *dare* you treat her that way. As if she was a toy, or your possession. She's a grown woman. How old are you?" She addressed Abby.

After a moment of stunned silence, Abby, wide eyed and bewildered, finally found her voce:

"T-twenty."

"Huh. At twenty, I was raising hell with Alex, planning our great escape from the twins. At twenty-one we both ran away from home, right after our own graduation party, and skedaddled all over the country. Look at me." She grabbed Abby's icy hands. In her agitation and righteous outrage for the girl, Nika forgot where she was and plowed right ahead. "I've been on my own ever since. And I've managed just fine. Both Alex and I have. Don't listen to anybody, Abigail. Follow your heart. If you want to paint and be an artist, then go and be one. Don't get married because your monster of a brother pressures you, and especially to a guy you don't love."

Too late it dawned on her what she just said. What she revealed.

Oh, crap!

The silence in the room was deafening.

Both Coleman siblings stared at her. Only, in Abby's case Nika read incredulous confusion. Eli's glance transmitted something entirely different. A stark, raging suspicion.

Nika burrowed deeper into the quilt that Abby had so tenderly put around her just a moment ago. More than anything she wished to become invisible and disappear from the picture as suddenly as she was dropped into it. She shut her eyes, said a little prayer, but when she opened them again, everything around her remained the same. Two figures, frozen in a pantomime, stared at her, Eli from above and Abby from the side. Her little prayer apparently went unanswered.

A wave of nausea swept through, making her clammy and miserable. She was stuck here, in this room, in this century, with this family for an unforeseeable future.

Oh, crap!

Nika's body shook from head to toe right before she turned numb all over, like after a shot of Novocain. She surveyed the intricate pattern of the parquet floor in front of her as if her life depended on it. Now she had done it. In her righteous disgust with male chauvinism, she let her emotions and her big mouth overrule common sense. She was doomed.

Nika held her breath and waited for the guillotine to drop.

"Well, I must say, it was a compelling and enlightening speech. Bravo."
Eli clapped his hands a couple of times in a parody of an applause. That dry muffled sound reverberated in Nika's ears like a cannon blast.
"I have one question for you, boy."
Just one? She almost laughed. Instead, she lifted her eyes, meeting the steely glint of his.
"Who is Alex?"

CHAPTER ELEVEN

Eli again found himself on horseback, galloping along the same narrow trail. Only now, he traveled toward Dungeness, whereas this morning he was escaping from it in a futile attempt to cool his temper and bring his frustration under control.

He was no less frustrated now, and even more agitated and confused. And all because of Abby. If not for her, he may have not left the Carnegie mansion this morning and not met that boy who dropped from high heavens just under Sultan's thundering hooves.

If not for Abby, he would turn around and go back, leaving the strange creature just where he had found him, and wash his hands of the whole affair. But no, she had to follow him, and seeing the boy in a middle of the road, started accusing him, her own brother, of God only knew what.

What choice did he have but to haul the boy's dirty, bony behind to the closest house that belonged to another member of the Carnegie family, and send for Doc Schmidt?

If not for his headstrong sister, he might not have been at a disadvantage or so befuddled. And that was worse than being agitated and on the verge of losing his temper. He, Eli Coleman, was about to lose his head. And how humiliating was that? If not for Abby, Eli fumed, he would never have met the strange boy. The blasted creature was the very reason he rode toward Dungeness now. He needed to speak with Doc. The old German was hiding something. Eli could feel it in his bones. Some secret the boy revealed to him, perhaps? Why else was Doc suggesting him to 'talk to Mr. Coleman'?

Who was that boy? Where had he come from? What did he want? Was he acting on his own, or guided by someone else?

He said his name was Nick. But was that truth or a fib? And what of his family? Had he confessed his true identity to Doc Schmidt?

And how on earth did he have possession of Eli's heirloom clock key?

Questions, so many questions. These questions were driving him insane. Even more so now, after that half-crazed, mind-boggling speech the boy had delivered earlier. Eli still couldn't find his bearings. A *tyrant*. He had the gall to call him a tyrant to his face! Not many a grown man had the sheer nerve to do that.

And who in blazes was Alex?

Eli cursed under his breath. He had reached his destination whilst his mind wandered. He dismounted and dropped the reins to the stable lad, then patted Sultan's flank absentmindedly. He almost ran up the stairs toward the sound of music and merriment, but curbed his agitation with an effort. He fumed embarrassed to have acted like an impatient and excited adolescent. Not a proper way for a grown man to behave, he lectured himself silently as he entered the room.

The gathering was large, as usual, with family and guests sipping the customary cocktails before dinner.

Eli plucked a glass from a passing waiter, not caring what spirit it contained. He searched the room for the small, rotund body of the doctor. He found his quarry nearby, in an animated conversation with some aging matron. Eli tucked his impatience under a cool nonchalant façade, made small chat here and there, all the while waiting for Doc to finish his tête-à-tête. Eli snatched the doctor by the arm the second he was free.

"Mr. Coleman!" Doc almost spilled his schnapps, but recovered well for a man of his advanced years. "What can I do for you, *mein Herz*? I hope our little patient is well?"

"Yes, he's well, thanks to you," Eli answered politely. "Physically, that is."

"Physically? What do you mean by that?"

Eli gave it some thought, deciding how best to proceed.

"I wanted a private word with you, Doc," he admitted at last, settling on the most direct approach. "Have you noticed anything...peculiar about the boy?"

"Aside from that he materialized out of seemingly nowhere, nothing," Doc replied with his eyes cast downward. Eli's suspicion multiplied.

"Doc? Is there something you're not telling me?"

"Whatever do you mean, Mr. Coleman?"

Doc stooped his shoulders, hunching even more, and lowered his head. All in all, he assumed a humble peasant to master posture that was so irksome to Eli, especially since he was positive the old German was play-acting.

"Drop that subservient mannerism, Doc, it doesn't suit you," Eli answered brusquely. "If you don't want to answer my questions, just say so, but don't insult us both by pretending."

Doc's features underwent an instant transformation, settling into his own shrewd self.

"Well then." He picked at an invisible lint from Eli's coat. "The truth is that the bo... uh, the patient is absolutely healthy, but seemed to suffer from a memory loss I hope to be temporary."

"But aside from that, nothing's wrong with the boy, is that what you're saying?"

"That is precisely what I'm saying, *mein Herz*."

"Did he tell you his name?"

"Yes, Nick. Nick Morris."

"Morris? Hmm," Eli pondered that for a moment. "Did he tell you where is he from?"

Doc peered at Eli over his glasses, his brows raised, his eyes faintly amused. As if he was having a private joke. Or did Eli imagine the mischievous sparkle in Doc's hazel eyes?

No, he was sure he hadn't.

"My patient said h-he was from Amelia Island," Doc Schmidt answered at last.

"Hmm, I don't know anyone by the name Morris." Eli frowned. "And I know almost everyone on the island. The boy doesn't look like a local lad. There's just something about him..."

"Yes?" Doc prompted.

"I'm not sure, but something *is* strange." Eli decided to keep the boy's unbelievable tirade close to the vest. What had set him off so? Abby's upcoming nuptials? Her reluctance to wed? Or Eli's actions?

You are such a tyrant!

"Okay, aside from that, did you learn anything else about him? After all, there's probably a family out there looking for him."

"No, my patient said h-he doesn't have a family, at least not the one h-he remembers."

The good doctor stuttered a bit, but Eli chalked it up to the effect of an excellent schnapps.

"Oh, and h-his grandmother is French," Doc added, as an afterthought.

"What?" Eli's cocked his head to one side. That accounted for the boy's faint and peculiar accent. He was speaking good, clear English, but...just in a slightly unfamiliar manner. "That's probably why," Eli murmured to himself. "Anything else?"

"No, *mein Herz*, nothing else of importance."

"Did he mention any twins?" *...Planning our escape from the twins...*

"Twins? Not that I recall, no."

"Anyone by the name Alex?" *...At twenty I was raising hell with Alex...*

"Definitely no."

"Are you absolutely positive?"

"I am, *mein Hertz*. No Alex, and no twins. Just a French grandmother," Doc answered frankly. Then he hesitated. "Have you noticed his toolbelt? It is of a great quality, and all tools are expensive."

"I noticed."

He also noticed several strange things he couldn't identify or the materials used to make them. A chill charged up Eli's spine.

"So, the boy must've come from a family with some money. Is that what you're saying?" he asked Doc.

"That, or he must have a wealthy benefactor."

"Hmm...." *Didn't consider that, did you?* The wealthy benefactor who supplied the boy with an excellent toolbelt and expensive tools of a trade. Possible. He probably was an apprentice. That, at least, made some sense. But what of his declaration about being on his own since he was *twenty-one*? My God, if the little urchin was a day older than thirteen or fourteen, he would eat his hat

"How old do you think he is?" Eli asked.

"Hard to say, *mein Herz*. My patient is young, but to tell you the exact age..." Doc shrugged.

"In your professional opinion, is the boy delusional?" Eli asked, focusing his razor-blade gaze at the older man.

"You mean, does my patient belong to an asylum?"

Eli nodded.

"Absolutely not!"

His relief was so considerable, his breath whooshed out. Of course, he failed to notice he was holding it in the first place. *Damn it all to hell and back.* The true nature of his feelings was too confusing to elaborate for right now. Something to ponder on later.

"If he lost some of his memories, as he claims, how soon can he regain them back?"

"Ah, *mein Herz*, no one can answer that question. Not even the greatest minds of psychology in Europe."

"So, it could be tomorrow, or in a year—" Eli muttered.

"Or never." Doc nodded, animated to the point of bouncing on his two pudgy little feet. "Oh, the mystery of a human brain, *mein Herz!* If only—"

"Can he be a fugitive?"

Doc blanched, did a double-take. "No-o-o, impossible! Absolutely impossible. Did you look at h-him? A wee thing like that? A criminal? No, Eli, absolutely not."

In his outrage, Doc forgot all the manners instilled in modern society, and for the first time called Eli by his given name.

Eli hid a smile. He kind of liked that Doc Schmidt took such a strong protective position toward the boy. Now, why *he* himself was feeling such a protectiveness toward the strange little creature, was another matter entirely, one he wasn't prepared to dissect at the moment.

"I will tell you, though." Doc cleared his throat after a pause. He was obviously uneasy. "That b-boy needs help." He coughed again, as if stumbling on the word 'boy.' And not for the first time. *Another item to file away for later.*

"Help? What kind of help?"

"Well, maybe protection would be a better word for it."

"What aren't you telling me, Doc?"

"I've told you everything I can, *mein Herz*," the old man answered earnestly.

His conversation with Doc Schmidt left him even more unsettled than before. Eli approached his host and hostess, tucking the matter of the strange boy to the back of his mind, and made some apologies for Abby's terrible behavior this morning. *The gall of the girl.* To announce to the Carnegie family that she will not marry their nephew Patrick, because she has decided to become an artist instead.

To *humiliate* him that way, in front of all his friends and peers. To challenge *his* decision, to undermine *his* will.

The insufferable, ungrateful girl, the one he had raised from the time she was almost a babe! Maybe he failed to do good job raising her. What did he know about parenthood? Next to nothing, really. He was twenty-four at the time, just four years older than Abby today, when their parents were killed in an accident and left him in charge not only of the vast Coleman empire, but a ten-year-old sister he barely knew. Maybe he should have sent her off to a private boarding school in Switzerland like many friends and relatives suggested, and washed his hands of her. But for the life of him, he couldn't abandon her. When the message of his parents' death reached him in London, Eli was half-dead himself. Just a few days prior to that, his wife of eleven months failed to live through childbirth. The newborn babe followed his mother moments later. And Eli was left alone, bereft, with his whole world turned upside-down.

That tragedy was something he wasn't prepared for, nor equipped to cope with. Always in control, arrogantly assured of himself and his own power, Eli had forgotten he was a mere man. The death of his young wife and his son taught him a hard and unwanted lesson. He was as vulnerable and defenseless against Mother Nature as any other person. All his wealth and superior intellect were useless.

He, Elijah Coleman, the wonder boy and the darling of fortune, was slapped in the face with humility. A hard truth to swallow.

His life turned into a single nightmare of the worst sort. One he was unable to awaken from. Young, defeated, and disillusioned, he contemplated suicide. What point was there in living when all he loved was gone? A day later he received a letter from his father's solicitor and overnight he became the sole heir to the Coleman estate. And the custodian of a sister he barely knew. God, as he figured, had given him another challenge, another way of escape. Determined to take control of his life once again, Eli left London for home.

His family's affairs were much more easily dealt with than his custodian duties. While he was on top of everything about finances, real estate, and running an empire the size of the Colemans', he was absolutely clueless in matters of child rearing let alone a girl. Life was much easier if he sent her to a boarding school for rich and privileged girls, but Eli never took an easy way in his life.

Abby had already lost her parents. Her life had shifted dangerously beneath her two tiny feet. To send her away, alone, was cruel and the equivalent to uprooting her, of robbing her of the life she was used to and entitled to. She wasn't an orphan. She had a home, and family even if it was just him. She was Abigail Coleman, and she was his only surviving family. And he was hers.

Eli was determined to keep it that way.

His little sister had everything money could buy, best tutors, best clothing, best food. Abby turned out to be a bright and intelligent girl, quite inquisitive and curious. Unlike him, she was sure the world was a marvelous place, and all the people deserved the benefit of the doubt.

She was incredibly sweet and funny, and had a heart of the size of the Atlantic Ocean. And every time she smiled at him, that huge heart shinned in her eyes.

They shared more than a family name, as he found out with time. They both had a penchant for languages and chess, loved Baroque music, and Shakespeare. They were crazy about fresh oysters and abhorred cruelty to animals.

They both were excellent equestrians and swam like fish. And they both shared a Coleman family trait: grey eyes and black wavy hair.

He couldn't pinpoint the exact moment when his little sister became so vital to him, nor could he imagine his life without her. He never confessed to her or, to be perfectly frank, to himself. It was just something private and deep and natural, almost on a primordial level.

No, he never said the words. Instead, he built her a butterfly garden after she had mentioned in passing how pretty the wings of the Monarch in her botany book were. And when she first began to show a talent for sketching, he sent her to Paris to see the paintings in the Louvre.

And that was the beginning of a disaster. Sending Abby to France was an act of overindulgence, but allowing her to stay there for three years to study art was the biggest mistake Eli had ever made in his entire life.

Instead of a well-behaved, curious, and funny girl, she had turned into an opinionated, self-assured, and quite passionate young woman. Passionate about her art, that is. The mere thought that his baby sister could be passionate about something or, God forbid, *someone* else, was sure to send him to an early grave.

Now, after that disastrous morning and Abby's terrible behavior, he stood in front of Lucy and Thomas Carnegie, trying to mend fences.

Calmly and with great conviction, Eli assured them the engagement of his sister to their favorite nephew was still on, but that in his opinion, it may be best to postpone the engagement for a short while, giving Abby time to accept the idea. Both hosts acknowledged his explanations graciously. More graciously than he had hope for, and certainly more than Abby, the insufferable girl, deserved. They agreed with him on a postponement. Thankfully, Patrick wasn't due for another few weeks, so it was mutually agreed upon to break the news to him then.

"And what was a few more weeks, or months for that matter, to youngsters like them, huh? Let them both enjoy their freedom before matrimonial bliss," Thomas Carnegie, the patriarch of the clan, said. His wife smiled and nodded her approval. Immeasurably relived and grateful, Eli shook hands with his host, kissed Miss Lucy's porcelain cheek, and, giving them both an abbreviated story of the strange boy, declined their dinner invitations and then left Dungeness.

He was impatient to return to Plum Orchard, the house of his best friend George who was the son of Mr. Thomas and Miss Lucy. Eli was grateful that Abby, the boy, and he were invited to stay another night. First thing tomorrow morning all three of them must return home to Fernandina. Whether Eli liked it or not, the strange, peculiar creature was his responsibility. Eli had no heart to abandon him now, especially since the boy claimed to be from Amelia Island. Maybe being in the familiar surroundings shall prompt his memory to re-surface. If the boy was really telling the truth, that is.

Well, there was only one way to find out. Eli still had time to report the boy to the police. But why? And whatever for? For materializing in the middle of a road, out of the blue? After all, he hadn't committed any unlawful acts. And his amnesia didn't threaten the members of the Coleman household.

Of course, there was that strange matter of the key, and some really peculiar items the boy had on his body, such as his toolbelt and ridiculous hat. But even taking all that into consideration, there were no criminal grounds, and therefore, not a single reason for the police department to become involved. The boy presented a puzzle Eli was curious enough to put together himself. And if the child was a spy or a thief, it was Eli's business to uncover and deal out the punishment. No, he refused to abandon the boy. Hence, take him home, give him room and board, and some sort of work around the house, all the while keeping his eye on him closely. Until the truth came out, or until the boy recovered his full faculties, whichever came first.

And then we'll see.

Eli set his lips into a thin line.

French grandmother, wasn't it? Alex, the one with whom he ran away from home? At twenty-one? Rubbish.

He shook his head. If the boy was older than fifteen, he would eat his hat. Weird and farfetched, that story, but Eli was up to the challenge. As a matter of fact, had there ever been another time he was so eager, or more energized and alive. That puzzled him. And then there was his own strange reaction to the boy.

What was it about him?

And who, curse it, was Alex!

CHAPTER TWELVE

For the second time in her life Nika found herself inside the infamous house that started it all. The Coleman house.

It was even more spectacular and amazing now than before. Or, rather more before than now, she corrected herself, since *now* was a hundred years *before* she stepped foot inside of it.

The splendor of the mansion took her breath away. Every aspect was just how she envisioned it in her mind's eye, and the way she planned to restore it. Which meant she had to find her way back and return to her own time. Or was that find her way *forward*? She was so confused with this century-jump thing, half the time the distinction between before from after eluded her.

The trip on *The Sea Princess,* the Coleman's luxurious boat, was something out of a fairy tale that Nika might have enjoyed if she hadn't been so scared and bewildered. Their small entourage consisted of five people, including the Colemans, Elijah's personal secretary Mr. O'Brien, Abby's French maid Claudine, and herself. And, of course, the captain and the boat crew.

Nika was dumbfounded by the amount of luggage hauled onto the boat. Her grandmother didn't take all those suitcases and trunks when she gallivanted around the globe. In no time at all, Nika found herself on the grounds of Fernandina's Marina of 1909. A dreamlike sensation seized her as she stared at the town she knew and loved. It was like peering at a familiar picture through a looking glass, or fog. *Or daguerreotype.*

Nika blinked several times to bring into focus the oddly distorted scenery. She recognized some buildings and landscape, but the familiar signs of the town she knew were mostly gone. The pain of that loss was almost physical. She was totally alone and scared.

Upon their arrival at the house Nika was ushered unceremoniously inside and thrust into the hands of Mrs. Smith the housekeeper. She was a stern stout woman of undeterminable age. Elijah gave her a terse order to find Nika decent accommodation. Nika cringed when the housekeeper asked who he was. Mrs. Smith was told he was a distant relative and guest of the house for the time being. Nobody clarified how long that time being implied. Nika glanced around the spacious foyer, her professional eye noticing all the tiny details of the original décor and craftsmanship. Then her eyes collided with the familiar form of the grandfather clock. It was in the same spot where she had found it before, in between the hallway and the living quarters. All six wooden feet of the elaborate masterpiece gleamed proudly and ticked away time like nothing was amiss. Nika froze, then prompted from behind by Elijah's slight push, she stumbled, but soon found her footing. She trembled from excitement, her eyes pinned to the clock. Then anxiety took over. She was so close to her goal, she could almost feel the rush of time passing by, as she hurtled toward her destination. All she needed was to find the key Elijah had confiscated. How hard could that be? Especially if he tucked it back in its hiding place behind the hidden panel? And if he hid it in any other place, well, she intended to find it, one way or another. Or, if he kept it on him, she had to devise a plan to lift it from his body. Nika shoved that particular scenario from her mind. The mere notion of touching Elijah Coleman, or approaching him closer than arm's length was daunting.

The man was bigger than life and colder than an iceberg. When his intense gaze was focused on her, which happened more often than Nika liked, she felt like a target that was about to be blasted to smithereens by a laser beam. Or a moth drawn to a flame of those incredible silver eyes...

Dammit, Nika, no!

But she was afraid it was too late. She was ridiculously attracted.

Or smitten, as they were saying in this time period.

He was the most handsome, dare she say gorgeous, man to come into her life. He was also the most dangerous. Nika was scared and bewildered and yes, smitten, dammit!

Madness, pure madness, girl.

You're telling me, Nika snorted and earned a stern frown from the formidable Mrs. Smith.

Yes, it was madness, especially since he mistook her for a boy, didn't trust her a bit, and was suspicious of her true motives. And, oh yes, he has been dead for half-a-century. At least from her perspective. Nika cast a quick glance in his direction. But he was so alive now, all six-feet-plus-a-few inches of exceptional musculature and surly disposition. He was as real to her as Alex or *Verochka*. He was flesh and blood, and could harm her if she weren't careful. She needed to keep her wits about her, to watch her every step, and control her every move and word, or else.

Physical harm wasn't a consideration or problem. There was something entirely different at risk here, something more fragile and vulnerable. Her heart.

And that she was *not* prepared to deal with.

One way or another, she must get back to her time.

But for now, she decided to behave as if everything were normal, that she was a lost boy with amnesia with no hidden agenda except to restore his memories. She vowed to familiarize herself with the house and its inhabitants, and learn everything possible about the original décor of the house.

Professionally, she was enormously, incredibly lucky.

Count your blessings, girl. This project is bound to be a smashing success!

Personally, she was miserable, bewildered and lost.

Nika decided to bide her time, keep her wits and escape at the first opportunity. But in the meantime, it was such a miracle. The magnitude of it all hadn't sunk in yet.

The house was superb. The gardens she had a glimpse of before she was ushered inside were lush and well-tended. Given everything she had seen so far, the butterfly garden with its gazebo and the pool area must be pristine and amazing. She promised herself to sneak out of the house at the first opportunity and satisfy her curiosity. After all, she wasn't a prisoner, but a guest of the house, right? At least for the time being.

Mrs. Smith herded Nika to a room on the third floor where all the servants of the house had their lodgings. Nika hadn't explored this floor during her earlier inspection and had nothing to compare it with. She went as far as the second floor before the chiming grandfather clock interrupted her. Considering the size of the household, there must have been a lot of servants. If memory serves, her research showed there were twenty live-in people on the premises. Or more? She counted ten doors on each side, twenty rooms total. No, her memory was still good. That cheered her up.

The shrewd Mrs. Smith probably guessed that her position as a 'distant relative' wasn't completely truthful, or else the strange undercurrents between Nika and the man of the house had made her suspicious. She apparently decided to place Nika in the servants' quarters, thus keeping a close eye on the unexpected guest. Her distrust was obvious. And why should she? More than likely, the woman was concerned for the family silverware. She spoke just a few words to Nika, but her eyes followed her like a hawk. Nika took no offence, and completely understood the housekeeper's misgivings toward her. But the unpleasant sensation of standing naked in a room full of dressed people was persistent and irksome to Nika.

Mrs. Smith gave the impression of a very sharp and astute person which scared Nika. Would the older woman see right through her façade? As soon as Nika was pointed to a door, she mumbled her thanks, closed herself in her room and relaxed the first time that day. The toll of her unusual situation had finally caught up with her. How long was she able to carry on this charade? Finding the key had become imperative.

So, this is my room.

Curious, she pivoted on her feet, surveying her domain. Rather stark, the room was small but clean, and had a natural light streaming through the tiny window. She poked her head into the postage-stamp bathroom. Bingo! It had a commode and a sink with running water.

Thank you, God!

The splash of cold water on her face was invigorating and brought some semblance of normalcy. Feeling much better, Nika braved a quick glance in the small oval mirror above the sink. And stopped short.

My God, I look absolutely... normal.

For some insane reason, she was shocked that her features hadn't changed while her life flipped upside-down. Her face was paler than usual, her eyes darker, but otherwise she was no worse for wear, so to speak. Well, aside from her hair. Her curls made a great impression of a corn stalk tasseling on a dry summer day. The hell with it. There was nothing she could do about her hair. Her overall hygiene, though, was another matter. As soon as she got a chance, she intended to talk with Abigail about a bottle of shampoo and a toothbrush. Did they have toothbrushes in this time? Did they just use soap to wash hair? She hoped not or the yellow dried out corn stalk tassel had to look like silk compared to her hair. Nika sighed, berating herself for not paying more attention to such details during her research.

Oh, well, she had to play it by ear. Nika sniffed the air and frowned. More than anything she wanted to take a shower. Did they even have showers? She wasn't a servant, but not a member of a household, either. So, how does one bathe? Ask permission? Take a turn? Who was responsible for the things like this in the house? Mrs. Smith? Probably. She resolved to find out. As soon as she overcame her fear enough to leave her room. *Her room,* Nika marveled, taking a closer look around. It was small, uncluttered, simple. Modest curtains in pale blue covered a single window overlooking the back yard. A sturdy little thing that doubled as a chest and a vanity with a mirror, small writing desk, a single chair, and a narrow bed with a pretty quilt. The wallpaper was an unassuming quiet blue with a darker border splashed here and there with tiny yellow daisies.

My God, it was probably designed by Andrew Fingar Brophy.

Nika had seen a similar design circa 1903 in a Victoria and Albert Museum catalogue.

Aside from the historical shock, everything about this room was serviceable and without any frills. A typical accommodation for a servant, but one higher on the totem pole. Probably a tutor, or a governess.

Well, beggars can't be choosers, right? She snorted. *Beggars-shmeggars, my boot. You're extremely lucky, girl, that Elijah didn't place you in an asylum, or report you to the local authorities. And then where would you be? In a padded cell, or in a jail cell, that's where, and that's in a best-case scenario.*

Nika shoved a worst-case impression from her mind.

She squared her shoulders, took a deep breath, and considered her next step. Her main goal was to find the key. Now, where had Elijah put it? Back in its hiding place, or someplace else? Nika started to pace, but managed just three steps before she faced the wall. Yep, the room was really small. Okay, scratch pacing.

Nika tugged off her boots, plopped on the bed, lay down, and tried to bring into her mind eye the house's floor plan. It had three floors. The first floor consisted of a foyer, a huge living/family room, a formal dining room, a combination of a musical room/library and a long hallway that led to the enclosed kitchen.

The second floor was divided into two distinct parts. The south wing had a spacious suite of four rooms with a luxurious bathroom, and three smaller guest suites. The north wing had a huge suite of three inter-connecting rooms with a modest bathroom, and another two guest suites. That part of the wing was attached to the Gothic tower that rose three stories up. She hadn't had a chance to explore it, unfortunately.

As she learned today, the south wing of the second floor was Abigail's living quarters. Nika wasn't surprised. Everything in that part of the house screamed female to her even in her time when it stood barren and derelict.

Elijah's domain was the north wing. The tower, Abigail warned her, was her brother's private retreat. No one was allowed to enter it without his personal invitation. Nika tucked that information in the back of her mind. She planned to snoop around that tower the first chance she got. The blueprints showed an elevator. Quite the novelty at the time. The tower had an entrance to the gardens via a hidden backdoor.

And what was he doing up there, in that forbidden, gloomy, turreted structure? Nika shrugged. Not her business. Let him do whatever he wanted, as long as he left her alone and hopefully ignore her.

Liar.

She heaved another deep sigh. Dammit, she craved his attention. She was deeply hurt that he mistook her for a boy. It was like a physical blow. Nika would give her left kidney to be able to stand in front of him as a woman, all spruced up, wearing makeup, teetering on high heels, and draped in her best evening gown. But the notion was idiotic and highly unlikely, not to mention dangerous. If Elijah Coleman got a whiff of her true identity, she could kiss good-bye to her plans for returning home. Because she may well be forever stuck in this time, incarcerated in a padded room of a local asylum. A chilling thought. Nika shivered. No, scratch the makeup and her cocktail Armani dress. She should be grateful for her jeans and boots. Not to mention her baseball cap that kept her unruly hair well hidden.

She should pray that he ignored her completely, which was exactly what he was doing since her ill-thought-out and impromptu explosion the previous evening.

Stupid, so stupid, Nika!

Yesterday when she had finally come to her senses and shut her mouth, Nika was struck mute with fear. She was sure Elijah Coleman would immediately tie her down and ship her to the crazy house. But, wonder of wonders, he did neither. After his single question 'who is Alex?' and her tearful response 'I don't remember,' he left the room without a word. Later that evening, Abigail told her that the Colemans were returning to Amelia Island in the morning. "And guess what? Eli has decided that you're coming with us, Nick!"

It sounded more like an order, but Nika was grateful not to be left behind, she didn't question his motives. But she guessed what they were. He wanted to keep an eye on her. Plain and simple.

Sleep eluded Nika the entire night. She spent the time sitting in a chair, fully dressed and alert, her ball cap and toolbelt clutched in a death grip. They were the only things that connected her to reality, and reminded her of her true identity. She worried about Alex and *Verochka*. What were they thinking right now? What were they feeling? Were they grieving? Hurting? Probably, both. Her sudden disappearance must have been hard on both of them, but him especially. He may blame himself and imagine all the terrible things that may have befallen her. He was probably moving heaven and earth to find her. Where in reality, she had been thrown a hundred years back in time and then tucked in a luxurious bedroom, waited on by maids and a wonderful doctor. The maid who brought her cleaned clothes told Nika she was a guest at Plumb Orchard, the mansion of George Carnegie, son of Thomas and Lucy Carnegie.

Mindboggling! And certainly, different than Mrs. Smith's less than warm welcome.

Nika had explored that marvelous house in *her* time in the twenty-first century, but oh, how she would have loved to see it in its original state. She didn't because she was afraid to leave her room and wander about, too uncertain of her own situation and her position in this house, in *this* time. She had never been so alone. Or so scared. After regaining her senses is when she plotted her escape.

Her goal number one was to find the key. Second, she had to get to the Coleman house and the grandfather clock.

Thanks to the mighty Elijah himself, she achieved the second goal quite easily and quickly. Now all she had to do was to find that darn key, insert it into its slot, turn the clock back, or is that forward, and return to her own time.

Piece of cake!

Nika closed her eyes and sighed. It was a tall order of things, but she must be vigilant and patient. She took a deep breath and blew it out on a huff. Patience wasn't her strong suit, not by a long shot, but she had to do whatever necessary, and that included wait and pretend to be a boy. For as long as was necessary.

You gotta do what you gotta do, girl.

She had to get back. The sooner the better. No choice. She had to find the key, and fast.

Nika jumped from the bed and tugged her boots back on. Then she finger-combed her hair and slapped on the baseball cap, bill backward, carefully tucking all the curls under it. She opened the door gingerly and peered out. Not a soul. The third floor was blessedly empty. Distant sounds of activity came up from downstairs. She stepped across the threshold and soundlessly closed the door behind her. Nika went to the staircase on tiptoes and, making sure no one was about, inched her way down the uncarpeted staircase. Elijah had left almost as soon as he deposited her and Abby inside. Trying not to speculate on his whereabouts she decided to search for the key. Without him on the premises, Nika was a bit bolder about her clandestine task. If only he had placed it back in its hiding place, behind the clock, she was then free to go back, or forward, immediately. Her hands shook as she hurried, quiet as a mouse, to the second floor. No one was about. Nika puffed out the breath she was holding, and, taking it as a good omen, continued on. Finally, she was on the first floor. Holding her breath, Nika scanned the scene.

Some noises from the kitchen area, faint footsteps from above. But no one had crossed her path. *So far so good.* She tiptoed down the hallway and approached the grandfather clock. She gasped. Its beauty took her breath away. The mahogany body gleamed. The gold inlay shimmered in the muted light of the hallway. The rich sound it made, soft, deep, and husky, as it counted the seconds away, had an almost hypnotic effect. Its golden intricately crafted hands showed the time of five-past-one. They had been standing still on twelve when she saw it first.

This grandfather clock was just pretending to be an object. It was a breathing, living entity.

It was alive.

Was it her imagination or had the clock really made a small humming sound, encouraging her to proceed?

"You brought me here, didn't you? I have no idea why, but now you have to take me back. It's not my time. It's not my place," she murmured quietly as if the clock might understand her. "I have a family that is worried sick about me. I must get back. Please. Help me."

The clock made another soothing sound, like it was agreeing with everything she said. Or did she imagine it? Gingerly, trying not disturb it, Nika crept closer, then closer yet, studying the clock face as if waiting its approval. The long golden hand smoothly moved lower to the number three.

Are you conversing with a clock? Have you completely lost your marbles?

Her inner bitch piped in, halting Nika in midstride.

Shut up, will you?

Her cheeks burned as she shook her head and slowly reached forward with her right hand. Her fingertips touched the mahogany case and then she snatched her hand back. She was startled that the clock was warm to the touch. The sensation of touching a real person increased tenfold and halted Nika's progress. She let loose a snort and called herself a fool before she leaned forward again, more boldly, to reach between the wall and the clock's back panel.

Please, please be there.

She refused to consider what might happen if the trick with the clock failed to work. If it worked once, to bring her here, it had to work the second time, to send her back to her own time and place. Otherwise...

"What in blazes do you think you're doing, boy?"

CHAPTER THIRTEEN

Nika yelped and sprang back.

She moved too fast, and banged her head sharply against the wall. Flashes of gold and silver spiraled before her eyes. Momentarily lightheaded, Nika steadied herself by leaning on the clock and grabbing it with both hands. When her heart finally dropped from her throat to her chest and her head cleared, she turned to confront the man who had turned her world upside down in one day.

"What's wrong with you? Do you have a perverse satisfaction to sneak up and scare the living lights out of me?"

"What is wrong with *me*?" Elijah lifted one brow in an arrogant manner. "Let me remind you, boy, I am in my own house. I can move freely inside these walls whenever I wish without asking permission. And I most certainly do not have a perverse satisfaction of sneaking or scaring anyone. You are the one who dropped out of nowhere. And now I catch you snooping around my house like a thief. What are you up to, I wonder?"

"I'm up to nothing. And I wasn't snooping, I was...looking for Mrs. Smith," Nika decided on the spot, "to ask about a bath."

"A *bath*?"

"Yes, you know, this big white thing called a tub? Where you pour water and wash yourself?"

"Don't get witty with me, boy, I know perfectly well what a bath is."

"Oh, good. Then, maybe you can point me to the direction of one?"

"Your room doesn't have one?"

"Would I ask for it if it has?"

"What room did Mrs. Smith place you in?"

"The one with blue wallpaper, on the third floor."

Eli frowned. "I must have a conversation with Mrs. Smith about it. I remember distinctly telling her you are a guest and a distant relation."

Probably afraid for the family silverware, the old shrew.

Nika glared at her host. Eli's trusted housekeeper was ornery as hell and probably stubborn as a pack of mules.

She must invaluable in her position which is why he tolerates her.

"She simply misunderstood me."

"Misunderstood, my boot," Nika muttered.

"I beg your pardon?"

"It's nothing," she said louder, "I'm okay where I am, honestly. Please don't rip into her on my behalf."

"Don't ...what?" Eli almost blanched. Wide-eyed, he stared at Nika.

Oops, no slang here, girl.

"Don't ...scold her?" Nika gauged his reaction. "Yeah, that's what I meant. Don't...trouble her with my humble persona."

Was it the right way to phrase it? She wondered, but since Elijah's face once again was drawn to its customary cool detachment, she deduced that it was.

Note to self: always keep my tongue leashed.

Eli's frown deepened. Not for the first time had the boy used peculiar verbiage. Even though he spoke clear English, his phraseology was sometimes...unusual, to put it mildly. What part of the country did he come from? Eli was dead sure the boy wasn't local, despite his insistence. But, considering his strange clothing, the boy was definitely from some faraway place. Then, how did he come to be on Cumberland Island? Had he literally dropped from the sky?

No, something was quite strange here. Something was amiss. He just couldn't figure it out. *Yet.* An urgency that Eli didn't quite understand filled him. He needed to uncover the boy's identity and his real mission. Before somebody else like his over-diligent housekeeper did it.

And until he uncovered that truth, he vowed to keep the boy close at hand. There was, he admitted not for the first time, something about him, something elusive that he failed to put his finger on.

That fact drove him mad. It made his mind wonder and his heart beat faster.

The boy was a puzzle, and Eli became quite impatient to solve this puzzle.

It also made his blood hum. Eli hadn't felt that alive in years.

That stopped him cold in his tracks.

No, he refused to consider such. Disgusted with himself, Eli glared at the small thin figure as his anger and frustration flooded through him.

The boy swallowed and took a step back.

Damn it, now he had scared the pitiful creature. It wasn't Eli's fault that the boy had reacted so strongly to his presence. It wasn't his fault, he admitted bitterly, that he had no enthusiasm while visiting Ernestina earlier today. And it definitely wasn't the boy's fault that he had embarrassed himself, unable to perform.

Or unwilling?

The horrid thought was more than Eli could bear.

Of course, he was willing! Eager even. For God's sake he was a man. A strong healthy man. But for a reason he was unable to comprehend, his eagerness lasted for only a shameful few minutes, if that.

He never had that problem with Annabelle. Was that because he had to leave money on her nightstand? Later he met Ernestina through mutual friends. She was a rich widow whose company he had enjoyed for the past two years, gracious and patient as she was lovely. She took his mishap in stride and chalked it off to nerves or fatigue after the trip. Eli was grateful she had made such an unlikely assumption.

Dammit all to hell and back!

And still, it was *not* the boy's fault.

Reining in his self-aimed anger, Eli closed his eyes and drew in and released three calming breaths.

Mesmerized, but wary at the same time, Nika couldn't tear her eyes from him.

He was seriously cute when he forgot to keep his mask in place and went with his emotions. What ran through his mind? The play of expressions on his face caused such a transformation, it took her breath away. And what a face it was. Strong, chiseled, patrician. Straight nose, wide forehead, high cheekbones. And those piercing silver eyes under the perfect black arches of brows. Her silly heart somersaulted in her chest.

Whoa! Down, girl! Keep your head straight and your glands in check.

She cleared her throat.

"Mr. Coleman? Sir? If you, or somebody else, can point me to the right direction of a shower...bathroom," she corrected quickly, "I will be out of your way."

"I'll talk to Mrs. Smith," Eli repeated coolly. "In the meantime, boy, I need to talk to you."

"About what?" Nika's shoulders sank.

"A lot of things, but first, about the rules of this household, since you'll be living here for the foreseeable future."

He turned and gestured for Nika to follow. She trailed after him, cautious at first, then bolder as she glanced around. Oh, the original state of the house! She would give anything for the opportunity to snap a few pictures.

That thought stopped her cold. Her iPhone! Where was it? She patted herself impatiently, then checked her pockets to no avail. Her trusty phone, her beloved companion and invaluable tool of trade, was gone. She probably dropped it somewhere on Cumberland Island. Or was it still in the Coleman house, but in her time, a hundred years ahead. She made an involuntary sound, something in between a moan and a groan. Her eyes misted with tears.

"Are you alright, boy?"

Nika halted, breaking her stride in the middle. Elijah stopped, too. A frown turned his full lips downward. But before she answered he set off again.

"Y-yes," she lied. She took a broken breath and followed after Elijah. In reality, she was far from alright. She was devastated.

The loss of her phone was the final blow that figuratively brought her to her knees.

For the first time in the last twenty-four hours Nika lost all hope.

The leaden weight of despair settled heavily around her heart, obliterating her resolve. It was silly to feel so strongly about the loss of her iPhone. After all, comparing to the loss of everything else—her family, her life, her own identity— it was a miniscule thing and shouldn't matter in a great scheme of things. But, nevertheless, it did. Like a proverbial last drop, it overflowed a receptacle, and opened up the flood. The reality of her highly unusual and downright scary situation, finally dawned on her with chilling and unmerciful clarity. She was alone and lost. She was doomed. She was stuck forever in this godforsaken time and place. More than likely, she would end up in prison, or an asylum. Or, in the event the Colemans threw her out, there was the great chance she might die from hunger on the streets. In any event, Veronika Morris now ceased to exist.

And at that pivotal moment of truth, Nika stopped caring.

She trailed after her host, strangely weightless, like all the substance was suddenly drained out of her.

He entered the library/music room and stepped inside. Nika shuffled forward one step after another, and then stopped, awaiting his further instructions.

"You wanted to talk," she addressed her host in a dull voice.

"So, I did."

Eli learned as a young child it was impolite to stare, but the boy was getting to him. What was it about him?

Thunderation.

Even though he was standing proudly erect and dry-eyed, something was amiss. His straight shoulders sagged as if he were defeated. And somehow...lost. Embarrassed that he unwillingly became a witness to something intimate, Eli averted his eyes toward his humidor. He took great pains to choose a cigar. Maybe to give the boy a bit of time to compose himself. Instead of lighting it, he took a deep sniff of the prized tobacco he had yet to develop a passion for despite the current trend. He whirled the fat cigar between his fingers just to keep them occupied. The boy was troubling him. A quick glance reaffirmed his concerns.

By God, he was getting more forlorn by each passing moment, poor lad.

Was the boy was grieving? What could possibly have caused such a pain? Only one way to find out.

"Be seated, boy."

It was an order, but given in a deliberately mild tone of voice. Has he gone soft? Eli wondered, then quickly disregarded the silly notion. He simply was putting his strange guest more at ease. That's all.

The boy, keeping his vacant gaze on Eli, stepped forward and sat in the chair across from him. His movements were somewhat mechanical. Like that of a puppet being pulled by the strings. Come to think of it, his face resembled the mask of a toy, deathly pale, cold, and distant. And his unusual violet eyes, currently focused on him, were dull and lifeless.

"I wanted to talk to you...ah, about..."

What did he want to discuss with the boy? The pause stretched like a rubber band.

Something important, something... But his mind remained totally blank.

Oh, for goodness' sake.

"About the rules of this household," his strange guest finished for him in a clear cool voice. The boy cocked his head, and his peculiar hat slid sideways, freeing a few yellow curls.

"Yes, precisely," Eli nodded. His fingers suddenly tingled from the burning desire to touch that sunny hair. He tucked his hand into a pocket.

"And the rule number one, you must remove your hat inside this house."

"The hat?" The boy blinked a few times and stared at Eli like he was talking in a foreign tongue.

"Yes, the hat." Eli pointed his index finger toward the boy's head.

"Oh, you mean, my baseball cap," he said after a pause, not moving a muscle to obey.

"You are to remove your headdress, boy, whatever it is you call it, inside this house," Eli repeated in a deep, rumbling voice, infusing a note of steely command. Usually, hearing this special tone of voice, all members of this household scrambled off as fast as they could to execute his every wish. The only one immune to it was Mrs. Smith. And now this scrawny little creature. The boy continued to stare at him with that dull, vacant gaze of his, irritating Eli all anew. Impatiently, he flicked his hand in a silent command, demanding his order to be carried out.

"Well, if you insist," the boy shrugged and tugged his hat off. The burning gold of tight curls literally exploded upward. Eli's breath caught in his throat.

A wildflower. A beautiful daisy.

Unwillingly fascinated, he couldn't tear his eyes away.

"Okay." Disturbed more than he cared to admit, Eli curtly nodded. "Thank you."

"You are welcome." The boy ran a hand through his hair and tucked one unruly strand behind his ear. But as soon as he did so, the curl sprung right back, bouncing merrily as you please. Eli's eyes widened. Such a gesture was distinctly feminine, one Abby did often.

"What's rule number two?" the boy asked after a pause.

Silence had stretched for a long moment while Eli's eyes were riveted on the boy's hair.

Snap out of it, he commanded himself, focusing once again on his young guest.

The boy sat still and looked straight at Eli with wide eyes, his head tilted, his mouth slightly open. He appeared to be profoundly fascinated.

Was the scrawny creature mocking him? Eli narrowed his eyes to slits. The boy had the audacity to keep his gaze level, his attention riveted, his pale, drawn face unsmiling and emotionless.

"Rule number two is really simple." Eli ticked the points off his fingertips. "No lies, no half-truths and no fibs whatsoever. It's not permitted. You are to tell the truth, no matter what."

"I am to tell the truth, no matter what. Got it." The boy nodded.

Eli's nostrils widened in irritation. The feeling that the boy was really mocking him intensified tenfold.

"You can start by telling me your real name," he managed through clenched teeth. "And the place you came from. Because that story about your amnesia? I don't believe it for a second."

Nika scooted closer to the edge of the chair, plucking absently at a single lose strand in the upholstery. Her trained eye almost absentmindedly recognized a silk brocade rococo chair circa 1900. She failed to remember the last time she was so grateful for being so tiny, otherwise she may have cracked the thin sculpted legs in two.

And that's your main problem now? Really?

Nika swallowed a lump in her throat. No, her main problem was standing in front of her, eyeing her suspiciously, waiting for her answer. She straightened her shoulders and held her head high out of sheer stubbornness. She would be damned if she let him see how scared she really was.

No, Nika Morris was one tough little cookie, if she said so herself.

"You know my real name. The place I'm from is Fernandina Beach, Amelia Island," Nika countered in a clear level voice.

Just not of this century, she wanted to add just for the hell of it. Just to see what reaction she got from the pompous ass, who stood there like he owned the world, by really telling him the truth.

The whole truth and nothing but the truth, so help me God.

But, since God wasn't helping her, not a single little bit, she decided to skip the *whole truth*, until absolutely necessary. Nika shuddered at the thought of the storm that might rage when her reality smacked Mr. Suspicious in the face.

"And the story about my amnesia, well, I can't help it if you don't believe me."

"You really don't remember anything? Your family? Your friends? Your life?" He squinted at her as if he still didn't believe her.

Her heart thudded. Thank God she was seated or that scrutinizing gaze would have knocked her to her knees. So much for being the tough cookie.

Oh, I remember, alright.

Instead, Nika cast her eyes downward and shook her head. She was never a good liar. Alex's voice rang in her mind.

Do not ever play poker, my girl. Your face is your worst enemy.

It was a private joke between them, the one that always made her laugh. She wasn't laughing now. She was grieving. Nika flinched from the unbearable pain. She closed her eyes to fight back the hot tears that threatened to flood down her cheeks and swallowed hard to regain control.

I remember everything, but I wish I could forget.

"Alright."

The entire situation had become too much. Witnessing the boy's obvious pain wasn't something Eli wanted to tolerate any longer. Maybe, he didn't remember anything. Maybe he was telling the truth. But, Eli decided, he needed to keep a close eye on him. Better to err on the side of caution. At least, for now.

"Any more rules I should be aware of?"

"What?" Eli was so engrossed in his thoughts that he almost missed the question.

"I asked, if there were any other rules I should know about," the boy repeated.

"Ah... there are, but for now these two will suffice."

"Okay. So, if that's all, may I return to my room?"

"If you insist. Or you may take a walk outside, just to get some air. You look unhealthily pale," Eli blurted before he thought out his words.

And what do you care how he looks?

He frowned. *Thunderation.* Because it suddenly dawned on him that he did care.

So what? Any decent person would. Just look at him. The boy is so thin and pitiful, he looks half-starved.

That thought brought him up short. Had Mrs. Smith fed him? By God, if that maddening woman failed to offer their guest, however strange he was, refreshments, he intended to have to have a heart-to-heart with her.

"Are you hungry, boy?"

"I'm not...I'm not hungry. I could use some water, though." At that moment, his stomach rumbled loud enough so that Eli had to choke back a laugh.

"I'll ring for tea."

Dammit, the boy was hungry, but too proud to admit it. And thirsty, and dirty on top of it.

"Do you have coffee?" the boy asked, his face aflame with embarrassment. "Just coffee would be fine. You don't have to feed me, or...or anything. I caused you enough trouble as it is."

Damn Mrs. Smith!

He should fire her on the spot. Right now! But he was the head of this house, so all the blame lay with him.

"As it happens, we do have some excellent coffee. And butter scones."

The boy swallowed involuntarily, betraying his hunger.

"Abby will be down soon." Eli glanced at the mantel clock. "It is almost half past one, and that's when she prefers coffee, too. Shall we?"

"Shall we what?" The boy was still seated in the leather chair that almost swallowed his thin form.

"Proceed to the dining room, of course."

Not waiting for the boy, Eli started onward, only to trip on something on the floor.

"What on earth...?" Eli picked up the small object that was...the boy's hat. He looked at it and was about to hand it over to its owner, when his gaze skimmed over the letters— *B & A*— that were intricately embroidered in gold on the front. His suspicions flared anew.

"What are those?" He asked, squinting. "Your initials, perhaps?"

"No, that's my company's logo." The words flew out of her mouth before her brain had a chance to catch up with it.

Oh no. What have I done?

Nothing much. That damned inner voice taunted her. *You've just committed the holy mother of stupid, that's all.*

Nika shook her head in dismay. That was just perfect. Just fan-fucking-tastik. She stole a sideways glance at Eli.

Maybe he didn't catch that.

But her wistful thinking was shattered when he crossed his arms across his chest, tilted his head to the side in an arrogant manner, and bore his hard silver eyes into her.

Yeah, and maybe you're the Queen of England.

A bead of perspiration trickled down her spine, but Nika forced herself to hold his gaze.

He held her cap between his thumb and index finger, like it was something vile and dirty, wagging it back and forth.

The bastard.

She wanted to leap forward and snatch it out of his grasp. And maybe kick his aristocratic pompous ass just for the hell of it.

So what if he did catch her slip of the tongue? What did it matter? This charade was bound to come to an end sooner or later. The constant tension. The tippytoeing around. The outright lies. It was all too much. She had had enough and at that point. She no longer cared what happened.

The hell with it.

Mind-numbing exhaustion slammed into her like a category 5 hurricane. She was scared, stressed to the breaking point, and tired to the marrow.

"Your...company? And what, pray tell, this company of yours is called?"

Nika broke eye contact, slumped her shoulders in defeat, and surrendered. "Before & After."

"What company is that?" His lips twisted into a smirk.

Nika fumed. Oh, what she wouldn't give just to wipe that stupid smug grin off his face.

His absolutely mindboggling gorgeous face.

And why was she so hung up on his face? It was humiliating, and irritating, and yes, embarrassing. She was a disgrace to her gender, plain and simple.

"I do not recognize the name." He arched his brow and curved his lips into a parody of a smile.

And sent her foolish heart into overdrive. Oh no, no, no, no. she wasn't just simply hung up.

Admit it. You're crazy about him. Her unwelcomed inner voice piped in, sly and gleeful.

I am crazy. Period.

"No, you don't," Nika snapped, half defiant, half petrified. "Because it does not exist yet."

She was so unraveled at the realization of her stupidity, Nika almost missed the rare treat of witnessing an expression of pure and undiluted shock on Eli's face.

CHAPTER FOURTEEN

As close calls went, this one was the granddaddy of them all, Nika decided while she and Abigail strolled along the gardens. The girl was simply too nice along with gracious, intelligent, and beautiful. She had the presence of royalty, with her impeccable manners, the kind inbred deep into her bones. Her dry humor came as a delightful surprise and reminded Nika of *Verochka*. Nika liked her immensely, and was indebted to her once again for arriving in time to save her. If not for Abigail's fortunate arrival, Nika would have been discovered for the fraud that she was.

"What company is that? I do not recognize the name." Eli turned the cap over and studied the lining before he glanced back to Nika.

"No, you don't. Because it does not exist yet." And Nika held her breath.

Abby, who came in at that precise moment, overheard their conversation.

"Of course, it doesn't, silly," she said, chuckling, "because it only exists in Nick's dream. At least for now. Isn't that right, Nick?"

Stunned but extremely grateful, Nika bobbled her head.

With a non-committal humming sound, Elijah left the subject alone.

"When you are fully grown, dear boy, my brother will help you to turn your dream into reality."

Nika blinked, unable to decide what irked the most, that she was perceived as a child, or the continuing gender mix-up.

"I will?" Elijah's eyebrows shot up in surprise.

"Of course, brother," Abigail smiled at him brilliantly. "You are a pillar of this community and very generous benefactor. What could be more important than to help one ambitious individual to embody his or her most cherished vision?"

She flashed him another one of her dazzling smiles, accompanied by a hot gaze and defiant head tilt, that left no doubt she wasn't talking about Nick's dream at the moment. Or, not only about Nick's dream.

Then she turned her more gentle but not less brilliant smile at Nika, and announced their afternoon coffee was ready and served.

The girl, as Nika discovered, was a great coffee lover and connoisseur. She was genuinely delighted to find a kindred spirit in 'Nick' because all other members of the household, as she explained, preferred 'that horrid' English tea. They spent a lovely hour, drinking excellent coffee and devouring spectacular butter scones with a homemade peach jam. That is, she and Abigail did. Elijah Coleman excused himself as soon as his sister put in an appearance, and wasn't seen since. Nika was relieved. Or was she?

She was almost disappointed the moment to tell the truth was lost.

And how screwy was that?

She was on the brink of telling Elijah Coleman that she was Nika Morris, a time-traveler from the twenty-first century. That she was a highly respected contractor nick-named a house whisperer who was hired by one of his descendants to restore the house they presently resided in. But most important that she was a woman, dammit and not a boy, or a 'lump of rags.' And that she had no idea how or why she was thrown backward to 1909, and that she desperately wanted to find her way back to 2019. In her jumbled mind past and future had traded spaces, and the present was as uncertain and precarious as sea breeze.

Her only anchor to reality was Elijah Coleman himself. Too bad how crazy that sounded. He kept Nika on her toes, and earlier, in a moment of acute despair, when she all but lost her hope and courage he reminded her that she was still alive, and challenged her by simply being his remote, cool and unapproachable self.

He was maddeningly aloof, infuriatingly infallible, irritatingly unfazed, with the domineering streak a mile wide, and a bearing of a commanding general. But he also became really angry at his housekeeper for treating Nick like an outcast. He demanded Mrs. Smith move Nick to the guest room on the second floor with its own modest but functioning bathroom.

He certainly held no trust for Nika, but he insisted on caring for her, and even suggested a walk outside, because of her pallor.

He managed the household and his various companies and enterprises with an iron fist, but he also built a hospital and a school for underprivileged children, and donated both to the town.

He was dead set on marrying off his sister to the man she didn't love or want, denying Abigail her God-given right to choose her own destiny. Yet he constantly brought home sick animals she learned and kept all his aging servants on the premises until their last days, even paying all their medical expenses.

The man was an enigma. He also set her stupid heart aflutter.

Don't even think about it.

Nika sighed. The truth was bound to come to light sooner or later, but thankfully not today. She was granted a reprieve, thanks to Fate in the shape of Abigail, and managed to keep her secret a while longer. But for how long, was anybody's guess.

Distracted by her thoughts, she managed a faint smile and nodded at whatever Abigail said What had they been talking about? Since they were outside, she surmised that she was given a grand tour of the premises. Thankfully, it was mostly a monolog carried by Abigail, and required no more than an occasional nod and a smile from her. Try as she might, Nika's professional curiosity refused to be up and running as before, let alone for her to admire the scenery. Probably, the aftermath of the stressful afternoon.

Try a really stressful day.

A day? Nika quickly calculated. Indeed, it had been a bit over twenty-four hours from the moment she had miraculously appeared in the middle of the dirty road on Cumberland Island circa 1909.

Just a day? God, it feels like a lifetime.

Abigail stopped, her brow furrowed and her lips turned down. Nika stopped short, wondering what had happened. The light bulb clicked on: Abby expected a response. But to what?

"I'm sorry, did you ask something, Ms. Coleman?"

"Please, call me Abby, my dear boy," she smiled. "And it appeared like you were miles away. Where did you go?"

"My mind was wandering, Ms. Co...Abby." Nika feigned a smile. "I'm sorry."

"Don't be sorry, it's okay." Abby patted her shoulder. "Were you thinking about your family, perhaps?"

"No, no, I was just..." Nika sighed. "Just daydreaming, I guess. So, you were asking—"

"Actually, I was wondering about this company of yours."

"My company?" Nika squeaked, a moment of panic froze her. Did she manage to blow her cover, after all?

"Yes, your *dream* company, the one you wish to establish in the future? I was just wondering what is it you're going to do?"

"Oh, that company," Nika let go of her breath and relaxed. "Well, I'm good with my hands, so I want to build things."

Abby linked arms with Nika and they resumed their stroll.

"Hmm," Abby made a noncommittal sound. "Like building furniture?"

"More like building houses."

"Houses?" Abby blinked at her. "But that's...a very big dream!"

"What's the purpose of dreaming small?"

"You know, dear boy, you are so right. So absolutely right, Nick. What is the purpose of dreaming small?" She laughed and threw her arms upward. "Let's dream big, shall we? You are going to build the grandest houses, and one day, maybe, you'll build me a castle where I will live and paint to my heart's content." Her pink dress billowed around her trim calves as she twirled several times. "And you will visit me in my beautiful castle often, and we will drink our beloved coffee and talk."

Nika smiled, delighted with the girl despite her gloomy mood.

"And eat scones," she added with a laugh. "Don't forget the butter scones, Abby!"

"Oh, no, we can't forget the most scrumptious scones with peach jam, can we?"

They faced each other, and then burst into laughter, carefree and joyous.

"So, you want to become an artist," Nika said as they walked along the garden path.

"No," Abby shook her head. "Not just an artist. The most famous artist for everybody to talk about. My paintings will be in all the museums, and all the distinguished collectors will scramble to buy my art." Then she smiled wistfully, and shrugged her shoulders. "It's just a silly dream, I'm afraid. But, oh, how I wish I can make it a reality. I wish..."

"You wish?" Nika prompted.

Abby took a deep breath before she continued in a fierce voice. "I wish to become independent, to make a name for myself, and to prove that I do have a talent. I wish I can have freedom to decide how to live my life."

"What's stopping you?"

"Not what. Who? Eli, my formidable, unbendable brother."

"Men," Nika snorted. "They always think they know better."

"Just so. And it's so disgustingly unfair." Abby's eyes flashed with anger.

"Tell me about it," Nika muttered, warming to the subject.

"Is it my fault I was born with a pair of tits instead of balls?" Abby slapped her hands over the swell of her impressive mounds.

Nika coughed to muffle her laugher. She had a hard time deciding what surprised her most, Abby's sudden transformation from a proper southern belle to a wet hen or her un-lady-like language. She was sure the Big Bad Brother would be outraged if he had witnessed it.

Abby stopped and whirled to face Nika, her face contorted with outrage.

"Tell me, Nick, what would you do if you were born a female, but wanted to build your dream houses, anyway? Would you quit your dream? Resign yourself to be miserable for the rest of your life, to meekly exist as another man's possession? Or be content to wake up every day, get dressed, and simply *be* a pretty thing?" Abby wind-milled her hands. "Or... go to the balls, dance, drink champagne and gossip?"

It might be amusing, if it were not so ridiculous.

To give herself time to come up with a response, Nika cleared her throat, avoiding Abby's eyes.

The younger girl couldn't even guess the impossible position she boxed Nika in with all these questions. She hated to shrug her off with some lame excuse instead of an earnest answer. Not because she had become very fond of the girl, but because Nika knew exactly what it felt like to be invisible and insignificant. She had been in Abby's shoes for the first twenty years of her life.

After racking her brain for the best course of action, Nika decided the simplest solution was to stick with the truth.

"To start with, I can't dance even if my life depended on it, and I don't like champagne or crowds very much, so balls are definitely out of the question. I can't sit still for more than a few moments, and I would die of boredom leading that kind of life." Nika took Abby's hand in hers. "So, to answer your question, I would do anything to find a way to achieve my dream, even run away from everything familiar and comfortable."

"Is that what you did?" Abby studied Nika for a long moment. "Did you run away to be able to achieve your dream, Nick?"

"In a manner of speaking, yes."

She left it at that. Abby wasn't ready to hear about Nika's and Alex's Grand Adventure. And she definitely wasn't ready to share it.

"You didn't lose your memories."

"No."

"You're just hiding the truth, right?"

"Yes." What was the point in denying it? "I remember everything, but I can't reveal the truth. It's too painful."

Not to mention, unexplainable.

"Please, believe me. I'm not a criminal, nor am I a fugitive. And I won't steal anything from you, I swear."

"I believe you," Abby answered earnestly.

"Thank you. But your brother..."

Your impossibly gorgeous, formidable brother I have foolishly fallen in love with.

"I don't think he trusts me, and he has a good reason not to. I don't want to lie to him, but I can't tell him everything. So, I don't want him to know that I...recovered my memories. Not yet. I just need some time to sort things out."

Like how to find a key and get the hell out of Dodge.

"After that, I will be out of your lives forever."

As soon as that the words were out, a pang of regret charged through Nika. Why was the mere thought of leaving so depressing? She wanted to go back, or forward, to her own time. Right? *Right!*

Of course, I do!

Why, then, was she so bereft? She wanted to return home, she really did. But, as crazy as it sounded, Nika also wished to be able to have more time here. To learn, to see, to explore. Abby and Elijah, Doc Schmidt, and even the formidable Mrs. Smith became a realty—her reality—and she longed to spend some time with them, but not as a strange boy, but as herself. *Impossible. Foolish. Dangerous.*

Her shoulders sagged. Her spirit took a nosedive.

Get a grip, girl.

With an effort, Nika shook off her mood.

"If I can't find the way," she continued in a quiet voice. Oh, God, she didn't want to consider that possibility. "Then I will tell him myself."

Tell him everything, and the hell with the consequences.

"So, would you please keep it between us for the time being?"

"I promise. Your secret is safe with me, Nick," Abby nodded solemnly.

"Thank you. It means a lot."

"You don't have to thank me, my dear boy," she smiled, "I am your friend and confidante, as you are mine."

Nika's throat clogged with unexpected tears. Abby's kindness almost undid her.

"And as a friend, I want to give you some advice."

"Yes?"

"Never lie to Eli. If you cannot tell him the truth, then try to keep away from him, or think very carefully before you say anything."

Nika had been doing exactly that from the moment she came to her senses and grasped a reality of her situation.

"For example, he would never let you get away with such a declaration as hating champagne, or dancing handicap." Abby grinned. "He would immediately initiate an inquest, and demand to know when and where such a young thing like you had ever tried the bubbly beverage, or danced in the first place."

"I'm not that young," Nika protested faintly.

Damn. What else did I manage to screw up?

"I know, my dear boy," Abbi shrugged. "But Eli would disagree. And he may well wonder about your family and your upbringing, and we do not want that, now, do we?"

"Definitely not."

"He's already curious about your grandmother as it is."

"My grandmother?" Nika blanched.

Abby nodded. "After Doc Schmidt revealed to him that she's French."

"Oh, dear God." Nika's closed her eyes. Her mind flew back to the conversation she had with Doc yesterday.

"So, is she really French, your grandmother?"

"Yes," Nika answered absentmindedly. Inside she was quaking with anxiety, furiously thinking of what else the good doctor may have revealed to Elijah under pressure. The most damaging news was her true gender, but neither brother nor sister questioned it, so that secret must still be safe. For now.

"I love France," Abby continued, oblivious to Nika's discomfort. "I lived there for three years before my big brother decided to summon me home and marry me off," she added bitterly.

"My grandmother was born in France, but she lives in the States now." Nika managed to reign in her fear. Her voice still sounded strained to her own ears, but Abby failed to notice.

"What is her name?"

"*Verochka*." Nika smiled despite her mood, a turbulent mixture of anxiety and sadness.

"Such an unusual name."

"Her real name is Vera, but we call her *Verochka*. It's an endearing form in Russian."

"Russian? I though you said she's French."

"She was born in France to poor immigrant dancers. Her roots are Russian, but she considers herself a true Parisian."

"What is she like?"

"Oh, she is..." How to describe *Verochka*? There were no words, really, to do true justice to her grandmother, at least, not to her. "She is the most amazing, most caring and most wonderful person in the whole world. She's strong, and kind, and curious, and just simply beautiful, inside and out. She never judges, never pressures, never makes you feel small and insignificant. She loves Alex and me unconditionally." Nika's breath hitched and her eyes misted. The thought she may never see her grandmother again was akin to a physical pain.

"I would love to meet her," Abby said wistfully.

"Oh, she would adore you, Abby," Nika smiled through a sheen of tears in her eyes.

"You really think so?"

"Yes, I really do."

"Maybe one day you'll introduce us?"

"Believe me," Nika answered earnestly, "I would love nothing better."

If only I could.

"Well, then," Abby cocked her head, frowning a little. "Don't look startled, but here comes Big Brother now."

"What?" Her heart stumbled, skipping a bit.

Don't let him see your tears.

With more strength than was warranted, Nika rubbed her face with both hands.

"Before he's here," Abby whispered. "Can you answer one more question for me?"

"Sure, what?"

"Who is Alex?"

CHAPTER FIFTEEN

The scene below the tower window was lovely. Abby and Nick easily conversed, animated, young and carefree. With hands clasped behind his back, Eli glued himself to the window. He was observing his sister interaction with the strange guest. That's all.

Humbug. Spying, that's what you are doing. Thunderation.

Self-loathing or cursing out loud didn't help. Try as he might, Eli failed to stay focused on business matters. His concentration abandoned him shortly after he sat at his desk, the documents that needed his attention spread out in front of him. He tried to keep his mind on the papers. He truly did. For as long as two minutes. Then he gave up. Yes, he spied on the pair below. So what? No one was the judge of him but himself. What were they discussing? Abby laughed and the boy joined her. Eli lips curved on their own. They were enjoying themselves from the looks of it, young, carefree, and oh, so beautiful.

That thought brought him up short.

His sister was, indeed, a beautiful young woman, but the boy...

How could he even think of this wretched, pitiful creature as *beautiful*? He was a mere stripling, puny and skinny, and funny-dressed, and...

Eli frowned. The boy was anything but eye-pleasing, with his odd hair and eerie eyes. Why he would even think of that child as a beautiful person was beyond him, and still...just for a moment—a very short, unguarded moment—Eli did.

What the hell is wrong with me?

What was wrong with the boy, he countered, because something definitely was. More accurately, something wasn't right about him. He used a queer language, although not a vulgar one of a lower class. He dressed oddly, with holes in his pants, for goodness' sake, but the quality of material and workmanship were excellent and bespoke of high-priced goods. His hat was made of fabric Eli never saw or touched before, and his working belt was superb, not to mention some of the tools Eli didn't recognize. Nothing added up. Eli rubbed his chin with his thumb and forefinger.

The pair below discussed something in earnest as they faced one another. And, if he wasn't mistaken, Nick was shaken or scared. Or both, he concluded as he studied the pale face of his guest. Even from the distance the boy appeared upset and in tears. Then he smiled and his face lit up with such an otherworldly beauty that made Eli's heart lurched.

Oh, hell.

Either he was the lowest kind of a pervert, or the boy was...

"Who the hell are you, anyway?"

Eli abandoned all pretense of work and marched to the door. The ride down in his private elevator took longer than usual in his estimation. Or was he simply too impatient to reach his destination? Eli bored down on the thought. He wasn't a youngster, but a man of four and thirty. His actions and thoughts were not seemly for him to act like an eager fool. Idiot. As soon as the automatic door opened, he sprang into action and stomped toward the garden.

Abby spotted him first. She tipped her head and murmured something to the boy. His skinny body tensed, then he rubbed both hands over his face. He turned his back to Eli, but it was unmistakable that he was trying to wipe traces of tears from his face.

So, Eli was right. The boy was crying. What about? Impossible that his sister, the gentle soul, was at the root of his distress. Abby could never hurt a fly even if she wanted to, not to mention another human being, especially one as unfortunate as this boy. No, it was something else.

Or somebody else?

One way to find out. Eli composed his features into a cool smooth mask he presented to the world. Yet his heart beat hot and wild.

"Well, my goodness, Eli!" Abby called out in a loud voice that oozed saccharine. "What brought you down to earth from the peak of your Tower of Gloom?"

"Abigail, you're needed at the house," he said as soon as he was a few feet away.

"Whatever for?" Abby arched one of her perfect brows.

"I've no idea, but Claudine was searching for you."

"And she came all the way to the Forbidden Tower to give you the message?" Abby slapped a hand on her hip as she cocked her eyebrow.

"Abigail, please return to the house at once."

Elijah repeated his order, dismissing his sister with the tone of his voice brutally polite and cold. He didn't bother to come up with anything close to an explanation about his obvious fib.

Abby heaved a deep, noisy sigh, but did as he bid. She drew closer to her brother, hesitated for a moment, then whispered, "Please take care with him, Eli. He's hurting."

Eli's eyes sought hers for a moment, then he gave an almost imperceptible nod.

Nick stood quiet and still, his gaze downcast. Eli drew in a deep breath. Abby's parting words echoed in his mind. Why was the boy hurting? What did she find out?

And why is this any of my business?

If it isn't, then what was he doing here? He deliberately and rudely sent his sister away. And now, for the life of him, he had no idea why. The uncomfortable silence stretched for too long, charged with his growing impatience.

Damn the scrawny creature, why doesn't he say something?

"Did you want something from me?"

Finally, he speaks!

"I certainty did." Eli clasped his hands behind his back.

"I'm listening."

The lad focused on something above Eli's left shoulder. Eli turned his head, expecting to see his sister lurking behind his back. No one there. The child was deliberately avoiding eye contract.

Doesn't want to look at me, does he?

Eli's temper started to simmer. By God, no one was able to try his patience like this pitiful ragamuffin. Furious and barely holding onto his temper, Eli clamped his teeth and glared at the boy.

"The rule number three. You are to look directly in my eyes when you're talking to me, boy." His voice was charged with indignation he failed to mask. "Or do you have something to hide?"

"We all have something to hide, Mr. Coleman," the insufferable creature answered, but for a change, glared straight at him.

Amethysts.

His eyes resembled amethysts. Eli swallowed the curse.

"Not me," he answered in a clip, icy tone. "I'm not hiding anything."

"What, no secret, or fear, or guilt? Or something in your past you'd rather not share with anybody? I refuse to believe that."

"Heavens forbid." The boy smirked and dared to stare into Eli's eyes. "Anything else you wanted to say to me in private?"

"Private? Why do you think I needed to say anything to you in private?"

"Oh, I don't know." He shrugged as if the conversation were of no importance. "Maybe because you abandoned whatever it is you were doing in that tower of yours, and came all the way down, or maybe because you sent Abby away under a most ridiculous reason."

"Abby, is it? So, you are on the first name basis with my sister?"

"Yes. She asked me to call her that."

"And what is she calling you?"

"Nick."

"Splendid! Abby and Nick. I wonder what's next."

"What do you mean?"

"You wrapped my sister around your little finger," Eli's voice dipped low. "But you cannot fool me, you little ragamuffin. Abby is a tenderhearted and impressionable young woman, so don't you dare to spread your fibs, filling her head with lies."

"Fibs, is it?" Nika literally quivered. She clenched her hands into fists and advanced forward, coming almost face-to-face with Elijah. He was at least a head taller, but in her current mood, Nika managed to look down her nose at him. "How *dare* you."

Eli blinked and took a step backward.

"Pardon me?" He regained his haughty attitude, arched one brow, and glared down at her. "How dare *I*?"

"Yes." Nika stepped forward then stopped when her boots tapped the tips of his shoes. "How dare you to belittle your sister that way, and to a stranger, no less? Tenderhearted? Impressionable? Get real, *buddy*. What you really meant is, malleable and simpleminded, which she is neither. She's smart, and strong, and kind, and so much better than *you.*"

"Temper, temper, my boy," Eli answered coolly, but his expression turned softer, as if he admired Nika's stance. "I meant no such things about my sister. She's an amazing person, but still a woman."

"*Still* a woman? And what that's supposed to mean? Huh?"

"That's she's inexperienced in some ways of the world."

"Oh, and a man is."

"Of course. Simply because he's the stronger sex."

"*Stronger-schmonger.*" Lord, this man could piss off a saint. "What baloney!"

"Excuse me?"

"No, I won't." Nika didn't wait for a response before she charged forward, "Give me one good example of why your sister is less experienced in the ways of the world, as you put it, than you?"

"Very well."

Eli's eyes crinkled at the corners and his lips turned into an almost smile. Was he trying to humor her?

"She lived her entire life sheltered, first under our father's protection, and then, mine. She wasn't exposed to the real world, and each and all of her steps were heavily chaperoned and guarded. She still believes in universal goodness and knows nothing of deceit and failure."

"So?"

"So, she's incapable of recognizing, or anticipating, matters as a man can."

"Oh, she can recognize and anticipate plenty. For your information, she recognizes that her brother's a *tyrant.* She also anticipates that said tyrant won't give her the freedom of choice as to how to live her life."

"Of course, not." And like an indulgent uncle, he smiled at her.

The moron dared to smile!

"And in your shoes, my boy, I would learn early on how to treat a woman, and be a master of a household, seeing as one day in the future, you'll be one yourself."

"Treat a woman, is it? Learn by your example, is it?" It was safer to spit the words in his face. But oh, how she wished to *really* indulge. "Do you really mean what you just said?"

"Of course. I always say what I mean."

"You know what." She puffed a breath. "You are not a tyrant."

"Happy to hear that." Eli gave her a mocking smile and nodded his head.

"You are a male chauvinist, and an insecure moron with delusions of grandeur!"

He blanched. The bright red color of his cheeks was probably unhealthy, but she didn't give a damn.

Let him croak for all I care.

"I'm not a chauvinist of any kind, neither am I suffering from any delusions or especially insecurities! How dare you accuse me of such vile things?"

"Oh, I dare. I call it as I see it, and somebody ought to tell you the truth."

"And that would be you." Eli blinked several times and then he burst into laughter.

"What's so funny?"

"You are, my boy. Now I know what's wrong with you."

"There's nothing wrong with me."

"Maybe wrong isn't the correct a word," Eli said between his laughter. "But there is something not right, either. You act as if you're not afraid, like you are above repercussion. One moment you are sniveling, the other you're spitting fire like an avenging angel. I'm starting to think you're not real, or not from this earth."

His smile disappeared. He narrowed his eyes at Nika.

"I wonder *what* are you, boy," he said in a threatening voice.

"Just...a person alive." Nika swallowed, petrified, and took an involuntary step back

"Interesting." Eli took a step closer. "A person alive, is it?"

Her nostrils flared up. She stared at him without blinking.

Mesmerized, Eli stared at the boy's face. How had he stooped so low as to inflict physical damage to another human being, even as a mock demonstration of power? But the boy tried his temper as no one ever had. Of course, he could never hurt him, but the boy must not know that.

Telltale signs of the boy's fear became obvious. His lips trembled. His eyes grew impossibly wide and luminous. The worst was the quivering pulse under his fingers on the boy's throat. Terrible self-loathing, along with brutal arousal, swept through him.

If he reasoned and explained the first, he refused to accept the latter. Bile rose in Eli's throat. But instead of releasing the boy, he tightened his grip on the tender flesh, sliding his fingers lower to Nick's collarbone. He was so tiny that Eli's palm, spread from bone to bone, almost encompassed Nick's shoulder. *He is so tiny, puny really.* And he was scaring the bejesus out of him. *Thunderation.*

With a great deal of effort, Eli drew his hand away. But his eyes refused to obey his brain command, and kept the pale drawn face of the strange creature in sharp focus. When he finally found his voice, he was pleased that it sounded as normal and unaffected as ever.

Inside, he was nothing of the sort.

"Call me anything you like, but in my universe called the Coleman household, I am the reigning king. Every blade of grass gets treated and watered because I said so. Every animal gets fed because I allow it. Every human under my roof depends on me for his or her livelihood. So, yes. my word is the *law*, and I am in charge. And everyone without exception inside the premises is under my protection."

"Your tyranny more likely."

"It is the matter of opinion, of course." He bared his teeth in a smile, deliberately mocking the little ragamuffin.

"I'm so lucky I don't belong in your universe, your Majesty."

"Wrong, *ma petite*. While you live under my roof, you *are* my responsibility." With those last parting words, Eli turned and walked away.

What in blue blazes just happened?

Eli's stride was unhurried and sure, his posture straight, his demeanor as cool as ever, but inside he quaked with emotions he was unable to identify even if he wanted to. He was, first and foremost, ashamed that he threatened a human being, never mind that person was a boy that stormed at him and accused him of God knows what. He was still a living, breathing creature, a person alive like he declared himself. Eli deliberately put his hands on him in demonstration of his superior power. Fool! Idiot! He was a man grown, a gentleman. What example had he presented for the young boy soon to be a man?

Poor, very poor. No, an atrocious example. He needed to apologize. Yes, the boy provoked him, calling him— him, Elijah Coleman! — a tyrant, an insecure moron, and even dared to accuse him of possessing delusions. And in his own home, no less, while being a guest under his roof, ungrateful little...

And you treated a guest like a villain, threatening to do him physical harm, he admitted to himself, ashamed and mad all over again. *Dammit, what the hell happened?*

Why did he get so angry over a silly boy's accusations and unable to control his temper?

You are a male chauvinist, and an insecure moron with delusions of grandeur!

Is that how the puny little urchin perceived him? Splendid!

Eli fumed as he climbed the round staircase to his tower. He purposely chose not to take the elevator, but to exercise his legs and cool off his temper.

Let him think whatever he wishes, but still it wasn't an excuse for you to put your hands on him.

He must apologize. And to demonstrate a much better example of gentlemanly behavior. After all, the boy was less fortunate, and any gentleman must behave kindly and demonstrate high tolerance toward the poorer class.

"High tolerance, my ass," Eli swore loud and clear. His words echoing off the plaster.

Stop waltzing around it and admit it. The boy got under your skin in more ways than one. He made you want and yearn. Damn his amethyst eyes!

One thing was clear to Eli, as long as the boy stayed under his roof, he needed to keep his distance from him. Or he was doomed.

He must keep a close eye on the youngster who dropped from the sky and almost landed under Sultan's hooves and talked in strange slang.

Get real, buddy? Baloney?

Something was off there. Eli knew it deep in his bones from the very first moment he met the boy.

Think, man, think.

Eli entered his office then sank into his favorite chair. He rubbed his chin with his right thumb and forefinger, and considered his problem.

What just happened?

Nika had stood frozen to the spot, stared into his silver eyes and drowning in them. His smell, something earthy and salty, made her head light and her knees go weak. To break the impossibly intimate moment, and break it fast before she was completely and irrevocably lost, she gathered all the strength she possessed and like a shrew blurted out:

"You *are* suffering from the delusion of grandeur, Mr. Coleman. Who do you think you are, King of the Universe?"

The moment was broken.

Left alone, with his half-warning, half-threat still ringing in her head, Nika started to quiver.

Oh my God. What just happened?

She shook her head to erase the last few minutes from her memory. She clamped her head between her hands, closed her eyes and tried to breathe slowly, in and out. No luck. His voice, his smell, his words imprinted on all her senses, left an invisible mark, as if he branded her with a hot iron.

What the hell just happened?

She wasn't afraid Elijah Coleman might hurt her physically, no matter what he said or did. But she *was* afraid— very afraid— of herself, of her reaction to him. She was afraid her temper might get the better of her, and the next time she may go too far, to the point of no return.

Clear as day she was attracted to him. It was also clear that she was in great danger of losing herself the longer she stayed here.

In my universe called the Coleman household, I am the reigning King.

He was. And, dammit, the longer she stayed, the harder it may be to resist her feelings. And to pretend to be anything but herself.

I'm so lucky I don't belong in your universe, your Majesty.

Wrong, ma petite. *While you're living under my roof, you are my responsibility. Ma petite...*

For the first time he had called her anything but 'boy.' It wasn't meant to be an endearment. But her stupid heart still pounded. And her skin where he touched her was still warm and tingling. She needed to get out of here, as fast as possible. The million-dollar question was, where the hell was that damned key.

No, the million-dollar question was, did she really *want* to find it, and escape from here to her own time.

Nika had no answer. And that scared her even more.

CHAPTER SIXTEEN

A knock at the door pulled Nika from a deep slumber. She was amazed she fell asleep after her earlier debacle with Elijah Coleman in the garden. But as soon as she entered her room and sat on the bed, she dropped dead to the world. How long was she out? Panicked, she shot up straight, disoriented, and listened again. Yes, it was definitely a knock at the door. Groggy, she managed to croak, "Y-yes, come in", then cleared her throat and repeated again, louder, "Come in."

If Nika ever wondered what 'heart in a throat' meant, she had her answer.

As soon as the door opened, she let go her breath. Abby poked in her head, and then entered the room, trailed by her maid, Claudine.

"Did you have a nice nap, Nick?"

"Ah, yes, thank you." Nika rubbed her face, then ran both hands through her hair. Since her fingers got immediately tangled up, she surmised that her curls went on strike without their usual high-maintenance treatment.

Tough. No Wen moisturizer mist for you, my pretties.

Nika slid out of bed, rotating her shoulders and neck. The pillow was much softer than the one she had at home, and it gave her a muscle ache. God forbid, she developed a neck creak. That was the last thing she needed. Her attention switched to Claudine holding clothes in her hands.

"What's that?" Nika asked the French girl.

"Why, your wardrobe, of course," Abby said. "We couldn't acquire anything new or made for you on a such a short notice, but, thankfully, Mrs. Smith has a nephew your age and build, so she lent us some of his clothes until we can properly dress you, my dear. I also must apologize as there are no men's shoes in the house small enough for you."

"But...but," Nika sputtered, amused and annoyed at the same time. "I can't possibly—"

"You can and you will, Nick. Look at you." Abby flicked her hand at Nika's legs. "Your pants have more holes than fabric. You must be very uncomfortable and cold."

Nika swallowed her laughter. Abby would never believe Nika's designer ripped jeans cost more than Abby's perfectly tailored dress.

"And it's unseemly to wear the same clothes day in and out." Abby laid out socks and toiletries on the bed. "Claudine, please hang Nick's wardrobe, such as it is, properly, and leave the undergarments on the dresser for him to deal with as he feels best."

"Oh, you don't have to," Nika mumbled and unsure of just what was happening.

The French girl curtsied smartly to Abby and went about her business, ignoring Nika completely.

"She doesn't have to," Nika protested, turning to Abby. "I'm quite capable of doing it myself."

"Of course you are, Nick." Abby smiled as if she were indulging a small child. "But you don't have to. Claudine is already here and more than happy to help you. Right, Claudine?"

"*Oui, mademoiselle.*" And the maid curtsied again.

Abby turned to Nika grinning from ear to ear. Obviously, she was accustomed to her orders carried out, no matter how silly they were.

So, brother and sister Coleman have something in common, after all. They both were steamrollers, sailing smoothly but surely over every and any obstacle on their way. Nika groaned.

What am I going to do?

"Dinner is at six," Abby said. "We dine early, so you'd better start preparing."

"Preparing for...what?"

"For the evening meal, silly. You must make yourself presentable."

Presentable. Right. Easy-peasy.

Obviously confused by Nika's response, or rather the lack thereof, Abby hesitated.

"Weren't you accustomed to cleaning yourself and dressing properly before dinner at your household?"

Nika barely suppressed her snort. At her household, dinner usually meant pizza, or take-out Chinese, which she shared with Alex on their deck all year round. So, even though the cleaning part was a must, especially if she was in the middle of a project, the dress code was always the same, typical Floridian high couture, shorts and tank-tops. Nika was confident that changing dirty, paint-splashed jeans to cut-off shorts wasn't what Abby meant for dressing properly.

"Ah, we were— are— very informal at my household," she finally answered.

"Oh," Abby furrowed her brows for a second. "I'm sorry, Nick, but in our home, we are rather fond of formality and etiquette. So, it's imperative for you to take a bath and change your clothes before dinner." Her long fingers picked at the fringe on her blue sash. "And if I may as a friend give you some advice?"

"Sure, why not." Nika's nerves took control.

"You'll need to tame your hair, just a bit. Nothing wrong with it," she hurried to add.

Nika touched her curls and wished she had the ability to command her mop to behave.

"As a matter of fact, they are gorgeous. I wish I could have such a curly mane of hair."

"Believe me," Nika grumbled. "You don't."

"It's just a bit wild, is all. You need to apply some egg yolk and glycerin water, and comb your curls while they are still wet. Here." She produced a small leather pouch from under her sash. "This is all you need, soap, rose water, glycerin. And, *voila!*" Abby gestured like a magician and slid an egg from her skirt pocket. "A fresh egg I begged off our cook."

Nika let her smile break through. This sweet girl was doing everything possible to help Nika through a difficult time.

"Thanks, Abby, but I'm afraid no egg and glycerin will make my curls less wild. I tried some very innovative...chemical solutions." Nika stood straighter, proud of herself for coming up with a substitute word for shampoo and conditioner. "But it didn't help. Nothing would."

"Oh, you of little faith." Abby smiled. "I'm willing to bet you a dollar this will help splendidly. I use it on my hair every day."

"Yes, but first, your hair is totally different." Nika envied the long dark tresses that hung heavily down Abby's back. "Second, I don't have a dollar to bet."

"You poor thing." Abby's eyes grew darker with pity. "Let me talk to Eli about—"

"No!" Nika's vehement protest stopped Abby mid-sentence. Nika swallowed hard to control the thoughts charging through her. "No, please. Don't say anything to your brother. I'm not a beggar. I don't want his money. I won't accept it."

"Will you accept mine? Just a small loan from a friend?"

"Thank you, I really appreciate it, but I don't need money. Honestly."

"Alright. But if you do, promise to come to me. I'll lend you as much as you need. I have my own funds."

"Thank you, I promise I will."

The girl's kindness was genuine, and Nika appreciated it more than she was able to say. But there was no need to borrow money here before she returned to her own time. At least she hoped so.

"Well," Abby shrugged delicately and, dismissed the subject. She broke into a grin and said, "Let me show you, my dear boy, how to mix the potion."

Nika was dressed in borrowed pants that were a bit long, but otherwise fit her surprisingly well, a white button-down shirt and a vest that Abby had insisted completed a traditional evening ensemble for a gentleman of his age. Abby had apologized repeatedly because there were no shoes in the house in Nika's size. She descended the steps to the first floor and self-consciously ran her right hand over her hair. The mixture of egg yolk and glycerin managed to do in just one application what all of her expensive products had failed throughout the years. Her curls were softer and silkier, and if not completely tamed, considerably less springy. She even managed to run a comb through her wet hair without breaking a single tooth or leave any bald patches on her head. Nika approached the dining room with caution, straining her ears. Abby had run off the list of who was to attend dinner besides the Coleman siblings and Nika. Along with Elijah's secretary Mr. O'Brien, who was more of a friend than an employee, and Abby's maid Claudine since they were responsible for the girl they brought from Paris. The only one who didn't take meals with them was Mrs. Smith, who no matter what, insisted on propriety and frowned upon intermingling of the classes. According to Abby, she preferred the rules of her late parents' household, and never got accustomed to the most modern ways of the twentieth century.

"But Eli still has high hopes to educate the old dear, and convince her to dine with us, at least on celebratory occasions."

So, the siblings proved not to be snobs after all. A huge plus in Nika's book. The responsibility for the less fortunate ran deep and true. They both were generous with their time and money. This was learned from her personal observation plus from her diggings into the historical archives.

But what truly earned her admiration was the way they treated their animals. They had four horses, five dogs and a slew of cats. Except for the horses, every animal had been rescued by Eli and nursed back to health by Abby. That was a serious ice-breaker for Nika. If nothing else, that fact alone was enough to melt her heart and win her respect.

All in all, both Coleman siblings were genuinely nice people. At least, Abby was. Regarding her older brother, the jury was still out.

And who are you kidding?

Shut up. Being a hunk has nothing to do with being a decent human being.

She ignored that irritating voice in her head that refused to leave her alone.

A huge mongrel dog of undetermined color greeted her on the last step. A wariness in its expressive eyes seemed to struggle with curiosity. The later won. Its strangely deformed stub of a tail jerked like a metronome. The poor thing was so ugly that it was kind of cute. As it braved its way closer, the dog sniffed Nika, then sat and grinned from its pointy right ear to its floppy left. Nika fell in love on the spot. Crouching before the hairy giant, she smiled back.

Another rescued soul, no doubt.

"Hello, there," she crooned to the dog, scratching beneath its ears. "Hello, baby. I wish I knew your name. So, you came to dinner, too?"

At the word dinner the dog cocked its head, then glanced at door to the dining room. The expression on its face could only be described as guilty. Probably not supposed to be inside, Nika guessed.

"You don't belong here, do you?" In lieu of an answer, the dog whined. "Me either, boy."

"It's a girl." Startled at the sound of an unfamiliar voice, Nika gulped back a yelp. The dog whined again, and scurried away, leaving her alone with Elijah Coleman's personal secretary.

She had met Mr. O'Brian only once, on their way from Cumberland to Amelia Island, but they never exchanged a single word. Now, almost face to face, Nika had a chance to make her first true impression of a young man. In his late twenties or early thirties, impeccably dressed, he was on the slim side, not exactly skinny, but rather slender. His intelligent blue eyes were patient and kind, and were currently sporting gold-rimmed glasses she hadn't seen before. For some reason, those little round spectacles put Nika at ease. Despite her predicament, she relaxed and smiled.

"What's her name?"

"Pardon me?"

His British accent was unmistakable and kind of sexy.

"The dog. You said it was a girl?"

He tilted his head and smiled mischievously. He had a perfectly sculpted face with all the right planes and angles. She wondered why this prime example of classical male beauty did nothing for her libido, whereas his employer, with his dark looks of a fallen angel made her blood run hot and fast.

"Yes, it is, and her name is Belle."

"You're kidding me!"

"Not at all. The poor dear is so hideous, it pains me to look at her, so." His grin blossomed into a full-blown smile. "Miss Abby named her Belle to strike a balance. Or more likely to thumb her nose at nature."

Nika laughed.

"Can you keep a secret?" he whispered like an actor in a Broadway comedy.

"Absolutely."

"Swear that Miss Abby won't hear it?"

"Cross my heart and hope to die." Nika nodded solemnly.

He blinked with surprise. He probably never came across that expression before, flashed in her mind. After a short moment, he regrouped and continued, "Between ourselves, we call her Quasy."

"Quasy as... Quasimodo?" Nika guessed.

"Exactly," he chuckled. "But you didn't hear it from me."

Nika laughed with delight. "Don't worry, I won't betray your confidence."

He smiled and said in a more formal voice. "I apologize, we weren't formally introduced. William O'Brien at your service." He bowed and offered Nika his hand.

"Nick Morris," she answered and offered hers in turn. At first, he appeared to be startled, but after a brief moment he clasped her hand firmly. She met his eyes, smiled easily into that handsome face. He was such a sweetheart, round glasses, sexy accent, and all.

"Daisy," he murmured under his breath.

"W-what?" She wouldn't have been more shocked if he doused her with gasoline and lit a fire. Or socked her right in the solar plexus. Instinctively Nika stepped back.

"Eli is right. With that hair you do look more like a flower than a boy."

His smile was crooked, but warm. If he was surprised at her reaction, he never let it show.

"He gave me something for you." William pulled a folded piece of paper from his breast pocket.

"For...me?" Nika stammered.

"Yes. Eli asked me to give it to the 'boy that looks like a daisy flower,'" he quoted.

"What is it?" Reluctant to take it, Nika clasped her hands behind her back.

"Mr. Coleman left for a business trip an hour ago," he answered on a serious note. "Before he left, he asked me to give you his written message."

"He left? But why? Where? For how long?"

The barrage of questions gushed out before she could stop herself.

"He left for St. Augustine, where he has some business to attend." The speculation in those shrewd blue eyes wasn't lost on her. "As for how long—he didn't tell me. For as long as he is needed there, I would assume."

He abandoned me. Just took off, and left me behind.

Disheartened, ridiculously upset, Nika finally accepted the note. And just like that, all the fun and delight from their earlier banter was gone. The prospect of spending the long evening in the company of strangers was almost unbearable. She would gladly return to her room and stay there until Elijah was back.

And how silly is that?

She should be happy that he left. Now she had an ample opportunity to search the house for the key. She might even sneak into his Tower of Doom without any fear of being caught. But there was no joy. The thought of searching for the damned key was the last thing on her mind.

He's gone.

The sudden emptiness of the house was overwhelming. Like all the energy, all the vitality was sapped out if it, leaving it hollow and desolate.

The chorus of voices carrying over from the dining room was short of the only one she longed to hear: that deep and silky baritone that was Elijah's.

Her foolish heart lurched to her throat. Her eyes misted and his note burned her fingers. A sharp sense of disappointment that was akin to betrayal enveloped her.

Get a grip, girl. You are alone, in this house, in this time. Now, think of how to turn this situation to your advantage.

Her hunger disappeared, but she still followed Mr. O'Brien, to the dining room. No excuses to leave came to mind.

Oblivious to her mood, William flung the doors open and nodded to Nika to proceed. With a fortifying breath, she stepped into the large hexagonal shaped room, and stopped dead.

It was lit up like a Christmas tree with slim candles on every possible surface. A huge dining table domineered the entire space. The centerpiece of elegant white roses in a tall Tiffany crystal vase perfumed the air. The cream-colored linen tablecloth hung low, almost touching the floor. There was more high polished silverware at each place setting than at any Five Star restaurants Nika had frequented. She was speechless.

"Is it someone's birthday?" she asked no one in particular.

"No, dear boy." Abby quickly scanned Nika from head to toe and nodded her approval. "Why would you think that?"

"It's so... grand," she mumbled as she tried to take it all in. She was just like a country bumpkin that was suddenly dropped in the middle of a Versailles ball.

"Oh, we just like to spend our evenings in a pleasant atmosphere, is all." Abby clapped her hands, delighted at Nika's reaction.

"Pleasant," Nika muttered. *Pleasant-schmesant*, it was spectacular! And breathtaking. Thank God for her upbringing, so no humiliating herself by choosing the wrong silverware. One never knew when childhood lessons in table etiquette might come in handy.

She was seated next to Claudine, with Abby and Mr. O'Brien across from them. Nika was so bewildered, she barely registered the food served, or what she ate. She was still reeling from Elijah's departure, and feeing quite sorry for herself. The one thing that worked its way into her mind was how William watched her like a hawk.

The conversation was lively, the atmosphere pleasant, and the company, especially Abby, was delightful. Little by little, Nika relaxed, and even managed to put a word or two into the discussion about Shakespeare and Mozart.

Then Abby mentioned her brother's absence. Nika's mood took a nosedive. Her appetite was gone, but her dismay was back with vengeance. He left. Just left, with nothing more than a stinking note, like she was...

The note! I almost forgot about the note.

"I had no idea he was leaving today, of all days!" Abby said, pinning William with sharp eyes. "And why didn't you accompany him, as usual?"

He took his time, blotting his mouth with a napkin, before answering. Nika was itching to kick him.

"Your brother's decision, Miss Abby. He wanted me here, in the house."

"Whatever for?"

"I cannot possibly know." And he cast his eyes downward.

William's innocent act wasn't lost on Nika.

The stinker!

Oh, he knew, alright. Elijah left him behind on purpose, but for what? To watch her? Ridiculous! But what if that were true, and he was left here to spy on her?

Well, we'll see about that!

Managing to swallow the last bite without choking, Nika plastered a false smile on her face.

"Thank you very much for a delicious dinner, Abby. I'm quite tired, so if you won't object, I'd like to... say good night and go to bed."

It sounded more like 'may I be excused, mother?' but she had no time to worry about that. She had a hard enough time keeping a leash on her tongue and not blurt her usual verbiage like 'I'm beat' or 'I'm going to hit the sac.'

Abby's brows furrowed with concern, but after a brief moment, her smile cleared it away. "Good night, Nicholas. Sweet dreams, dear boy."

And with that Nika hurried from the room like the hounds of hell were chasing her.

She took the stairs two at the time, running the last few feet to her room. As soon as she was inside, Nika bolted the door shut, and took the note out of her pocket. Bracing herself, she opened the folded piece of thick and expensive stationery.

Her head swam, her breath hitched and a small moan escaped her lips.

Nika's legs folded and she sat down, right there, on the spot, hitting the floor with a dull *thump*. She wrapped her arms tight around herself protectively.

If she had even the slightest doubt of who was the author of the first note, the one that she read on the beach with *Verochka*, the same one that commanded her to 'find the key,' she could rest easy now.

The same familiar, bold handwriting in stark black ink teased her eyes as soon as she opened the note.

> I must apologize for my earlier behavior. It was uncalled for, and unbecoming of a gentleman. I hope you will forgive me, if not right away, then in time.
>
> Elijah B. Coleman

Just like the first letter.

Nika blinked, unsure of his intent and just what the hell was happening.

Just what the hell does the B stood for?

CHAPTER SEVENTEEN

The next several days followed the same monotonous pattern. Nika woke with the first rays of light, went outside to explore the gardens, gazebo, stables and all other buildings memorizing everything as best she could. After an hour or two she cleaned up, then enjoyed breakfast with Abby and Claudine. Later she either posed for Abby, who decided to paint 'Nick,' or toured the house unobtrusively to familiarize herself with the original interior. At night she prowled every nook and granny in relentless pursuit for the key.

In short, she went through the motions: ate, slept, dressed up, cleaned up, and explored the property, day in and day out, with nothing really to occupy her hands. And that left her mind free, which was never a good thing. She was bored, sick at heart, and frustrated. She needed to keep busy, to do something—anything—to fill the void Elijah's absence had created.

She even tried to offer her help to the formidable Mrs. Smith to no avail. She was shooed out of the kitchen by the cook, who proclaimed that she did *not* need help from the likes of her. When she suggested something to the carpenter, who showed up to fix a leak in the attic, she was snorted at and threatened with boxed ears. The other servants kept their distance, too, but whether because they were ordered to do so, or because they didn't trust the strange houseguest. All this drove Nika nuts.

What am I, a leper?

Even when she was quarantined with chickenpox at the tender age of eight, Nika wasn't as isolated as now. She was never treated as a useless makeweight. If not for Abby and Belle, Nika would have gone stir crazy from sheer loneliness.

She counted days like a prisoner in a cell, visualizing a calendar in her mind and putting a virtual 'X' on a virtual square every evening. But if prisoners counted days until their freedom, she tracked days from Elijah's departure. *And how pathetic is that?*

"I don't care."

Let's be frank, Nika, you are moping like a schoolgirl.

"I don't care."

Dammit, wake up. You're acting like a fool. The man is long dead.

"Oh, shut up."

He was very much alive to her. And bigger than life. And he left.

God knew when, or even *if* she would see him again.

Nika touched her pocket where she had tucked Elijah's note. She got in a habit of reading and rereading it daily, like some simpleminded, smitten maiden. No not matter that he wrote it to the *boy,* or that it was a formal apology and not a love letter. She cherished every word, blushed every time she read it, and carried it around, hidden in her pocket. She even wrapped it for protection with a piece of butcher paper she snatched from the kitchen.

You are in trouble, Veronika Margaret Morris. Like with a capital T. No ifs or buts about it.

Yes, she had it bad. So bad that she daydreamed what may have happened if she belonged here, in his time, or if he were in hers, if they met under the normal circumstances, and she didn't have to pretend to be anyone but herself...

Silly dreams, girl. Silly, dangerous dreams.

Nika drew a deep breath. Today marked the sixth day of Elijah's absence. Dull and monotonous like yesterday, and the day before that, and the day before that...

It also marked one full week since Nika had been thrown back in time to 1909.

The whole week, and she was no closer to finding her way forward to 2019. Moreover, instead of a curious observer, she had become a willing participant, and that was most troubling and disturbing.

And very dangerous. She didn't belong here. She shouldn't be here.

It was unnatural. It was risky and unsafe, and not only for her own wellbeing. Nika was familiar with The Butterfly Effect theory, according to which a small insignificant change can trigger a much bigger effect and impact on the future. The term, if she wasn't mistaken, came from an apt analogy where a butterfly flaps its wigs and causes a typhoon.

But if once upon a time she considered it just a curious fact, now she seriously contemplated the reality of such theory. Time wasn't linear, and everything in the universe was sensitively connected and interdependent. So, what if some smallest, most innocuous act on her part here and now affected all future events? Could she hurt someone? Could she change inadvertently an outcome of history? The responsibility was enormous. Mindboggling and scary as hell. Nika didn't want to say or do anything that might screw up something in the big scheme of things. Just being in the wrong time was bad enough. She wanted no ramifications that might weigh heavily on her conscience.

All the more reason to get out of here as fast as possible.

Truth be told, she missed her own world. Her iPhone, books, computer and internet, even her own clothes and comfy flip-flops. She wanted nothing less than to be in her home with her own bathroom. And then there was pizza and cold beer. Nika's mouth watered for just one more taste. Then there was her car, her baby. And her job. Was Alex able to keep the business going or had her disappearance ruined that, too?

But most of all, she missed her family. Alex and *Verochka*, her mother and siblings, even the twins. Her stomach tied in knots with the painful thoughts.

What were Alex and *Verochka* doing? Were they still searching for her? Or mourning her? Nika shuddered. *Verochka* and Alex couldn't keep her disappearance from the extended family indefinitely. Her mother and siblings, her aunt and cousins— everyone must have been notified in the hopes Nika had contacted one of them. New York was more than likely buzzing, wondering what had befallen the black sheep of the Morris family. The twins were sure to be more outraged than surprised. They probably came down hard on Alex and blamed him for her disappearance. The twins' voices rang in her ears, "You're the older cousin and a man! You should've kept her in stride.' *Verochka* would defend him and get her fair share of blame, too. What a mess! Guilt swept through Nika, even though the mysterious time jump wasn't her fault.

Listen to yourself! You even started to think in Victorian English.

Distressed and irritated, Nika rummaged in her closet until she found her baseball cap. She outlined the letters B&A embroidered in gold with her index finger, then plopped the cap on her head, and immediately felt better. She was sick and tired of being a boy. She missed her old—real—self.

Nika hated pretending to be someone she wasn't, but she had no idea how to stop the charade. She shook her head. Was stopping it even safe? A few times, when she was at her lowest, she almost confessed to Abby. But always, for one reason or another, she stopped herself.

Abby's first allegiance was to her brother, as it should be. To confide in her and ask for help was the equivalent of asking her to lie to Elijah. Nika hated to put the girl in that position.

Would Abby believe her? Nika genuinely liked the girl, but they were literally and figuratively a world apart. No, as fond as she was of Abby, Nika couldn't enlist her help. Or anybody's help, for that matter. She must count on herself and act alone. She must locate the key and pray that the grandfather clock's time-jump trick was reversible. Otherwise...

Don't go there. Just search for the key.

And that's exactly was she'd been doing, night after night.

Fiercely. Doggedly. Desperately.

Every evening was the same. At nine-thirty, she went to her room after wishing everybody good night, then on the first strike of midnight she went about her clandestine activities.

To learn everyone's routine was a piece of cake.

Abby, Claudine, and Mr. O'Brien retired for the night by ten.

At precisely ten-thirty, Mrs. Smith, accompanied by a servant girl, walked through the house, top to bottom, preparing the fortress for the night.

By midnight, even the animals were down for the count.

And so, at midnight, Nika, dressed in her black t-shirt and ripped jeans, silently began her nocturnal excursion.

First, she inspected the main floor, reasoning Elijah was more likely to keep the key in his secondary office or in the library. However, she thoroughly searched the whole first floor, from corner to corner, including the dining room, library-slash-musical room, Mr. O'Brien's office, Abby's studio, kitchen, and all the nooks and crannies. She even poked her head into the fireplaces and rummaged inside the enormous stove in the kitchen. It took her two whole nights to accomplish the task. As a result, Nika had a bruised hip, a skinned elbow and scratches on both hands to show for her efforts, but no prize.

The hidden back panel of the grandfather clock, the point of origin so to speak, was the very first place she inspected, but found it empty.

Every room on the third floor yielded a similar result, but Nika hadn't expected anything from the servants' wing, anyway. She searched it during the day when the occupants were about their duties just to be thorough.

She tried the attic and found a treasure trove of late nineteenth-early twentieth-century household items, enough for opening a couple museums, but no key.

The second floor came next, and dismissing Claudine and Abby's rooms as the least likely places for Elijah to hide the key, Nika went straight to his bedroom. She spent several memorable hours there, snooping to her heart's content, touching his personal belongings.

She was so busy admiring décor and his taste in clothes, she almost forgot the real reason why she was there. She gave herself a mental shake and continued her methodical search for the key.

But her gaze strayed to the four-poster canopy bed that ruled the room. Nika knew her furniture. And this one was hands down a spectacular object of art. An unmistakable Chippendale, the bed was mahogany probably of the Honduran mahogany especially favored by Thomas Chippendale. It had the ball-and-claw feet design and a solid headboard with a traditional pediment, decorated with hand-carved acanthus and anthemion leaves, the symbol of endurance and immortality. All four posters were shaped in spiral-turns with flower carvings and flame finials for dramatic effect. Two impossibly thin sheer curtains the color of early-morning fog draped casually over the magnificent frame. Nika swallowed hard as she surveyed the wooded glory. It was a true masterpiece, a resting oasis for a king. Or an oasis for his sensual enjoyment. Her unruly imagination overlaid an image of Elijah, half-naked, over it that made it impossible for Nika to concentrate.

Finally, abandoning all pretense of searching, she walked closer to the bed. As beds went, this one was the granddaddy of them all. The large mattress was covered with soft cream-colored sheets and a silk coverlet in deep ocean grey.

The wispy curtains above created the illusion of whimsical, blurring the edges of the whole picture, making it slightly out of focus. The sight of this bed made her uncomfortable. Nika averted her gaze, but not before a flash of... something like smoke, or a shadow of two figures, male and female, moving sinuously in an ancient dance of lovemaking.

A small helpless moan... a deep satisfied male groan.

"Daisy, my Daisy..."

Frozen in trance, Nika stood at the foot of the bed, unable to tear her eyes off it. She shook her head—shock? denial? —and the sensual vision slowly faded.

Shaken more than she was willing to admit, Nika almost ran from the room. After that she was unable to sleep that night. As soon as she closed her eyes, a faint whisper reached her ears, *"Daisy, my Daisy"* and two bodies undulating on the canopied bed.

Tonight, she decided to search Elijah's sanctuary—the tower.

She was jittery inside and out, which earned her several concerned gazes from Abby and a polite inquiry about her wellbeing from Mr. O'Brien. She was jumpy, and agitated, and dammit, plain scared.

And sick to her stomach.

Like a thief, she sneaked into Elijah's private domain, and invaded his privacy. She would go ballistic if someone— anyone— dared to do it to her. But she reasoned with herself, it wasn't a normal circumstance, and she wasn't going to do it out of sheer curiosity. Her survival depended on it.

The tower was the last logical place for Elijah to hide the key. Granted, there were three other small cottages on the premises, and the stables, but Nika doubted that he ever thought to use them for that purpose.

No, the tower was the last resort. If Nika didn't find it there, she was doomed. Plain and simple.

Nika fought to keep her fears at bay as she tiptoed to the hidden panel on the second floor that led to the elevator. She inched the panel open and sighed in relief when it eased back without a sound. She closed the door and was plunged into a total darkness. Good thing she wasn't afraid of the dark. In a matter of moments her eyes adjusted and she was able to distinguish the latch that opened the elevator doors. Nika took a couple of deep breaths to calm her galloping heart, and, after a long moment of debating the wisdom of her action, proceeded with her plan. She needed that damn key. The sooner she found it, the better for everybody.

"Liar."

"Shut the hell up," she answered to her bitchy, argumentative self, and went inside. As soon as she stepped into the elevator cabin, the dim overhead light flickered to life, startling her.

"Dammit, Nika, get a grip." The row of round golden buttons glimmered on her left. They were numbered 1, 2 & 3. She pushed number 3. With a faint mechanical groan, the elevator started its slow ascent. Holding her breath, fascinated, Nika slowly turned around.

Wow. Just...wow.

It was a prime example of Otis brothers' early masterpiece: opulent, elaborate, uniquely created for every commissioned unit. There were no two elevators alike, from what she had learned. She must try to commit to memory every single detail of the interior, that elegant mix of dark cherry and brushed gold, in order to restore it later to its original décor. But before that she must find the key and return home, in one piece preferably. Thus fortified, Nika grabbed the latch and, when the elevator finally stopped, slid the door open.

"Wow." Her breath hitched in and out a couple of times in awe and wonder. She didn't know what she had expected, but definitely not this. She did a slow 360 to take everything in. The room was spacious, perfectly round with a high vaulted ceiling, making a classical pointed-tip-up cone. It was lit by the full moon streaming through the drape-less Palladian windows. She nodded in satisfaction. It made her job much easier. Creeping closer to the windows, she took a quick peek outside. *Huh!* The room was the perfect observation point. Eli was able to see every single corner of the estate spread below. Elijah's words came back to haunt her.

"Call me anything you like, but in my universe called the Coleman household, I am the reigning king."

Yes, it was a true king's domain.

She turned and gasped, as her gaze fell upon the unusual fireplace. It was shaped like a lion's mouth, gaping open with two protruding fangs. Its warning roar was all but palpable.

"Wow," she repeated again.

The room was fascinating. The writing desk that dominated the room was antique, adorned with beautiful moldings, burl wood inlays on the top and intricate brass handles. The lamps and chairs belonged to late nineteenth century. The clock on the corner of the desk was a large egg-shaped masterpiece in royal blue, inlaid with mother-of-pearl and gold, was an original Faberge. She was sure of it.

Everything about the décor was classy, even elegant, but unmistakably masculine.

It suited its owner. Elijah's image flickered in and out of her mind's eye, making her shaky and ashamed of herself.

What am I doing?

He saved her, brought her here, under his own roof, fed her, clothed her, cared about her in his own way. This is how she paid him back? By snooping, spying, and pawing at his things? Feeling lower than dirt, and slimier than sludge, Nika drew a broken breath. She needed to stop while she still could, and the hell with the key. After all, she could always ask Elijah for it, explaining to him her situation. She must tell him the truth, all of it and make him believe her. Somehow. Relief swept over Nika like a huge weight was suddenly lifted from her shoulders. She inhaled a calming breath, and resolutely turned around, ready to leave. The paintings grabbed her attention. The walls were peppered with them.

Her heartbeat accelerated. All the paintings were watercolors, picturing the ocean in its different moods, from tranquil to raging mad. She could almost hear the sound of waves, feel the texture of foaming water as it rolled onto the shore. And the energy! It was pulsing, raw and primitive, like the ocean. She held her breath, almost reverently, and studied the images. Her arms and legs were covered in goosebumps. Her unique reaction when she was in the presence of great art. Those paintings were certainly masterpieces. She squinted, searching for the artist's signature, and found it in the lower right corner of every canvas, A. Coleman. Nika did a double take. A. Coleman—Abigail Coleman? Were they Abby's paintings? *Oh, God, they were.* After all, what was the chance there were two artists in the same family with the same initials. Nope, they were Abby's alright, she would bet her prized toolbelt. The girl had a gift from God, and her brother must have recognized it. Somehow, Nika doubted Elijah covered the walls of his most private domain with Abby's art just to placate his baby sister. Why, then, deny her the most cherished desire? The notion of taking away her paints and canvases, and marry her off to a man she didn't love was the equivalent of cutting off her arm! Both arms, she corrected herself. Worse than that, it was equivalent to amputating her soul. Nika shook her head. Elijah's reasoning was beyond her. It was barbaric and inhumane. Her future husband may indulge his bride, and send her off to France to paint. *Probably not.*

Sad and deflated, a lump formed in Nika's throat. For Abby, for herself. The notion of confiding in Elijah was no longer a great idea. If he refused to bend under his own sister's pleas, why do it for her? Why would he believe her, when she had no proof? She might provide ample evidence that she was a female, but that was as far as her proof went. And then? What were the words to convince him? No, damn it, she needed that key. Now more than ever. All her emotions aside, the rational part of her pushed her to continue searching. Not only for herself now, but for Abby, too. Because more than anything at that moment Nika wanted to help the girl. But how? What could she do, being stuck here, a hundred years behind her time, and mistaken for a boy?

You can't even help yourself.

But if she found the key, she could snag one of Abby's paintings, and...

And what? Take it with you? To what purpose? What would it accomplish?

"I don't know, but I'll think of something," she vowed. "Right after I find that blasted key."

Energized, Nika started her search in earnest.

CHAPTER EIGHTEEN

And she failed rather spectacularly.

Not only did she not find the key, she almost got caught. Fortunately, the operative word was almost. Unfortunately, she lost her beloved baseball cap during her escape. *Damn!*

Who knew that Mr. O'Brien was allowed to enter the tower at any given time, middle-of-the-night-time included? Certainly not Nika, or for that matter, Abby. On numerous occasions she warned Nika that her brother absolutely forbade any member of the household to enter that room, especially in his absence. Obviously, William O'Brien wasn't included in that group. *Or else, he missed the memo.* Somehow, Nika doubted it. She suspected Elijah had asked his secretary and friend to keep an eye on *the boy* in his absence.

More accurately to *spy* on her. She fumed.

And what were you *doing in his bedroom, or his tower? Checking the plumbing?* She huffed a breath and frowned. The events of previous night were still fresh in her memory. Her intruder had materialized quite suddenly when Nika was on her knees in front of the fireplace with her right arm all the way in the lion's mouth searching for the hidden key. Something alerted her, and trusting her instincts, she rolled and ducked under the desk before William entered the room. He was dressed in a silky robe over his nightshirt, and held a candle in his left hand. His feet were bare which was why she hadn't heard his stealthy approach.

Canny bastard.

He stepped into the room, lifted the candle, and peered into the darkness. Thankfully, he didn't find anything amiss. He turned to leave but not before a brief pause near the desk where she was hiding. Once he exited the room, Nika counted to one hundred before she fled to safety. She sucked in the first full breath of air once she reached her room and bolted the door. As an extra precaution she propped a chair against it. Silly? Yes, but it cocooned her in a veil of safety.

Nika raised her left hand to whisk off her baseball cap, and horror struck. No cap. It was missing. Switching from praying to swearing and back, she ransacked her room to no avail. Without a doubt she had lost it somewhere in between the tower and her room. Nika retraced her steps to the hidden panel, kneeling at every corner and patting every floor board, but all in vain. To add insult to injury, the resonant chime from the grandfather clock as it struck the hour reached her. The sound was muffled, but no less threatening. Nika's heartbeat stumbled then shifted into overdrive. She wasn't a coward, but neither was she brave enough to go back to the tower. Defeated and disheartened, Nika returned to her room. Misery took over. Her skin was clammy with cold sweat, her hands shook.

You are in trouble, girl. With a fat capital T.

Tell me something I don't know. So, what now?

But even her inner smart-alecky self was at a total loss.

Nika sat on the edge of the bed, and brooded until dawn like a prisoner awaiting execution.

When the first rays of sun peeked through the purple sky, Nika changed into her boy clothes and crept out the back door, thankfully undetected. She didn't want to see or talk to anybody. She had no heart to interact with people. Nika headed to the stables, where everything smelled of horses and grass and hay. She found Belle and they went through their established greeting of her crazy barking and licking and kissing while Nika rubbed the dog's belly. But today even Belle's antics failed to lift Nika's spirit. Haunted by the events of the night, she burrowed her face into the dog's fur, sank to her knees, and finally let her emotions fly free. Her eyes burned from unshed tears, her throat was scratchy and parchment dry. And worse, her body ached from exhaustion and fatigue. She was so close to a breaking point, like brittle glass. Except for Belle, Nika was totally alone, tired and scared, and lost in time.

Mounting fear that she was stuck here, in this century forever, took control like a deadly virus, eating at her spirit, destroying her resolve.

Calm down. She hugged Belle tightly. *Think, Nika, think and plan.*

Belle chose that moment to lavishly lick Nika's face, and then butted her shoulder, none too gently.

"You're right, girl. My pity party is over. Time to get up and do something." She smiled at the dog and kissed its wet, cold nose. "Thanks for reminding me."

Nika couldn't afford the luxury of wasting her time on self-pity. She needed another game plan, another course of action.

She took a deep calming breath, and tried to sort out what she had accomplished so far. The short list depressed her.

She didn't find the key, her only real hope to return home.

She had inspected the Coleman house top to bottom, and knew it now like the back of her hand. Considering she had no means to return, it was unlikely she could ever apply her knowledge.

She made friends with Abby, and wanted something fierce to help the girl to achieve her dream and succeed. But how? She raked her hair with her fingers. How could she help Abby? Talk her into running away, and go with her? Where? To Paris? Maybe. She had experience in convincing people to follow her crazy plans. Alex and their Great Adventure popped into her mind. *Don't go there.*

Hot tears pressed against her eyelids.

Alex. My God, will I ever see him again? Don't! Don't think about your family, or else you will fall apart. And what purpose does that serve? Better think about getting away and returning home.

Home, the place where everything was familiar, where people she loved and trusted were waiting for her, out of their minds with worry about her. Home, where she belonged. Truly belonged.

And just like that, her thoughts turned to the Coleman house. No, it wasn't her home, but for the past several days it had started to feel like one.

Nonsense!

It was Elijah and Abby's home, not hers. She was an outsider, a strange creature that dropped out of nowhere. Brooding, she stopped by Sultan's empty stall. Today marked a full week from when Elijah left.

How much longer he's planning to travel? She felt like crying. She was crying! *Dammit.*

You better pray that he stays away for as long as possible, you idiot.

Because as soon he came back and visited his tower office, he would know that she was there.

And then all hell will break lose.

Belle chose that moment to nudge her hand, demanding attention. Absently, Nika scratched the dog between her ears.

"Guess we'll cross that bridge in due time."

The dog made a little sound, halfway between a moan and a grunt, and Nika smiled. How could she stay miserable, where the pair of almost human eyes were gazing at you adoringly?

And just like that, her mood switched, and everything was much better. Hugging Belle one more time, Nika rose to her feet. "Thank you, sweetheart. I can't imagine this life without you."

Digging into her pocket and finding it empty, Nika cursed under her breath. She had forgotten to scrounge a treat for the dog that morning, dammit. Guilt hung heavily on her shoulders.

"Oh, baby, I'm so sorry, I have nothing tasty for you today. I promise to bring a double treat next time, okay?"

Belle snorted, then tilted her head before jumping and prancing around Nika, asking to play.

"Sorry, girl, not now." Nika smacked at her legs to clean her borrowed pants of dust and hay. "It's time for me to go back and face the music."

The household was probably already up and ready for breakfast.

Belle whimpered, but remained in the stables.

Nika approached the house with trepidation. She sensed something was about to break loose. But what? An invisible dark cloud hung low over her head, making her jumpy and twitchy. Like a dead man walking, she closed the last few feet to the back of the house and entered through the kitchen door. And immediately was plunged into chaos.

Shouts, cries, confusion.

What on earth?

Nika squeezed in between the wall of people, who were gathered in the kitchen.

"Let me in." She shoved at someone, and finally was inside the human circle.

Was there an accident? Did someone cut themself? She made a quick scan around the kitchen.

Steam from the open pots and pans billowed. The sounds of boiling water and sizzling bacon filled the room. But all the servants were huddled together, gaping at the floor. Mrs. Smith. She laid on the middle of the floor, her blotchy face twitching, her eyes rolling madly, her hair loose from her usual severe knot and fanning her head in a salt-and-pepper mess. For a split second, Nika stood as petrified and frozen as everybody else. Then her first aid training kicked in. Nika jumped forward, issuing orders right and left.

"Get out of the way! Get me a glass of water and a pillow! Don't just stand here. Call 911! We need an ambulance and a doctor, fast! Get moving, people!"

Kneeling in front of the older woman, Nika quickly assessed the situation. She gently turned Mrs. Smith's face and looked into her eyes, then touched her forehead. No fever. Her pulse was too fast, but strong, so not a heart attack. No deformity of the face, thank god, because a stroke was something Nika was afraid of the most. The discoloration of the skin, clamminess and difficult breathing all pointed to some kind of an arrest. Dammit, it looked familiar. Where did she see something like that? And then it hit her. Anaphylactic shock! Of course! One of her crew members had terrible allergies. Nika has witnessed one of his allergic reactions, and after that she made sure to carry antihistamine in her toolbelt for such emergencies.

Oh, God, of course!

Abby and Mr. O'Brien ran into the kitchen.

"What's going on? Oh, my…" Abby covered her mouth in horror.

"Abby, come here," Nika jumped to her feet, grabbed Abby's hand none too gently, then pulled her closer to Mrs. Smith. With a yank she dropped Abby to her knees. "Keep her head elevated. Here, put it on your knees, that's right."

When Nika was confident everything was done, she turned to William O'Brian.

"You! Don't just stand there like a statue. Call 911! Get a doctor here, pronto."

"Call…what?" He gaped at her, blinking in confusion.

"Oh, the hell with it!"

Nika ran toward the doorway. She reached the stairs and ran up, two steps at a time. Every second in an allergic arrest was essential and precious, and Mrs.

Smith's time was ticking down much too fast. God knew how long ago she had collapsed before someone stumbled upon her. Back in her room, Nika ran to the wardrobe and rummaged in it, searching for her tool belt.

"Damn, damn, damn," she muttered, as one piece of clothing after another fell on her head. "Where is it...?"

Finally, she located her prize. She grabbed it and raced to the kitchen, discarding one item after another, covering the staircase with her tools.

"Please, be here, please, please," she prayed breathlessly, all the way running as fast as her legs would go.

"Yes!"

She finally found the syringe. She threw her toolbelt aside, and then burst through the door into the kitchen.

"Out of my way," she shouted as she raced to the older woman now suffocating in earnest.

"Oh, Nick, she's dying! We sent for the doctor, but it's too late." Tears flowed down Abby's cheeks, but she continued to hold Mrs. Smith's head on her bended knees. "Poor Mrs. Smith, poor darling."

"No one's dying, not today," Nika announced, and praying that she was right, plunged an EpiPen into the older woman's thigh, right through the clothing.

"What are you doing?" Abby face was awash with horror.

"Saving her life. I hope," Nika muttered.

For the next several seconds time stood still. Everybody stared at the prone figure on the floor. One second, two, three...

Mrs. Smith gradually stopped convulsing. Her face became even paler, but lost the angry red blotchy marks, and finally she made a tiny sound and took a labored, shaky breath.

"She's alive! You saved her." Abby cried out, whipping the tears from her face with one hand. Her second hand still supporting Mrs. Smith's head lying on her knees.

Nika, who had lost ten years of her life, sitting on the floor in front of the older woman and debating the wisdom of her decision to inject an EpiPen, took her own shaky breath.

The quiet that followed Abby's statement was so absolute it was deafening.

Raising her eyes, Nika slowly surveyed the room. All people gathered in the spacious kitchen were huddled together, and all of them was stared at her.

Their faces reflected a gamut of expressions from open curiosity to guarded suspicion. Some faces wore masks of animosity mixed with disgust.

Some people tend to be afraid of things they do not understand. And who could blame them? The main thing was, Mrs. Smith was alive and well. Everything else was secondary. Nika raked both hands through her messy curls, blew out a breath and was about to lift herself up when she noted a commotion. She turned her head toward the short rotund body of an older gentleman with a satchel, shooing people left and right, approached her. The doctor had finally arrived.

"And what is this? Clear the place this instant! You hear? Where is my patient?"

Nika left Abby in charge of the situation, and stood. Her legs were so wobbly, they barely supported her weight, still reeling from the near-disaster.

"What on earth is that?"

That came from the doctor who held up the empty EpiPen and squinted at it.

"Oh, it's an amazing potion that Nick gave...or injected, rather, into Mrs. Smith's leg," Abby explained when no one answered.

"Nick?" The doctor turned his shrewd eyes in her direction. "And where did you get this magic potion, young fella? And what, I repeat, on earth is that?"

"Good question," rumbled a deep baritone behind Nika. "I, too, would like to hear the answer."

She froze, then slowly turned around and lifted her gaze. There, in the middle of the kitchen, stood Elijah Coleman, gorgeous and larger than life.

And he was watching her. Fixedly.

The incredible joy slammed into her like a fist to a solar plexus, stealing her breath.

Unable to move, feeling shackled to the spot by the heavy, unreadable stare of his eyes, Nika froze, but didn't lower her eyes. He was back, he was here. *Finally.*

She smiled, letting go the broken breath. He was back, and everything was going to be okay.

A moan cut into the haze of her delirium, returning her back to the moment. As reality penetrated the fog in her brain, Nika's smile faded. The adrenalin jolt that had kept her on edge during Mrs. Smith's ordeal had dissipated. A cold dread rushed in, turning her blood to ice.

"Well, boy? The cat got your tongue?"

Elijah lifted one of his brows in a mock gesture, but his eyes were dead serious.

Shaky and freezing, Nika swallowed a couple of times with great effort.

"It's an EpiPen," she answered after a long pause.

"An epi what?" asked the doctor.

"An EpiPen, a medicine for allergies. It's ah...applied in emergency situations such as this." She pointed at Mrs. Smith. "She was suffocating."

"And how did you deduce it was an allergy, and not an asthma or a heart failure, pray tell?"

"Maybe it would be better to relocate poor Mrs. Smith to her own bed?" William O'Brien cut into the doctor's interrogation. His quiet but firm voice spurred everybody back into motion.

"Of course, of course," the doctor muttered, returning his attention back to his patient.

The onlookers moved, clearing the path for Elijah, who lifted Mrs. Smith effortlessly into his arms and exited the kitchen, followed closely by the doctor and Abby.

Mr. O'Brien was the only one who stood exactly where he had been all this time, with his hands clasped behind his back. His pose was deliberately negligent, his enigmatic eyes unreadable. And they were glued to her face.

They were alone in spacious and usually orderly room that now resembled a scene after a hurricane.

"Well," he said.

"Well," she echoed.

"You have a lot of explaining to do, you know." His haughty British accent was more pronounced than ever.

"Yeah, I figured." She swiped at her clammy forehead.

"You saved her life, and he will be forever grateful."

"I don't need his gratitude."

"Maybe so." His expression as unreadable as that of a sphinx. "*What* do you need, then?"

"Excuse me?"

"You won't answer." His lips curved into a crooked smile. "To me, anyway. But to him, you shall. You must."

Then he unclasped his hands from behind his back, and moved toward the exit. Then he hesitated, and turned back.

"By the by, what's 911?"

Befuddled, Nika frowned.

"A... what?"

"You ordered me, twice, I might add, to call 911. What's that?"

"Dammit." She closed her eyes. *Of all the things!* "It's a..." *What? Stupid, Nika, so stupid.* "It's an emergency service," she finally managed. "We call it 911 where I come from."

"Huh." He lifted his brows. "I thought you were from Fernandina."

"I am."

"We don't have any emergency services here, save for the firefighters' squad. But we do not call it 911."

When he was almost at the threshold, he turned to her one last time.

"May I suggest? When you talk to Eli— Mr. Coleman—don't spin your tales with him. Either tell the truth, or don't tell anything at all."

CHAPTER NINETEEN

"I assume this belongs to you."

She stood before a scowling Eli in his Tower office. To say Nika was anxious was an understatement of her and his centuries combined. Her stomach roiled and she trembled like the proverbial leaf. And that was why she barely noticed the item he held in front of her face.

So, that's where it is.

Her beloved baseball cap, so absurdly small and fragile in Elijah Coleman's outstretched hand.

And what beautiful hands.

Nika always was a sucker for nice looking hands. His were quite exceptional, with strong but elegant wrists and long fingers that were at the moment clutching her priceless ball cap.

Well then.

Frustration, confusion, anticipation, fear, joy—all her conflicting emotions that had been warring inside her since the morning debacle in the kitchen, evaporated as if magic dust. Instead, an icy calmness came upon her, because the moment of reckoning had finally arrived.

She took a breath and released it slowly.

Well then.

She knew it was coming. Sure, she wished to be more prepared for it, but, then again, more preparation equals to more frustration and confusion. Nika always preferred an honest spontaneous reaction to a well-developed strategic action. And she was insanely glad that the weight of her deception will be lifted from her shoulders soon. Like right now.

She took another breath, her gaze never wavering from her beloved baseball cap, her talisman and time-travel companion.

"Yes," clear and steady, her voice reverberated through the high-vaulted V of the room.

"Care to explain how it ended up under my desk?"

"No."

"No? And that's it?"

He was still seated behind his massive desk, more curious than angry. Nika took it as a good sign.

"What there is to explain? Obviously, I was here, and lost it."

She was treading a tightrope, and knew it. Each and every word could mean either her liberation or her doom.

"Huh," he tilted his head, "and?"

He was looking at her, enigmatic and oh, God, so handsome, he quite literally took her breath—along with her sanity—away.

The hell with it.

She was so tired she didn't care anymore. "And what?"

"Don't pretend to be dense, boy. I know better."

Eli unfolded his long frame and stood up in one smooth, fluid movement, graceful like a panther. Nika's heart did a quick somersault in her chest, and when Elijah came to stand near her, started a happy drumbeat.

"If I didn't know anything about you at all, today's episode in the kitchen would be a great revelation by itself. By the way, you saved Mrs. Smith's life. It was indeed an allergic reaction to a bee sting. Who knew," he muttered, rubbing his chin between his fingers. She almost smiled, eyeing the small shallow dent in his chin she absolutely adored...

What? Are you out of your mind, girl? Get a grip, Nika!!

"So, she's feeling better?" She asked hurriedly, interrupting her inner voice that was presently screeching at her own self.

"Much." Unaware of her dilemma, Elijah continued in a mild, even tone. "The doctor prescribed her bed rest for a few days, but knowing Mrs. Smith, she'll be up and about tomorrow, ordering her troops like a commanding general."

"I'm glad."

"Me, too. We all are, and will be forever in your debt."

"I don't care."

"And I don't care to be indebted to you," Elijah countered smoothly, "or to be lied to," he finished on a suddenly ominous note.

Nika's heart skipped a bit, and then started galloping a mile a minute.

"I...I never lied to you," she swallowed, pinned to the spot by his steely stare.

"No?"

"No."

"What about your strange device? Or your knowledge of medicine?"

"You never asked."

"I'm asking now. How did you know that Mrs. Smith was having an anaphylactic shock?"

"I saw something similar once. A friend of mine collapsed and was saved by the injection of an EpiPen. Since then, I took it as a rule to carry one with me at any time. As a precaution."

"Okay," he frowned, obviously unconvinced, "but *what is* this medicine, this EpiPen? Where did you get it? Our doctor said he's never heard or seen anything like that before, and he's been practicing medicine twice as long as you have been alive."

"It's a...an advanced device, with a very strong agent against allergy. It was produced quite recently."

"Produced where?"

"All over the world," Nika answered honestly.

"Hmm. It's possible that we are so isolated from the outside world we didn't hear anything about it. Even probable. But what's not even remotely possible or probable, is for a young boy like you—you are what? Fourteen? Fifteen? —to have such an advance knowledge in science, whereas you can barely remember your own name or your place of origin."

Enough was enough.

"I remember my name very well, and my place of origin. But regarding my age," she paused and regarded him with an open, humorous gaze, "you are wrong, Mr. Coleman. I'm not fourteen or fifteen. I'm twenty-nine years old. Also, I'm not a boy. Quite the contrary. I'm a girl. A woman, rather. My name is Nika—not Nick, but my last name is indeed Morris."

Her voice sounded calm and steady even to her own ears. Maybe because she was calm. Deadly calm.

Elijah, on the other hand, was anything but.

At the beginning of her speech, he was standing in a gracefully negligent pose, her baseball cap still clutched in one of his hands. At the end, however, he dropped heavily into his chair, and gaped at her in wonder and something close to an incredulous fascination. Then he started to laugh.

That silenced Nika as nothing else could.

Momentarily concerned for him, she was about to step forward, but her legs simply froze to the spot. Surely, her eyes were deceiving her, or else Elijah Coleman was really shaking from uncontrollable merriment. For as long as she had known him, he never so much as cracked a smile in her presence, not to mention laugh almost hysterically. Was he having some kind of a break-down? Did her revelation manage to send him over the edge?

Ridiculous!

What, then?

"Mr. Coleman." Nika closed the distance between them and put her hand on his jerking shoulder. At the moment his face was buried deep into the palms of his hands. "Mr. Coleman, sir? Please, don't. I don't know what have I done, but I am sorry, sir. Very sorry."

"Sorry? You're sorry?" He lifted his face then and, still laughing, glared at her. His eyes sparkled with steely glitter.

Danger!

"You are, aren't you?" he murmured, still chuckling.

He seized her hand, the one she had foolhardily placed on his shoulder, then rose to his feet in one fluid motion.

"Well, I am not," he finished almost savagely. "Do you have any idea the hell you put me through? Do you?"

In a split second, his face underwent an incredible metamorphosis.

Facing up, with her head thrown back, Nika was helpless to move. His eyes held her. A willing prisoner, she was entrapped in them, as they grew hard and dark as steel.

She would be afraid, probably should be, if she hadn't been so caught up in the moment, in the incredible symphony of emotions that played on his face. And the shock of hair that fell to his forehead. How she longed to smooth it away. Run her fingers through his thick black hair. Feel the silkiness of the strands.

"A woman, you say?" His voice sounded harsh, hot. "Twenty-nine years of age, is it?"

"Y-yes."

A yelp squeaked out when he jerked her up, lifting her to her toes. Both her wrists were imprisoned in his vise-like grip. No hope for Nika to break free, even if she wanted to. God help her, the last thing she wanted was to get away from him. She reveled in the moment, trembling with anticipation, soaking up his heat. The scent of Eli – strong, masculine – filled her. The energy that radiated from his body flowed over her in powerful, potent waves. His eyes burned into her. For an eternity of a few charged moments, they were frozen in time, hands and eyes intertwined, bodies almost touching, emotions barely leashed. She was balancing on a tightrope over the abyss.

Her inner voice screamed to pull away while sanity still ruled. But she craved to see him naked and savor every glorious inch. But she wanted him to see her naked first. Prove she was a woman. A woman with desires and needs. Desires and needs only he could satisfy.

"Prove it," He whispered, his voice deep and throaty. Sexy as hell.

"Let go."

He released her. Rough as his action had been, she regretted the loss of his warm fingers and powerful hands on her.

With determination, and the tease of a talented stripper, Nika took her time to undo each button on her shirt. When they were free, she inched the coarse fabric apart, baring herself to him. She reached for his hands and then laid each warm palm on top of her aching breasts.

Elijah blinked, glanced at his hands, then at her. His eyes widened.

"You are not a boy!"

Triumph. Relief. Awe.

"No shit, Sherlock."

"But neither are you a lady!" He dropped his hands as if he had been burned.

"And thank God for that!" She kicked off her boots then whisked the belt from her pants and let them fall to her ankles. His eyes darkened as he scanned her nakedness. She stood straighter, shoulders back, and not an ounce of shame tweaked her conscience. More than anything she wanted to see his body. What the hell, she had nothing more to lose. She stepped clear and reached for the top button on his shirt.

He brushed her hands away gently and then ripped his shirt off and tossed it aside. Somehow his shoes clattered across the wooden floor. Next his trousers and underwear dropped. He stepped free and then kicked them aside.

She gave a sharp intake of breath. He was beautiful. Everything she ever wanted in a lover and more. Before she said or did anything, he fused his mouth with hers and they became one, in every sense of the word.

CHAPTER TWENTY

But they didn't talk at all that day. Or that evening. Or that night.

More accurately, they failed to talk about *the thing* uppermost on their minds. Almost as one they seemed to agree to ignore the reality, and enjoy the brief intermission the universe had granted them.

By an unspoken mutual agreement, they locked away the outside world, cocooned themselves in the sanctuary of a single room, and simply savored one another. They missed dinner, a fact that bothered Nika a bit, and not at all because she was hungry, but because Mr. O'Brian knew they were supposed to be together. She pointed out to Eli that William had fetched Nick and escorted her to the tower, to the meeting with 'the man of the house.' She was concerned he might get worried, or suspicious, and decide to investigate. And what a disaster that might be.

But Eli brushed her concern off. William was a trusted friend, he said, and left it at that. There was nothing she could have done, and quite frankly, nothing she wanted to do but stay imprisoned in Eli's bed, in his arms, and enjoy for as long as Fate allowed the current state of delirious, mind-boggling and oh, so sinful bliss.

So, no, they didn't discuss anything serious, troubling, or anything that might destroy their fragile paradise.

They made love as soon as they fell in bed. And again, in the middle of the night when Eli roused her from her slumber. And when the dawn slowly bled into the darkness, they turned to each other again, still drowsy and sleepy. She wept from the sweetness of it, that lazy and unhurried lovemaking that broke her heart and stole her breath.

Even if she was destined to die tomorrow, she would go a happy woman.

She never imagined there was so many ways to make love. Nika wasn't a novice, nor was she a prude, but some things they did that night made her blush. Eli proved to be an ardent and generous lover, and innovative. He was physical, sensual, thorough.

And his stamina was unbelievable. Yet, he was always careful of their weight difference He supported himself on his hands and elbows to protect her smaller body. Nika smiled through the haze of awakening. She was a goner before, but after last night...Nika couldn't imagine any other man as her lover. *Every woman deserves an experience like that at least once in her life.*

Her body was delightfully sore in some interesting places. Her breasts were tender to the touch. She drew her index finger along her lips. Her mouth was puffy and sensitive. She was alive and loved, and used in the best meaning of the word.

Can it get any better?

She was happy and satisfied. Delighted and amused at herself, Nika finally decided to join the ranks of living.

Time to face the world, Daisy-girl.

Her eyelids fluttered open and there he was.

My Eli.

She almost smiled, until his face— guarded, cold, remote— sharpened into focus.

Eli was propped on his elbow, lying on his side and staring at her with his silver eyes. His face was like a mask in the early morning light. Gone was the passionate lover of the night. Instead, a stranger who watched her intently as if she were a specimen on a scientist's glass slide.

A cold shiver soared through her. She drew the covers around herself higher and tighter, unsure of this man and now self-conscious in her nakedness.

"Why are looking at me like that?" It sounded more like an accusation than a question to Nika.

"Like what?"

"Like you don't know who I am and what I'm doing here."

"Oh, I know what you're doing here, alright, but as to who you are—I wonder..."

"Wonder about what?" She bristled when his silence hung like a heavy cloud.

"Your eyes," he answered. "They are the color of amethysts. Very peculiar color. I've never seen eyes like yours."

Nika swallowed, taken aback by this strange statement.

"They are also very expressive You could've been a mute and still talked with your eyes."

It was merely an observation nothing more.

He didn't reach out, didn't touch her. Nor did he smile. Fear squeezed Nika's heart. What had happened to the man who was a gentle lover? Who seemed to put her satisfaction above his own?

"That's the only thing on your mind right now? My eyes?"

"No, not only. Your hair is also quite unusual. Coils of tarnished gold, and there's your language. Your command of it is very good, but the verbiage at times seems to be almost foreign."

A shadow moved over his face. Was it regret? Remorse?

Nika shivered again and clutched the quilt in a bare-knuckled grip. Did he regret their night together? Was he sorry? Disappointed?

"You are so tiny and slim, you passed for a boy quite easily, fooling everybody."

"I didn't intend to fool anybody. You mistook me for a boy, and I chose not to correct you."

"Why?"

"It's a long, complicated story. And Doc Schmidt knew my true gender, by the way."

"Huh." Eli chuckled without amusement. "That old fox. "

"What about Abby?"

"No." Nika lowered her eyes, ashamed for not confiding in the girl. Will she consider Nika's behavior a betrayal of her trust?

"Who are you?" he asked coolly. "A spy?"

"A what?" Nika choked and sputtered when her saliva went down the wrong way. She sat up, all modesty forgotten, and coughed to clear her throat.

"Jeez, Coleman, I didn't expect that one coming," she managed, finally. "Why do you think I'm a spy? Why would you think something so outrageous?"

"What am I supposed to think?"

Eli's voice thawed a bit, losing its flat edge. Nika sighed, grateful things might be better.

"You dropped out of the open sky." His fingers busily plucked at his chin, betraying his agitation. "Didn't remember who you are, or where you were. You wore peculiar clothes and had strange items on your body. Unusual things, and at the same time, don't know some elemental facts!"

"You searched my home every night while I was away."

Nika sucked in a quick breath.

"Yes, I know all about it." Eli's eyes grew steeler with every word.

"He was spying on me, wasn't he? Your Mr. O'Brian? I knew it!"

"He was watching you, yes, per my instructions."

"I suppose, it does seem rather strange, when you put it like that. My behavior, I mean. But a spy?" She shook her head and drew her lips tight. "What was I supposed to think?"

"I don't know, but..." she shrugged, lifted her hands in a helpless gesture, then dropped them. "I don't know."

"Did you find what you've been looking all over the house for?"

"No."

"I don't suppose you'd tell me what it is?"

"You won't believe me."

"Try me," he laid back on the bed, pillowing his head on his bent elbow. The covers fell to his waist.

"I don't even know where to start," Nika muttered under her breath.

"How about at the beginning. A long and complicated story, is it?" Eli repeated her own words. "Well, I have all the time in the world."

Nika took a deep breath.

"Before I tell you my story, I want to ask you one thing. It's super important to me to know the truth."

She didn't spare him a single glace, but just sat quietly, tense and quivering as a drawn arrow.

"What is it?" he asked, his voice crisp and cool.

"Are you..." Nika closed her eyes, hating herself for self-doubts and vulnerability, but she had to know. "Are you regretting last night?"

"No. Not at all." He repeated more forcefully.

She let go of the breath she held and drew encouragement from his monosyllable answer.

"My name is Nika, or Veronika Morris. I was born in New York, but currently live in Fernandina Beach. Recently, I was hired by Senator Lauder, one of the descendants of yours, to do a complete restoration of his family home, now a historic building." She drew in a deep breath. "Your house. The Coleman house. I am the head of the construction department of the company Alex and I started eight years ago, Before & After, Inc."

Eli cocked his eyebrow and stared at her for a long moment.

Please, believe me. Please.

"Your hat. The letters B&A mean that name."

"Yes. It's our logo, our name. Rather the name of the company."

"Who is this Alex?"

"My cousin. And best friend."

"Go on," he prompted, non-committal.

Nika hesitated, searching for the best way to say the truth and not sound crazy.

Nika took another fortifying breath and decided to stick to dry facts. "When I entered the house for inspection, it felt almost familiar, as if I knew it, was there before. But I had never stepped a foot in it.

"Along with the keys to the house, Senator Lauder gave me a letter that was addressed to me." She stole a quick glance at him, then turned away. "A letter from you, written in 1909. I was supposed to read it in 2019. September 2019, to be precise."

She expected a reaction. Anger. Ridicule. Disbelieve. But not this, not a complete and utter lack of any response whatsoever. Dammit, her earthshaking confession warranted some sort of a comeback.

Nika darted another quick glance at him. He made a superb picture that she almost forgot she was in the middle of an unbelievable confession.

Unmoving, unfazed, with his head on the bended elbow, Eli exuded absolute calm. His eyes were half-closed, his muscles relaxed. The sheets bunched at his waist, baring his magnificent torso.

A stillness of a jungle cat before it jumped.

A trickle of uneasiness slithered along her skin. Before she lost her last nerve, Nika plunged ahead. "The letter that I was so reluctant to open because it was written a hundred years ago—"

"A hundred and ten," he corrected absently.

"Well, yeah, hundred and ten. Trust the engineer to know his numbers," she muttered under her breath. "Anyway, when I finally read the letter, it confused me even further."

"What did it say?"

"'Find the key. You know where it is. Hurry, for goodness' sake.' And you signed it, Elijah B. Coleman. The exact way you signed your apology note your Mr. O'Brien gave me a few days ago. The same handwriting, the same stationery, same ink. By the way, what does B stand for?"

"Benjamin."

Now she knew. Elijah Benjamin. "Okay."

And that is so freaking important right now because?

"Carry on," Eli prodded, his face an unreadable mask.

"Well, the first thing I recognized was the grandfather clock. Even though I didn't know what key I was supposed to find—and in a hurry, mind you—when the clock began to chime, the same clock that had stood unwound and neglected for half a century, I had a flash of vision, or burst of memory. I don't know how to explain it, but I knew that the grandfather clock had a little hidden space on its back panel and the key was there. I found it, took it out, and inserted it into the clock. Don't ask me why. And then..." She plowed both hands into her hair, and closed her eyes for a moment, feeling again that dizzying sensation of being pulled into the dark tunnel of time. She shrugged it off with an effort.

"I don't know how better to say this, but the truth is, I turned the key in your grandfather clock, in your house, in 2019, and was thrown back a hundred years, into 1909."

"Hundred and ten," he corrected again automatically.

"Hundred and ten, yes. That's all," Nika finished in a flat voice. "I swear I'm telling the truth. I just don't know how to prove it. Or how to prove that I'm not crazy, or delusional." Her heart banged against her ribs. "Do you believe me?"

"I don't know, and that is the plain truth. But neither am I doubting your story, which means, if you are delusional, so am I. The key, then, you were looking all over for the key to my prized grandfather clock?"

"Yes."

"You think the key that brought you here, can take you back in time, to your place?"

"I hope so, yes. You do have the blasted thing, right?"

When he didn't answer, Nika took it for a yes.

"Can you just give it to me? Please?"

"Why? You want to return back home so badly? Are we treating you horribly here?"

"No, no. I don't belong here." Unbeknownst to her, she had moved all the way to his side of the bed, and was sitting on her haunches, before him. "Please, Eli. I have family. People are missing me, probably crazy with worry! People that I love and care about. I have to—"

"What about me?" he interrupted her plea, "What about us? You asked me if I regretted last night. Do you?"

"Never." Nika looked him straight in the eyes. "Never."

"Good."

Quick as a tiger strike, he grabbed her wrist and hauled her against him. And then he kissed her.

Hot.

Urgent.

His tongue swept along the seam of her lips and burned her alive.

"One more question," he asked in between kisses. "You turned the key in my house in Fernandina, but you ended up in Cumberland Island, in another state entirely, in the middle of the dirt road. How do you explain that?"

"I have no clue, except..."

"Except?"

"Except that I somehow connected to you. Internally. Deeply. Miraculously."

"Daisy," he growled, "my Daisy!" And rearing up, Eli sized her around the waist and reversed their positions. In a split second Nika forgot her own name.

And only later, much later, that nagging thought in the back of her mind had finally crystallized, *Verochka was wrong, after all.*

Because Nika wasn't Daisy Coleman reincarnated—she *was* Daisy Coleman.

PART THREE
Daisy

CHAPTER TWENTY-ONE

The next day, Eli took her by the hand, and asked all the members of the household to gather in the great room, where he calmly explained to everybody that 'Nick' was actually Daisy, a long-lost relative from New York, a twice removed cousin of his. She came to Amelia Island, incognito, seeking Eli's help because of an unpleasant situation. No one dared to ask why she didn't have luggage, or why she chose to live a whole week camouflaged as a boy. He asked for their loyalty and swore everyone to secrecy.

"If anybody starts asking questions, you are to refer them to me." He finished his speech in firm order no one dared to disobey. "The situation is too delicate. We are talking about the safety and well-being of a lady. Please, everyone, be considerate." He concentrated, one by one, on every member of the staff in turn. "I trust you will make Miss Daisy's stay with us as pleasant as possible."

And that was that. The God had spoken.

They both agreed that the true story of her miraculous journey was better kept in secret from everybody, Abby included. Nika just had to stick to the truth as much as possible, but omit her time travel experience. It was a challenging endeavor she was ill equipped for, but she had no choice. After all, how many people would believe her? Truth be told, she wasn't sure Eli had believed her completely.

The most daunting part, however, was approaching Abby.

The stricken expression on her face during Eli's speech was Nika's undoing. She wished she could erase it, to spare the girl, but it was already too late. Pale and drawn, Abby appeared to be befuddled, then appalled. And hurt.

As soon as Eli dismissed everyone from the great room, Nika sprang into action. She went after Abby who simply disappeared. *Dammit.* She truly cared about the girl. Abby's friendship was essential to her during all this time. Her opinion mattered. *She* mattered. Just as simple as that. More than anything right now, Nika wanted to mend fences.

Like a person who was about to face a firing squad, Nika approached the door to Abby's suite. She knocked once, then again, louder. Silence. Nika scowled, eying the door. A muted 'Come in' sounded just in a nick of a time, as she contemplated kicking the door in.

Nika took a deep breath. Entering Abby's room was, hands down, one of the hardest things she had done in a long time.

"It's me."

"Did you want anything?"

"I wanted to explain."

"What is there to explain?"

"Many things. Abby—"

"Why?" The girl dropped whatever she was holding in her hands and then whirled to face Nika.

"Just tell me why? Why did you make a fool of me, lying to me, pretending to be my friend?"

"I am your friend!" Nika went with her heart, and closed the distance between them in a few strides. "I am, truly. I never meant to hurt you, Abby."

"Well, you did. And when I think of how you talked about dreams and men, and building that castle for me..."

"I never lied to you, and I will build that castle for you, I swear, I will. Someday."

"What a great fool I am," Abby shook her head.

"You are not! You are the smartest, most talented, and kind person I've met in my entire life. I like you, Abby, and respect you greatly."

"So much that you pretended to be a boy who lost his memory?"

"I'm sorry." Nika lifted her shoulders in a helpless gesture. "I really am, Abby. Please, just let me explain."

Abby wiped a single tear from her face and strode to the window.

"I don't know where to begin, but..." she spoke to Abby's stiff back.

So, she isn't going to make it easy. I deserve that, I suppose. Hurting for them both, Nika forged ahead, "I came here looking for your brother." That much was true. Kind of. Nika decided to stick to the facts as much as she could, and improvise a little but she refused to lie to the girl.

"I really hit my head, and was disoriented for some time. Since I've never seen Eli in person before, I didn't recognize him at first. Later I lost consciousness, and woke up in an unfamiliar house, with strangers all around me. I didn't know who to trust. So, I decided to keep my identity hidden for a little longer. After all, a young woman traveling alone in men's clothes was more suspicious than a boy."

"And when we arrived here? What stopped you from revealing your true identity then?"

"Fear." That was the truth. Partially. Mostly. "Eli was acting unfriendly toward me. He was suspicious and mistrustful. So, I decided to wait, but then he left. For a week. And..." Nika lifted her arms, palms up, and then dropped them, helplessly.

"But what about me? I wasn't unfriendly or mistrustful, was I? Why didn't you confide in me? I thought we were friends."

She was magnificent in her anger. Hands on hips, one foot tapping impatiently, pewter eyes shooting fire. Even with her face paler than usual, and with twin red splotches riding high on her cheekbones, Abby was a personification of royalty. A majorly pissed off royal.

"We were! Are. I hope." Nika lowered her gaze. "I am sorry, but I felt like I had to talk to your brother first, and let him decide whether he'd let me stay or turn me away. If he showed me the door, I would have left and you'd never hear from me again. In that case, I didn't need to subject you, or anyone else, to the unpleasantness of the situation. You have your hands full as it is with your upcoming engagement, and I didn't want to add weight to the disagreement between you and Eli. Please, believe me."

"He would never turn you away. My brother is the most honorable man," Abby said defensively.

Nika smiled. Nothing pleased her more than Abby's jump to defend her brother, even when she was mad at him. There was nothing like a true sibling's loyalty. Her own relationship with Alex was a great example of that. *Oh, Cuz, I miss you so much.*

"I know. Now," she continued quietly. "But I'd never met him before, just saw his pictures and heard rumors about him, so I didn't know what to expect."

"Hmm," Abby left her post by the window and went to sit on a sofa. She was mulling over Nika's explanation, still a bit guarded.

"He said you asked for his protection."

"Yes."

"When? How? Why?"

The girl doesn't miss much.

"Some time ago. When it became obvious that my situation at home became... unbearable. You see, my father and his twin brother are very wealthy men. Bankers. They rule our household with an iron fist, deciding what's best for everybody."

That was honest-to-goodness truth. The image of her father and his twin's faces, closed and autocratic, flashed in her memory. Their almost identical voices whispered in her inner ear, "We are so disappointed in you, Veronika." She quickly tuned them out.

"Did they want to marry you off?" Abby asked with some empathy.

"No," Nika swore not lies, even though this angle was more comfortable to pursue. "No, but they both wanted to rule my life—rule me—telling me what to do and how to live, what to wear and who to trust, what to like and not like. In short, I was smothered. I felt like I was slowly disappearing as a person, as a free human being. It couldn't go on like that anymore. I couldn't obey, but neither could I live under their roof if I wouldn't toe the line. So, I ran away."

"Alone, without money or any help?" Abby's eyes widened. "You are so brave, Nic...Daisy!"

"I'm not, not really. And I did have help. My cousin Alex and my grandmother, *Verochka*." Nika didn't elaborate. After all, did it really matter *how* or *when* they helped her? The most important part was, they did.

"So, there really is a French grandmother," Abby murmured.

"Yes. Everything I told you about her is true."

"And your cousin, Alex? What is he like?"

"The best. Kind, and funny, and loyal to a fault. He's my best friend," Nika's heart squeezed tight.

"I thought *I* was your best friend," Abby said primly.

"Oh, Abby," Nika chuckled despite the tears clogging her throat, "you are my best *girl*friend. Alex is..." She closed her eyes, took a deep breath. "He's family, and best *male* friend."

"And Eli?" Abby cocked her head. A small mischievous smile bloomed on her face, "I've couldn't help but notice you're calling him Eli now, not Mr. Coleman, or Mr. Elijah."

Nika could laughed it off, or deny it. But she was determined to tell Abby the truth.

"Eli is the best of them all," she answered quietly. "And I'm so much in love with him, it hurts."

Abby was visibly startled by her admission, but quickly took it in stride.

"Well, he *is* the best of the best, his tyranny and impossible stubbornness notwithstanding."

Then her pewter grey eyes became serious and troubled.

"My brother seems remote and cold, but he's nothing of the sort. He's just shielding his heart as best as he knows how, Daisy. You see, he was terribly hurt a long time ago. Eli suffered a tremendous loss when his wife died in childbirth. His baby died, too. I don't remember him before he went to London, because I'm so much younger, but I heard from Mrs. Smith and others that he returned a changed man. Cold, withdrawn. Guarded. What I'm trying to say is," she smoothed the invisible wrinkles on her skirt, then resolutely rose from the sofa. "Don't hurt him. Please. His heart is tender. It was broken before. If you truly love him, take care. Take a great care with my brother, please. And if you hurt him, well, then." She shrugged and smiled. "I'll have to kill you, Daisy, even though I would mourn your passing every single day. Because I like you very much. So there."

And then, Abby turned to the practical matters at hand such as a new wardrobe for Nika 'because you simply cannot traipse in men's clothing anymore'.

And just like that, they were, once again, the friends of the very best variety, girlfriends.

The following days were both the happiest and the weirdest in Nika's life. Like Alice, her favorite childhood book heroine, she found herself in a parallel universe of Wonderland, Fernandina circa 1909.

She now lived in the same house she was hired to restore in 2019, or a hundred and ten years in the future. And, if that wasn't enough, she had fallen in love with a man who had been dead for half a century.

She still hadn't found the key to the grandfather clock that was, she was sure, the portal between her time and this. Did she really want to find it? If she did, might that not tear her apart? Guilt and common sense warred with her heart and reminded her of the family left behind.

*Alex, Verochka...*Her head swam, and her stomach knotted at the memories of them, two people in the whole world that were most dear to her.

Until now.

Now she had Eli who had become the center of her universe, her rock, her anchor. Her lover. She was Daisy now, his Daisy. Nika Morris was slowly stepping aside, becoming a distant memory. She was disappearing. Slowly, inevitably.

Terrified, Nika fought for her every day, reminding herself of *who* she was by touching her toolbelt and beloved baseball cap. But every night, as soon as Eli took her into his arms, she became Daisy, willingly and without any regrets.

She never knew it was possible to love like that. Nika had been infatuated a couple of times in her life; surely was in lust, especially in her misspent youth. But she never was in love—true love—with a capital L, where nothing else mattered, except the person who become your life, your air, your blood. Your reason for being. That was the effect Eli had on her.

He was the reason she was alive and had her sanity intact.

Nika had no idea who could have listened to her absolutely unbelievable story and not committed her to a padded room. Instead, he made love to her like she was the most desirable, most beautiful woman on the planet.

She was worried how they were going to explain her story, and her true gender, to the members of the household, but Eli told her not to worry, that he had it under control. And he did, as easily and effortlessly as he did everything else.

Everybody accepted her presence in the house without a question, taking it in stride. Everybody that is, except William O'Brian.

While he was cordial and pleasant toward Nika as the boy, he became almost hostile to Daisy. Nika didn't know what to make of it. He was constantly watching her, as if waiting for her to make some dire mistake, or commit a crime. His mistrust was palpable. His silent accusing glances in her direction became impossible to ignore. No telling how long Nika could hold her temper before getting in his face and demanding an explanation.

But for now, she tried her best to ignore him and act normal.

For everybody's sake.

But all others were kind to her. Some were even protective. Even the formidable Mrs. Smith warmed toward her considerably. Was it because Nika saved the woman's life, or because Mrs. Smith trusted that Nika, being a daughter of wealthy New York bankers should know better than to disappear into the night with the family silverware?

One day, she placed two of Nika's favorite pastries on her plate without being asked, and muttered gruffly for her to 'eat every single morsel or else.' Nika had finally won that battle, too.

Abby brought up an idea that they needed to introduce Nika to the society. "The rumors will soon start running amok, no matter what," she said primly. "I think it best if we prevent that happening by acting first. We need to put together a welcoming party, and introduce our Daisy to everybody."

"Hmm," Eli pondered it for a brief moment. "I think that's a brilliant idea, Abigail."

And so, with Eli's blessing, Abby and Mrs. Smith put their heads together and started planning a grand party to welcome Nika to the community.

To say that Nika was a nervous wreck was a gross understatement of this and her own centuries combined. She was sure everyone knew her for the fraud and impostor she was. Nika begged both Coleman siblings to forget about the silly idea to no avail. Even Mrs. Smith turned against her, shushing her smartly, and going about her business of putting together an evening menu.

Everybody ignored her, rolling over her pleas, inviting people all over Amelia Island to introduce them to 'Daisy,' a visiting cousin from New York. There was absolutely nothing she could do to dissuade them, and with a heavy heart Nika gave up. The party was taking place with or without her agreement, so she just threw in an imaginary white towel. The hell with it. There was nothing she could do to prevent it from happening, so might as well accept the inevitable.

The grand event was supposed to take place on the last Sunday in September. The Coleman house was buzzing with activity, humming with anticipation and excitement. Everyone was busy with something to do.

Except Nika.

Eli was out of the house, overseeing his various business enterprises. Mrs. Smith was planning the party, commanding her troops like a general before the major battle. Claudine was running back and forth, doing God knew what. Mr. O'Brien stayed in his office, closed off for hours at time. Abby took care of the necessary tasks of ordering new evening gowns and choosing the jewelry for them both.

So, Nika was left alone, her idle hands and troubled thoughts as her only companions. With nothing to do, she spent most of her time outside with Belle, forlornly awaiting the night of the greatest embarrassment of her life. The dog commiserated by following Nika around like a shadow.

The night before the party, she and Eli had their first big fight.

It had started from a small thing, a disagreement about something insignificant that quickly snowballed, one word after another, into a full-fledged argument about women's rights in general. And Abby's situation in particular.

That afternoon Abby had approached Eli, demanding to call off her upcoming engagement. It was supposed to be announced on Thanksgiving, and with every passing day the girl was more frantic about it, begging her brother to reconsider. Eli refused her demands. Abby became enraged, then burst into tears and ran from the room, locking herself in her studio. She refused to allow anyone inside, even Nika. She also was absent at dinner that evening.

After they retired for the night, Nika decided to bring the subject up and try to reason with Eli. They talked a bit of tomorrow's party, and Nika again expressed her fears that everybody would see through her charade, exposing her for a fraud. Eli chuckled, and told her not to worry about a thing, that everybody will simply adore her. Nika doubted it, and his placating tone suddenly pushed the wrong button.

"What if they ask me about my family? What do I say?"

"Nothing." He shrugged. "Refer them to me, I will take care of everything, *ma petite*."

Nika bristled.

"So, let me get it straight, Coleman, I am to keep my mouth shut, smile and point everybody in your direction to answer all the questions, correct?"

"Yes, precisely."

He beamed like a proud teacher at the simpleminded student that finally got the lesson.

Nika barely kept her irritation in check. She bit her tongue, and reminded herself that she needed her cool for the conversation about Abby's future. *Hold your temper, girl.*

But it didn't last for long. As soon as Nika brought up the subject about Abby's engagement, Eli coolly and carelessly dismissed her concerns, like swatting an irritating mosquito.

"We shall not talk about it anymore, Daisy." He drooped a kiss on the nape of her neck, and then turned her around to face him. "Abby's marriage is a *fait accompli*. She needs to get used to the idea."

Fed up with his king of the manor attitude, Nika wrenched herself from his arms.

"Who put you in charge of the universe, huh? Did God suddenly retire, and leave you Her chief executive? Why wasn't I included on that bulletin?"

"I am absolutely sure that it's a blasphemy to talk about Lord this way, especially addressing Him as Her." Eli was taken aback, but made an effort to lighten the mood. Nika was having none of it. All the stress of the last few days had finally caught up with her, exploding in a flash of temper.

"What are you talking about?" She slapped at his hands when he tried to reach for her. "Of course, God is a woman! Who else would have been able to create a Universe out chaos in seven days flat?"

"Jesus was a man." Eli frowned.

"That's the matter of opinion!"

"What about disciples? What about Judas?"

"Now, Judas was definitely a male." She crossed her hands over her chest.

"Why? Because he committed a betrayal?"

"Because he was a moron suffering from insecurity!"

"If I recall correctly, some time ago you called me an insecure moron." Eli brought his hand up and tapped on his chin.

"I rest my case."

With that, Nika marched out of his bedroom. That night, for the first time since Eli had returned home, she slept alone in her old room.

CHAPTER TWENTY-TWO

The next morning Nika was wide awake and brooding. She had slept badly, tossing and turning half the night. She missed Eli's warmth, aroma unique to him, and the sound of his soft snores.

Stop it! Just stop it this instant!

She was disgusted at what she had become. There was nothing attractive about a needy, whimpering nincompoop.

Oh my God, now I'm talking like I belong in 1910!

Their fight saddened her more than it angered her. He was set in his ways, stubborn and controlling.

She needed to make him listen, sway him to see Abby's side of the story.

She must motivate him to relent and reconsider.

You are a fool, Nika.

She cursed under her breath and squared her shoulders. Fool she might be, but she had to forge ahead, because she, too, was stubborn enough to push and pursue her course if that course was important. And this one was super important, even vital. Abby's happiness depended on it.

Nika was on a quest to save the girl she had learned to love like a sister. Unfortunately, to win that quest, she needed to defeat Abby's brother, the man who meant everything to her. The man she loved.

And where would it bring them? What was the cost? The constant discord around the house, the arguments, the fights...How long could she endure it? How long before they were able to live in the atmosphere of continual disagreement and unhappiness?

There was no way in hell a sane person could tolerate that.

She needed to speak with Eli. Plead with him. Make him understand.

She missed him, damn his stubborn, tyrannical hide. Nika whipped the rogue tear rolling down her face. She would give everything in her power to make the siblings to reconcile their differences. What could she, a total stranger, the time traveler from another century, do? She couldn't even help herself. She was totally dependent on the Colemans for everything from the food she ate to the clothes on her back. Her hands were tied. She was limited in every aspect of her existence. But like *Verochka* said, we all have our limitations. The trick was to learn to use them to your advantage. If she failed to convince Eli, then she needed...to talk to Patrick Carnegie.

That stray thought popped into her mind out of nowhere. A small smile turned into a huge grin. If Eli refused to listen, then she needed to find another ally. A direct path to the goal might be the shortest, but not always the safest, or more successful. If Patrick was as unhappy about the upcoming nuptials as Abby, maybe he might be convinced to cancel. A brilliant solution to all their problems! She just had to snag him at the party, and pretend that she needed to talk to him about something important, and then...

I'll think of something.

The main point was to intercept Patrick before Eli did, and talk with the young man. If he was as kind and decent as everybody gave him a credit for, she just might make him see the truth. But first, she had to make herself ready to face the music, so to speak. Time to prepare for the party.

Nika jumped to her feet and raced to the bathroom. She twisted the bathtub knobs and deftly adjusted the water temperature. She took a moment to congratulate herself at how adept she had become with this century's way of doing things, bathing and personal hygiene included.

But she longed for a hot, steamy shower and the smell of her favorite body wash. Oh how she missed the minty taste of toothpaste and convenience of deodorant. Her hair weathered best, despite all her worries, and grew accustomed to a mixture of glycerin and egg yolk. But washing it for the first time? That was a challenge alright.

And the trial of wearing long skirts on a daily basis. Shirt waists were okay even though not her cup of tea. Thank God she didn't have to endure the torture of a corset, since those tools of Satan had gone out of fashion.

She missed her shorts and sandals and air conditioning. Oh, the cooling bliss of AC, especially on the hot muggy nights! All the things she took for granted once upon a time.

When Nika finally glanced at herself in a mirror later that evening, her eyes widened in shock. Who was the woman staring back at her?

Dressed in a ball gown of warm ivory tones and adorned with Coleman's family pearls, she resembled an image from a daguerreotype, softly blurred and old-fashioned. Even her unmanageable curls that Abby had parted on the side and clipped with a pearly comb, gleamed like an antique burnished gold, quiet and classy.

Who are you? What is your name?

Her bubbling panic grabbed her by the throat, making her lightheaded.

Because the woman in the mirror wasn't Veronika Morris. Frozen, she couldn't tear her eyes from the image. *Who the hell are you? Where is Nika?*

Fear of losing her identity was paralyzing. Her breath hitched, her heart beat like a trapped bird.

Where is Nika?

God only knows how long she stood in front of the mirror, searching for herself, before Abby, dragged her away.

Nika was still in grips of panic when she was thrown into the midst of the jolly crowd, and introduced to the friends and neighbors gathered in the brilliantly lit Great Room. Tongue-tied at first, she felt like Alice in her special version of Wonderland.

She bumped shoulders with the wealthiest men and women in America, ones she had once upon a time read about in her history schoolbook. That was enough to render her mute.

And deaf. And blind. And start questioning her own sanity all over again.

But soon she loosened up enough to carry a conversation with David Yulee, the father of Florida railroads, who turned out to be an intelligent and pleasant, if a bit stern looking, gentleman He was, according to Senator Lauder, Eli's uncle on his mother's side.

Her attention perked up when she was introduced to members of the Carnegie family. Miss Lucie and Mr. Thomas were not able to make a trip from Cumberland Island as they had a 'previous engagement.' Their son George and his wife Margaret, the owners of Plum Orchard mansion, were in attendance. But where was Patrick? She eyed the crowd. Did she miss him? She jerked herself back to reality when Abby introduced her to George and Margaret. Nika smiled, and thanked them both for their hospitality, praising their home and staff. They stayed reserved for a while, and eyed her a bit suspiciously, but both soon became talkative and carefree. They even laughed freely at some joke Nika managed, thanks to the third or fourth flute of champagne, to tell.

Where on earth was Patrick? Nika wondered for the umpteenth time. She was sure he must make an appearance.

Abby was clearly on pins and needles, her hands always in motion, her brow knitted. Probably bracing herself for the meeting with her future fiancé. The girl tried to hide her mood as best as she could, acting nonchalant, being a perfect hostess. But Nika knew her friend well enough by now. Abby was tense, and stretched to the point breaking point. She made an effort to stay by Abby's side, sticking close, just in case. At that moment Abby laughed at something, and turned her eyes to Nika. Only a blind person couldn't see they were dark and heavy like a rainy cloud. Nika's heart squeezed. Poor Abby.

She was such a classy thing, almost like royalty. Tall, beautiful, proud. A bit reserved. Her modestly cut baby blue gown hugged her body lovingly, making it long and sinuously fluid. Its color contrasted beautifully with Abby's black hair and accented her exotic pewter eyes.

Abigail Coleman was a looker, alright. Had she lived in the twenty-first century she would be called a traffic-stopper. No wonder all the young men watched her eagerly, fighting for her attention. And young Carnegie was still missing in action. Nika frowned.

Darn it, where was he? And what if he was in love with Abby? flashed in the back of her mind. *What if he truly wanted to marry her?*

That possibility hadn't crossed her mind. As inconspicuously as possible, Nika scanned the room. No Patrick anywhere.

Where is Abby?

Nika gave a nonchalant glance over her left shoulder. Abby was talking to an older gentleman, who was trying unsuccessfully to suck in his enormous belly. But even this funny picture failed to lighten Nika's mood.

She needed to find Patrick. Pronto.

If there's nothing I can do to dissuade Eli, then, I must discourage Patrick. Beg, lie, or threaten if I have to. Anything short of murdering the poor kid. If I ever meet him, that is.

The grandfather clock came to life, announcing the hour.

Ten o'clock. Where in blazes is this guy?

She stole his breath. From his chosen remote spot Eli observed every person in the room, but his eyes were only for her. Their argument the night before didn't sit well with him. Several times he was about to go to her room, but pride, and yes, hurt, stopped him. How can she question his decision? How can she take Abby's side? How *dare* she leave him standing like a fool, in the middle of his bedroom?

Stubborn, infuriating, perverse female! If she wished not to be bothered and sleep alone, well then, let her. There is no female born who will make me beg. No one. Until Daisy. Thunderation

He looked across the room. She was laughing and sipping champagne and thoroughly enjoying herself. His heart broke into a thousand pieces because he wasn't the one bringing her pleasure.

Eli shook his head, resigned to the truth. She had the power to make him do anything. Begging included. Because, damn her, she was the one for him. His mate, his other half, his destiny.

As soon as she entered the Great Room, she left him breathless. She was a vision in her flowing silk gown and his grandmother's pearls. Her silhouette shimmered, in and out of focus, whimsical, enchanting. One moment she was real, the next—a dream-like, shadowy image, ethereal, otherworldly, overwhelmingly fragile.

He barely contained himself from running to her, scooping her into his arms and whisking her away from all these people. He longed to tear her gown off and make love to her until his last breath. He wanted to stake his claim. If that made him a savage, he didn't give a fuck. He wanted her, pure and simple. She was *his* woman. His salvation. He had recognized her even in her ridiculous clothes, even when she was masquerading as a boy. Even when his eyes deceived him, his heart knew, and recognized its second half. Even when he ran away, tortured by the thoughts of his depravity, his soul recognized her and demanded reunification.

In his entire life he had never felt for another woman, not his late wife, what he felt for Daisy. The depth and intensity of his emotions were scary, overwhelming. He wanted to take care of her, protect her. From what?

Whom? His silent curse was born out of resignation. He followed her every move with his eyes, his shoulders stiffening, anger mounting inside him.

Look at her, smiling and talking with guests like an enchantress.

She wrapped them around her little finger. His mouth curved in a rueful smile. He expected nothing different. He almost laughed aloud when thoughts of Daisy, sick with worry about meeting his neighbors and friends, and fretting they may see her for a fraud.

A sip from his tumbler went a wrong way when Daisy laughed at some joke.

Who was she talking to? Ah yes, General Fitzpatrick.

The old gent was flirting with her. It was absolutely harmless, and then he dared to kiss her hand. Blood boiled in Eli. His vision turned red. He clasped the tumbler so hard it cracked.

Everyone was taken with her. They all sought her company. Animated, she talked, drank, and joked with every male in the room, no matter his age or status. But damn it, not him.

She was already accepted in the circle of rich and prominent citizens of Fernandina as an equal. And not a single soul guessed that she was *special*. A time-jumper. A guest from the future.

He wasn't sure he was fully convinced of it himself. Eli set the cracked glass on an end table at his left.

Time-traveler. What folly!

But she saved Mrs. Smith with an amazing medicine. Didn't she speak of things— troubling things, such as two great world wars, along with fascinating things, such as television and wireless telephones.

How could it be possible?

Eli was an engineer and a scientist. He dealt in numbers and cold, hard facts, not fantasies.

Time-travel. What nonsense! And still...

Eli accepted another drink from a passing waiter. He must be honest with himself. He either believed her or not. It was that simple.

If he didn't, then he must accept that Daisy was either the greatest liar, or dangerously delusional. But she was neither one of those things.

Damnation, she wasn't!

If he did believe her, then he must accept that she really is a woman from the future who was thrown back by a whim of his heirloom grandfather clock.

Eli was torn. His rational mind and his feelings were at war. He loved Daisy like he had never loved anyone in his thirty-four years on earth. But did he trust her? Did he believe her story? Completely, utterly? He shook his head unable to make a decision.

But even acknowledging this, Eli still kept the key to the clock hidden.

He nursed his second whiskey, but his mood darkened as he watched his Daisy.

Nika was tired. All the tension of maneuvering between total strangers and answering their questions, carefully censoring every word she spoke, and all the while searching for Patrick Carnegie, finally caught up with her. Eli's silent treatment worried her the most. Throughout the evening she sensed him watching her. He stood by the fireplace, drinking, but never approaching. At first, she was upset, then irked, then she became pissed off and then upset all over again. Nika was jittery to begin with, but by the end of the evening she was a quivering mass of nerves, hot and sweaty, irritated, and absolutely disheartened. She failed to talk to young Carnegie because he, by circumstance or design, never showed. The fact Eli was obviously avoiding her broke her heart.

On the other hand, she passed her first major test. She spoke clearly and with caution and acted like she belonged to their society. But most important, she neither fell on her face nor tripped on the hem of her ballgown.

The food was plentiful, the atmosphere joyous and carefree. The guests were quite nice, simple and kind, and not at all what she imagined the uber-rich were like. The upper crust society of Amelia Island had accepted her. By the end of the evening everyone believed her to be the wealthy daughter of a banker from up north visiting Florida. It was a huge relief, and a great victory. Yet she wanted to cry.

When somebody carried a gramophone into the room, and started the music, Nika decided it was high time for her to make a stealth exit. She couldn't dance if her life depended on it, so before some brave soul invited her to waltz, and cause her imminent embarrassment, she set her drink down, and slipped away toward the exit. Many guests began dancing to the lovely tune she didn't recognize, creating an unfortunate obstacle on her path to freedom. Nika plastered a smile to her face, and pretended to enjoy the festivities, all the while gliding out of the room. She was almost at the doors, and about to make a run for it, when a hand grabbed her upper arm, halting her progress. Cursing under her breath, she turned around.

"Going somewhere?"

Eli's deep baritone reached her ears before his face came into her focus.

She whipped the false smile off her face, and tried, unsuccessfully, to shake off his hand.

"As a matter of fact, I am."

"But the evening's still young. The dances just began."

"I don't dance," she answered hauntingly, glaring up at him.

"Why not?"

"Because I can't."

"Can't waltz?"

"Can't anything: polka, waltz, Charleston, boogie. I was born with two left feet, or so my family say."

"That's a shame. I'm not sure what Charleston or boogie are, but I hope we can manage a simple dance together. I'll teach you."

"You don't know what you're saying. I'm going to ruin your perfect shoes." She pointed at his shiny, obviously very expensive, footwear.

"Don't you worry about my shoes, *ma petite*. I have plenty," he said, dismissing her objection easily. "Will you do me an honor?" He bent his arm at the elbow, offering it to her in formal invitation.

"Don't say I didn't warn you," she muttered even though she was dying to try to dance. Especially with Eli.

The tune changed. Familiar first chords of Strauss' *Tales from Vienna Woods* filled the room. Nika paused, and was about to tag her hand free from his but Eli was having none of it. He tightened his grip on her hand, leading her along, then smoothly turned her to face him. Nika held her breath. They were in the middle of the brilliantly lit ballroom. The conversation ceased, and all eyes were on them.

And suddenly time stopped.

The sounds, the lights, the people, everything disappeared, leaving the two of them in an enchanted place between time and dimension.

She gazed at him. He was staring at her with a reassuring smile on his face. She stood there, hovering on the brink of something magical, too mesmerized to breathe, too stunned to move.

Then Eli blinked, and broke the spellbound moment. The present rushed back at Nika in a flood of dazzling lights and sounds, making her dizzy. She took a breath, then another.

"Don't look now," Eli murmured quietly into her ear, "but you are dancing, *ma petite*."

"I am?" Still bedazzled, she glanced down and snorted loudly, making a few heads turn in their direction.

"Ha," she chuckled. "It's cheating, that's what it is!"

Her feet were piggybacking on top of Eli's shiny shoes and moving in smooth steps to the rhythm of the waltz. *Verochka's* words sounded in the back of her mind, "It takes two to tango, my dear."

Or waltz. Oh, Verochka, if you could only see me now.

"You are sad. Why?"

"I'm not."

He lifted his brows, clearly unconvinced.

"Well, if you must know, I just remembered my grandmother. I miss her."

Eli just tightened his grip on her waist.

"Do you wish to go back?" he asked after a long moment.

"No. Yes. I don't know."

She was torn, and when she lifted her eyes, she read the pain in his as clearly as an open book.

And why are you so surprised, chump?

"I don't want to leave, but...I wish I could give my family peace of mind. They must be going crazy with worry about me. I just— *puff!* — disappeared into a thin air."

He frowned and remained silent.

"Are you mad at me?" Nika asked after an eternity of a heavy silence.

"Mad?" Eli tilted his head. "No. Why do you think that?"

"Well, after our quarrel last night, and... everything." She shrugged. "You ignored me all evening."

"I wasn't ignoring you." His lips curved into a half smile. "Well, maybe a little. You are a hard woman to ignore, Daisy. Or stay mad at for long."

"So, you are no longer angry?"

"No."

"Good. Then, maybe we could talk—"

"Maybe we could just dance and enjoy ourselves a bit? We will talk later."

"Promise?"

"Promise."

"Okay. Can you please put me down? People are watching."

"Let them."

"Your feet are going to get numb," she protested.

"You don't weight but a pound," he countered smoothly.

"Well, thank you kindly, sir." Nika batted her eyelashes like women did in old movies. Then in an exaggerated southern accent she added, "It's a fine compliment, indeed."

A carefree chuckle burst free from Eli. They were still entwined in each other's arms even after the final sounds of the Strauss waltz dissolved into the night.

CHAPTER TWENTY-THREE

He must be mad. Truly mad. Or else she bewitched him. How was it possible that he, a man of four and thirty, shook like a boy at the mere glance at her? The smell of her. The taste of her. The feel of her. No matter how many times he made love to her it was never enough.

How pathetic that all he thought of was the color of her unruly curls when they caught the sunlight? And what folly was that?

Eli looked up from the business contract he failed to grasp and let loose a string of swear words to stop himself from daydreaming.

Land sakes, man, get ahold of yourself.

But he couldn't stop thinking of her any more than he was able to command his heart not to beat.

He was addicted, and Daisy had become his drug of choice. *Thunderation.*

There was no cure to it save one.

Eli shoved back his desk chair and then stormed out of his office.

A few minutes later, he found her in her old room. The door was ajar and there she was sitting on the bed, pensive, lost in thought.

So small, tiny actually, and so sad. So unbelievably vulnerable.

Lord, how he wanted to cradle her in his arms and make everything all right again. Protect her from the world. Make her smile. Mostly he wanted her with him forever. He needed her with him to feel whole.

Eli tapped on the door to no avail. He walked in and glanced at the short, narrow bed, more suited for a child than an adult. Eli managed to ease his hip onto the corner. The bed groaned as it adjusted to his added weight. Still, she didn't acknowledge his presence.

"Daisy? What are you doing here?" Eli slid his eyes to her. No woman had ever moved him like this slip of a girl coiled into herself. He was afraid to touch her. Afraid to scare her. He sat there with his hands at his sides unsure of what to do. He decided to wait because she needed to act first.

"I searched the house from top to bottom before I found you. Are you hiding from me?"

"No. Yes."

This wasn't the conversation he had intended. "So, is it yes or no?"

"I don't know. Just needed some thinking time."

"About?"

"You. Me. Us."

He stopped short. More than anything he wished to know what she was thinking. Did she have doubts? Regrets? Or worse, had she decided to leave? Fear stopped his heart for a moment.

No, no way in hell.

He regained his senses and asked, "What is there to think about?"

A small smile trembled on that unholy mouth of hers as she turned to face him.

One glance, that was all it took to set him on fire. His blood began to churn. For God's sake, he would go raving mad if he failed to taste that mouth.

Why this woman? Why her? She incited his passion like no one before her. And her eyes.

My God, those eyes.

Cotton Mather, and his fellow Salem Puritans, may have ordered her burned at the stake once upon a time.

"Oh, Coleman, you are such a guy." His beautiful little witch shook her head.

He had grown accustom to her peculiar use of words, but this one confused him. Had she accused him of being a man?

"I am, yes. And very glad of it. And you are such a woman, *ma petite*."

She grinned, the wench, then burst into laughter. But her merriment was short-lived. She caught his gaze and held it. Like a magnet, her siren's eyes pulled him into their amethyst depth. He was drowning and didn't give a damn. All his senses sharpened, focusing on her. Afternoon sun streamed through the single window and turned her curls into a halo of burnished gold. He could swear he heard her heart beat, fluttering in her chest like a hummingbird's wings.

His nostrils flared as he inhaled her unique fragrance of warm honey and wild flowers, sweet and earthy and incredibly fragile. *Like magic. Daisy smelled of magic.*

Enthralled, he couldn't tear his eyes off of her. She slowly untangled her bare legs from under her full skirt.

Silk shimmered. The bed creaked. His need for her exploded.

Daisy scooted closer, and then looped her hands around his neck. Her amethysts eyes darkened as she gazed into his.

"You know what, Coleman?"

He had to swallow hard before he was able to answer. "What?"

"My thinking time's over."

And with that she began unbuttoning his shirt. Her nimble fingers moved slowly, grazing, and then she brushed her knuckles against the sensitized skin of his chest. He hardened more with each stroke.

Little tease. So, she wants to play.

But he needed to know.

"And did you come up with an answer?"

Harsh even to his own ears, his voice stopped her mid-motion. She tilted her head and eyed him.

"About?"

"Me. You. Us."

"I have. Yes, I have indeed."

And she continued to work the buttons open on his shirt with one hand while her other laid on his thigh. The heat was scorching him and making him harder than he had ever been.

"Tell me," He barely choked out.

Eli leaned back, his hands supporting him on the little bed, and soaked up the pleasure of her touch. It was pure torture. Sweet, hot torture.

Thank you, Jesus.

"Nope. I'd better show you."

His shirt came undone. Daisy moved it out of the way, spreading her warm hands over his chest. His heart hammered and Eli prayed a heart attack didn't steal his pleasure. She lowered her hands and hooked her thumbs into his belt right before her hot lips began to play along his throat.

He was burning alive. The anticipation was akin to pain, but he revealed in it. Undone, tethering on the brink, Eli sunk his shaking hands into her hair. Smooth as silk, soft as breath.

A low moan broke free when those soft golden curls brushed against his hot skin.

Agony.

Torture.

Bliss.

He would die if he didn't touch her. But when he reached for her breasts, she smacked his hands away, and proceeded to kiss a wet path down his torso. She was driving him mad.

Daisy still had on all her clothes while he was almost naked. The image struck him as the most erotic picture he had ever seen. He was excited, hard as a rock, frustrated, and ready to beg. She tugged her blouse free, and then dropped it to the floor. Her skirt and panties went next, leaving Daisy gloriously naked.

"Now it's your turn to tease me."

And that ungodly mouth of hers covered his, stealing his sanity.

CHAPTER TWENTY-FOUR

September gently faded opening the way to October that, in turn, unhurriedly and gracefully bowed out to November. The days were still balmy, but nights became crisp and breezy and long, as was customary for Amelia Island. Two months had passed since her arrival. Some days it was all like a dream, and she vaguely recalled her own time. And some days the reality hit her like a sledgehammer, leaving her sad and lost. And somehow, somewhere along that blended line between a dream and reality, she stopped her quest for the key.

What was the point? *Was* there a point to begin with?

Some days she brushed it away as easily as her unruly curls. The other days she almost doubled over with shame and remorse.

She wasn't mistreated, or wanted for anything. Far from it. Nika was well fed, well dressed, and treated with kindness and respect, but she was guilt-ridden, and that guilt weighed heavily on her.

She disappeared even though by no design of her own, and hurt the two most important people in her life, Alex and *Verochka*. They were constantly in her thoughts. Did they still search for her? Did they miss her as terribly as she missed them? She dreamed about them often, waking up in tears, inconsolable in her grief. If not for Eli, Nika well may have fallen into depression.

Eli. Elijah B. Coleman. The man who wrote her the mysterious letter.

The man who somehow was responsible for her time traveling journey.

Nika was convinced she had jumped through the century because of Eli. Because they were meant to be. They belonged together. Sometimes nature made a mistake, an oopsie-daisy, and two halves of the whole were born as far as one hundred-plus years apart.

She loved him more and more with each passing day, so much that soon it was all she felt. That infinite, overflowing love, deep and true and profound.

He brought her so much happiness. Guilt swept through her for being blue and maudlin. He was her joy and hope, even though they often butted heads, mostly because of Abby's upcoming engagement. He treated her like she was the most precious thing in the world, and even though he never said a word, Nika was sure he loved her as desperately as she loved him.

They never spoke of the key, or her time traveling adventure. Yet it hung between them like an invisible barrier that they were too wary to approach. Did he believe her confession? He never said, and she didn't press for the answer. More than likely, he was as reluctant to discuss the subject as she. She just hoped he kept an open mind, which was all she could ask for.

They talked for hours on end, and spent a great deal of time together, learning about one another. She told him about the twins, about her Grand Adventure, and of course, about her grandmother and Alex.

He told her about his life in London, about losing his parents and raising Abigail. But he omitted the tragic story of his wife and child.

They often went for walks, strolling along Main and Centre Street in downtown Fernandina. Nika told him about the new businesses and stores that in her century were occupying them. She recognized the courthouse, the railroad station, and the big building on the corner of the 4th and Centre Street that became the Nassau County Library, her favorite research place. But the *Chao*, an Italian restaurant, or *Jack & Diane's,* a charming café that had a slogan 'Food with Attitude' on its sign of course were not yet built. At number 310 Centre Street she stopped and gazed at the display window with longing and sadness. In her time, it was home to her most favorite store, *Celtic Charm,* a quaint boutique where she bought Christmas presents for *Verochka* and Alex.

But when they approached the future building of Before & After, Inc. she fought to keep her tears at bay. Heartbroken, she begged Eli to take her home, where she spent the rest of the day in the company of Belle and horses, well-hidden in the stables.

Did she want to go back? Did she want to leave the man who had become the center of her universe, and return to her own place and time? Even a month ago, the answer was yes. Now? She was confused. The simple truth, she was happy here, but she missed her own time. Her life had splintered into two parts, the before and after. The apt name, the one she gave their dream company a long time ago, now became her personal slogan.

Or the story of her life.

Before she was Nika. Now she was Daisy.

Before she had a profession she loved and was successful at. Now she had idle hands, and too much free time to do nothing productive but reminisce.

The only thing that remained the same was the main trait of her character. She was a rebel, and a strong defender of an underdog. She never tolerated an injustice on any level, social or domestic. Hence, her constant arguments with Eli, and their never-ending battle about Abby's future.

She loved him to distraction, so much that it hurt. He was the only man on earth who could make her ecstatic one moment, and mad as hell the next.

He was the only one for her. He was her destiny.

They became inseparable, day or night. After that singular incident on the evening before the party, they hadn't slept a single night apart. They tried to keep it a secret, for propriety's sake, but Nika was sure no one was fooled, and that everybody in the household knew.

But no one dared to contradict Eli.

No one that is, except William O'Brian.

One day, in early November, he asked Eli for a meeting. It was such a formal request, that Eli lifted both brows in surprise, but obliged nevertheless.

"What's on your mind, William?" he asked without preamble as soon as his secretary and friend entered his tower office.

"That woman who lives in this house and shares your bed."

Eli pondered that for a moment, then answered, his voice dangerously soft. "Her name is Daisy, and who I chose to share my bed with is entirely my business, and no one else's."

"You have your sister living under the same roof, so I think you'd be more considerate of her feelings, if not others."

"Are you, by chance, accusing me of impropriety, my friend?"

"That's exactly what I'm doing, *my friend*."

If it were anyone else, Eli would throw that person out without question, but not before enjoying a punch or two. Since it was William, the man he liked and respected, the man he had known for a long time, Eli paused and chained his temper.

"What truly troubles you, William? Why are you acting this way? I know you, know the man you are, and that's why I am more concerned than insulted. So, out with it."

William glanced at the floor then straight into Eli's face. "I apologize for crossing the line."

"Never mind that, just tell me what's bothering you so?"

"That...Daisy. You said her surname is Morris, and her father and uncle are twin brothers who run a bank in New York City."

"Yes." Eli tensed. "What of it?"

"I sent some inquiries, and guess what? There are no bankers with that name in New York City, or anywhere if New York state, for that matter. She's lying to you, Eli. She's just some opportunist that came to you under a false pretense. God knows what's on that woman's mind, but she's playing you for a fool!"

"You know me, what? Eight, nine years? And during all those years, have you ever seen me played for a fool? Do I look gullible to you?"

"No, but there is a first time for everything, my friend. Women in general are clever and dangerous creatures, and this one—"

"William, please sit." Eli debated between the fib and truth, and decided to follow his heart. "What I am about to tell you, will seem preposterous at first. It is a secret no one is privy to except Daisy and me. And now, you will be too."

And he told him the whole story. When he finished, the silence was oppressive.

"And you believe her?"

William's face wore an incredulous expression bordering on pity.

Eli's gut knotted, and he regretted his foolhardy decision to reveal the truth to William. But it was too late.

"Yes. I know it sounds unbelievable—"

"Crazy! It sounds absolutely insane." William jumped from his seat. "Eli, the woman is a lunatic."

"She's nothing of the sort," Eli exploded in a rare spurt of temper. "And you'll do me a great favor if you refrain from addressing her in a similar manner in the future."

"Have you forgotten that she was searching the house, while you were away, looking for God knows what?"

"I know what she was looking for. This." Eli went to the fireplace and put his arm deep into the lion's mouth. When he withdrew his hand, he held the brass key. "She was searching for this key. That was what brought her here. She was hoping to use it and get back to her own time. But she didn't find it, since I had it with me all of that time. And she will never find it." He reached into the lion's mouth again, and secured the key into its hiding place. "Because neither I nor you will tell her where it is. Correct?" He pinned William with his eyes.

"If she's so keen on getting back, just give her the key and be done with it."

"Never."

"Listen, just listen, Eli. Give her the key, and see what happens. If she's lying, then you'll know it, and act accordingly. If she's telling the truth, then she'll disappear and—"

"Never!"

"But she's an impostor, if not worse."

"She is my fiancé. My future wife!"

As soon as he said that, a great deal of weight slid off his shoulders. He hadn't broached the subject to Daisy yet, but he knew without a doubt that she loved him. Their destiny was to be happy together. They were created for one another. They were meant to be. Of that he had no doubt. None whatsoever.

William's mutinous face was closed and guarded.

"What about my cousin? Have you forgotten her already?"

"I'll never forget Mary for as long as I live. And I was a faithful and good husband."

"I know, Eli, but..." William took a deep breath. "She was my family. And I loved her. When she died..." he turned away, "I thought I was going to lose you, too. You were hurting and acting like a man who didn't want to live."

"I didn't. I was about to end it. I was very close to doing it, too, but then the message about my parents' demise came, and I was needed home, so I returned. And there was Abby."

Eli closed the distance between them, and touched the younger man's shoulder. "For the first time in ages I'm happy. I have a purpose and reason to wake up every morning. I have hope. Please, don't spoil it."

The silence in the room hung in the air.

"And William," he said in a softened tone. "Please don't make me regret my decision of confiding in you. I trust you with my life, and now I have entrusted you with the life of the woman I love. Please take care."

"I'll honor my word to you. I won't betray your trust or your confidence. But one day, Eli, you'll remember my warning. One day you shall regret your blasé attitude in this matter, and learn the truth the hard way. I pray it won't be too late."

With that, William turned and marched out of the office.

More pensive than disturbed, Eli touched his chin with his fingers, and pondered his friend's final words. Then he dismissed the nagging feeling of doubt they evoked, and resolutely strode out of the room. He had many things to do in between now and Thanksgiving Day, when Carnegies were descending on Amelia Island for Abby's engagement. He had three weeks to settle his own affairs of the heart, so the shine wasn't stolen from Abby and Patrick's special day.

The ocean was gentle, cool, and smooth like a silk sheet with fringes of lacy froth. Warm sand slipped between her toes. The salty air tickled her nose. Home.

She shielded her eyes with her hand, and lifted her eyes to where the sky blended into horizon. Then she turned around and tilted her head, expecting to see the familiar hexagonal form of her house. But instead, up ahead, above the dunes, a gorgeous white and cream structure, tall and imposing, with the single turreted tower, met her gaze.

The Coleman house.

She smiled. How clever of Eli to move the house closer to the sea and to hers and Alex's home. Her home? But wasn't the Coleman house her home now? So, where did she live? Where did she belong? Behind her the ocean rolled, regal and majestic. Above her a lonely sea gull circled, lost and forlorn.

Nika woke with a start. Quiet. Too quiet. And empty. The room had that special vacant vibe. She was alone. Strange. Usually, Eli, a habitual and annoying early raiser, moved about, waiting for her with a cup of coffee. But she preferred those mornings when he engaged her in lazy and sweet lovemaking. But not today. Disappointment threatened to take control. She pursed her lips tight. Something was off. She sensed it ever since Eli's meeting with William yesterday. He became more withdrawn than usual, and at times distracted. Long stares, apprehensive frowns.

Why is he looking at me like that? Almost like he's afraid. Of me.

Which was absolutely ridiculous. Eli never feared anything or anybody. Least of all her.

Nika stretched and blew off the annoying curls out of her eyes. Her hair had grown too long. Two months without a trim, and her curls were almost unmanageable. The next time she went to a salon, her stylist would have a heart attack.

Next time? And when might that be?

Maybe never. She shrugged. Did she really care? Nope. She wasn't a high-maintenance girl like her mother, or her aunt and cousins. She could always hack it herself, if it came to that. Or let it grow. Eli was quite fond of it, and twirling up a stray curl around his finger became his habit. And her pleasure.

But her hair, annoying as it was, was far from her biggest problem. Her semi-annual birth control shot was due soon. If she missed that then trouble loomed ahead. With their super active sex life, she might get pregnant the instant her protection stopped working. What if she conceived?

And what of it? Was it be too horrible to become pregnant with Eli's baby?

Her hand crept lower to cover her belly. How did it feel to have a life growing inside of her, unfolding, moving, expanding?

Nika bolted upright in bed and yanked back her hand as if she had touched a live wire.

A baby?

What was she thinking? She wasn't, that was the problem.

"Idiot," she muttered. "You are nuts, Nika-Daisy. Like totally and certifiably." Her position in this house, and in Eli's life, was questionable. For all she knew, he was quite content sleeping with her without any further obligations.

They hadn't talked about it, not the future. Did they even have a future? All Nika had was her present, in 1909, and her past, in 2019. Or vice-versa.

She was afraid to entertain the notion of a future. Oh, God, it was so mixed up and confusing! Nika kicked the covers off then swung her legs over the edge of the bed and hopped down. She grabbed her robe, stuck her feet into slippers, then stomped to the bathroom. The main point was that they didn't talk about them as a couple. Come to think of it, they failed to discuss anything lately except Abby's engagement. And talk, Nika chuckled humorlessly, was a ridiculously inappropriate description for it. What they did was constantly argue. And every time during those arguments, Eli became colder and more withdrawn. While she grew madder than the proverbial wet hen. Yet every night they made up, albeit silently, when he took her into his arms.

But as fantastic as their lovemaking was sex didn't solve the problem, and the next day everything was repeated all over again. Nika was sick of it.

"This has to stop." She frowned at her reflection in the bathroom mirror. "You have to break this crazy pattern, Nika-Daisy. You must!"

And she would. Or die trying. Furiously, she attacked her teeth with the long wooden toothbrush that was impossible to get used to. As soon as she found Eli, she planned to inform him that she was sick and tired of their constant quarrels. An apology was needed, not because she had something to apologize for, but to rake in some brownie points, and offer a solution. A compromise. Just that, a compromise between two intelligent, civilized people that implied talking about things they disagreed on openly and calmly, without any sulking or yelling. She intended to promise to stop defying him. She vowed to do her damnedest to stick to that promise, even if it killed her. And he must promise to stop treating her like a simpleminded female, or a convenient body. She was an intelligent human being, dammit! She had her own opinions, strong ones. She had her own mind, sharp and smart, if she did say so herself. She was an independent, successful businesswoman.

You're getting bent out of shape, Nika. Is that how you compromise?

Ashamed of herself, she worked to slow her breathing.

In and out.

In and out.

Truth be told, Eli always treated her with respect and kindness, even when she was 'the boy.' He never made her feel cheap, Nika admitted, ashamed all over again. Just the opposite, in fact. He made her feel cherished and valued. He just kept things from her, like the real reason for that meeting with William O'Brien. Nika grabbed her brush and dragged it through her hair, wincing and cursing because the tangles refused to be tamed. She exercised the wisdom of grabbing the sheers and cutting it herself, here and now, but reconsidered. The heck with it, she scowled and dropped the brush. Her mind circled back to yesterday's meeting between Eli and William. Eli glazed over what was discussed, "nothing of importance." However, they both behaved quite unusual afterwards. Eli was distracted and pensive, and William simply disappeared. His seat at the dinner table was empty. Mrs. Smith informed them that 'young Mr. O'Brian has begged off,' claiming some important engagement in town. Nika suspected that his 'important engagement' was a convenient fib to get out of the house.

She blew out a breath. There was only one explanation. She was the main reason for that meeting. William was probably trying to warn Eli against her, or to convince him to...what? Kick her out of the house? Report her to the authorities? Probably, all of the above. She drew a deep breath, and noisily let it out. Honestly? It was more baffling than aggravating. Why? She genuinely didn't get it. What did she do? Or didn't do? William never tried to cover it. Whenever they were in the same room, he either openly ignored her, or shot poisonous glares in her direction. If eyes had the power to kill, she would be dead ten times over by now. God knew, she did her best to avoid the confrontation. It was hard, and she was literally biting her nails, trying not to get in his face and demand an explanation. But no more. Her avoidance tactic obviously failed, so it was time to change it. Time to get aggressive.

Yes, he was Eli's friend, and yes, he was a part of the family, but enough was enough. Her patience had finally run out. If William wanted a war, she was happy to oblige, but first, she needed to find out what that war was all about. Pumped for action, Nika nodded at her reflection in a mirror.

Ready, set, and go, girl, go.

She had her morning schedule all lined up. First, find Eli and have her important talk with him. Second, corner William O'Brian and get their grievances aired out. Once and for all. Satisfied, she belted her robe, and went to dress for the day.

CHAPTER TWENTY-FIVE

Eli was impatient. After he retrieved the ring from the family vault at the bank, he wanted nothing more than to get back and get it over with. He galloped all the way home, giving Sultan the pleasure of running fast and hard. The horse sensed excitement, and flew as if he had sprouted wings. By the time Eli dismounted, they both were sweaty and winded, but well satisfied. He handed the reins to the stable boy and then looked deep into the horse's intelligent black eyes.

"I'm sorry, boy, for not taking care of you myself. I'll bring you a carrot later, I promise." He kissed Sultan on the nose and patted his sweat glistened neck. "Wish me luck, boy."

Sultan blew warm air into Eli's face and then made a gruff sound that Eli took as a horse's blessing.

He turned and walked to the house, taking a shortcut through the gardens.

Eli found Daisy sitting on the grass in the middle of Abby's butterfly garden, with Belle's head on her lap. The ugly mutt seemed to gaze adoringly at Daisy while licking her hand. As soon as he approached, Belle tensed, moved closer to Daisy, and remained as if she were consigned to guard duty.

"You're going to ruin your skirt, you know. Those grass stains are stubborn, and impossible to get rid of," Eli said and plopped down beside her.

"I'm sorry." She raised her tear laden eyes to his. "I'm so sorry, Eli."

A sudden realization that she would definitely try to go back *if* she had the grandfather clock key disturbed him.

Will she go back forever? Or for a short visit? He had no answer, and that bothered him even more.

"I am so sorry," she whispered brokenly.

"For grass stains? Daisy, I was just joking. Please, forget I ever mentioned it." Eli's heart stopped when he noticed the shattered expression in her eyes. He cursed himself for being so clumsy. "Daisy, please, *ma petite*, forget about it. That was plain stupid of me."

"No, it wasn't." She moved to stand. "I really am going to ruin this wonderful skirt, and you are going to ruin your pants."

Eli took her hand, tugged at it, and stopped her.

"We have more where it came from, both of us. God knows, we keep the tailor in this town quite happy."

"Supporting local business?"

"That I am. You weren't crying because of the skirt, were you?"

"No," she admitted, but failed to look at him.

"What then?"

"Oh, I don't know. It's silly, but I woke up alone, after a strange dream; and then I went to breakfast, and no one was about, and I felt...abandoned."

"Abandoned? Look at your champion here." He nodded toward Belle who was cowering behind Nika's back, whining softly. "This one would never leave your side."

"No, she won't." Nika smiled at the dog and scratched behind her ears. "So, where did you go? I was looking for you, but Mrs. Smith said you left in a hurry at breakneck speed. Her words. I was afraid something happened."

"No, nothing happened. I...I made a short trip to my bank." He touched his breast pocket. "I needed to take something out of the family vault."

"Oh, well, that's good then. I needed...I wanted to talk to you. Very seriously."

"I want to talk to you, too, Daisy. Very seriously."

"Okay, then, you go first."

"No, ladies first."

"But I'm no lady, you said so yourself."

"I did?"

"Yep, on several occasions." Nika motioned with her hand "Go ahead."

"Maybe we should move to the house."

"Why? The weather is perfect, our garments are soiled anyway, so shoot, Coleman."

"Shoot?" He hesitated. "Why would I want to shoot you?"

"It's just an expression," Nika laughed. "It means, go ahead, start— shoot, understand?"

"Oh, alright, if you insist."

God knew, he wanted to do it properly, like he had done it the first time, with Mary. But proposing to his first wife was different, he decided for a lack of better description. The situation, time, and woman were all different. What was proper and right for Mary, wasn't for Daisy. Eli cleared his throat.

"First, I must ask you if there is anyone who I need to ask for permission."

"Anyone? Like who?"

"Like your father, or uncle, or brother."

"A male member of my family, you mean?"

"Yes."

"Huh. You know very well I do have a father, and uncle, but both of them are not..." "Wait, hold on, you said permission?"

"Correct."

"You lost me, Eli. Permission for what, exactly?"

"To marry you."

Daisy seemed to freeze. Her eyes became huge and round like two saucers.

"But...but...did you say...marry? Marry me...?"

"That's what I said." Eli's mood boosted at her surprise.

"But...that's impossible!"

"Why? Give me a single reason."

"I'm...I'm...I don't...I can't..."

"Don't love me?"

"Of course, I love you!" she shouted fiercely. "I love you more than...than... anything!"

She threw her hands wide as if to encompass the world around her.

"I love you so much it hurts! So much that it's scary."

His heart beat heavily, almost painfully against his ribs, as if trying to escape its confinement. She loved him. Deep in his heart he knew it, but hearing her say that changed everything. It broke him to pieces. It made him humble. It gave him wings. And once again, everything was right with the world. He took her hand, kissed it, entwined their fingers. Yes, this was right.

"Then, what?" he asked, smiling at her.

"You know, what! I came from...another time!"

"So, what?"

"So...so, I don't belong here!"

"You belong with me, Daisy. That's the truth. I don't care where you came from, or who your parents are. Look at me, look at me, darling."

And when she did, tears spilled down her cheeks. All the love in the world shone back at him from her eyes.

"I love you. Deeply. Desperately. I never thought I was able to feel what I'm feeling for you. Not after...after my wife died. I thought that my life was over. But then, one fine day, you dropped out of the sky, right in the middle of my path, and changed my world forever. I loved you when I thought you were a boy, a street urchin who tempted me with feelings so dark and forbidden, I felt ashamed. I cursed myself, I fought with myself, but was powerless to erase you from my mind. When I discovered the truth, I lost my head. My heart, as it happened, was already lost to you. So," he took the small velvet box out of his breast pocket, and opened it. "When I first looked into your eyes, they reminded me of my grandmother's amethysts. She was quite fond of them." He took a ring out of the box and placed it on her finger. "I went to the vault today to retrieve that ring. It reminds me of you. I hope you like it."

The pale solitary amethyst, large and oblong, set on a simple gold band, sparkled and pulsed with a deep lilac fire. The beauty of the ring captivated Nika.

"Oh, my God," she murmured, mesmerized by the ring's exquisiteness.

"Well, say something."

"Like what?"

"Like: yes, Eli, I'll marry you."

"You didn't ask me to marry you."

"Come again?"

"You said you loved me, and many, many nice things." Nika managed tremulous smile. "But you didn't ask me to marry you. Not officially."

"So, I didn't." Eli hefted himself onto one bended knee, and then took both of her hands into his. "Daisy, my own wild, beautiful flower, my unexpected gift from the universe, my everything. I want to share my life with you, wake up beside you every morning, make babies with you. I promise to cherish you, take care of you, and protect you until my last breath. I love you. I want you. I need you. Will you marry me?"

Nika went with her heart. She kneeled, facing him, brought their joined hands up, and turned them before she kissed his knuckles.

"Yes," she answered. And then threw her arms around him, laughing and crying at once. "Yes, yes, yes!"

He tugged her into his arms. The movement propelled her forward, and pushed him backward. They lost their balance and collapsed onto the grass in a laughing, rambunctious heap.

The dog, forgotten now by both of them, jumped back, then tried to squeeze in between, barking loud and furious.

"She thinks I'm hurting you," Eli managed in between kisses. "Tell her to stop chewing my foot, or you'll have to marry a cripple."

"Belle," Nika found her voice, "Eli's a friend. Friend, Belle. Stop it this instant."

The dog stopped her mad antics, and sat, still quivering and growling, but didn't move away. She was clearly intimidated by Eli, but her devotion and love for Nika overweighed her fear.

"She hates me."

"She doesn't trust you."

"That's even worse."

"She'll learn to love you."

"She will?" Eli lifted one brow skeptically.

"Absolutely."

He glanced at Belle, who answered with a deep guttural growl.

"I applaud your optimism, Daisy."

"That's not optimism—an intuition rather."

"Okay, if you say so," he turned his laughing eyes at her. "Now, it is your turn."

"My turn?" Puzzled, she cocked her head, puffed impatiently at her curls, and arched her brows in question.

Just look at her!

She was so ridiculously adorable: disheveled, slightly out of breath from their impromptu romp in the grass, with a tiny patch of dirt on the end of her pert nose. Delighted with her. With them. With life in general. When was the last time he had been so joyous and carefree? *Never before Daisy, that's when.*

It was liberating to laugh when the mood struck, or smile because why the hell not?

"My turn...? Oh, right! My turn, of course." She leaned forward and planted a hot, hard kiss on his mouth.

"Mm-mm," her taste lingered on his lips long after the kiss ended. "Exquisite, *ma petite*. Not exactly what I meant, but..."

"What *exactly* did you mean?" She eyed him suspiciously. That look made his blood sing.

"Well, we both declared that we wanted to talk to each other. I stated my business." Her pulse bit strong and true where his fingers pressed against it. His kiss just below the place where his ring now adorned her finger, was gentle, almost reverend. He smiled at her. "Now, darling, it's your turn. What is it you wanted to talk to me about? Not that I'm complaining about the kiss, you understand."

"I wanted to offer you a compromise, and totally forgot about it!"

"A compromise?" He gave a short bark of laughter. "Darling, I'm afraid the meaning of the word is absolutely foreign to you."

"I can compromise," Nika pouted, then seemed to catch herself and forced her lips into a straight line. "I can, it's just..."

"Just?"

She shot a quick glance at her hand where his ring now encircled her finger.

"Yes, I was about to propose a compromise as a peace offering, because I'm sick and tired of our constant fighting—"

"We do not fight," he corrected. "We argue."

"Well, fight, argue, quarrel—no matter what you call it, it still sucks. Big time."

"It does?" Eli asked cautiously. He already opened his mouth to clarify the meaning of the phrase, but smartly closed it. *Better not.*

"Oh, boy, does it ever!" Nika wind-milled her hands to demonstrate, then yanked at the lock of hair that continued to fall into her eye. "But you know what I realized?"

"What?" Fascinated, Eli rose on his elbow, and then tucked the offensive curl behind her ear before she pulled it clear from her scalp.

"That compromise I was about to propose? Scratch that."

"Okay, I will."

At that moment he would do anything she asked of him. Even if he had no idea whatsoever how to 'scratch' a compromise. He resolved to find that out later, and pray to God it wasn't anything embarrassing for a man of his stature.

"What we need is a partnership. A partnership!" Nika exclaimed triumphantly, grabbing both of his hands. "It sounds right, it feels right. It's just perfect for us. Don't you agree?"

"I have never had a female partner before."

"Well, you have now. A marriage partner." She winked at him then lifted her left hand and made rolling motions with it. His priceless amethyst sparkled in the sunlight. "Because a marriage, as I see it, is a partnership between two individuals. I might be bad at compromising, but I'm very good at partnership deals. Just ask my cousin Alex."

As soon as she said that her expression plummeted.

The dog pressed into her hand as if offering sympathy

"Do you miss them? Your family," Eli asked gently after a pause.

"Yes." Daisy wiped a single tear away. "Very much. I know you don't believe me, but I wish you could meet them, my grandmother and Alex. He's more like my best friend than a cousin. I put him in trouble more times than I can count. And still, he always stuck by me. And my grandmother...You would get such a kick out of meeting them both!"

His heart was breaking. Eli hugged her gently, offering all the comfort possible. He wanted to do anything— give her anything— just to make her smile at him again.

No, not anything, he corrected himself. Not the key. Not the one thing she wanted the most.

And he regretted not giving her back the members of her family she missed so deeply: her cousin and her grandmother.

But he vowed to give her his home, his family, and, God willing, his children. He promised to give her stability, comfort, and independence. And his wealth, so she never wanted for anything She was to have the best of everything money bought. He had already given her his heart, broken and mended, and his love, unconditional and unbounded, and everything in him he had to give. Until the day he dies.

"I wish we could invite your family at our wedding," he said, a twinge of guilt biting at him.

Wedding?

Nika froze in the warm cocoon of Eli's arms.

"Wait, wait, what wedding?" She pulled from his embrace. "Who said anything about any wedding?"

"I did. And not about *any* wedding—*our* wedding. You know, the day when the engaged couple are going to church, and..."

"I know what wedding means," she interrupted, "I just don't understand what it has to do with me?"

"With *us, ma petite*, with us. Remember? Partnership?"

"Yeah, but—"

"What's wrong? Changed your mind already?"

"Of course, I didn't change my mind, but, Eli..." she swallowed audibly, "a wedding? *Our wedding?*"

"Yes, soon-to-be Mrs. Coleman, that is correct. Our wedding. You are going to make such a splendid bride."

"Splendid bride, my boot." She squeezed her hands together to stop them from shaking. "Listen, let's simplify, shall we? Let's just go to the church, get hitched, and then come back home. Okay, okay, we can make it a special family dinner, if you insist, but just us. Just family. Please?"

"Get...hitched?" Something in between confusion and horror flashed on his face.

"I don't know what you think I said, buddy, but 'get hitched' means get married, make it official."

"Dear Lord, Daisy," Eli blew out his breath, then shook his head. "One of these days you'll be the end of me."

"One of these days, Mr. Coleman, I'll teach you the modern slang of the twenty-first century." She grinned more relaxed now that they were on her turf. "But don't try to change the subject. I am serious about this big wedding deal. I don't want it."

She had no idea why she was so opposed to the idea of a large wedding. The mere thought of it nauseated her.

What's wrong with me?

Better ask what's right with you. Her nasty inner voice was always there to cheer her on.

Bitch.

"I thought every woman dreams of a big, splashy wedding."

"Not this woman."

"Obviously not." Eli sucked in a deep breath, and let it out. "Are you sure, Daisy? Nothing would make me happier than giving you a traditional wedding with all the guests and trimmings."

"I know." She stretched up and kissed his dimpled chin. "I'm sure I want to marry you. Just without all the pomp and circumstance."

"Very well, then.," Eli rose to his feet. "Since we don't have a guest list and reception to plan, we don't have to wait to get married. I will arrange with our priest for the ceremony on Saturday."

"Saturday? But that's in three days!"

Eli misread her distress. He tipped her chin with his index finger and then placed a soft gentle kiss on her mouth.

"I know, darling, I am impatient too, but I just got word that I'm needed in St. Augustine."

"You're leaving?" Nika grabbed Eli's hand. Panic clawed at her throat, suffocating her. Drowning her. "Please, don't. Don't go, Eli!"

"I am sorry, Daisy, but I must. It's business. I will be back before you know it, *ma petite*."

"How long?" She clutched both his hands until her knuckles turned white.

"A day, two at the longest."

Fear of never seeing him again paralyzed her. She wanted to beg him to stay, to cling to him, to plead with him. But instead, she smiled through the sheen of tears that made his face slightly out of focus. "Just get back as soon as you can."

She always despised clinging and needy women and she'd be damned if she started acting like one.

CHAPTER TWENTY-SIX

Before he left, Eli once again gathered everyone in the parlor, like on that memorable day two months ago, when he introduced 'Daisy' to the family.

This time, however, he announced the news of his and Daisy's upcoming nuptials.

"The wedding will take place in three days. Everybody is invited, of course." With his arm around Nika's waist, he tugged her closer to his side, and kissed the top of her head. And then he smiled.

And such a sweet smile it was. Mrs. Smith sniffed. The glow on her face proved she believed her boy was happy and at peace, finally. She crossed herself as if she was thanking the merciful Lord that she lived to witness this wondrous moment. The household erupted in loud cheers and well wishes for the bride and groom.

The groom grinned like a man who just had his first glimpse of paradise, and happily accepted congratulations.

The bride, however, was subdued. Nika hid her eyes from everybody. Her smile, if anybody cared to look was forced.

In the circle of Eli's arms, unsettled and uneasy, Nika shut her eyes. What was the reason of her dismay? As a testament of her enormous will, her smile was still plastered on her face.

Something is wrong. Correction: something awful is about to come.

A storm was brewing, slowly but surely. Her gut told her so. But what was the problem? They were happy, they loved each other, and were about to get married.

Yeah? How about the fact that you are marrying a man who's long dead?

Stop it! He's alive and well. He's right here.

But for how long?

"After the small ceremony in church," Eli continued in his velvety baritone, interrupting her troubled thoughts, "we will celebrate privately, in the tight circle of our immediate family, as per my bride's wishes."

He took Nika's left hand, smiled down at her, and kissed it.

"Is that what you wanted, *ma petite*?"

His smile lit up his face, making him appear younger than his years. And how old was he?

Thirty-four? Five?

I don't know, don't remember. And how strange is that?

She forgot all the details on the subject of her research about Elijah B. Coleman. Because he was no subject to her any longer. He was a man, her lover, soon to be her husband.

"How old are you?" She blurted, startling herself.

"Thirty-four. Too old? I'm afraid it's a bit late now to change your mind, Daisy, my flower. Look." He turned her around.

Abby yelped and jumped up and down; misty-eyed Claudine chirped fast in French; other servants clapped their hands and grinned, while some swiped tears from their cheeks. Even the formidable Mrs. Smith shed a tear of joy. Only one member of the Coleman household was absent. Since William O'Brien was still missing in action, Nika didn't know what his reaction might be, but she had a feeling that it wasn't a happy jubilation.

"You are just right for me," she answered quietly. "Just right. Just you."

Suddenly overwhelmed, she buried her face into his chest, inhaling the painfully familiar smell of him. He wasn't in the habit of using any colognes or fragrant soaps; he wasn't a smoker, so he smelled just like the air and skin and... him, just Eli. Nika wished she could cry, but her eyes were hot and dry.

"Please, come back soon," she choked out. "Come back to me."

Eli left a moment or two later. His small suitcase, thanks to Mrs. Smith, all packed and waiting. That brown satchel with its unmistakable classic Louis Vuitton pattern that hadn't changed for a hundred-some years squeezed Nika's heart with panic. The feeling she may never see him swept over her.

Ridiculous. He'll be here tomorrow night, Friday morning at the latest. He promised. Eli always keeps his promises.

She didn't see him out. The urge to grab him and beg him to stay, or take her with him, was too strong. Too desperate. Too scary.

Nika stayed inside, locked herself in the library and pretended not to hear the door had closed after him.

And just like that, the vibrancy and energy of the house was gone. Sucked out.

The vacuum became abysmal.

How will I survive two days?

You must.

How?

Just suck it up, Daisy-girl. One step at the time, one day, one hour, one minute...

The house was too quiet, too empty and forlorn. Or was she projecting her own emotions? She paced aimlessly around the room, touching this and that. Missing him. Fretting.

This was so not like her, the old Nika Morris, who shook off her gloom, and found something to do, something productive, such as...such as...

Nothing came to mind. Nika shook her head in defeat. What was there to do here? Re-do this gorgeous, professionally decorated mansion? Build an outbuilding? Or a doghouse for Belle? Frustrated, she paced the room again. If she planned to live here, she had to kiss her profession goodbye, because no one would accept a woman contractor.

If she planned to live here, she needed to find something new to occupy herself, so as not to go stir crazy. She wasn't a southern belle, or house-wife material. She was a modern, independent woman with a successful career who knew how to stand on her two feet.

Yeah, sister, but that was in the twenty-first century.

The million-dollar question was, what could she do here, at the dawn of the twentieth century, being the wife of a rich man? Hold tea parties? Organize balls? Volunteer in church? What?

Distressed by the prospect of her future, Nika dropped onto the piano bench. She was tired, and disgusted with herself for moping around. It was so not like her. She ordered herself to shake it off. Tomorrow Eli will be back. On Saturday, they'll get married, and together they'll definitely think of something for her to do, to stay busy, and productive.

Everything will be back to normal as soon as Eli returns.

But deep down, she knew that there was no more normal. Not for her.

And what was *normal*, anyway? Nothing was normal since the day she met Senator Lauder and accepted his restoration project. Nothing was the same after she read the letter written to her by the one and only Elijah B. Coleman, ordering her to find the key and '...*hurry up...*'

So much happened after that. Her normal life ceased to exist, and Nika Morris had first transformed into 'the boy', then Daisy. She met new people, made new friends, even a new enemy in Mr. O'Brian, and saved a life. She fell in love for the first time. And somehow, her life here, in the Coleman household circa 1909 became her new normal.

Nika calculated: forty-nine days. She'd been here forty-nine days. Just a tad under two months.

A lifetime. Or a brief moment.

Forty-nine days. Such a ridiculously short period of time for such a mind-boggling, life-changing journey. The longest forty-nine days of her life— a century and a decade long.

Nika shook her head, trying for an umpteenth time to sort it all out in her mind. This time warp was so confusing. The past, the future. Her past was Eli's future, her future Eli's past. What was the present?

Her brain struggled to catch up with her emotions, because deep down, in her heart, she knew she was exactly where she was supposed to be.

Where she *wanted* to be.

But in her mind, she was still trying to figure out all the whys and hows.

In her mind, she was still wrestling with reality and fiction, with science and myth. With cold hard facts of physics and seductive dreams of fantasy.

But her heart didn't care. It trembled, and loved, and was sure, and content.

It was a balance, a very tentative one at best, but Nika managed to keep it.

Until today.

Until Eli put his grandmother's ring on her finger.

Until this freezing dread crept inside, and her mind signaled to her heart that something was wrong. And her heart skipped a beat.

Silly. She was just being silly. But silly or not, Nika was seriously freaked out. She caught herself on the verge of wringing her hands. So instead, she laid them on the piano keys and started to play.

"I didn't know you can play." William pushed away the drape he stood behind and stepped into the room.

Nika jumped. Her fingertips slammed onto the keyboard. But she managed to recover quickly. "You don't know a lot of things about me, Mr. O'Brian."

"I know a lot more than you think I do," he countered smoothly. His face was drawn, his lips pursed as if he were keeping a tight leash on his emotions. "Eli told me everything."

"Everything?" She cocked her head. "Well, that's probably for the best. So, tell me, Mr. O'Brien, what do you think? Am I a liar, an opportunist, or just crazy?"

"What I think," he said as if he were measuring his words, "isn't important. It doesn't matter. But what matters the most is what Eli thinks. And he seems to be blind and deaf, and totally under your spell."

"You make me sound like a witch. Or some kind of a femme fatale."

"Let me assure you." He came to stand in front of her with his hands clasped behind his back. "I don't for a moment believe you're either. You are," he tilted his head as if he were mocking her, "just a woman with an agenda I have yet to decipher. At first, when we met, and you were masquerading as a boy, I thought you were a con artist, but a harmless one. So, I wasn't very concerned. Even when Eli insisted on bringing you here, and giving you a room and board. But I kept my eye on you just in case. Something about you was...unusual. Your language, for one. Your exceptional belt with all those tools. Or your painted toes."

"My...toes?"

"Yes. I've noticed your red toenails. You removed your shoes once, when you were frolicking in the grass with the dog. And it immediately caught my attention. The boy who lost his memories and paints his toes? No, something was definitely not right, I thought. But I kept my doubts to myself. I didn't want to frighten Miss Abby, or Mrs. Smith, but especially Eli. So, I took it upon myself to follow your every step. I became your shadow. When you started your systematic search of the premises, my uneasiness intensified. What kind of a con artist, or a thief crept, night after night, around the house, and not steal anything, even a silver teaspoon?"

"I wasn't going to steal anything. I was searching for one particular item."

"I know. The key."

"So, you know about the key."

"I told you, Eli revealed everything to me."

She closed her eyes. Her enemy was the demon she anticipated.

"Then you saved Mrs. Smith's life in front of my eyes, and I started to think that nothing about 'the boy' was as simple or harmless as it might seem to the naked eye. And I was right. Turned out, our boy 'Nick' was actually a girl 'Daisy,' a daughter and niece of rich New York bankers by the name Morris, who, after I made some inquiries, were a figment of someone's imagination. Or another lie."

He turned and came to stand in front of Nika, his blue bespectacled eyes as hard as sapphires. Because she was sitting down, he towered over her, giving him an advantage.

Nika hated it. She rose from the bench and backed away. All her bravado aside, she was suddenly frightened. They were alone in the room, with the doors shut.

Even though not as big as Eli, William O'Brien still had a few good inches on her, not to mention his sheer physical strength. Lithe and slender he might look, but the bulging muscles on his arms were quite impressive. What scared her the most was the barely controlled menace in his eyes as he stared at her.

"I came to Eli with this information," he continued smoothly, his cultured British accent more pronounced than usual. "Hoping to open his eyes, and make him see the truth, but—oh, wonder, —he knew all about it already! It seemed, you were one step ahead of me, my dear. Remind me to never play chess with you."

"I don't play chess."

"Pity. You would make an excellent Grandmaster. Or Grand Mistress? Anyway, where was I? Oh, yes. So, Eli sat me down, and confessed the truth about 'Daisy' that was even more unbelievable than Jules Verne's fantasy novels. As it happens, you, my dear, are a time traveler from the future, the one that jumped from one century to a hundred years back, to find her true love and her destiny." He smiled, but it had a mean streak that gave Nika chills.

"Hundred and ten," she added automatically.

"I stand corrected." He made a formal bow that meant to insult. He succeeded.

"What if I can prove to you that I really am from the twenty-first century?"

"How?" He lifted his eyebrow.

"Here's how." Nika took a small item out of her skirt pocket and offered to him.

"What is that?"

"A trail mix. My usual snack I always keep on hand. It so happens, when I was hurtling through time, from my century to this, I had a couple of these snacks in my toolbelt you admired so much. So, they came with me. I found them later, when I was searching through my tools for an EpiPen, the one that saved Mrs. Smith's life. That medicine, by the way, was invented in 2004, if I'm not mistaken." She nodded at the tube of a trail-mix in his hand. "This is a mixture of different nuts and dry fruit that if not unusual by itself, has packaging that isn't known to any manufacturer yet. And here, look at the expiration date." She pointed with her finger at the small black letters and numbers. "See? 'Best used by 10/15/ 2019.'"

"What...what is that?"

"The proof. I came here from the year 2019, William. I don't know why or how. Well, I can guess why, but not the how part of it. I swear, one moment I was standing in the Coleman house in my time, and the next—I was lying on the road, and Sultan was barreling toward me, with Eli on his back."

"You are...telling the truth, then? But...but how? How is that possible?"

"I wish I knew." She shrugged and wished this entire afternoon never happened.

"Do you wish to go back? To your time?"

"Yes, but not forever. I just wish I could see my cousin and my grandmother one more time, and reassure them that I am well and happy."

"And for that, you need the key from the clock."

"Yes."

"What if it won't work?"

"Well, then, I will forever miss them, and feel guilty for giving them so much worry and pain. I can't even imagine what they're thinking by now."

She sat back on the bench, spent and sad, all her fright about William forgotten.

"But that's a moot point, since I never found that damned key, and Eli refused to give it to me."

He stared at her as if weighing his remarks. "What if I can bring it you, would you still wish to go? Abandon Eli, even though you're soon to be his bride?"

"I will not abandon Eli for anything in the world, William. But I need to take a quick trip back in time— or forward in time—to reassure my family, and then return. Eli is the reason why I'm here. He is my destiny."

"My, my, how melodramatic." He almost spat those words in her face. "I know your sort, so don't try your act on me, my dear."

"I'm not *your* dear, and you don't know jack about *my sort*." More curious than hurt, Nika studied him for a moment. "You know, I've wanted to ask you for a long time. Why do you hate me so much? What did I ever do to you to deserve that?"

"I don't hate you."

"Could've fooled me," she spit back.

"I just don't like you."

"You liked me enough as a boy. You were kind and considerate. Even funny. But when I became Daisy, you turned on me like I was a leper. So, what gives?"

"What gives what? You're confusing me with your unorthodox language."

"Translation: what happened to make me," she pointed a thumb toward herself, "your number one enemy?"

"You want to know the truth? Okay, here is the truth: you are a woman with an agenda. You slithered by a deplorable means into this household, then you lied, pretending to be a boy. Then you seduced Eli, no doubt bestowing your sexual favors on him. Now he wants to marry you. You! The woman with questionable pedigree and no manners to speak of, not to mention body or face."

"My, my, so much passion, and so little sense. I would get it if I were the reason his marriage to your late cousin was destroyed. And I'm guessing, ever since her untimely and very tragic demise, Eli wasn't living like a monk. So, he must've had mistresses."

"And what of it? He is a man in his prime! Of course, he needs his...satisfaction...now and then. But his mistresses were just that: a convenience, a tool to achieve a physical release. No more than that. But you..." he took a deep breath and turned away, visibly struggling to calm himself down. "You enchanted him. Put him under a spell. You completely turned him into a different man. He looks at you, and he lights up. From within. He lost his head, his heart. He lost himself. Because of you. All because of you." He turned his eyes toward her. They blazed fire. "I don't just hate you. I abhor you. I wish you'd disappear."

"Ha," she said, keeping her eyes on him. "William, if you were a female, I' swear you're jealous." She smirked, meaning to crack a joke and lighten the atmosphere that had become thick with tension.

William recoiled like she had slapped him.

And then Nika knew.

"Oh, my God." She took a couple tentative steps toward him. "You're in love with him!"

CHAPTER TWENTY-SEVEN

Suddenly bleached of all color, his face contorted with pain.

My god, of course.

"Oh, William, I didn't know. I thought...but, oh, God. I'm sorry, so sorry. I can't even imagine..."

"No, you cannot."

"How long?"

He gave one harsh laugh that broke on a low moan. "All my life."

"Does Eli—"

"No!" He screamed, and spun away. "No. He doesn't. He cannot know. Please! If you have an ounce of compassion in you, you won't tell him. I know I don't deserve it. But... I beg you."

"It's okay, don't worry. It's okay. I won't tell, of course I won't." Nika went with her heart and touched his arm. His muscles bunched under her fingertips before he jerked back, averting his face. She wanted to give him some comfort, but didn't know how. And what could one say in a bizarre situation like this? Sorry you love the man I'm going to marry? It was unbearably sad, not to mention humiliating. For both of them.

William averted his eyes. He was standing erect, with his back to her, but his shoulders were slumped in defeat. Nika's heart was breaking for this proud man, who was born a century too soon. Fate, she mused sadly, was a fickle bitch indeed.

"You don't have to be afraid, William," Nika said softly. "Your secret is safe with me. God, it must be terrible for you to watch Eli and me together, to be his confidante, all the while...No wonder you hate me so much."

"I don't hate you," he added wearily, rubbing his eyes with one hand.

"Of course, you do."

"No, really, I just..."

"You just love him."

He hung his head low in defeat, and pressed his fingers against his shut eyes.

"I tried to fight it," he uttered. "God knows, I tried, but..."

After a pause, William put his spectacles back on, and took a broken breath.

"And here I am, as pathetic and pitiful as ever."

"You are neither. You're just in love."

Nika didn't know what to do for this torn man. She felt his pain and shame as acutely as if it was her own. Ridiculously guilty, she tried to come up with something to say, something to do for him, but had nothing. And what could she, the woman who was his rival, say or do to ease his struggles?

"My love is shameful," he whispered after a long pause.

"There is no such thing as shameful love!"

"Forbidden then."

"In my time, the love between same sexes isn't forbidden. It's quite normal, William. There are marriages between two men, or two women. Official marriages."

"And the states allow it?" His gasp was inaudible. It broke Nika's heart.

"Yes. Absolutely."

"It's a wonderful time you live in, then."

"It is. It was," she sighed, "it surely was. But even here and now, maybe you can find someone who shares your... preferences. Maybe someday you too will be happy."

"Are you laughing at me now?"

"No! God, no. But there must be more men..." She wanted to say *gay*, but was he familiar with the word in her context? Very unlikely. "Like you, even in this century."

"There might be. But it will not do me any good, even if I met someone like me."

"Why not? In time, you may meet someone you can respect and love."

"Respect? Maybe. Love? Never."

"Why not?"

"Because there's only one Eli Coleman."

They both fell silent. The silence grew, until it became uncomfortable. Nika tried to come up with something to say, but William beat her to it.

"I know where the key is, Daisy."

That stopped her cold.

Was it possible?

Bewildered, frightened, she reminded herself to breath.

"The... key?"

"Yes, the key to the grandfather clock. Eli swore me to secrecy, and he would never tell you where it is. But I can bring it to you. Tonight. You can go, see your family, and return while Eli is away."

"Really? You would do it for me? Even if it means lying to Eli?"

"I don't look at it as lying. Just doing something that he wouldn't approve. But you should be back in no time, so he might not even know about it. And if he finds out, I'll tell him the truth."

His tormented eyes were impossible to look into. Nika's heart was breaking for the poor guy. She longed to touch him, to bring him some comfort, but was afraid to be rebuffed. So, she curled her fingers, clasping her hands together.

"Why?"

"I want to do something for you. Please, let me. Accept it as a gesture of my gratitude, and my deepest and sincere apology."

"Oh, William." Overwhelmed, Nika ran forward and hugged him hard. "I'm so, so grateful! You don't know what you just did for me."

"I'll go fetch it. Meet me by the clock at midnight. Everybody will be in bed and fast asleep by that time."

Nika still had trouble grasping the truth. Was it possible that in a matter of hours she might be back in her own time and place, and see Alex, and *Verochka*?

On the heels of that jubilation came a really sobering thought. What if the clock failed to work? Or, what if it did, but inaccurately, and sent her tumbling through time to some other place? What if she ended up in the eighteenth century?

Or twenty-second?

Well, I guess there's only one way to find out.

Nika squelched her fears, and squared her shoulders. She had been searching for the darn key for too long to refuse the opportunity. Especially when that opportunity was dropped into her lap.

No time to chicken out, sister. You have to try it.

If she didn't, there was always what if and regret for her indecision.

"What was that piece that you played? I didn't recognize it."

She blinked a couple of times, tilted her head, and then shook it.

"It's called *'The Wings,'*" she answered in a moment. "Did you like it?"

"Yes, even though the melody is...very unusual. It's sad, but uplifting."

"Huh, 'sad but uplifting,'" she repeated, smiling. "You described it wonderfully, William. This piece has an amazing story, you know. An amazing *love* story. One great musician composed it for the little girl he saved. Both her parents perished in a hurricane, but she survived. He found her by a sheer miracle." *And wasn't that the truth.* But Nika doubted William would believe that her good friend Al Gabriel found and saved his future wife in his dream. Not many people did, even in her time.

"She was badly injured, and wanted her mom and dad. And so he lied that they grew magic wings and flew away. When she asked to see the magic wings, he promised to show them to her one day. And so he did. With his music."

"What happened to them?"

"They lost each other for a long time, and then they met again. She became a doctor, a surgeon. He is one of the world most famous pianists. They fell in love" Kira and Al's smiling faces swam in her memory. "And they lived happily ever after."

"A doctor? A woman became a doctor? A surgeon?"

"Yes," she chuckled. "In my time, there are women doctors, women pilots, even women senators. We almost had a woman president, if you must know."

"Now you're mocking me."

"Not at all, William. Time comes when a woman can do anything, be anything, she wants. A woman in my century is free to choose her own path and her destiny."

"If that's the truth, I don't understand why you want to live here."

"Don't you?"

She stepped closer and stood in front of him. She raised her head, and sought his eyes. Then she reached out and touched his face with her fingertips. Her caress was brief and soft. Like the touch of wings. Like her melody.

"And you didn't recognize *The Wings* because it was written in the year 2000. A hundred years from now."

"A hundred and nine," he muttered.

"You're okay for a guy," she said with a wink and lightly punched him in the arm. "When I'm back, we need to talk, you and I. You know, to air our differences, so to speak. I hope with time we can become friends. I'd be happy to call you my friend."

And she offered him her outstretched hand. His eyes shot open wide. After a long moment, he lifted his own hand and took hers gently. She laughed again, and pumped it for all she was worth. William seemed surprised to find such a strength in her grasp.

"So, midnight by the clock?" she asked eagerly.

William lowered his gaze and stared at her hand still clasped in his.

"Yes, midnight," he replied finally.

"Daisy?"

Maybe because it was the first time he called her by her name, or maybe it was something in his voice, but Nika's body jolted like from an electric shock.

"I hope you will forgive me one of these days. For everything."

For a long-charged moment, he stared at her as if he wanted to commit her features to his memory.

And then he was gone.

Finally, after an eternity of waiting, pacing and dreading, midnight descended.

Well, almost midnight. Unable to sit and wait in her room, dressed in her own black jeans and t-shirt, Nika crept downstairs well before their rendezvous time. She paced in front of the grandfather clock and strained her ears for William's footsteps. The curtains on the corner window were drawn halfway so the moonlight gently streamed inside, creating an otherworldly atmosphere. But at least it helped to navigate in semi-darkness. Nika took it as a good omen. She preferred to tolerate the eeriness of the moonlit room than risk the use of an oil lamp she yet had to master. She looked at the golden face of the clock for the umpteenth time, fretting, fidgeting. What if William didn't find the key? What if he changed his mind? What if he wasn't coming? She looked at the time again, but it was still short of twelve. If he wasn't here at midnight sharp, she decided to hunt him herself and wrestle the darned key from him by force.

"Come on, William, don't do this to me, not now!"

She had no doubts that William told her the truth. No doubt he knew where the key was. But what if Eli got suspicious, and changed the hidden place? Then what?

Eli...

That gave Nika a momentary jolt, and stopped her in her tracks. Just thinking about him made her weak at the knees. All her nervous energy that had her moving for the last few hours dissipated and left her nauseated. That nagging feeling of looming disaster she experienced earlier. Only stronger.

His face swam in front of her eyes.

Oh, Eli, I hope you'll forgive me.

Nika entertained a notion of leaving him a short note just in case and then firmly dismissed that thought. She decided not to insult him with a written explanation of her transgression. She planned to tell him the truth, face to face, when she came back. And accept all the blame. Confess that she blackmailed William into giving her the key. Eli wasn't a cruel man. He would forgive William, she was sure.

And you? Will he forgive you?

Good question.

He'll understand, if not forgive. I hope.

Hope springs eternal, my girl.

Oh, shut up.

Even if he returned later than her, Nika still decided to tell him everything.

Her quick zip back and forth, as she calculated, should take no more than eighteen to twenty hours, max. Her plan was to return home tomorrow by six, just in time for dinner.

Home.

As revelations go, this one was of a quiet and pleasant variety. Somehow, somewhere along the way, the Coleman house became a home. Her home.

As if seeing it for the first time, Nika slowly turned around the room.

What once was a dream project, and could be the most successful achievement in her professional life, was now simply home.

And that thought wasn't alarming or surprising anymore. Somewhere, somehow Nika accepted the fact that here was where she belonged. Accepted and embraced it. As simple as that.

She took another deep breath, let it out and checked the time. Ten to midnight. She almost groaned, but caught herself. Sounds carried well this time of night, considering that there were no hums or noises from nonexistent household appliances. And the only disturbance of silence came from the hypnotic *tick-tock* of the grandfather clock. It was unnerving, and irritating. *And scary as hell.*

Nika shivered, crossed her arms over her chest in a protective gesture. She strained her ears for a sound— any sound— but there was none.

The Coleman house was ominously quiet.

Like it's holding its breath.

Where did that come from? Nika shrugged.

She shivered, chilled to the bone. What the heck? Did the temperature inside the house suddenly drop? Or was it just sheer nerves and excitement?

What was that sound? Her gaze flew up the staircase. Was that William? No, there was no one up there. Just darkness. Strange, there was definitely a creak and a footstep, Nika was sure of it. Irritated that she jumped at shadows, she checked the time again. Five to midnight. Where was he?

"Come on, William. Hurry up!"

And suddenly, as if conjured by her will alone, there he was, right there, standing so close to her, she jumped.

"Jesus, why don't you just whack me over the head, and be done with it?"

"A...what?"

"Nothing. You scared the living lights out of me, is all. Where were you? I was afraid something happened, and you didn't get the key."

"I retrieved the key. Not a thing happened. Here it is."

The shape of the antique brass key was painfully familiar. Lying on William's outstretched palm, it seemed so small, dull, and ordinary, it was almost impossible to believe it could be anything but a simple key. If there was a classic example of the phrase 'appearances can be deceiving', this was it.

Mesmerized, Nika stared at it, afraid to hope, terrified to touch.

"Changed your mind?"

And like a slap in a face, William's voice brought her out of her trance.

"No." Sucking on a breath, Nika snatched the key out of his hand, and moved toward the clock. Its golden face gleamed in the dark, encouraging her. Or daring?

Unable to force herself to take that last step forward, Nika cursed under her breath.

What is wrong with me?

Torn apart, she was impatient to move, but reluctant to insert the key into the keyhole.

Swearing out loud to bolster herself, Nika tightened her grip on the key.

"Daisy?"

Nika almost jumped out of her skin. She was so intent on her inner battle, she barely paid attention to William. As a matter of fact, she all but forgot about him. She flicked a quick glance over her shoulder.

"Yes?"

William was almost at the staircase, one hand on the banister.

"Be happy. And..." he hesitated, like he wanted to say something else, but then just shook his head, and repeated: "... just be happy."

And he was gone. Alone, with his parting words hanging in the air, Nika tried to shrug off the sudden chill.

Be happy?

What a strange and unexpected farewell, especially since she expected to be back in a few hours. Why not 'be safe,' or 'see you soon'?

She didn't have time to reflect on this, before she was grabbed by her arm from behind. Nika yelped, jumped, and brought both fisted hands up, ready to fight. And got another shock to her system, as she faced the person who ambushed her.

"Abby! What are you doing here?"

"I know everything, Daisy. I know who you are."

"What are you talking about? Of course, you know me."

"Stop pretending! I heard you and William today, in the library. You are...from another time!"

Nika really didn't have time for this. "Listen to me: I'm kind of in a hurry, so let's discuss everything when I'm back."

"No, we won't discuss anything, because I'm coming with you."

"What? Wait! No, hell no!"

"You are supposed to be my friend! You said you wanted to help me!"

"Of course I do, but coming with me isn't the solution."

"If you won't take me with you, I'm going to scream bloody murder and bring the whole household down, and then you won't go anywhere!"

"First, eavesdropping, and now blackmailing? Well done, Miss Coleman."

"You left me no choice."

Nika glared at Abby. She was dressed in her best overcoat, sporting a jaunty French hat, and clutching an oversized travel bag with both hands. It appeared to be heavy and cumbersome.

What the heck did she pack for a journey to 'another time'? *Her entire dowry?*

In contrast with her ridiculous appearance, Abby's face was dead serious, paler than usual, but determined. No doubt she'd scream 'bloody murder.' What was she supposed to do? Desperate, Nika stole a glance at the clock— almost midnight—then at Abby, and cursed like sailor. A movement in her peripheral vision caught her attention.

William. Thank God.

"William!" Nika didn't bother to keep her voice down any longer. "Help! Please, take care of her. Now!"

With that, she pushed Abby out of the way, and then jammed the key into its opening on the grandfather clock.

CHAPTER TWENTY-EIGHT

"Well, it's about time." Nika spit out the words as she fisted her hands on her hips.

A moan slipped from Abby as she turned her head and blinked. A dazed look filled her eyes.

"What happened to me?"

"You fell and conked your head. And if you ask me, you deserve it. What were you thinking, pulling a stupid stunt like that?"

"You're angry."

"No shit, Sherlock!"

"I'm...Abby. Don't you remember?"

"I do. Unfortunately."

"Well?"

"Well what?"

"What happened? What stupid stunt did I pull? And what does that even mean?"

"It means you stuck your curious little nose into something that you were not supposed to, and now we're stuck."

"Stuck? How? Where?"

"Where? In Fernandina Beach, in 2019. How? Because I dropped the key when you tried to wiggle it out of the clock, and lost it."

"Lost it? But...we... we can find it. I'll help you."

"You helped enough, little Miss Trouble." Nika glowered at her. "Just do me a favor, and stay away from me for a while."

Abby scrambled to a sitting position and winced.

Her headache must have intensified with her movement, but Nika had no sympathy for her.

"Where could it be, really? We're still at the house, so we can find it here, somewhere."

"Where could it be?" Too aggravated to keep still, Nika jumped to her feet and kicked Abby's carpetbag out of her way. "It could be anywhere in between 1909 and now! Shit!"

She kicked at something under her foot, and almost rejoiced at the sharp, crunchy sound of glass breaking.

"We are still at the house? Look around, Abby. Does it look like your house?"

"Well, now that you mentioned it, it looks like our house, but much dirtier, and shabbier. What happened to it? Did it get mugged? Burned?"

"Nothing so dramatic. It got old, that's all. Hundred and ten years older."

Abby's eyes widened as realization slowly sank in.

"We've made it, then? To your time?"

"Oh, yeah. We've made it."

"But that's good, isn't?"

"Good? Abby, wake up! I've lost the damned key to the clock!"

"So?"

"So? She's asking 'so'!" Rolling her eyes was safer than pounding her head against the wall. "So, we're never, ever going back."

"I don't want to go back."

"But I do!"

Hot rage and cold panic were a combination from hell Nika never experienced before. She wanted to break something—anything, and scream at the top of her lungs. But even more so she wanted to wake up from this nightmare in bed with Eli.

"I do." Nika reined in her temper. "I need to. I have to. Eli will be home tomorrow. I promised to marry him. I gave him my word. I must go back." Despite her best intentions, her voice soared to a desperate crescendo at the end.

"But the clock is right there. Look! That means, you can go back, right?"

"Wrong. The clock is here, but the key is lost. The key opens the portal. Without it, this," Nika jerked her chin at the antique clock, "is just a piece of furniture."

"Daisy, darling, don't despair, we'll find a solution, I promise."

She promises. Nika almost laughed. Her eyes stung. Her throat burned. She was a mess.

Gotta hold it together.

Or else she was afraid she might disintegrate. Physically and mentally.

Abby moaned, then massaged her head with both hands, and whimpered like a whipped pup.

Like a drunk with a hangover, Nika thought dispassionately. *Dammit, if not for Abby...*

Nika refused to feel sorry for her, or to offer help when Abby slowly dragged herself upright, and hobbled closer. So what if it was mean and small of her? She felt mean and small and desperate.

Then Abby gingerly touched her shoulder.

"Don't cry, *ma petite*, we'll find the answer."

And broke hear heart.

The bubble of mean and small and desperate burst, bringing on a flood of shame.

"Oh, God, Abby."

Much taller than Nika, wearing a hat and heels, Abby practically towered over her. In comparison and nine years her senior, Nika really was a small thing. But that endearment, the very one that Eli always used, simply undid her. The meltdown Nika had kept at bay by sheer will finally broke through. Like a ragdoll, she folded, dropped to her knees, and dissolved in tears. She hadn't cried in ages. She hated crying. She despised weak women who cried over anything and everything. But this was no simple crying jag. It was an agony of the soul. Grief, pure and raw and primal. Nika's sobs racked her body from within, hurting and breaking. At the end, she was an empty shell. Her head, eyes, even her bones ached, but that was nothing compared to her heart. The pain that lodged under her left breastbone was white-hot and razor-sharp.

And incurable.

If not for Abby, who held Nika and rocked her like a baby, she would probably just lie down right there, close her eyes and go to sleep, exhausted and empty. This horrible void that took residence inside of her was deceptively soft. It lulled her to sleep, seducing her to give up and flow away.

Snap out of it! Now!

Nika jerked back to reality, following that inner voice in her head. Abby still held her, a bit harder than was comfortable. She was probably scared as hell, but instead was comforting Nika.

Slowly, she pulled from Abby's embrace, and focused at her face. And almost laughed. With her feathered hat askew, buttoned up in overcoat, and her hands covered demurely by long gloves, Abby was a visual definition of ridiculous. Her usually neat and glossy hair was now a dusty, sweaty mess; her lips trembled; her eyes wide and round, and a little wild on her white-washed drawn face. But her steel will and determination that made her clutch at Nika's hand and hang on for dear life in a desperate attempt to escape her fate, shone through. She was clearly scared, but holding it together. Stiff upper lip and steel backbone. Resigned, Nika shook her head. Could she really blame the girl? After all, it wasn't her fault: it was Nika's. She was seduced by William's offer to see her family one last time. She took the key and inserted it into the clock, even though Abby's unexpected and shocking arrival made everything much more complicated. She should have scratched the whole scheme right then and there, but instead, she forged ahead and turned the damned key in its hole, not once, but twice. And she was the one who dropped the key, not Abby. Instead of holding it in a death grip like her life depended on it, because it really did, she carelessly let it slip from her fingers without realizing it. Stupid, so stupid! She had no one to blame for this fiasco but herself.

No, not fiasco. Disaster. Of major proportions.

Nika pulled away, disengaging herself from Abby.

"Well, girl, here we are, you and me," she said, stating the obvious.

"You and I," Abby corrected automatically. Nika chuckled without any mirth.

"You and I, right. So, what do we do now?"

"I think we should get up, get our wits about us, and decide where to go from here," Abby answered primly.

"Yes, well, good advice, Miss Clear Head," Nika muttered as she rose to her feet and wobbled. Abby put her hand under her arm to help Nika. When they both were standing, Abby slowly turned around.

"So, here's our home."

"Yes, here it is."

"It's in shambles, all dark and dirty."

"It just needs some paint and some work. A lot of work, actually. But it will be as good as new." Nika had a sudden urge to defend the Coleman house, the one she fell in love with two years ago.

"Will it?" Abby asked, wistfully.

"Yeah, it will. After I'm done with it."

"So, you will be repairing it?"

"More like renovating, but yes, I will. I was hired to do so before I...well, before."

The fact of what she promised was like a slap in the face. She might very well be out of this project, for all she knew. With her disappearance, Senator Lauder may have pulled it from Before & After, Inc. Damn. And if he didn't, did she really want to do it? Did she have a heart for the project? Could she do it?

What project? I have to get back to Eli. I have to find the key!

"Oh, look, there on the floor. What is this thing?" Abby pointed her gloved index finger.

Nika's heart lurched. There, in the middle of a room, lay her iPhone. She lunged for it, grabbed it, pushed the home button, and—wonder of wonders! —the screen lit up immediately, showing her the familiar screenshot of two smiling faces: hers and Alex's.

Weak with relief, Nika kissed the small gadget, and grinning like a loon, started to push buttons.

"What is it?" Abby came closer, a combination of curiosity and shock written on her face.

"It's my cell phone."

"Your... phone? A telephone? This small object? What can it do?"

"A lot of things," Nika answered, impatiently, bringing up the phone log. Strange. No missed calls, no messages, and no texts. Like, absolutely nothing. That was more than strange, it was simply unbelievable! How could Alex, or *Verochka*, not try her phone when she first disappeared? No, it was impossible. They should have called every five minutes, trying to locate her. Especially *Verochka*. But where were all those attempts to connect with her? Where were their frantic voicemails and texts? Very strange. No, it was more than that, it was bizarre.

The thought something might have happened to them while she was incommunicado hit her like a torrential downpour.

"Quick, we need to go!"

"Go? Where?" Abby bent to retrieve her case.

"No time for that." Nika grabbed Abby's hand, and together they sprinted toward the door. "We need to go home. Fast. Something happened. Something terrible happened."

"Like what?" But Abby ran for all she was worth.

"Don't know. But my family...they didn't call me. Not once. It means only one thing: something bad happened. We must hurry!"

They hit the main door together, and ran outside. Nika turned toward the place where she parked her truck, Abby fast on her heels. She stumbled once on the folds of her long skirt, but quickly righted herself, and followed closely behind. But when they came upon Nika's truck, a gleaming dark-red behemoth, Abby came to a screeching halt.

"What is this thing?" she asked, breathlessly.

"A truck, my truck. Hop in." Impatient now, Nika flung the passenger door open and unceremoniously pushed Abby inside.

Running to the driver's side, she jumped in, and turned the ignition. It came to life with a familiar deep purr. Nika pressed the gas pedal and took off like a rocket, recklessly navigating the narrow path. Gravel pieces crushed under her tires and exploded upward like fireworks.

"You can operate this vehicle?" Abby whispered, awestruck, then clutched at the handle with both hands after one mighty lurch of the truck.

"Yes. It's called a truck. It's a car—automobile—only bigger." She was babbling and knew it. Hell, she would sing an opera aria to get her mind off her fear.

"Much, much bigger, I'd say." Abby swallowed audibly. "You are going too fast, Daisy."

"Not fast enough," Nika muttered, flooring the gas pedal. The mind-numbing fear for her family overshadowed all else. Her botched return trip, the loss of the key, and Abby's presence— all was forgotten in a flash the moment she powered her phone and found her call log blank. *Alex, Verochka*...What happened to them? A million different scenarios, one more horrible than the other, chased each other in her head. They were mugged, or run over by a car, or kidnapped for ransom...Or they were badly injured, lying in a hospital...Or...

Don't even go there. Don't think about them.

But, of course, she did.

The trip from the Coleman house to her home took an unprecedented ten minutes instead of the usual twenty. But for Nika it seemed like an eternity. As soon as she was on their driveway, she jumped out, and, without turning the engine off, ran pell-mell toward the staircase, taking two steps at a time. At the doors, she paused, briefly considered which one to push open, hers or Alex's, then bent over, shaking and nauseous, took a couple of fortifying breaths, and grabbed the knob. Turning it slowly, Nika prayed, promising God all sort of things, from her firstborn to the last drop of her blood.

Just keep them safe, God. Please, just keep them safe.

The picture that met her eyes was so ridiculously absurd, her jaw dropped. Squinting, Nika tried to focus her vision, concentrating first on a piece of something pink in the middle of the room. A...mat. Her mind went blank. A pink yoga mat?

No, the color wasn't pink. *Verochka's* reprimand rang in her mind's ear, "Dusty rose, my girl. The color's called 'dusty rose.'"

Soft music, something primitive and ethereal, with a lot of strings and flutes, came from hidden speakers. In the middle of that oasis was her grandmother, sitting on the mat with her eyes closed and her hands resting on her intricately entwined legs in a perfect Lotus position.

Am I hallucinating? Verochka was doing yoga, as serene and unperturbed as a lotus flower itself. *What in the world...?*

Her mind clicked off and went to stupor. For a moment she stood glued to the spot, unblinking, unbreathing, and unable to comprehend what she really observed.

When a movement on her right caught her attention, Nika expected anything but not her cousin with a steaming cup of coffee in hand. And he was grinning.

Is that how they coped with my disappearance, by pretending everything was normal? Did they even notice that I was gone for two months? Did they even care?

When her rational mind finally started functioning again.

Something's not right with this picture.

She probably blurted it out loud, because *Verochka* abruptly stopped and turned toward her.

"Nika! We weren't expecting you so soon."

"So... soon?"

"Usually, you're lost to the world for several days when you're starting a new project," *Verochka* said, rising gracefully to her feet in a single fluid motion.

"Several days," Nika parroted, blinking in puzzlement at both of them. "How long..." she had to swallow a couple of times before she had her voice back. "How long was I lost this time?"

Verochka's brows winged up.

"Just two days, darling." Her surprise quickly turned into concern. "Well, today marks day three, but you said not to bother you unnecessarily, so..." Her hands rose helplessly, then fell, as she turned to Alex.

"Yeah, brat, your last text said it was a lot of work, and you practically ordered me to stay away for at least three or four days. I was going to come and fetch you tomorrow, if you didn't resurface first. Saved me the trip. So, how was it?"

For a split second, Nika blanched. Was he asking about her time-travel journey? Realization hit her. He simply inquiring about the status of their new project and her initial inspections. She almost laughed. Hysteria and panic bubbled in her throat.

"What day is it?" she asked, bracing for the answer.

"September sixteenth. Why?"

"Oh, God, oh, God... Time moves differently! Here and there! Time..." she shook her head, finally coming out of her stupor. "I was there for two and a half months, while here... only two days passed. What am I going to do? Oh, God!"

She grabbed two fistfuls of her hair.

"What are you talking about? Are you okay, Cuz? You look funny."

That was the understatement of the century. Nika's cheeks grew hot and sweaty. Confident she was green around the gills, Nika swallowed hard to keep the bile at bay. Her emotions ran rampant, fear, grief, sorrow, and others she was unable to identify they flitted through her so fast.

"What happened?" He took her by the shoulders and shook her none too gently. "Tell me, dammit!"

"Oh, nothing much." Her fake smile hurt her face. "Nothing much, except that I traveled back in time, to 1909, and fell in love, and now I'm back. And, oh, I ruined everything!"

"You did what?" *Verochka's* voice rose an octave.

"I ruined—"

"Before that?"

"I traveled back—"

"No, the other part of it?"

"I fell in love." She focused on her grandmother. "I mean really and madly in love. He proposed, and I said yes, but I had to come back and see you both, to say good-bye, and then I was going back, but I... I lost the key."

The entire scenario sounded crazy even to her own ears. Two faces, wearing identical expressions of shocked disbelief, stared back at her.

"I came back to see you both, to say that I was okay. I felt so guilty. I thought you were frantic with worry because I disappeared, but when I realized that you weren't searching for me—I checked my phone and there were no calls or messages—and I thought that something terrible must've happened to one or both of you! And I panicked. I broke all the speed limits, driving here. When I opened the door, I was afraid of what I might find, but thank God, you both are safe and sound. Time," she choked, then found her voice again, "it moves differently, here and there. You see, I thought I was gone for two months, but here it was just two days, so you didn't even notice. And now I can't return, because I lost the key! My God, what have I done?"

"Daisy?"

CHAPTER TWENTY-NINE

The ensued silence was deafening.

"Oh, and I forgot to tell you. I didn't come alone. Everybody, meet Abby, my unexpected travel companion."

"You brought a friend."

Verochka quickly regained her equilibrium. She smiled and walked to Abby who hovered uncertainly by the door.

"How delightful! Hello, dear. My name is Vera, but everybody calls me *Verochka*. I'm Nika's grandmother."

"You don't look like anybody's grandmother," Abby blurted, then flushed furiously.

"Oh, you are so kind, my dear," *Verochka* laughed, tugging her gently by the hand all the way inside. "The girl has great taste."

"Who's this?" Alex was still gripping Nika's shoulders.

"I told you, this is Abby."

"Why is she dressed like...like that?"

"And what is wrong with my state of dress?" Abby demanded primly, patting at her badly wrinkled skirt in an attempt to smooth it. Her hat that she had removed earlier was hanging by the ribbons around her arm. She still had her gloves on, covering both her arms up to her elbows. The lacy collar of her tailored shirtwaist was high enough to brush her delicate chin. She might have stepped from some nineteenth century painting.

"Nothing wrong with it." *Verochka* rubbed her arm gently, and shot warning glances at Alex. Of course, being Alex, he chose to ignore them.

"Nothing wrong with it, except it belongs in a museum. Are you an actress?"

"I am no such thing!" Abby straightened her shoulders. Even though she was several inches shorter than Alex she managed to look down her patrician nose at him. "I am Abigail Suzanne Coleman, the daughter of Peter and Madeline Coleman, and the sister of Elijah Coleman," she announced hauntingly, sounding like a royalty.

Nika stifled a nervous laugh.

A very pissed-off royalty.

"Yeah, right, of course. Well, Miss Abigail Suzanne Coleman," he presented her with a mocking nod. "It's nice to make your acquaintance."

"Pleasure is all mine," Abby answered in a saccharine voice as false as her curtsy.

"Well, children, if you finished with your mutual taunts, how about we all sit down, and have a cup of coffee with the pastry? I ordered such delightful little chocolate cakes from the Ritz's bakery. It's simply decadent!" *Verochka* explained to Abby right before she turned her narrowed eyes to her cousin. "Why don't you take our guest's jacket, my boy? Let's make her feel welcomed."

His glowering gaze was her only answer. But in a moment, his good manners took over, and he assisted Abby reluctantly in removing her overcoat. He even hung it up, eyeing it curiously. Then he shrugged as if dismissing the matter of the strange coat, and walked back to the kitchen, where *Verochka* was already pouring coffee and arranging the small round cakes on China plates.

"Well, girls, drink up. Abby, you must tell me what you think of this scrumptious chocolate delight. Isn't it wonderful?"

"It's quite tasty," Abby managed, spooning the tiny piece and tasting it delicately. "It really is marvelous, Grandmother."

"Oh, dear child, call me *Verochka*. Please."

"Very well, *Verochka*," Abby repeated softly.

Nika watched Alex's reaction to Abby with interest. He tried to be unobtrusive and failed miserably as he stared at the woman so out of place in her old-fashioned clothes and her holier-than-thou manners. Obviously, he had trouble believing their time travel story. No doubt, she piqued his curiosity. And when he was curious, he turned into a bloodhound. History proved he chased and sniffed, until he found the answer to satisfy his nosiness.

"Okay," he put his cup down with a loud clunk. "We had our coffee. We had our cake. Now, how about we hear the whole story. And, Nika, the truth, please."

"Whole truth and nothing but the truth," Nika muttered, and took a deep breath.

"Okay, then. *Verochka*, Alex, meet Abigail Coleman, the baby sister of Elijah Coleman, an incredibly talented artist. She was supposed to be married off to a man she doesn't love, forget her dream and abandon her paintings, and that's why I brought her with me all the way from 1909."

She didn't add that Abby kind of brought herself, or forced her way into the future.

To a horrified Abbigail, Nika said in lieu of an apology, "Sorry, Abby, I don't have secrets from these two."

"Abigail Coleman?" Alex croaked, staring at Abigail.

"Yes. I told you my name already, didn't I?"

"The baby sister of Elijah Coleman?"

"The one and the same," Nika answered two steps away from total exhaustion.

"Have you lost your freaking mind!" he exploded in a half-shout, half-roar and leapt from his chair.

It was so unlike him to raise his voice in general, but especially in such a dramatic manner. Nika gaped at him in surprise.

"Are you nuts? What were you thinking, bringing her here?"

"Don't yell at me, Alex!"

"I'm not yelling!" he bellowed. "I'm just asking what was going on in that convoluted brain of yours when you decided to bring her here."

"I didn't decide—it just happened."

"Just happened! Oh, that's just great. Fucking fantastic!"

He paced back and forth, his hands jammed into his pockets and his lips twisted in a no-nonsense expression.

"Well, there's only one thing to do. You have to reverse it somehow. You have to return her back. The sooner the better."

"Return?" Abby cut into his rambling, her voice cool and razor-blade sharp.

"Return?" she repeated coolly. "What am I, a parcel? A *thing* to be handled? I am Abigail Coleman. A human being, a grown woman of free will."

She rose from the chair. Her head tilted, her brows lifted. She was, once again, the personification of an insulted, enraged royal.

His eyes widened but he soon regained his senses.

"Well, pardon the fuck out of me, your Highness. What was I thinking? Where are my manners?" He stooped in a mock curtsy and then saluted her for a good measure.

"Miss Coleman, would you be so kind as to do us, and yourself, a great favor and return to your time as soon as possible? Like, immediately? Pretty please?"

"Your behavior is utterly absurd and childish. You, sir, are no gentleman!"

"Oh, that's just rich." He laughed and threw his hands up in the air.

"Children, children," *Verochka* interrupted. "You both are behaving childishly. Instead of bickering and insulting each other, let's think of something constructive."

"By all means, let's!"

"It's obvious that Abby came here for a reason. Didn't you, sweetie?"

"Yes."

"Whatever her reason, she must go back." His eyes blazed as he fired back at her.

"I won't. I can't. Even if I wanted to, which I don't, I couldn't do it."

"And why the hell not?"

"Because we lost the key. Didn't you hear what Daisy said?"

"What?" He turned to Nika. "What the hell is she talking about? What key?"

"The key to the old grandfather clock inside the Coleman house. It somehow opens a portal in between our time and 1909. That's how I turned up in the original Coleman household and that's how we came back. But I lost it. I lost the key."

"How?"

"I don't know. It just happened. I must've dropped it. But I don't have a key to the clock anymore."

Alex swore, rich and loudly, and raked both hands against his scalp. Nika bit her tongue so as not to remind him that he had no hair to rake.

"Alex!" *Verochka* exclaimed, shaking her head. "What's wrong with you?"

"What's wrong?" He muttered a few more expletives, obviously unconcerned by the presence of three women. "By God, Nika, I've witnessed your crazy shenanigans during the years too many to count, participated in some of them just to save your reckless hide, but this one is so outrageous, so absolutely, fucking irresponsible, that I'm losing my vocabulary trying to describe it! How could you?"

"How could I what?"

Nika's short fuse had finally ignited, and she jumped to her feet to face her cousin. "How could I save the girl from being married off against her will? How could I give her a chance to decide her own fate, to be someone, to reach her dream? How could I help her to run away from a world where she has to depend on overbearing, stubborn, rich men? Sound familiar, cousin? We did the same. Remember? We revolted and made a run for it. So don't you dare stand here, look me in the eye and ask me 'how could I'!"

"Dammit, Nika, that's not the same."

"Why the hell not?"

"Because we ran away to another city— not another century. We didn't change anything in the great scheme of things except the quantity of seating places at a dinner table in our parents' homes. But you did. You snatched her from one particular moment of time, hundred and ten years ago, and dropped her here and now, changing completely the course of history. God only knows how many lives and destinies you overturned, or even ruined, in the process. Think about it."

"Sir, stop this at once!"

Abby, trembling from head to toe, stepped between the cousins. She glared at him. "It's not Daisy's fault. Please, stop shouting at her. If someone is at fault here, it's me. I asked her to bring me here. No, let me be absolutely frank: I begged, and blackmailed, so your wrath should be aimed at me directly."

"How did you call her?" *Verochka* asked quietly.

"Daisy. We call her Daisy. Brother says with her sunny curls and violet-blue eyes she reminds him of that wildflower," Abigail replied with her eyes glued to his face. Nika watched Abby's reaction as a grimace of horror disfigured his handsome features. He became sickly-pale and glared at Abigail like she had sprouted horns and tail.

"I have to... get away."

He turned, knocked against a chair, and all but ran from the room.

Nika clutched two fistfuls of her hair in both hands, and made some unintelligible sound. "Fuck! Shit!"

"Nika!"

"Daisy!"

Verochka and Abby exclaimed simultaneously.

"Sorry, sorry. I have to..." and she ran away in the opposite direction of the deck. Through the open door Nika overheard the rest of the conversation.

"What did I do? What did I say?"

"Nothing, child. It's not you. Or, more accurately, not about you. Alex will calm down, and so will Nika, don't you worry."

"But they are mad at each other because of me. They yelled and fought and—"

"And that's what they've been doing since they were in diapers."

"D-diapers?"

"Nappies? Oh, never mind, sweetie. They both will take a walk on the beach, wear off their mad and come to their senses. I assure you, they'll be back in less than an hour."

"Are you sure, Grandmother?"

"Absolutely, and it's *Verochka*, remember?"

Nika hated when she and Alex argued. It didn't happen often, but when it did her stomach twisted into knots. She stepped onto her deck to face the calming water. And there he was, kicking his way through the sand. Apparently, his walk on the beach did nothing to calm him. If anything, it seemed to have made his temper run hotter. With every step along the hard packed sand his face turned a deeper red as his blood seemed to upgrade from simmering to boiling.

Nika understood. It wasn't every day a regular guy was confronted with the reality of traveling through time. He knew she wasn't crazy or delusional, so her claim to have spent two months in 1909 at the original Coleman household just might strike him as the truth. Even Nika failed to figure out how two months in the past only equaled two days in the present. How did that happen? No logic in that but it certainly was a fact.

Her heart broke as she studied her faithful cousin, the guy who was always there for her. It must be hard for him to accept she returned to say her good-byes because she was marrying Eli. Did he feel abandoned? Deserted? And what about her guilt of leaving Alex and *Verochka* forever? Did she really love Eli that much to never see her favorite people again? Another set of thoughts she needed to shove from her mind.

Of course, Abby tagging along certainly set him back a few paces even though it didn't shut him up.

A satisfied smile tugged at Nika's mouth. Abigail Coleman, a beautiful woman who called *Verochka* Grandmother in a voice that was pure dark honey. Nika let loose a chuckle remembering the look on Alex's face when Abby called him sir in the same voice, but while the first time sounded like an endearment, the second was more an insult. When she called Nika 'Daisy' he stopped, did a double-take. The startled expression on his face proved he finally realized that Nika wasn't a reincarnation of Daisy Coleman, as *Verochka* claimed all along. She *was* Daisy Coleman.

The crashing waves and screeching seagulls drew Nika from her reverie. The time had come to act. One way or another, she must go back, because she had a wedding to attend. How? The grandfather clock was the portal. To activate it, she needed the key that was lost somewhere between now and 1909. She needed to find a solution for this mess and return to Eli. Nika charged off the deck onto the beach. The stress was eating her alive.

CHAPTER THIRTY

She ran. She didn't think, didn't feel, she just ran. With no destination in mind, she ran like all bats of hell were at her heels. The wind whistled painfully in her ears. She ran until her legs simply refused to carry her weight any longer, and then she collapsed, face-down, onto the wet cold sand. Breath heaved her chest, her heart thrummed, her blood swooshed. Her guilt was heavier than her weight, deeper than the ocean. Darker than a black stormy cloud. Was it possible to survive that guilt?

At that moment, she didn't know the answer, and didn't care.

You are not a coward.

Leave me alone.

You have people who love you. Have you thought of them?

They will survive.

What about Abby? Will she survive, too?

Irritated, Nika shrugged. Abby will be fine. She's strong.

But is she strong enough to find her way in this time? *With no one familiar, alone and lost, and penniless. How will she support herself?*

That thought stopped Nika cold. Can she support herself here? She had no other skill except painting and knew squat about this place and time. Was it possible for Abby to survive? The simple answer was: no. Without Nika acting as her guardian, or more accurately a shepherd, Abby's chance of survival was slim to none. Even with Alex and *Verochka's* help. After all, it was Nika who spent over two months with her, lived under the same roof, shared the same meals. Nika alone knew Abby's story and was her confidante. Willingly or not, but it was she, Nika, who brought Abby here. So, she was responsible for the girl, whether she liked it or not.

You become responsible, forever, for what you have tamed.

She never fully understood that famous Saint-Exupery quote until now.

Nika fisted her hands. The cold wet sand squished between her fingers. She sat up resolved to face the situation head-on. Abby was like a blind person without a cane in a foreign place. She needed Nika. Until Abby became acclimated and got her bearings, until she found her way and steadily walked on her own two feet, Nika must be strong. And after that, she might allow herself the luxury of falling apart for as long as she wanted. Or until doomsday.

But for now, she must pull it together whatever the cost. If for no one else's sake, but for Abby's.

She rose to her feet, stumbling a few times before she regained the feel of her legs. Her eyes were itchy and dry. She wiped her hands on her shirt then rubbed them across her eyes, and blinked away the excess grains. Enough. Her pity party was over. Time to return to reality.

Turning around, Nika started to walk. Home. She just had to get home. The image of the Coleman house circa 1909 flashed in her mind. *Home.* Her imagination by volition of its own conjured the image of one place she had called home for the past two months.

Home, where Mrs. Smith lorded over the staff.

Home, where Belle sneaked inside, to get some treats.

Home, where in the stately, lonely tower its owner supervised his many enterprises.

My friends and family call me Eli...

Eli, who even now was hurrying back home to wed his bride.

Daisy, my own wild, beautiful flower, my unexpected gift from the universe, my everything...

Eli, whom she may never see again.

I want to share my life with you, wake up beside you every morning, make babies with you...

"Eli!"

Doubling over, Nika retched until she has nothing left in her, until she was empty and brittle as a broken seashell.

Get up, Nika. Get the hell up.

Standing upright took some effort, but she did it, thinking of Eli. There was nothing she had the ability to do for him except take care of his baby sister. After all, at this point, she was the only family the girl had left.

The house that was no longer her home was blessedly empty. Where had they gone? What time was it? Nika squinted at the clock. The digital display of the modern wall clock showed eleven. Morning? Night? Who cares? And what difference does it make? Thirsty, she drank water right out of the kitchen faucet and then wiped her mouth with her dirty hand. Her bare feet were caked in sand. Where were her boots? Did she remove them?

The hell with the boots.

Her black jeans were almost beige from dust and dirt. She lifted her hand to turn the brim of her ball cap, and touched hair. Where was her favorite hat? Did she put it on when she was changing clothes? Yes, she surely did. Nika distinctly remembered she clipped the toolbelt, then removed it, and hid it underneath her everyday wardrobe. The belt was too heavy and clunky, and she was afraid to lose her most prized possession during the time travel. But not the ball cap. Nika refused to make herself part with her favorite hat. She had plopped it on her head, and turned the bill backwards as usual. And now it was gone.

The toolbelt was lost to her, too, but it was the loss of the hat that made her sick at heart. She wished she could be angry instead. Like raging, hopping mad. And she will be. Tomorrow.

But not right now. Disheartened, Nika trudged to her room. She dragged along sand everywhere she went. *The hell with it.*

Tomorrow, she promised to apologize for the mess, and clean everything up. Tomorrow, she was soon enough to make an effort to care. But not right now. Right now, she was totally wiped out. Spent. Useless. Like an electric gadget with no juice. The tiny charge of energy she had left was just enough to carry her to the bedroom. Nika longed for a long hot shower, but had no power to indulge. Tomorrow, she vowed.

Need to recharge those batteries, girl. Need to snap out of it. Remember your backbone?

Yeah, yeah. Tomorrow, everything tomorrow.

Get rid of temporary funk, get back to her own self, start thinking about the future. Because she must get back. No ifs or buts about it. She must find a solution.

And I will, but not right now.

Still fully clothed, dirty, Nika dropped onto the bed, and was out in a second.

CHAPTER THIRTY-ONE

The finest single malt whiskey tasted bitter as it slid down his throat. Eli slammed his tumbler onto the side table and cursed when the noise made his head throb. Determined to forget the woman who made a fool of him, he poured another generous drink. And gulped it down. A wave of nausea swept over him. Eli was drunk, beyond reason. To move his arms and legs was a chore at best. But his head, even though throbbing like a rotten tooth, was clear as day. His mind worked like a well-oiled mechanism, refusing him the stupefaction he sought.

He ached all over. His head was about to explode from the harsh pounding inside of it. His eyes were dry and hot, his throat scratchy. He was feverish, shaky, and miserable. And sick to his stomach.

But the pain that crept under his left breastbone was the worst. It was excruciating. White-hot, razor sharp, soul deep. He wished for oblivion.

Every moment of the past three days, he had wished for it, begged the merciful Lord to bring it to him. But his prayers went unanswered, and his torture continued.

Eli sat and drank, locked inside his tower, every day since his return. He prayed for his heart to burst in his chest and end his torture. But no such luck.

Once, long ago, when Mary and his newborn child had perished, he had contemplated ending his life. But now? No way in hell.

What was the point in committing such an ungodly act? He deserved the agony that ate at his soul.

He deserved to be punished. For being a gullible idiot. For falling for an act. For being blind.

He couldn't forgive himself for trusting an accomplished actress, for turning into putty in her hands. He hated himself for letting his guard down, and believing her lies. He lost his head. Completely. He still tried to find some excuse— any excuse— for her actions. Was she threatened? Did she fear for her life? Did she have to run to save herself? Those and a myriad of other possibilities raced through his aching head.

But none of them explained the theft of his grandmother's pearls, or the other pieces of family jewelry she helped herself to.

She took all the money he kept in his desk for the household expenses along with his most prized and dear possession—his father's breast pocket Swiss watch.

The list of purloined items was as long as his arm, but Eli only cared about his father's watch and his great-grandmother's amethyst engagement ring that he slid onto Daisy's finger a few days ago.

Was she already planning her escape when she accepted his proposal and pledged herself to him? Or was it a spur-of-a-moment thing? He filled his tumbler to the brim, and then choked down the dark liquid. He hissed through clenched teeth, but welcomed the fire that burned his stomach. Eli closed his eyes and willed the liquid fire to turn his insides to ashes. Was that even possible? Maybe. Hopefully. With the amount of liquor he consumed, it ought to happen.

But not soon enough.

He still could feel.

Think.

Remember.

Damnation!

He scanned the room, stopping his gaze on his desk. He first learned of her true gender here, in this room. He kissed her here. Made love to her. Her ghost lingered, lurking in the shadows, driving him insane. Eli pressed his hands against his ears to shut out her voice, her laughter, the little sounds she made when he loved her, and that funny noise she made when she snorted. And that tiny sigh when she woke up in his bed.

He still smelled her. Everywhere. Anywhere. His fingertips still tingled from touching her hair...Daisy...Daisy...*Daisy!* Pain sliced him in half, sharp and brutal.

She made him whole. She gave him purpose to live.

And then reality stung him. She had abandoned him. Stole from him.

But the things she took were of no consequence. She betrayed him. That was the hardest thing to comprehend. To forgive.

And in essence, she destroyed him.

Eli brought the tumbler to his mouth, sloshing the whiskey with an unsteady hand, gulping the remainder in three swallows. The burn in his gut became an inferno. His rage ignited with it, and he threw the empty tumbler against the wall. The breaking glass reverberated in his head like a slammed door.

She ran away. Like the thief she was, in the middle of the night.

His memory took him back, to the day of his return.

It was early Friday morning. He was eager and impatient to get back home, only to find his household in uproar. His fiancé and sister had both disappeared. Half-crazy with dread, Eli conducted his own investigation, asking multiple questions. Mrs. Smith, the cook, the gardener, and William O'Brian—everybody was of the same mind that Daisy acted sad and forlorn after his departure, but not alarmingly so. She spent some time in the library, then went for a walk in the gardens with that ugly mutt she favored. After dinner, she bid everybody good night, and went to her room. And no one saw her after that.

The next morning, after both Abby and Daisy failed to come down to breakfast, Mrs. Smith sent someone to fetch them, only to find their rooms empty.

Abby had cleared her own bank account, took all her valuables, and some of her clothes. Somehow, Daisy had convinced his beloved sister, his own flesh and blood, to follow in her footsteps. To betray him. To abandon him. To shame him.

At least Abby left him a note.

"Brother, I'm going away with Daisy. I only took what belongs to me, my jewelry and gold. Hope with time you can forgive me. Don't despair, and don't search for me. I love you.

Forever yours, Abigail."

After he read that note, Eli halted the police investigation into their disappearance and recanted his original statement.

They had left of their own accord and had no desire to be found.

In his heart he knew they were never coming back.

Returning home from the police station, he locked himself in his tower, and started to drink. He lost all meaning of time. Day? Night? What did it matter? It was all the same to him.

He couldn't face the bedroom, where everything reminded him of Daisy.

Would he ever be able to spend a night in that room, sleep in that bed?

Eli sat in his chair, in a drunken stupor he inflicted on himself, day after day, too drained to move, too clearheaded to sleep.

The first visitor who appeared in the tower was William. Eli watched dispassionately as his friend wrinkled his nose and clasped his hand over his mouth.

What a picture I must present.

A humorless chuckle broke free, hurting Eli's alcohol abused throat.

The look of disgust on William's face quickly changed to what Eli recognized as guilt. Even in the room's semi-darkness the expression was as distinguishable as the moon on a clear night.

Strange. Why should William feel guilty? Or am I imagining things?

Eli hadn't had a drink since the previous night when he finally decided his drinking binge was pointless. Moreover, it was playing havoc with his mind, turning him into an imbecile, or worse, a weakling. He wasn't yet sober, but not inebriated either. He floated somewhere in between. Eli watched William skulked into the room, stopping short as if he was afraid to face him. And that irritated the hell out of him.

"Welcome, my trusted friend. What brings you to my private realm?" Eli swept his arm to encompass his office and the empty bottles lined up on his desk. "Have you more news to share?"

Eli squinted his eyes to study William. Slightly out of focus, but there was definitely something wrong with his friend and secretary. Was it just guilt or... pity?

Damnation.

Had he sunk so low that he was now an object of pity? Anger simmered in Eli's gut and then burst forth before he was able to regain control.

"Get out! Just get the hell out and stay out!"

"I'll go, but first I have to tell you that I'm very and truly sorry."

"Sorry? You? Whatever for?"

"For not being brave enough to press my case, to convince you—"

"Convince me that the female I was so enamored with was a fraud and liar?" Eli let lose a cruel laugh. "No one was able to convince me of that, William, not even the Lord in heaven. So, you may soothe your conscience, and go away. I wish to be alone."

If anything added to his decision to shake off this dreadful weakness and pull himself together, it was the look on William's face, a combination of sympathy, guilt and disgust.

It was plain shameful, and pitiful, to be shattered like this because of a woman.

What's wrong with you, man? Pick yourself up by the boot straps and remember who you are!

But dear Lord, the task seemed almost inconceivable at the moment. William's words cut through Eli's inner debate with himself.

"You've been alone for several days now. Drinking."

"So?"

"Did it help?"

"Nothing helps." Eli dragged both hands through his hair and glared at William. "My own sister has chosen a stranger over her flesh and blood. My fiancé abandoned me, choosing gold and jewelry over me. I am cursed."

"Eli, listen to me. Abby is gone, because she fell under Daisy's lies—not because of you. You are the best brother a sister could dream of. Daisy lied to her as she lied to all of us. It has nothing to do with you. You are not to blame for any of this. It's Daisy. It's all her fault."

Eli switched on the desk lamp desk and squinted at its brightness. He looked up at William. Was that a sheen of sweat on his forehead? And why was he looking to the side, hiding his eyes?

"If you are guilty, then all of us are, too, because we all liked her, and believed her," he said passionately. "Even the stupid dog had fallen under her spell. She's gone now, Eli, but life continues. Business continues. In time, you will understand that you're better off without her. In time, you might even be glad that it happened. Time, my friend, heals all the hurts."

"Do you know that for sure? Do you, William?"

"I do," William answered with his eyes now cast to the floor.

"Time," Eli muttered. "Time goes on...time can heal. Time..." He blinked at William not sure of anything anymore, but something still seemed off.

"She told me she was from another time, from the future. And like a fool, I believed her. I believed every word. I even hid the key from the grandfather clock in fear she may want to return to her own time."

It shamed him to admit that the first thing he did was to check the secret hidey-hole in the fireplace. Because if the key was missing, there might be a sliver of hope that she was telling the truth, and might return one day. But the key was there, proving him the greatest fool on earth.

He let lose a brittle chuckle "What does that say about me?"

"It says you're a trusting man."

"Well, I wish I were less trusting. What am I going to do now?"

"One step at the time, my friend." William walked closer and laid his right hand on Eli's shoulder. "I'll be there, right beside you, offering you my strength, my belief in you, my devotion."

Eli stared into William's misty eyes and was taken aback. What on earth was that? Devotion? Loyalty? If he was sober, he may think it was...love. Eli shook his head appalled at the thought.

Must be drunker than I realize.

William bent down on one knee. "I'll do anything for you, Eli, I swear. We'll pull through this together, I promise."

"Go now." Eli pushed William's hand from his shoulder. "I need to be alone."

"But, Eli—"

"Don't worry about me, my friend. I won't drink anymore."

"Let me at least clear away the bottles."

"No," Eli answered, more tired than he had ever experienced. "I'll do it myself. Later. Now I wish to be alone."

William slowly rose to his feet.

"Do you need anything? Water? Food?"

"I need some quiet," Eli snapped. "Sorry, I really need to be alone to sort things out. I promise to come down soon. Just not right now."

"Can I fetch you later? You could be unsteady on your feet."

"I'll come on my own," Eli countered with quiet dignity. "Please, leave."

When William was about to exit the room, Eli called his name.

"William?"

He turned, his hand still on the doorknob. His face ashen in the harsh desk light. No, Eli hadn't made a mistake. He recognized guilt when it stared at him.

"Thank you. For everything."

William winced as if he were slapped and then left the room.

True to his word, Eli emerged from the tower the next morning. Cleaned up, freshly shaven, and clad in his perfectly tailored clothes.

Before breakfast, he gathered the staff, and made two announcements: they were never under any circumstances to mention Daisy's name under his roof. She was as good as dead. Period. As for Abby— if anyone asked, she had moved north, on her own volition, under no influence from anybody else.

"She has enough finances to set her for life," he added for Mrs. Smith's benefit. She stood just to his right wringing her hands together and sniffing. . "She won't starve."

"But, Master Eli, won't you look for her?"

"No, I won't."

"But she's so young. Alone, in the world."

"She's of age. She is strong, and resourceful. She'll manage quite well on her own."

"But, Master Eli—"

"That's enough, Mrs. Smith," he cut her off. "We won't talk about it anymore. I wish my sister all the happiness in the world, but that's all."

And that was the end of it. The old Master Eli, the cold and unyielding ruler, was back. God help them all.

The next morning, Eli ordered Sultan to be saddled up. He needed a ride, fast and mindless; needed to get out of the house where everything reminded him of Daisy. She had spent just a little over two months there, but managed to put her stamp on every inch of his property. *Damnation!* He hoped with time he might be able to banish her ghost. Hope springs eternal. Dressed in his riding clothes, Eli left the house, took a turn toward the stables, and stopped dead. Belle, the ugly mutt who became Daisy's shadow, was lying nearby, still as death, with her face on her front paws.

"Hey, girl," he called softly. "Are you alive?"

The dog lifted her shaggy face, and made a mournful sound that covered Eli's skin with goose bumps.

"Missing her, aren't you?"

Another heartbreaking moan answered him.

"Master Eli, I am sorry, sir." The stableman hurried toward him. "This darn dog, begging your pardon, sir. Just sits here like a statue, and whines all the time. Git, git, you ugly bitch." He windmilled his hands at Belle. She rolled her eyes to him then looked away.

"Have you been feeding her?" Eli frowned at the young fellow.

"Yes, sir, but she's having none of it, sir, that I know of. No food for almost six days now. Just drinks water once in a while, and that's it. I'll wager, she's a goner, this one. Pro'bly more merciful to shoot her, and be done with it."

"Do not dare to touch this dog! If someone takes a strap to her, or kicks her, or hurts her in any way, he will answer to me. Understood?"

"Yes, Master Eli, sir." The stable hand stumbled backward, all the while staring at Eli with wide eyes.

"This dog is mine," Eli said as the meaning of his own words sunk in. Belle's anguished eyes tore him apart. He crouched beside her and then laid his gloved hand on the dog's enormous head. She whimpered and closed her eyes.

"Don't even think about it," Eli muttered. "Don't you dare leave me, too, girl. I need you. You hear? I need you as much as I think you need me. Let's try to survive, Belle. Let's try together."

With that, Eli lifted the half-starved dog, and carried her toward the house.

CHAPTER THIRTY-TWO

Brutally awakened, Nika bolted upright in bed, with her heart in her throat. She heard something. What was it? Whining? Keening? The sorrow, the pain...almost human-like, but not. Dog. She heard a dog. She heard...*Belle*?

"Belle! Here, girl, here, sweetie."

And then reality crushed her like a rogue ocean wave.

Nika pulled the covers over her head, and closed her eyes tight. The effort to ease her mind and memories was fruitless. Belle's mournful cries were as real and clear as her own breathing, or the sound of the rolling waves behind her open window. Sometimes, even being fully awake, she smelled the lemony fragrance of wax Mrs. Smith used around the house, or heard the deep murmur of the grandfather clock.

As soon as she closed her eyes, Eli's face appeared. His voice called to her. His unique scent permeated the room. Every night she was transported back to the Coleman house circa 1909, but only in her dreams. Nika began to spend more time in her bed, anything to maintain a contact with Eli and happier times.

Two months had passed since she and Abby made their way back to 2019, almost as long a time as she spent in 1909. She had come for a few hours to say her good-byes, but Fate, that fickle bitch, decided differently: without the key she was lost. Nika was stuck here forever, and the antique grandfather clock was dead and useless, just an old relic with no purpose.

At first, fueled by hope multiplied by determination, Nika jumped into action, searching for a way to beat Fate. At Abby and *Verochka's* suggestion, and Alex's enthusiastic approval, she made a mold casting of the key and ordered duplicates from the best clock masters and locksmiths all around the country. But not a single one of them, no matter how closely it resembled the original, managed to start the clock. She spent countless hours inside that old house, sitting by the grandfather clock, waiting for a miracle; she prowled the rooms, touched every nook and cranny, searching for an answer, to no avail.

When one month had passed and Nika was still no closer to her goal, she stopped caring about anything. She barely ate, and only when food was forced on her. Her initial concern about Abby dissipated. Enamored with her grandmother, Abby found her own footing.

And *Verochka*, delighted with her new charge, took an active hand in Abby's introduction to modern society, her education and overall fate. They became inseparable, almost attached at the hip, and knowing her grandmother as she did, Nika was sure that Abby was on her way to achieving all her dreams. Even her beloved cousin, who still doubted the wisdom of Abby's presence here, was helping with more official matters such as applying for the ID and social security card that was presumably lost. He also took Abby on long walks and day trips, showing her around the town she had known from before, helping her to assimilate and ease her way into the world of the twenty-first century.

In short, Abby was in the best possible hands, so Nika no longer worried about her.

Abigail Coleman would survive. With all the gold and jewelry, she had stashed into her satchel and brought with her from 1909, she was set for life. And Nika was free to fall into pieces. Which she did with abandon and flourish.

She sulked, moped around the house, slept a lot.

She dreamt every night about the man she loved and home she lost, Belle and Sultan, William O'Brien and Mrs. Smith...but even in her dreams, she was back in her own time, and the Coleman house, once again, was out of her reach.

But enough was enough. She woke two days later disgusted with herself and ready to scream. What was she doing? Had she lost her freaking mind? She had plenty of time to grieve, to come to her senses. To snap out of her funk. Time to stop feeling sorry for herself, and start acting.

Nika wasn't inclined to moping, or crying, or waiting like some damsel in distress for the knight in shining armor to come to her rescue. If someone did the rescuing in this family, it was her. She wasn't one to fold without a fight, definitely not the one to accept the shitty hand that Fate had dealt to her. Nika flexed her muscles, rotated her neck, and mentally pumped herself up like a boxer before getting inside a ring.

Giving up was *not* an option. Not today. Not tomorrow. So life spit at her and broke her heart. Happened to many people. The strong ones get over things, even if it eats away at their soul. Time for Nika Morris to get her ass in gear and come back to the living.

She walked to the bathroom and stared in the mirror. Holy cow! The image looking back was pathetic. Nika barely recognized herself. Disgusted, she flipped on the faucet and contemplated just shoving her head under the cold water. A good soaking should remove the cobwebs and clear her thoughts. And then the hot shower. And coffee. In that order. Nika barely had time to rearrange her thoughts when the bathroom door flew open. She scowled at her cousin's grinning face.

"Since when did you stop knocking? What if I was naked?"

"But you are not. And I saw you naked. A skinny-dipping dare, if you recall."

"We were six, you moron, and that's not the point. You must always knock, especially on the bathroom door."

"I did knock. You didn't hear me. The water was running, so decided to come in."

To check on her, most likely. Even appreciating his concern, Nika's irritation flared.

"Well, you can go away now. I'm busy."

"Doing what? Drowning your sorrows? Well, allow me to help." And pressing his hand to her nape, Alex pushed her head under the running cold water. And the moron had the gall to wink at her. Nika went livid.

"You chicken shit! You...you disgusting egg-head! Moron!"

"And she's back," he sing-songed, nimbly evading her elbow jab. "Okay, okay, but on a serious note, you need to hurry up. There is something I have to show you, Cuz. Something important. Dry off. Time's a wasting."

And wasn't that the truth.

Too much time had been lost: a hundred and ten years.

And two months that you've been playing ostrich, you idiot.

When Nika emerged from the bathroom, Alex offered her a steaming mug of coffee, doctored to her liking.

With downcast eyes, she took it, and nodded her thanks. After a couple of sips, Nika muttered under her breath.

"What's that?"

"I'm sorry."

"For?"

"For calling you names. You're not a disgusting egg-head." She shrugged, avoiding his eyes.

"Just a chicken shit, then?"

"And a moron," she sighed, "but you are my moron."

"Okay." He nodded. "I can live with that."

"Where's everybody?"

"*Verochka* and her sidekick are visiting some educational establishments today, such as Fernandina Museum of History. Then they were planning on refreshments at the Ritz-Carlton, then a shopping expedition, but don't ask me where."

"My, my." Nika feigned a smile. "They're quite a pair, aren't they?"

"Are you kidding me? They're like twins separated at birth who've finally found each other."

"I'm glad. Abby never had a real friend. She's starved for companionship, for affection. And who's better than our *Verochka*?"

"Yeah, *Verochka* is a champ. But you're not a slouch, yourself, brat. You found her, brought her here."

"She kinda brought herself here." Nika shrugged. "Frankly, it was Abby who found me, not the other way around."

"Yeah, she told us the story about 'the boy.'"

"Oh, well." Nika lost all the interest in her coffee. "Anyway. You said you have something to show me?"

"So, I did. Grab your ball cap and let's go."

"I lost my cap." Her eyes welled. She had lost so much. It was ridiculous the mention of her cap still shattered her composure and reduce her to pieces. But there it was. Not for long, she vowed. Nika squared her shoulders as she blinked her tears away.

"Hey, we'll get you another one, no biggie." He fluffed her hair. "Let me grab my car keys."

"Are we going somewhere?"

"Yes."

"Where?"

"You'll see."

"Alex?"

"Yeah?"

"I really didn't mean that. You know, the egg-head and everything else."

"I know, brat." He hugged her, holding fast and hard. Nika sighed and leaned into him.

"I love you, baby," she whispered.

"I love you, too, Cuz." He broke the mood when he tickled her sides and made her giggle, like when they were children.

"Let's go."

"You must be kidding me," Nika exclaimed after Alex had stopped and parked the car. "Seriously? A cemetery?"

"I have something to show you."

"Here?"

"Yes." He exited the car and, without waiting for her, started toward the main gate to Fernandina's oldest cemetery, Bosque Bello, established in 1798. Still dumbfounded, Nika unclasped her seatbelt and scrambled after him.

The magnificent live oaks that gave the cemetery its name—*Beautiful Woods*—stood like sentries between the graves and tombstones, some of them dated to the early eighteen hundred. She had visited Bosque Bello a couple of times on a Saturday tour, when they first arrived on Amelia Island. But as beautiful as this place might be, it was still a cemetery, and Nika, even though not finicky by nature, was still not comfortable strolling between graves. She couldn't shake the guilt of intrusion. The dead were entitled to their privacy, too.

"Wait, wait! Why did you bring me here?" She grabbed his hand, halting him in mid-stride. "Is this some kind of a joke?"

He turned to face her. "Do I look like I'm joking?"

"No." She searched his eyes for an answer. "You look like a man on a mission."

"Bingo."

"Start talking, cousin, and fast, or I swear I won't take another step." She dug in her heels and crossed arms over her chest. "Well?"

"You'll have to take another, oh, fifty or so steps, Nika. Because you really need to see it with your own eyes. To believe. To understand. Trust me?"

She was about to turn around and leave him in the middle of the old cemetery, but then curiosity got better of her. That, and the deep, quiet sincerity in his lilac eyes. Taking her silence for agreement, he tugged her by hand, veering right from the main path. They walked another fifty-three steps and then stopped in front of a group of headstones. The tallest one was made of gray granite. It towered over all others, dominating the space.

Very close to it was another one, a bit smaller and lighter in color. It was almost bluish-gray, and had some intricate carvings on its granite face. *A feminine grave.* Chills raced up and down her back.

She turned toward the weathered gray headstone and focused on the inscription.

Elijah Benjamin Coleman,
a great man, beloved husband and father.
December 7th 1873 - March 29th 1954.

Silver mist swam before her eyes. A wave of grief swept through her. Nika swayed, and almost fell on her knees, thankfully Alex caught her in time.

"Easy, baby, easy. Breathe, Nika, breathe, dammit."

"I n-never thought..." she started, but had to stop and fight down the sob that filled her throat. After several deep breaths, Nika faced her cousin. "I never thought you were cruel. But this..." She pointed to her left. "This is beyond cruel. It's brutal. Is that what you wanted me to see?"

He held her gaze for a long moment. Not one sign of remorse in his eyes. "No, I wanted you to see this."

He laid his hands on her shoulders and then gently turned her toward the second, smaller, headstone.

"Look at it, Nika. Read it."

Daisy Coleman
beloved wife and mother, the timeless miracle
Died January 29th, 1954.

Nika read it twice, then slowly a third time, to let the words sink in.

"I don't understand," she whispered, "I don't..." She raised her eyes to his. "What does this mean?"

"It means, you got back. Somehow, you got back to your Eli. Look at the date: only one, without a date of birth. Because, hey, he couldn't put your real birthday, May 27, 1990, now, could he? And besides, how many Daisies were running around Fernandina in 1909 who qualified for the role? On top of it, being the 'timeless' miracle? Get it?"

"I got it." Nika broke into a smile as big as the sun. After a moment she whispered, "So, she died first."

"He outlived her by two months, and then died on the same date, the 29th." Her gaze lingered on the two headstones. Even in death they made a union: two graves, side by side, identical in shape, but different in height and color and defying all logic and laws of modern science.

Alex bowed his head, saluting the man who loved Daisy.

"You'll find your way back, Nika. I don't know how or when, but you will get back to your Eli."

"You really think so?

"I know so." He hooked his arm around her neck, and then kissed her on the forehead.

Nika wiped her eyes with both hands, and sniffed loudly. Smiling, he offered her his handkerchief.

"Okay, I'm okay. Just...give me a few minutes alone?"

"Sure."

Once she was alone, Nika allowed herself a moment before facing the headstones.

So close together. *Elijah Benjamin Coleman.... Daisy Coleman...* Was it strange that she felt nothing looking at her own resting place? Maybe. Probably. She had no time, or desire, to dwell on it. But when she turned to Eli's grave, Nika bit her lip hard to silence a fresh sob.

She stepped closer to it, laid her forehead on the dark cold stone, and closed her eyes. The amethyst engagement ring she wore on a thin chain around her neck began to pulse.

Hidden under the layer of clothing, always close to her heart, that ring was her only tangible connection to Eli. Until now.

Elijah Benjamin Coleman...

She leaned forward and kissed the stone, caressing his beloved name with her fingertips.

Visions of their time together danced through her mind. Beautiful memories that brought a smile to her lips and warmed her soul. She had been loved with tenderness and devotion that too few women have the pleasure to experience.

She glanced up at the snowy clouds rolling across the bright blue sky.

"You were my everything," she whispered. "You always will be. I love you, Eli."

And as if he were standing nearby, his voice whispered in her ears:

"*Daisy, my Daisy...*"

A spray of rain, gentle and light as her sorrow, brushed Nika's face.

"*Hurry for goodness sake...*"

She closed her eyes and smiled. And let go of the past. Time to move, to find her way back to Eli.

Whipping away her tears, Nika turned to leave, welcoming the calm that embraced her. With the last glance at the grave, she whispered:

"Good bye, my love. Until we meet again."

ACKNOWLEDGMENTS

To come up with a story and write it down is easy. To make it into a book—now that's entirely different story.

The creative process is a lonely road, sometimes straight and smooth, often like a hike in the hills, but always solitary. And that's how it should be. But every road, no matter how long or hilly, comes to an end, and then...

...you realize that it's not the end— far from it! — but a crossroads, and you need to choose carefully where to turn, or how to proceed and not to get completely disoriented. You need help to choose the right path, a map to orient yourself, a guidance and a gentle nudge (or a mighty push) to start moving again. In short, you need other people. Then, the real adventure begins.

I've been truly blessed. By the time I came to my crossroads, I was so lost, I was about to turn back. But fate decided differently: she sent me Sloane Taylor, my editor, who very soon became my mentor and my guardian angel. She took me by my hand and dragged me to the right path, showing me the way. And all the time while I stumbled along the thorny path, she was walking behind me, cheering me on, whipping my tears, or kicking my behind. I've never had so much fun, or been so frustrated, in my life, but every second of it was worth it.

Thank you, Sloane Taylor, for sticking up and not giving up on me. Thank you for everything. This book is as much yours as it is mine. Without you it wouldn't see the light of a day.

My heartfelt thanks to Kelly Shorten, who created such a beautiful cover.

And as always, my sincere gratitude to the men in my life, my husband Leo and my son George. Thank you for believing in me, guys.

Don't miss out!

Visit the website below and you can sign up to receive emails whenever Stella May publishes a new book. There's no charge and no obligation.

https://books2read.com/r/B-A-COXF-OBQRB

BOOKS 2 READ

Connecting independent readers to independent writers.

About the Author

Stella May is an author of the family saga/ trilogy Once & Forever, and romance-fantasy Rhapsody in Dreams. Love and family are two cornerstones of her stories.

When not writing, she enjoys classical music, reading, and long walks along the ocean.

She lives in Jacksonville, Florida with her husband Leo and son George, her two best friends and partners in family business.

Read more at www.StellaMayAuthor.com.

www.ingramcontent.com/pod-product-compliance
Lightning Source LLC
Chambersburg PA
CBHW020440270626
47155CB00022B/759